MAN
OF
CLAY

VICTORIA OSBORNE

First published in 2015 by Victoria Osborne
ISBN: 978-0-9942181-1-7
© 2015 Victoria Osborne

National Library of Australia Cataloguing-in-Publication entry
Creator: Osborne, Victoria, 1959- author.
Title: Man of clay / Victoria Osborne.
ISBN: 9780994218117 (paperback)
ISBN: 9780994218100 (ebook)
Subjects: Marriage—Fiction.
Man-woman relationships—Fiction
Interpersonal communication—Fiction.
Dewey Number: A823.4

Cover sculpture: Sam Jinks 'Small Things' www.samjinks.com/
Cover design in collaboration with Risa Liu Paperdino
www.paperdino.com.au/en/
Victoria Osborne
www.ourrelationshipwithnature.com

21 And the LORD God caused a deep sleep to fall upon Adam, and he slept; and he took one of his ribs, and closed up the flesh instead thereof:

22 And the rib, which the LORD God had taken from man, made he a woman, and brought her unto the man.

23 And Adam said, This is now bone of my bones, and flesh of my flesh: she shall be called Woman, because she was taken out of a man.

Genesis 2

Chapter 1

Torso

We met over a dissection. With every cut, every unfolding, every pin, Jude did nothing less than reveal to me the mysteries of the inner workings of life itself. I've remained spellbound ever since.

It was a hot summer morning at the beginning of the university year. The professor, a man with dark eyebrows and grey hair who had surely never been young, spoke from his position near the blackboard. His sandpaper voice was monotonous and not quite loud enough for everyone to hear. The room smelled of acid, sulphur and strong cleaner. The bench varnish bubbled with age and tessellations of gouged initials. The lab was housed in a solid, sandstone building. From where I sat, halfway back near the window, I could see a sharp-faced gargoyle crouched on the edge of the roof.

Sudden action in the airless room, purpose hummed as students got up to move. Uneven wooden stools clattered on the floor, shifted by the oval handholds carved out of their concave seats. The professor summed up the activity of the class as he scrawled point by point on the blackboard. I stared at the list, willing myself to comprehend the chalk marks. After a few moments it became clear: I was expected to kill and dissect a frog. That instant. Constance

Sonnenberg. Me. Murder. Cold bloodedly. Right now. I was expected to suffocate a poor little frog.

I looked for escape. The windows were arrayed in a grid of square panes framed in white. They marched most of the way along the wall, barring the space from bench top to ceiling. All the windows were firmly shut.

I moved on automatic as I collected the kill ingredients: chemicals, dissecting kit and living being. Overwhelmed, I sat down again. The victim sat in front of me in a square, glass dish covered with a bell jar. It was as if I could see its heart beating in its throat. The frog was olive-brown with gold patches on its back. It was shiny. It had large, round eardrums. The creature was pale underneath and each little foot was like the tip of a fern frond. The webbed fingers were spatulate and somehow smoothly connected to the dish surface as if the creature's feet had melted. The frog's eyes glistened like the deepest billabong. It blinked at me. There was a dark streak running above the eye and a paler stripe from eye to arm. The legs were bright greeny-blue.

The yellow summer sun began to warm the bench top and the room smelled even more of chemicals. I wasn't sure how to kill the frog with the chloral-hydrate solution and I began to envisage a future where I might not only dread attending labs but also become terrified of lectures. I had done well in science at school but now I was feeling young, frivolous and nervous.

The frog's throat throbbed, the yellow light glowed, and time slowed down. I no longer heard the jangle of scalpels, the muttering of students absorbing knowledge, or the prof with hair in his ears chewing his words.

The frog's throat beat a tattoo. A panic beat. There was only the dark-eyed frog and I in that mote-laden yellow sunbeam. I was so sorry for the little creature. I picked him up. He wriggled and pushed off with his legs so I made a cup with my hands to prevent him escaping. He was slimy. I bent to look at him closely. We stared into each other's eyes. I kissed him on the lips. Then I heard laughter.

Someone opened a window and cool, fresh air flooded into the room. I could breathe again.

The man beside me had blonde, wavy, out-of-control hair. It flopped over his face into his eyes and he was a man and not a boy. His eyes were sky-blue and as deep as the atmosphere; his smile was warm and sweet; his face was slender. A new beard was a gentle sparkle over his jaw. His crimson lips were perfectly formed, tantalising and sure. His jaw was strong, not quite square, but trustworthy. He stood and watched me, sucking his lips back to his teeth thoughtfully. His voice was chocolate concern. He reassured me. He asked if I needed help. I most certainly did.

I felt his charisma tuned to me alone in that yellow, foetid biology lab: a frog in hand, the gargoyle out the window, and that young man was Jude.

He killed the frog.

Once its life had gone, Jude stayed with me and translated the slime and guts for me. With his help and knowledge, I found the dissection fascinating, even sacred.

He showed me the frog's skin was thin and covered in mucus. Its skeleton was made of bone and cartilage. He pointed out the frog had humerus, scapula, femurs, tibia and feet. The skull protected the tiny brain. The frog's heart circulated blood around the body. The lungs worked like a human's, exchanging gases, until the frog went into hibernation and could absorb oxygen through the skin. The liver also worked just like a human's. Jude explained that all adult frogs were carnivores. He told me frogs had an intestinal tract and a urinary bladder, just like humans.

He told me we had a lot in common with frogs.

I remember that dissection clearly, Jude's lips and mouth talking about the liver, the eyes, the stomach, the bones. Every single word intrigued me and each word was another nail in the coffin of my science career.

~~~~~

Now I sit as if meditating. Can't interpret the indistinct atmosphere. It's as if ghosts echo in the space. They perform memories. Here are echoes of Simone, Zita and Jude. They bubble through the children's lesser whisperings. They live, just more faintly than I do.

Many of Jude's belongings used to be mine. Ours. The furniture is pale, modern, slender pine with long legs and smooth surfaces. The walls are hung with framed wilderness photographs. A framed print of Dombrovskis' *Morning Mist* swirling around Rock Island Bend in the Franklin River hangs like an idealised window cut into the white wall expanse.

Faded gold Tibetan brocade is laid over the back of the couch, which is plumped by cream cushions. Drifty sheer curtains float over the real windows. Worn floorboards are almost covered by pale rugs. The carpet we carried all the way back from Iran is milky coffee with faded blue flowers and clay-coloured leaves curling from charcoal stalks. Pale shelves hold examples of my earliest pottery; bent bowls and a cracked plate. Even though I've never lived in these rooms, they feel like home. Nearly all the objects are permeated with me. Except for the frogs.

Grow restless and begin to wander. Pick things up. Put them down. Snoop, for what I do not know. Jump when his mobile phone rings. Go to it and stand there, not answering, watching it vibrate and shift slowly over the surface of the desk. Don't want to know who it is. Hope the batteries die soon. A light blinks on his answering machine: on, off, on, off… Don't touch that, either.

As far as the rest of the world knows, Jude has gone to Minnesota for something to do with frogs. It's always something to do with frogs.

Frogs provide decoration, colour and punctuation here. There's a large, framed photo on the wall by his desk: a black and yellow frog nestling into a huge, green, spongy plant that could only be a moss. A bookmark green-frog-with-white-lips sticks out of a book. A card on the bookshelf shows a frog clinging with all four hands, stretched out between two stalks, almost to the point of hopelessness. Jude's mouse mat is also graced with a frog: a green one with red eyes.

Heaps of papers and books are on top of the table, piled onto chairs and stacked on the shelves, everywhere around the room. A mountain of unbound pages is piled in the centre of his desk. The top page is entitled *Declines and disappearances of Australian frogs*. The margins are marked with his small, neat handwriting. Different coloured sticky markers make a jaunty frill along the side of the heap. Because I'm aimless and there's no reason not to, I flip through it.

Apparently, it's a collection of typed papers and articles to be proofed and printed. Titular words such as *instability, impacts, threats and disappearances, loss and degradation* build up in me the way DDT builds up in predators as they eat their poisoned prey. Sit at Jude's desk and consume victim pages from the beginning. What on earth is all this about? Need my glasses. Go upstairs to fetch them.

Have found new purpose. I read page after page. I remember Jude's trip to the UK ten years ago, in 1989. Simone kicked up a fuss about being left behind, but someone had to look after the baby. Hadn't heard the reason for the trip. Must have been busy with a commission. Now I read that frogs in 1989 were declining at an alarming rate around the world. You'd think he might have mentioned that, being alarmed, just in passing.

It's all here, in his notes. I read he went to the First World Congress of Herpetology in Canterbury, in the UK. He'd been one of the scientists meeting to acknowledge, for the first time, that frogs were disappearing.

Disappearing? What's happening to them? Can't understand much of the scientific jargon. Taxonomy confuses me. Like another language.

Can feel my brain exercising. Absorb ideas behind the complex words. Deliberate, careful scientists from around the world are in agreement about the perils facing frogs. Climate change, habitat destruction, changes in the direction of waterways, mutation-causing chemicals and introduced feral species threaten the very existence of frogs. Not pandas, not elephants, but the small things in life; tiny, little frogs.

Sit back, push my glasses to the top of my head and sigh. So that's what's kept him late at work. No wonder some of his students think it's the end of the world. If there are no more frogs in the wild, all those student herps, experts in frogs, will have to become zookeepers. Or historians.

When I jostle the mouse by mistake his computer monitor flickers into life. Have no hesitation. With my recently acquired skills I can open files and I do. There's an article called *International Declining Amphibian Populations Taskforce*. They need a taskforce to study frogs? Prop my glasses back on my nose. The article asks, 'Why care about amphibians?' It points out that most people don't care if frogs live or die. It says herpetologists believe that the decline in frog numbers is a catastrophe. A catastrophe? What sort of word is that? Catastrophe?

Way back in Biology One, when I couldn't kill a frog, I made a choice to avoid science as a career. The scientific search for 'truth'—reliable, repeatable, testable theories, together with weighing possibilities and balancing probabilities—is beyond me. But, science, particularly biology, is more than Jude's interest. Science is his passion, whereas I find my comfort in mud.

Begin to digest the words. Understand the quest for knowledge is a dangerous thing, particularly for frogs. Imagine those countless frogs killed by scientists testing out their theories.

Learn the type of frog I once dissected is now an endangered species. Now there's a word: *endangered...* in danger. Faced with danger. Clearly my particular frog had been facing such danger it had died. I had chopped it up. Peeled it. Dissected it. From my reading, it was probably a green and gold bell frog; they were as common as clouds back then but now are rare. So rare they are endangered.

When a species is endangered it might become extinct. Find a note in Jude's handwriting: 'I have held the last known individual of

Taudactylus diurnus in my hand and watched it die. There was nothing I could do.' Know the feeling.

Sleep in Jude's chair by the computer. Sleep in his bed. Shower in his shower. Drink his tea. Weep. Read about frogs. Cry some more. Frogs begin to fill me.

Go down to studio. Open freezer and pull out plastic bag full of ribs. Will incorporate them into a work of pottery. Seems fitting that ribs should become a woman. She will be every woman and no woman. She will be the other woman. She will be a torso.

Dry the ribs in kiln overnight. Grind them. Wedge them into clay to give strength and texture. Coil torso, paying particular attention to rib cage. Deliberately sculpt her with twenty-three ribs although I discover in my *Anatomy for Artists* that the biblical story is just that, a story. In reality, the number of ribs can vary from individual to individual, not necessarily by sex.

Seems that ribs are protectors of the body, shielding our lungs and heart. Ribs are part of our superstructure, shaping and support-ing us.

Jude's books tell me that frogs don't have ribs, only vestigial spines on their vertebrae. Frogs have soft, unprotected bodies. One great difference between us. Possibly frogs cannot bear the weight of a human-powered planet.

As I work, I think of frogs. Think of the frogs I have found on Jude's computer. Read more about the frogs in his books. Study the frogs that decorate his walls. Even examine the pottery frogs that the children—Peter, Leaf, Fern, Francis and Emma—made for him during their school years. They knew the one thing that would always please him, that would garner his certain approval, would be a frog.

Frogs lead my thinking to metamorphosis. My own experience with ceramics overlays Jude's: fire, evolution and adaptation. It's fated that the other woman should take on the colours of an endan-gered frog.

Choose *Philoria loveridgei* because it has 'lover' in the name. It's known as the masked mountain frog. Jude found specimens in the wet forests bordering Queensland and New South Wales. With her mask, this frog has the right anonymity to be the other woman. Has a smooth white belly with brown flecks, like a borlotti bean.

The woman's back is burnt biscuit brown with scattered ridges and sunken wart shapes. The dark band of the frog is echoed on her shoulders. Her chest is pale borlotti cream and leans back slightly to reveal the floating ribs. Takes three firings to get the glaze right.

Late one night after closing the kiln, go upstairs to my own flat. Turn on lights. Cold. Begin to tidy up. First time I've been there since... since Jude's...

Clean everything and remake bed as though for a motel. Blinking light tells me there's a message on my answer phone. When I push play, William's voice shouts from the machine. Shocked by volume I turn him down and push replay. William is moving back to Sydney to reopen the gallery. He wants to start with the missing exhibition, my exhibition, *The touch of earthly years*. And, he adds with no detectable change of tone, would I join him to watch the Mardi Gras parade this evening?

At one time this was all I wanted. Now it's different. Impossible. Finish tidying the flat. Bring tinned baked beans, soup and biscuits down to Jude's bedsit. I'll stay here for now.

Eat half a tin of baked beans. Do not bother heating it. Did not realise how hungry I was. The sauce is cloying. Tip rest of tin into a cup and refrigerate. Rinse tin and place into recycling bucket before I ring William. Refuse him. Have no time for tinsel and gyrating this year. Have work to do.

Lead William to believe I need some time to myself. Tell him I require space. Tell him I have things to think about. Reassure him I will call again another time, and hang up. Think about frogs. Frogs bring me closer to Jude.

Philoria loveridgei will soon disappear under the weight of climate destabilisation and direct human activity. Just as we all will. Survival of the fittest means some are born losers.

He chose me in the end. I was the last wife.

When I look out my window, the glimpse I have of Sydney Harbour glows in the new day. If I rise above it, it is warped in the liquid style of a Brett Whiteley painting. The water shines ultramarine. The flooded river valley is pulled and stretched. It is polished, spread out and anaesthetised ready for dissection.

Chapter 2

Gargoyle

In 1961 we went to the Royal Easter Show at the showgrounds in Paddington. It was a year after we'd met and Jude and I were 'going out'. A tentative understanding was developing between us, reinforced by his ambition to succeed in academia and not get 'involved'.

We watched the grand parade, we admired the sheep, and we laughed at the chickens. We grew hungry looking at marmalade and those fruitcakes with sultanas and currants so evenly dispersed. We admired the fruit and vegetable display representing an agricultural map of Australia. We were there for ages before he took my hand. His hand was warm and he was tall beside me. It was one of the happiest days of my life.

He walked me to my bus stop. He put his arm around me. There was a press of people waiting there. When my bus arrived, I turned to smile my goodbye to him. His arms hooked around me and he bent and kissed me on the lips. It was my first kiss, and over so quickly, I'd had no time to savour any anticipation. I watched his lips closely as they smiled, then they kissed again. This time his tongue licked my lips lightly as though I might have fairy floss stuck there. I had to pull away from him to clamber onto the bus. I took a seat by the window. I thought of dogs kissing each other, licking their tongues in amicable tasting. I smiled out the window at Jude. He watched me intently as the bus drove away. He was serious.

~~~~~

The earth shook as I ran a piece of chamois over her cold, clay lips. I was in the studio finishing a commission for the triangular garden outside Wollongong library. The sculpt was of a mother holding a child—the shape of love and care. The mother had good bones. No sculpture can live until the bones are true. This clay woman was pleasingly alive, calm and still. I was completely absorbed in her expression. Her embrace of the smaller form, her love, her bending over and into, all flowed through her face; smooth planes focused on her responsibility. Her lips were slightly curled in a maternal smile. Her jawline was gentle.

The earthquake sounded like a muffled explosion. I was jolted into alarm. My hands shook as I searched the studio for my glasses. Where were the infernal things? As I looked, my mind raced for possible explanations. I knew both kilns were off but perhaps there had been some kind of gas leak? Would it be safe for me to investigate? I didn't like to ring emergency services. What could I tell them? I would wait until I had a clear idea of the problem. I located my glasses by the sink. I put them on. I rushed to see what had caused the blast.

My acute awareness gave my surroundings new vibrancy. The kiln was intact. The woodworking space immediately outside the studio was undisturbed. The storage area leading into the garage was a melange of cartons and sporting equipment that looked as if it might have been blown up, but then, it always looked like that.

I entered the garage to find Peter's car hard up against the cinderblock wall, its bonnet bent into a V. One headlight dripped from its socket anchored by different coloured wire-veins. There was no sign of Peter. He'd left the scene. That's what they call it in police procedurals, don't they? The scene.

The yellow afternoon light seared down onto the injured vehicle like a spotlight. I surveyed 'the scene', picking drying clay from my fingers. Had he been hurt? Peter didn't normally behave like a member of Oasis. There was obviously something wrong. My urge was to rush to his flat but, as he'd not come to the studio immediately, I thought I'd better give him some time alone. I went back to the studio and put the kettle on.

My studio, Peter's bedsit, and garaging for four cars were at ground level. I would sometimes commandeer a car space to build framework for a larger piece. Any extra space around the walls was used as storage: garden tools, Jude's windsurfer, the children's bikes, and for the assorted boxes, which were piled up wherever they would fit.

Now, Peter's grey Datsun 120Y lay across two parking spaces. Luckily, he'd missed my old Volvo. Then again, thinking of the potential insurance payout, maybe not so lucky. I returned to the clay mother to wrap her in damp rags and recycled dry-cleaner's plastic to protect her from drying out in the heat. The kettle began to steam.

When I first moved in, I planned my studio carefully, fitting workbenches around two walls with shelving and storage above and below. The space had rewarded my efforts for a decade and a half. A large gas kiln with a chimney to the outside stood in the woodworking area and there was a smaller electric kiln inside the studio, good for running tests, also vented to the open-air. I might store pieces in the garage, but they rarely stayed there long because they were built on commission and had somewhere else to be.

The space faced south so I could work in even light all year round. The studio's windows folded open, concertina fashion, to a courtyard lined with crimson and purple bougainvilleas. This display of colour together with a bas-relief mural hanging on the white painted brick wall, a trio of terracotta pots erupting with tall flax leaves, and a couple of swirling sculptures suggesting flame or falling fabric, coalesced to a peaceful refuge. When there was time, I would take my cup of tea and a sandwich out to the ceramic table there.

After washing my hands, drying them thoroughly and applying hand cream, I replaced my rings and prepared to meet my son. Thankfully, I still had a packet of biscuits in the cupboard—macadamia nut and white chocolate—that Simone had given me. I made a pot of tea, put it on a tray with the biscuits, and took the tray over to Peter's flat. He didn't answer my knock (or rather my kick for my hands were full with the tray). I called through the door, 'I've made tea. I'll leave it here for you, shall I?' Bending down to place the tray on the ground, I noticed paint was flaking from the walls.

Slowly, Peter opened the door. In this brief glimpse of his face I could see no obvious injuries but he screwed up his eyes as if in reaction to the light and retreated back into the gloom of his cave. No help with the tray, then. What was going on? I picked up the tray again and followed him. I put the tray on the kitchen counter and went to open the curtains.

'Leave them,' he said.

'At least let me open a window.'

The small flat was stuffy and smelled of dust and old sweets. The kitchen joined the living room and the bedroom and the bathroom were on the other side of the mini hall. It was a Granny flat really, but all that a young single professional academic required at this stage of his doctorate. I did open the window but only twitched the curtain aside a few centimetres in deference to his cave-dwelling mood.

Peter slumped on the couch. It was brown tartan with black vinyl sides. He'd found this couch left out for hard rubbish collection by the side of the road. He should have left it there. His hair, the colour of sandstone, was getting longish, and was strangely unkempt.

I found pottery mugs in the kitchen cupboard and put them next to the teapot.

'Are you hurt?'

'No.'

I poured tea into one of the mugs and sweetened it. Considerably. I put the mug and the biscuits, still in their packet, on the table in front of him. I waited. Hovering, mothering. Not as calm as clay.

'Sit down, Mum. Have your tea.'

I poured myself a mug and sat. There was no cushion and quickly my bum ached almost as much as my back did from having to sit up so straight in the rickety wooden chair (another hard-rubbish find). I distracted myself by examining the pottery, funny how I could see into the past with each sip. The mugs were fine with a casual grevillea design sprayed over the glaze. Slightly crazed now.

'Insurance up to date?' I offered, conversationally.

'Typical,' he said. 'All you ever think of is practicalities.'

'I don't see the harm in practicalities. For instance, how do you expect to get to uni?'

'It'll still go.'

'You hope.'

Peter finished his tea and most of the biscuits. He picked up the packet and stared at it. He'd always been one of those children who'd read everything in front of them. He would read the cereal boxes, window-cleaning advertisements, Neighbourhood Watch notices and now here he was, reading the biscuits. 'Trying to kill me?'

'I've had them for a while.'

'That explains the use-by.'

'And the car? What explains that?'

I watched him slump, silent and unmoving on the couch, for a while and I let my attention drift around the room. A CD called *Frogstomp* was top of the pile by the stereo. 'Better not let your Dad see that.'

'He'd probably like it.' The muscles in Peter's jaw worked as if he were an actor in a soap opera. I waited and it finally arrived. 'He's doing it again.'

'What?'

'Dad.'

'What? What's he doing?'

'Take a wild guess, Mum.'

That's how my son reported that my ex-husband was seeing yet another female. How can a person cheat on his third wife? When do you push your luck right over The Gap? Aren't you also cheating on your first and second wives?

Somehow, I thought intellectually, I should be over petty jealousy, but it was strange… the green bile did plunge into my mouth, it caught hold, and suddenly I was afraid for us all: my husband, his three wives, and all our children.

I was flooded with dread. The rules had changed again. I didn't think I could bear it. Fighting the bile lunge, I collected the mugs and put them into the sink. I put the teapot back onto my tray. 'It may be none of your business, you know.'

'Then again, it may be. It just may be my business, Mum.'

'Why should your father's love life matter to you? It never has before.'

He flashed me such a look, then said very clearly, 'Oh, why do you think, Mum?'

Peter stared at me and his eyes were hard, as though I should know something. His look asked me, wasn't it obvious? Nope. I had no idea what he was talking about and it was clear the interview was over. I took my shaky tea tray back to the studio, wondering just what he was trying to communicate.

Why would I think my son would be caught up in his father's escapades? For me though, that wasn't the point. I was more concerned with another question: why should I have to think about his father's escapades at all?

~~~~~

Construct the gargoyle. The twisted snarling mouth issues from somewhere deep inside me. Hope it will be built into guttering so the mouth will vomit a stream of cold, roof water filled with rat shit and rotting leaf debris. Use coarse-grained clay from Pugoon, near Mudgee. It's good for large outdoor pieces. Grind up lips and tongue and mix them into a slurry. Blend them into the clay.

Take care to bash out any explosive air pockets but it's mere habit. Will accept any explosion. Will deserve it. Will take it as my due. Will be confirmation I am incompetent. Not quite a widow, not quite a wife. Not an able craftsperson, nor a skilled artist. Someone who struggles with words. Struggles with my husband, the man who is not my husband. Oh yes! Surely those myths should explode.

Leave gargoyle to dry for a week. Fire it slowly. Gently increase and then decrease the heat, over twenty-four hours. Burn teeth and lower jaw in the smaller kiln. Add them to the glaze. Do not think about what I am doing. Cannot think about it. Am simply doing. Working my memories in clay. Hope, and fear, maybe the golem will stir into life, much as my memories are stirring. When it comes to colouring the gargoyle, creature of myth and caricature, I find a little frog with tusks like a walrus, *Adelotis brevis*. It's found in rainforests and open grassland, all threatened by habitat loss, degradation, chemicals and disease.

The oxide pigment is my own invention. Gargoyle has a dark-brown lumpy back. Shifts into black with white spots developing at its front. There's a butterfly mark between the eyes. The base flares into two bright-red patches to imitate the colour found on the frog's groin and on the back of its legs.

Two large teeth protrude from the lower jaw of the male-tusked frog. Most frogs have little teeth along the edge of the upper jaw. Some have no teeth. Few frogs have teeth on their lower jaw apart from this strange, tusked frog. These lower fangs disappear into small cavities in the upper jaw when it shuts its mouth.

Frogs generally use their hands in water because their tongues lose their stickiness when wet. Frogs might use their teeth to hold food while shoving it into their mouths with their little hands. They are like small children with chunks of watermelon. Food is crushed rather than chewed. They swallow dinner whole. It's not just dainty little insects either. Jude once saw a green tree frog eat a baby rat.

~~~~~

Sheryl used to make pressed tongue. We would have it with other cold meats and salad for summer lunches. It would be greyish-pink in colour, set in aspic, with a soft juicy meatiness. It went well with iceberg lettuce, tomato and an apple cucumber. Often there was a dressing made from sweetened condensed milk and brown malt vinegar. Sheryl kept a tin of condensed milk in the fridge. When it became crusty and crystallised we would lick the edge of the tin. We were lucky not to cut our tongues. At least that's what Sheryl would say when she discovered us.

William and I would touch tongues in the bath. He tasted like soap. The living pressure of another tongue is so strange. Wouldn't we giggle! Wouldn't we be grossed out!

~~~~~

In ancient Mesopotamia there was a goddess called Mami. She was responsible for making the first seven men and the first seven women. She made them out of the flesh and blood of some poor old god mixed up with clay and spit. I suppose that makes humans a kind of sacred mud pie. Seven of each seems a reasonable hedge against destruction in the kiln. Risk management by the gods.

Chapter 3

Rainjar

Throw round base of the rain jar on the wheel. Shift base to the bench and build up the side with coils until it stands about waist height. Shift it down onto the wheeled trolley. Continue up with the coils. Smooth and comb surface with a toothed, bean-shaped card as I go. Easy to extrude several links of clay at once. Move to build wall, working continuously with the required ammo piled at the ready. Check with plum line. Want a thing of elegance. Relatively easy to transfer piece into the kiln but I'll need help once it's been fired, when it's time to pack and get it on the truck transporting it to wherever it goes in the end. Who knows where that will be?

Dig into clay. Dig into my skills. Reuse my stock of craft. Digging into memories of Jude, thinking of frogs and shaking my head every now and again. Now, as I type, I am accounting. Recounting what I have done to him.

Rain jar survives the kiln again. Glaze is okay. It's chocolate brown with black flecks. Dark stripes on either side flare into a white edge. The yellow band, also with black flecks, grows from the white. Two, bright, bluey-green stripes along the sides, again with black flecks, are the glory.

These blue-green patches on thigh and groin distinguish the green-thighed frog.

~~~~~

Jude used to have a pair of olive-green corduroy trousers that smoothed thin and pale over his thighs. As he moved, the long line of quadricep would flex and I would press the back of my hand into his leg as we walked along to feel the warm muscles stretch and shorten against my hand. The reliability of his strength was life affirming. I miss that pair of trousers. I miss that thigh.

One of my biology drawings still hangs on his study wall. It's captioned, 'Tie me amphibian down, sport.' It depicts a frog pinned out and half-dissected; the Rolf Harris-esque caption because I imagined frogs as hairless kangaroos. One of their great talents is the ability to jump, probably even better than a 'roo. The word 'femur' is Latin for thigh. The femur is the longest and strongest bone in a human.

And in a frog.

~~~~~

I remember when Jude took me to meet his mother for the first time. He called for me one Sunday. Dad walked us down to the wharf where the little dinghy was moored. He was wearing faded green shorts and a paler green shirt; his uniform for work, a kind of bush camouflage.

Jude held the dinghy steady as I clambered in. I sat down immediately, feeling ignorant and scared. A seagull screeched and splashed a large white donation over the bow. I was only too glad it missed me. I looked up when Dad burst into laughter. His enjoyment broke the ice and I relaxed, trying to make myself comfortable on the cold wooden plank and trying to forget that shortly there'd be very deep water beneath this flimsy craft.

Jude told us he and his brothers had restored the dinghy over two summers. It was made of pale wood, varnished to light caramel. The mast looked impossibly tall but Jude hoisted one main sail and a smaller triangular one with seemingly little effort. The sails might once have been white but were now degraded to a dirty lilac.

Dad smiled at me encouragingly as I sat with my feet in a puddle. I felt useless. I'd never been in a sailing dinghy before. The neighbourhood kids all mucked about with rowing boats around the sailing club but I'd done nothing so serious as going right across the harbour. Jude assured Dad he would get us there in one piece. He comforted me, too, as he showed me how to lace up my life jacket. It was dirty yellow, cracked and smelled of oil. I did not like it.

I was nervous of the water, the wind and the rocks along the shore. There was all the other shipping to consider: ferries, cargo boats and pleasure craft. A male rowing pair, with a small girl as cox, veered across the water in front of us. One of the men shouted in alarm as they came close to the shore and then, in a lower voice that carried across the water, encouraged the girl to say the correct coxing terms. As they rowed on, the men cast nervous glances over their shoulders, bound to vigilance for the rest of their trip. From the other direction, a yacht with a bright red hull moved smoothly out towards Watsons Bay, her white sails full and regal.

As we set off, Jude concentrated on pulling various ropes to best catch the gentle wind. Out in the middle of the harbour, the wind was laden with the oily portent of roiling machine and industry. The chugging harbour water was impending and seemed bottomless.

Dad, with his arms folded across his chest, stood watching from the wharf. Gradually he grew smaller and eventually faded into the landscape. I knew he would be watching even when we sailed into Balmain. From there, it might have been possible to see him with a strong pair of binoculars but we had no such thing.

The sailing was easy compared to meeting Jude's family. In that tiny kitchen with the green walls and tattered red linoleum, the first question Queenie asked me was where I went to school. I remember my hand next to Jude's warm thigh as we stood side by side and I told her I had been to SCEGGS. Of course, Queenie knew of the Sydney Church of England Girls' Grammar School and she didn't like it. She smiled and ever so slightly shook her head. I was dismissed.

We got through that lunch, I don't know how, and walked back to the water to find the dinghy where we had left it. Then we became business-like, and together hoisted the mast and sail as if we'd always been a team. During the trip back into Greenwich, Jude had me reaching for ropes—sorry, halyards—making sheets fast to cleats, and helping like a proper sailor.

We arrived back late afternoon and, avoiding the wharf, tied up at the sailing club. I'd been concerned about getting my dress too wet and Jude was only half-joking when he offered to carry me to shore. We sat and stared at each other across the little boat. Our legs were touching and a bit cold, and the wind teased the sails even though we had lowered them. The jib flapped gently. Jude told me it didn't matter that I wasn't a Catholic. It didn't matter what his mother said. I felt less shivery then.

Jude stepped out of the boat and held it steady as I disembarked. The water came up to my thighs and my dress did get wet. He kissed me and asked me to wait until he graduated, because he wanted to marry me. I shivered again, but not from the cold.

~~~~~

Dry out meat over two days until harder than leather. Grind. Blend into the clay. Makes the bisque firing a darker colour and the clay porous. Bone ash is calcium phosphate. Not only does it provide a reddish tone to the glaze but it also creates bubbles in the surface. In a chun glaze, for instance, the addition of just a tiny percentage of ash creates bubbles that trick the eye into seeing blue. With a greater percentage of ash, a chocolate colour develops, as does warty skin quality. Use plenty of bone ash to invoke the texture of *Litoria brevipalmata*, the green-thighed frog.

~~~~~

We had a family barbecue the day before Peter pranged his car; it was a lovely February afternoon, not too hot, with a sea breeze gently teasing the jasmine flowers outside my bedroom window. In the morning I walked in to the laundry where Jude waited for his washing to finish. He leaned against the spinning machine and stared out at the terrace.

'Anything special?' I asked as I handed him a cup of tea.

'No, no, just wanted to see all the kids.'

'So you thought you might as well have the mothers along too?'

'Exactly.' He grinned. 'Might as well.'

He had green tea, for the antioxidants. We sipped quietly, companionably. He was using an old mug from my callistemon phase, its splash fired surprisingly bright for a red. Its final firing had been in a reducing flame, the smoke causing the metal to burnish in the glaze.

On the day of that family barbecue, Jude was fifty-five. He was stocky and muscular with gingery-blond fuzz all over him. It was more wiry than fluffy. He went to Bondi to run and swim every morning except in the dead of raining winter. Then he'd use the uni pool. He went sailing whenever he could. He was less often found windsurfing and hang gliding these days but he still loved the silent prayer of wind. He went to the gym three times a week but also had a treadmill at home. A machine, that is, not just us three wives.

He used to have infinite eyes the colour of a summer sky but, as I avoided looking at them much anymore, I could not be sure if they had faded. He had big earlobes but his ears did not stick out. He listened to women in an interested way. He appeared mesmerised by them. He loved children: babies were just as adorable as frogs. Well, ask yourself, what do frogs and babies have in common?

Jude wore jeans and bush shirts. He wore solid boots. He still enjoyed regular field trips. He'd been a biologist at the same university for over twenty years. He published enough to hold his head up and he helped start Frogwatch. He was an academic. He was under pressure to question assumptions and to test every theory. I had noticed, though, that for some time Jude had been distant and distracted, more so than usual. Generally though, he was a considerate man, thoughtful and contemplative. I loved him.

The spinning stopped and he dragged his cream sheets from the machine and stacked them into the cane basket balanced on the sink. When the machine was empty he paused, leaning on the wet, cool washing, and looked at me seriously. 'Connie, how are you?'

I smiled, looked past him to the door and said, 'Fine.'

He said, 'Really?'

'Yes. Fine.'

'You'd tell me, wouldn't you? If there was anything?'

'Sure.'

He grinned at me as he left but I knew he wasn't reassured. He hoisted the washing basket to his hip like a woman and carried it to the line outside. I took our cups to rinse in the sink and got on with some sketches at the kitchen bench. Five or so minutes passed before Jude re-appeared. He said he'd see me later to warm up the barbecue. Off he went out the front door in his sport shorts and his freckly legs. The skin at the back of his legs was crepey and he wore huge sports shoes. I noted, too, that he had a new sports bag—just do it. Later, at the barbecue, he looked tired but smiled all the same.

~~~~~

I return to my golem of memories. After kissing my frog prince, I finished with biology, dropped out of university and enrolled in the new ceramics certificate course at East Sydney Technical College. While Jude completed his degree and postgraduate work, I became adept, studying with local potters, Peter Rushworth and Mollie Douglas. We knew Japan was the place to learn about pottery and admiration of nature and it was almost a royal visit when the British potter, Bernard Leach, came to visit us. He was inspiring, bringing old ideas from Japan, China and Korea fused into his British intelligence. He came to class and not only gave a demonstration himself but also discussed some of our work. He picked up one of my bowls and was not exactly flattering—he pointed out I'd over-worked the pattern somewhat—and I had.

I took over Dad's garden shed and started a cottage industry. I remember approaching my first shop, L & C's Treasures, in Lane Cove, with a set of six mugs. The owner was reluctant, doubting she could sell them. But she could. She rang the very next week with a repeat order and I started to make money. It was the early sixties and a pottery mug was 'in'.

My mother wanted to disinherit me. She couldn't believe I would waste my expensive education not only on pottery but also on a poor dirty Mick. She predicted I would end up pregnant, bashed, with ten kids, an alcoholic brute of a husband, and living on the wrong side of the harbour. She hardly ever spoke to me again, nothing meaningful, no real communication. Well, she was busy: rarely in the same city much less at the same table. Though she was always generous. She paid for our wedding, after all.

I took Catholic instruction from Father Brian at St. Augustine's Church in Eaton Street, Balmain. I'd been filled with trepidation at the thought of having to spend six sessions immersed in religion, but as it turned out, Father Brian became a friend. It transpired he had his own reasons for being intrigued by pottery. He not only covered the business of good Catholic-wife-and-mother duties, as expected, but also searched out relevant passages in the Bible about clay and creation. Obviously he was trying to make our educational sessions germane to me, but at the same time he was teasing out his own problems with intelligent design.

I cleaned spiderwebs from the garden shed wall and painted, in black paint, none too neatly: *Hath not the potter power over the clay, of the same lump to make one vessel unto honour and another into dishonour?* It helped me focus my thoughts. It made me think pottery was a honourable business—take that, Mother-mine. I even etched into a series of bowls: *We are the clay and thou our potter; and we are the work of thy hand.* It was difficult for me to imagine anyone's hand forming the people that I knew, but then, I thought, if a god made in our image had made us humans, that might explain all the mistakes.

I invited Father Brian to my studio in Greenwich and gave him clay to play with. I tempted him to make a little figure of a man. Just a bit more detailed than a gingerbread man, it did not breathe. We laughed at our minor blasphemy. Then I taught him how to make a simple pinch pot. After succeeding at that, he made a charming little desk container for his paperclips, which I later fired for him. He soon forgot he was wearing a floral pinny. It didn't cover the white collar.

As my potting career progressed, I explored different clays and found better ways to push the limits of wet dirt. Stretching to the utmost or firing too thick a piece was risky. Unfortunate cracks and even explosions in the kiln lead me to realise I had to let the clay behave how it needed to. I had to work within the limits of the constituents. I would have to rethink, allowing a subsidence where I had planned a rise, a bend where I had worked for a straight, and those verses expounding the potter's power over the clay would creep into my mind. I reasoned that as God is like a potter, so too I was like God. Father Brian saw no harm in such thoughts. He was even amused that my theology could be so literally based in clay. It made my life so simple; so earthy.

I held my clay very carefully. The tiny organisms inherent in the mud could be precursors to the next evolutionary step. Was it possible these invisible life forms might conceive my actions as godlike?

In celebration of my forthcoming marriage to Jude, I presented Father Brian with a ceramic nativity scene. After our discussions about power and creation, he understood that I had made him a little kingdom and enjoyed the joke.

Who knows, I thought in those, my hopeful, young days, perhaps there is a great, bearded old man sitting at a clay-splattered wheel with mud under his fingernails and a mind filled with designs and forms. In his beautifully lit, heavenly studio he cries out for more fluid clay, a smoother wheel and an infinitely more pleasing shape. And the wheel groans on.

~~~~~

People tell you things in all sorts of ways. Sometimes they mean to let you know, other times it's a mistake. Peter's fury and his announcement, 'He's doing it again,' told me more than enough, although I don't think Peter knew for sure. I think he just guessed. When he told me, I knew something that might not even be true. When does supposition or instinct become certain knowledge? When does theory become fact? Is not husband innocent until proven guilty?

~~~~~

Providentially, I inherited this three-storey block of flats in Bellevue Hill. Its name, *Bindiwurra*, was picked out in black tiles along the low front wall. The very word *Bindiwurra* had such resonance and promise. I read it out loud, repeating it, enjoying the roll of vowels. I never did find out what *Bindiwurra* meant. I invoke Providence, but Lord, paying for never-ending maintenance was stressful beyond belief. I hated pushing up rents but there you go, got to pay the bills. The flats seemed to suit everyone. As I've said, my studio, Peter's bedsit and garaging were downstairs, and Simone, sparkly wife number three, lived on the first floor with her two kids.

Simone was a photographer, known mainly for her commercial work. She also did portraiture. Apart from her flat, she used a bedsit down the hall as a darkroom for smaller jobs. She rented space elsewhere if she was working on a big shoot. Meetings with clients were conducted in her front room. Whenever I looked at Simone I thought, all that glitters is not gold. I couldn't help it, I tried to stifle it, I didn't want to be judgmental, but it just kept sliding into my mind. Does that make me a bitch?

Zita, my friend, and Jude's second wife, was a florist. She lived on the second floor with her two teenagers, Fern and Leaf. She kept early hours, wanting to maintain hands-on control of her business. She used a supplier and no longer enjoyed visiting the flower market regularly, competition having become too fierce years before. Her popular wedding floristry, Zed to Wed, was based in Double Bay. She did very well, still featuring regularly in the special wedding edition of *Vogue Australia.*

Jude's airy bedsit was on the same floor. He was just down the hall for the teenagers, should they ever need him. The question was, if the need ever arose, would they ask and how would he realise that he was wanted?

Zita and I were still friends, thankfully. I'd been there for her and the kids and she'd always helped me with Peter. All the kids would come to any of us mothers for comfort after a skinned knee or a bruised ego. (Maybe not Simone.) Ideally, a mother will always mother another's child. Especially when they've got the same father. Ideally.

I lived upstairs, above them all, mother hen, in a two-bedroom flat opening out onto the roof garden. Jude, Zita and I had laid terracotta tiles to make a Mediterranean-style balcony. The ramparts of *Bindiwurra,* mainly chest high, stood all around the roof providing shelter. Sliding glass doors led into my kitchen cum living area. We planted an olive tree, a lemon tree and an orange tree in giant pots. Smaller pots overflowed with bougainvillea, Jasmine crept up the wall around the bedroom window, and grapevines covered the arbour, under which stood a circular table. Shaded by grape leaves in the summer and a suntrap in the winter, the table was the heart of family gatherings.

Over the tips of the glossy trees in Cooper Park we could see to the harbour, Shark Island and beyond. Bellevue Hill had been a picturesque picnic area for the gentry in the early 1800s. Governor Lachlan Macquarie gave the beauty spot its name, being unimpressed with the earlier name, 'Vinegar Hill'. Though the park is much smaller now, we still have picnics here, although none of us knows any gentry. We can pretend.

Up on the roof garden, everyone arrived for the barbecue. When the father called to see his children, the mothers were only too grateful. The wind was fresh and the washing on the line was dry. Jude's sheets billowed in the breeze like butter spinnakers.

Jude was in charge of cooking the meat. He knew I wouldn't touch it. He'd stabbed a leg of lamb with chunks of garlic and rosemary, swashed it over with red wine and sprinkled it with black pepper. He closed the lid on the barbecue and opened a couple bottles of Syrah to allow them to breathe.

I, first wife, was in the kitchen. I pushed finger holes into focaccia dough and pressed in olive oil, rosemary and garlic before placing the baking trays in the oven. Zita, second wife, provided a green salad plus a tomato and mozzarella plate strewn with ripped basil leaves. Zita had hair like black candyfloss which she had a terrible time controlling. Nevertheless, it always looked magnificent, and gave Zita the appearance of a model in a Fellini movie. Her eyes were a profound ocean-green.

After swirling gold oil over the red tomato, green basil and white mozzarella, Zita flung ground black pepper flecks across the platter, then gathered up knives and forks and went out to set the table.

Simone, wife number three, followed by her Siamese cat, Nuri, was late. She brought potato salad straight from the supermarket. She laughed as she spooned it out of the containers and into a bowl. 'Don't tell anyone, will you, darls?' She also brought sweets that I put into cute little bowls her kids had made with me during school holidays. After making as much mess as she could, she went outside to the table to check on Francis and Emma. I wiped up mayonnaise splashes from the bench and was rinsing the plastic containers in the sink when Jude popped in to the kitchen. 'Anything I can do?'

I said, 'Under control,' and put the potato salad containers into the recycling without looking at him.

'Sure?' He looked to Zita. She shrugged.

I said, 'Why don't you help Simone?'

Jude smiled generally at both of us, meaningfully at neither of us, and left the kitchen to see what he could do for Simone and the children.

After he'd gone, Zita poured cokes for Fern and Leaf. 'You know,' she said, 'I don't know why I bother. They're only interested in wine and beer. Actually, they're only interested in what they can get away with. Just like their dear old dad.'

'Zita, it's not that bad. They're just teenagers.'

'It is that bad.'

I handed her a bottle of Chardonnay. She took it gratefully and filled a glass to the brim. Then, after she'd drunk half, she added a splash of soda and smiled at me. 'We need some semblance of dignity here.'

All of us were wearing sunhats selected from an assortment I'd stored for just these occasions. Except for Simone and Emma. Francis, at twelve, wouldn't have cared if St. Vincent's op shop had kitted him out entirely, but Simone and Emma were most particular about their labels and knew what worked for them. Simone looked in the mirror and adjusted her hat—if you could call that folded, cubist object a hat—over her shiny ponytail. 'What do you think? Akira threw this together for me last year, you know, when we were working on the *Dance Alive!* Calendar'.

I must have had my stupid look on because Simone stared at me in wonder. I had absolutely no idea what to say. Then she snapped. 'Oh, come on! You know Akira, don't you? Akira Isogawa? Sydney Dance? Oh, Connie, it's as though you're asleep half the time.'

I apologised for my ignorance but that didn't matter to Simone. In fact, her knowing something I didn't know was fuel to her. She became more energetic, bustling, purposeful, grabbed salt and pepper, chili sauce and dashed outside.

We congregated at the circular table. I sat opposite Zita and tried to avoid rolling my eyes too obviously. Akira Isogawa! Where was the function in that hat? It was not to keep the sun off. I would have unfolded it and used it as a table napkin. What would I know?

Jude helped Emma unpack her homework at the large round table now covered with my best yellow tablecloth and set with knives and forks. They moved aside a couple of settings and Emma sat with her legs swinging while she arduously wrote a couple of sentences about the start of the Sydney to Hobart yacht race on Boxing Day, and how no one could have foreseen the tragedy that would unfold. She read out her work so far and Jude could not help but grin at her effort. Her tongue poked out between her lips as she shaped each letter. Jude assisted with her spelling. I found it difficult to believe the other preps would have chosen so difficult a subject but Jude wasn't fazed. He seemed delighted by her understanding of current events. Once Emma had completed a rough draft, Jude left her to do the good copy and went to chat to Francis.

Francis had moved a chair into the shade in which to slouch and read a book. His blonde curls bent low over the paperback. The boy was slender with knobbly knees. His lean thighs jutted from his shorts just as I imagined Jude's might have at that age. Jude and he murmured together. I heard Jude's comment, 'They work in teams, driving fish into the shallows...' I craned my neck to see what Francis was reading. Of course, *Storm Boy*.

'Do they only eat fish?' asked Francis.

'Interesting question,' Jude said. 'Australian pelicans aren't fussy. They'll eat anything: frogs, snakes and even other birds'.

'You mean babies? Fledglings?'

'And not so small. They're a big bird, a pelican. They can kill their prey by holding them under water and drowning them'.

Zita unfolded the Sunday paper. She was just getting comfortable with her spritzer and the letters page when Leaf sprayed her with his water pistol. With a clatter of cutlery Zita jumped up, shrieking. *Mascalzone!* You little rat! Come here.'

Leaf, laughing, came to her. She looked up at him, her face shiny and wet. Water dripped from her dark, spun hair and ran down her nose. Leaf grinned cheekily down at her.

'Little, you say… little?'

'You take that right away from me, okay. I really mean that, Leaf. You can easily go home.'

Jude smiled at his son. 'Listen to your mother.'

Leaf looked up briefly, nodded and then patted Zita on the head. 'Yes sir, little mother.'

Zita shook off his patronising pat and flounced back to her seat. She snapped out her newspaper and held it up as a barrier.

Leaf and Fern took their pistols round to the clothesline where Jude had hung his washing. He didn't seem to mind. I figured it would quickly dry in the heat after they lost interest. They couldn't be contained for long and Francis stayed composed when they squirted him. He grinned at them and shook the worst off his book.

In her turn, Emma was not happy. 'Oh, excuse me, what am I supposed to tell Ms Dickens about this?'

' Really!' Simone rushed over to dab at the exercise book with a tea towel. 'You two are worse than babies. Can't you find something constructive to do?'

I called, 'Hey, what about watering the plants?'

'I'll take the olive,' Fern said.

Leaf shrugged. 'Better than being yelled at.'

Nuri yowled as he took a blast on the face. He shook his paw delicately and began licking water from his feet and legs.

'Leave the cat alone!' screeched Simone before she, too, rushed into the kitchen. I followed her to attend to the bread and saw her reach for an empty wine glass and the bottle. She poured herself a hefty glass and looked up at me. 'How the hell are we going to get through this, I ask you?' I wondered if she meant the children or the wine. Her sunglasses perched on top of her smooth blonde hair like a tiara. She turned her face to the bread and inhaled deeply before looking up at me. 'You're such an earth mother, Connie.'

'So are you, Simone.'

'Never.' She laughed then, as if she were imagining something completely absurd. 'Impossible, baking bread from scratch! Never ceases to amaze me. I don't know how you do it.'

'I'll teach you, if you like.'

'Me? I could no more bake a loaf of bread than fly to the stars.'

Emma turned up in the kitchen holding out her completed story. 'Simone, here's the good copy. Can I play with Nuri?' Simone took the story and signalled for the child to wait.

Emma had just started school that year. I hate to define kids, but that child gave every impression of being precocious. She was already adept with her reading, writing and counting. I suspected Simone had high expectations and that there might have been some home-schooling going on to make sure Emma could cope with the school environment; enough to cope really well, or at least better than the other girls her age.

Simone nodded to Emma, said 'Good job, darls,' and put the exercise book and pencil case into their basket. Emma then took a carrot with leaf attached and went to torment the cat. She squatted on her haunches and laughed as Nuri rolled over onto his back and batted lazily at the dangled feather-frond.

Simone and I went outside to the table to join Jude and Zita. We all watched the game as if we were happy. We sipped chardonnay spritzers and read the nonsense weekend magazines.

'Unbelievable,' Zita exclaimed, looking up from her paper, 'Did you know Auckland still doesn't have power?'

'The whole city?' said Simone.

'Just the CBD,' said Zita.

I'd heard about it as well. 'They're putting on extra rubbish collections to get rid of the rotting food.'

'Suppose hospitals would have their own generators,' said Jude.

'They'd have to,' we all agreed. 'Wouldn't they?'

Jude asked, 'Wasn't there a power outage in Canada recently?'

'Have the governments sold off the utilities there, too?' Zita asked.

'How's Auckland going to survive without power?' asked Simone.

'They'll get it back on,' said Jude.

'It's been off for weeks now,' said Zita.

'Imagine if that happened here,' said Simone.

'I think Sydney is more organised than that,' said Zita.

'You hope,' I said. We all laughed and Zita turned another page.

Bored with her cat baiting, Emma drifted up to her mother and leaned on her. 'Simone, I'm hungry.'

'We're eating soon, aren't we?' Simone asked the table.

'No point holding up lunch just for Peter,' I agreed.

'Why don't we feed the kids first?' said Jude.

'Because there's only Emma who's a kid, that's why,' said Leaf. 'We can wait.' The two adolescents slid around the side of the building again.

'I want you two at the table,' Zita called after them. 'Come on, guys. Talk to your father.'

'Mum!'

'You don't see him enough as it is.'

'Whose fault is that?'

'We're here now, so can you please make an effort?' Zita came back to sit beside me at the table and, with dramatic flair, leaned her head into my shoulder.

I gave her a little pat. 'Teenagers!'

'Tell me about it.' She sat up, shook her head and went back to her paper.

Jude dragged his eyes from the paper and said, 'Don't worry, Zita. They'll talk to me in their own time.'

Zita hooked up an eyebrow. Her tone was dry as she said, 'Will they, indeed?'

We all heard the car in the driveway revving up. 'That's no way to treat an engine,' I muttered.

'It's a Ferrari,' came Leaf's retort from behind the sheet spinnakers the colour of pale butter. 'They're supposed to be revved. Music of the Gods.'

'Car Gods,' said Zita.

There was a squeal of tyres as the car roared out of the driveway. Peter's girlfriend, Leela, drove the Ferrari. She was a successful copyright lawyer with a perfect bum. She went to the gym five days a week to make her strong enough to harness the horsepower of her bright pink sports car.

Zita shared my amused exasperation. She knew how much I'd willed this silly girl to piss off. Having met in first year, Leela had been going out with Peter for most of their law studies. Now she was working her way up in a large multi-partnered firm and, while he was still embedded in academia, she was itching with ambition and focused on developing her budding share portfolio.

When Peter finally arrived, he quietly said to me, 'Leela apologises. She won't be coming to lunch.' I looked at him hard. 'She just dropped me off. She's busy.'

She dropped him off? Or just dropped him? Is that what I heard? A mother is allowed one question at least and I phrased this one carefully: 'Is everything okay?'

'Sure.' He looked right back at me. There was a slight pause as he considered what he would tell us. It was possible to see him phrasing His Official Position before he spoke. 'We won't be seeing her around here too much any more.' He slapped hands with his dad and went off towards the kitchen.

Hurray! Hopefully that would be the last we'd see of Leela and her bum. What a relief! Zita and I shared a signal of covert triumph as Peter clattered in the kitchen, probably looking for a beer. It didn't take long to transmit a message to a friend like her. We were on the same wavelength.

Jude went into action, stabbing the glistening, browned leg with a barbecue fork, then slicing and arranging the meat on a platter. His action was the signal for us all to troop into the kitchen to grab salads, plates and serving spoons and commence the feasting. Emma carried jars of chutney and mint sauce. I found some batik table napkins I'd bought in Kuala Lumpur. I called out to Leaf and Fern, 'Grub's up, kids!'

'On our way,' said Leaf. Was there some giggling there? Zita shrugged her shoulders and we sat. Jude began to serve the meat and the others helped themselves to salads. There was much reaching, and passing of plates, hot bread and sauce. No one said Grace.

Simone picked over her meat and turned to Jude. 'Is some of this a bit bloody?'

'It's perfect,' said Jude.

With a general murmured agreement, Simone passed her plate back for redevelopment. I ate my chickpea salad while Jude picked over the bone and found an edge well done for Simone.

As we chewed, I watched my son. At twenty-seven, Peter had grown into his bones. His thighs were covered in old jeans. He had Jude's baby blonde hair, and a decent tan after the holidays. He was a legal academic. I suppose he took the studious bent from his father. He was writing a thesis on changes in custody arrangements while he earned a basic living tutoring in Family Law. He liked to follow the adage of eight hours sleep, eight hours play and eight hours work, but tended to work when he should be playing. He did play: saxophone in a jazz band of variable membership. He was playing that night, so would be leaving right after lunch.

Peter had been with Leela for five years. He seemed subdued, possibly a little despondent, in that he didn't tease the kids or joke with his father in his usual cheery manner, but his heart wasn't broken. No way. I wondered who had done the dumping. He wasn't one for change but this apparent lack of emotion was somewhat surprising. I guessed it was he who'd initiated the breakup.

Peter had never forgiven his father for stealing our family life and giving it to Simone, but he mellowed once he met Francis. Francis's sincere grey eyes latched onto Peter; Francis's sticky baby-fingers latched onto Peter's finger, and a bond was formed between them that defied explanation. Leaf and Fern, too, when they first met the baby Francis, were completely enchanted. They burst into laughter. They caught glimpses of each other's eye lights and peeled with merriment.

Francis was sensitive. When a kid bullied him, Francis did not want to go back to school ever again. Jude and I, for Simone didn't want to get involved, met the teacher and the other parents, trying to resolve the situation. That particular case only ended when the bully left the school and then Francis was able to enjoy his sandwiches in peace without having to search for his hidden lunchbox every day.

When he slid down Cooper Park hill on a piece of cardboard in the rain once, and only the once, he broke his femur. When he went to the dentist he had more fillings than anyone else. When we played cricket, he would want to stay home and read a book. He wasn't as robust as the other kids but everyone loved him solidly. He was both the one everyone looked after and the one everyone listened to.

It was Francis who discovered that Leaf and Fern had appropriated a bottle of wine and were hiding behind the olive tree quietly making use of it. I'd noticed Francis fashioning a sandwich with lamb, salad and sauce in a chunk of bread. He repeated the operation, and then carried his two creations over behind the spinnaker washing. Peter, intrigued, followed him. There was a slight pause during which adult conversation stilted and creaked over the table. When Francis and Peter returned, Peter held an empty chardonnay bottle in his hand. 'Been missing something?' Peter plunked the bottle on the table and sat down beside me while Francis resumed his seat by Jude.

The bottle took Zita's attention. 'Where did you find that?'

Peter gestured to her kids, now standing by the clothesline, gnawing on their Francis-made sandwiches. 'Private party'.

Zita took a deep breath before getting up. Then she walked quickly to the outside tap, turned it on, and swished the hose over her children. The washing got drenched yet again. She spoke slowly and from great depth. 'Get downstairs now.'

'Mum…' said Fern.

'If you can still stand.'

'But, Mum…' said Leaf.

'Just get out of my sight. *Vattene!*'

Fern pushed Leaf. 'You drank more than me.'

Leaf opened his mouth to retaliate but Zita slashed him with her hose water sword. 'I don't care what or how much. You're both under eighteen! I have to struggle to find your brain cells as it is. Go have a shower. Go on, get out of my sight.' Leaf and Fern got. The hose water splashed onto the terracotta. I started stacking plates, Francis assisting, but paused when I saw Zita had turned her sights on Jude, still holding the hose. I moved to turn off the tap just as Peter disarmed her. He coiled the hose back to the wall. Zita didn't seem to notice. She put her hands on her hips and glared at Jude. 'What is it with you, Jude Baldwin? Can you only relate to the younger children? Or maybe it's just Simone's children?'

Simone gasped. 'Zita!'

Jude said, 'That's unfair, Zita.'

'No, you tell me. You tell me what's happening for them… your children. Anything. Go on.'

I watched as Jude looked at her, fearing he would provoke a raging that would wash him from this roof if he said the wrong thing. His eyes appeared to search his memory for something concrete to say, something that would appease this torrent of a woman. He looked to the sky, he looked to the olive tree, and he looked to me. He apparently found no clues wherever he looked and Zita continued. 'Anything at all? Go on. Tell me. What did Leaf do last week? You don't want to hear about Leaf's Year Ten camp and Fern's netball team, do you? They know that, you arsehole. They know you don't care.'

'Zita!' hissed Simone, gesturing to her young wards.

'Zita… come on, dear,' said Jude. 'I know Fern's team lost yesterday.'

'Okay, that's something. Right. What's Leaf's band called?'

'Something about enemies, isn't it?'

'Enemies? Is that a Freudian slip? They are the Mortal Enemas. Enema, not enemies. How about Fern's latest love?'

'Okay, I'll admit I didn't know she had a boyfriend. When did that happen?'

'It's a pony, Jude. Her friend Tilly owns it. Star's the only thing she's been talking about for the last three weeks. You've got to start taking an interest. Or at least pretend you're taking an interest. They need their father to pay attention. Starting now. Starting last year, actually. You've got to be responsible, if that's at all possible. Otherwise,' and this came with a rush of emotion, 'I don't know that we can continue living here. I can't cope by myself while pretending that you're helping. We may as well live separately. It's a joke. Don't you think?'

Jude closed his eyes. A gust of wind lifted his fringe and ruffled the grapevine. Jude's policy had always been one of least said, soonest mended. He thought it better for Zita to get it all out of her system and let bygones be bygones. He opened his eyes when he thought she'd finished. He looked at her and said cautiously, 'Zita, I'm sorry. I can't be everywhere but I can try. I'll pop down and see them in a minute. Okay?'

Zita shot a glance at me, and then looked back at Jude. 'It will have to do, won't it?' She took her salad bowls and went home.

Jude moved closer to Simone and reached for the bowls of lollies she held to place into her basket. The diamantes on her tee shirt coruscated as they caught the glare of the sinking sun. Jude held up his hand as if to shield his eyes from the blinding flashes. The two of them even began to laugh. The newly responsible father figure encouraged Francis to go with Emma, off to the bath with them, while he and Simone gathered the cat, all happy families. All except

Nuri, who could never be happy in that yearning way of the yelling Siamese.

Peter and I washed the dishes in my kitchen where, if I stood on tiptoe, I could just see over to the tall green pines of Manly Beach. I said to him, 'You know, your father loves all of you children'.

I don't know why I was surprised at the silence.

Peter said, 'Mum, he left us'.

He didn't, I thought. I did not say a word but I thought, he didn't, you know. I pulled out the plug and swirled the water down the drain. He's still here. He's still here, with me.

Chapter 4

Bird bath

Back then Queenie was deeply upset by Jude's determination to marry me. The old lady stopped eating and began to fade away with disappointment because she believed her youngest child was to endure a mixed marriage. Even though I was happy to convert, I could never be a proper Catholic in Queenie's eyes.

At the time, when Father Brian asked me, I believed I was freely entering into marriage with Jude. No one was forcing me. I envisaged a partnership of love for a lifetime and was open to the possibility of bringing new life into the world. I wanted to honour and obey my husband. I wanted to be the heart of the marriage, and I wanted him to be the head. The heart and the brain can never be separated; they are the shape of the body: veins, arteries and nerves. I believed Jude was clever enough for both of us. I believed he would know best.

Of course, all these things mean nothing now that my marriage has been annulled. According to the church, it never happened. But it did.

It happened like this: it was the very end of 1963 and a liquid sun morning in Balmain when we married in the Catholic faith. As we arrived, a willy willy skittered leaves across the road. Dad and Sheryl were there together and my mother was away. Jude's sister,

Stella, and two of Jude's older brothers were also there. William was swanning around Roma, the eternal city, so he missed my commitment to the man I loved.

In the dusty rear of St. Augustine's church, Mary held the body of her broken son taken down from the cross. Her eyes were raised to heaven and his knees were grazed.

~~~~~

Knees develop differently in boys and girls. A baby has only a sort of cartilage kneecap. By the age of three, females have developed a bony patella. Yet little boys take about five years to grow their bony knees. Why such a difference, I wonder? Both boys and girls surely fall over and graze their knees at much the same rate? This is why we need science—to answer all our mysteries. Everything unanswerable is left to religion.

~~~~~

After the service we had a right royal shindig, a good old knees-up, with our uni and tech friends and our families. Not long after that, Queenie died. People said she died from a broken heart because of me. Or perhaps it was the ovarian cancer.

Jude and I didn't think we'd been particularly lucky with our mothers-in-law, but we could always rely on Sheryl. Ever since my childhood, when Sheryl had lived next door, she had been my proper mother. Sheryl's son, William, wasn't in Sydney and I was. Sheryl helped me with the entire wedding business: dealing with Father Brian and Queenie, negotiating fittings with the dressmaker and arranging the florist. Sheryl, steadfast C of E, was a magnificent stage manager, a true friend and a better mother.

So I was surprised when Sheryl whispered to me as we stared at my white-dressed reflection prior to leaving for church. With a wry look she told me she couldn't help wishing it was her son but that's just a mother's foolishness. Then she kissed me and reassured me Jude was absolutely the right man, as if I didn't know that full well! There was never anyone else for me. Her wish was nothing more than an amusing aside. I'd never considered William in that light and he paled into insignificance in the face of my Jude.

I would follow Jude anywhere and that's just what happened next and it happened quickly. A chance meeting at a conference at Sydney University, Jude's excellent academic record, a recommendation from his professor, and he was offered a research assistant position in the genetics and embryology department at Cambridge University. I had only just found buyers for my products in Sydney. I was successful and now Jude was leaving. I didn't want to leave my Dad alone. I thought maybe I could follow on in a couple of years when Jude was more settled and we were more financial.

My mother was the one who put the clincher on it. She pointed out that my 'little pottery hobby' could be pursued anywhere. Even though she maintained two years separation might be the best thing for us (given her distaste for my new religion) she could see the idea of parting made us miserable. She bought tickets for us to travel by sea, for she believed flying was extravagant and that we would enjoy the time to relax after the fuss of our wedding. Jude was taken aback by her impulsive generosity, believing she wanted nothing to do with him ever but I think she actually liked him by then.

There was a whirl of packing and farewells and then we were on the deck of S. S. Peripetia holding handfuls of multi-coloured streamers. Dad and Sheryl and Queenie and the family, looking small and far away, all looked up at us and walked along as the ship began to move and held the other ends of the crepe paper strings and the huge foghorn blew and I jumped and burst into tears. The streamers stretched out across the water, providing that last fragile connection between those on the ship and those on the wharf. They broke and fell away and the thin criss-crossing lines of colour sank into the sea and I couldn't see for tears and Jude hugged me and we were on our way through the Heads.

~~~~~

A few days after Jude's family barbecue, Emma spent an afternoon painting in my studio. She was one of the most prolific painters I'd ever known and I've seen a few young artists in my time. It didn't take her a minute to finish a work. Even when I'd suggest she take more time or add more detail she'd declare the next one finished and demand more paper. I'd slung a rope across the garage so we could peg her many works out to dry. After the rope had been hung end to end with curious grinning faces with explosive red hair, with purple cats and tall green buildings, and with one particularly energetic work featuring fat, green, criss-cross lines that she informed me was the Sydney Harbour Bridge, I suggested she hop into the shell pool in the courtyard to remove the worst of the paint. She held the hose over the pool and when I judged it full enough, turned it off.

'Constance! That's not fair. It only comes up to my knees!'

'It will do.'

Emma got in and splashed and the droplets sprayed through the sunshine. She found her inner three-year-old and remembered we used to play tea parties with plastic measuring jugs. She happily poured until she started to drink the painty water she sat in. When I remonstrated with her, she insisted she had to drink as much as she could. 'I'm being Tiddalick,' she said.

'What's a Tiddalick?'

'He's the frog that drank up all the water and the other animals had to work out how to get the water back and they had to make Tiddalick laugh so he'd spit out the water so they could all share it again.'

'Where did you hear about this creature?'

'Charlotte's.'

'Charlotte? Who is Charlotte?' I asked innocently, thinking Charlotte would be a friend from school. But no, I had the wrong friend and the wrong school.

'You know. Daddy's friend.'

'Was Daddy there?'

'Course he was. Helping her with homework.'

Helping her with homework, was he. Good old daddy. Sharing again.

I asked Emma, 'Can't you just pretend to drink the water?' She did pretend and Tiddalick laughed and flung measured jugfuls of water into the sun and watched the rainbows arch against the crimson bougainvillea.

So, Charlotte did exist and she was telling our children dream-time stories.

~~~~~

Up on rooftop, tip dirty birdbath water out. Scrub with old dish-washing brush. Run clean water into it with the hose. Jude's next piece will be a birdbath. He'll like that. Or not. Don't really know what he'd like. Less and less sure what I know about him. Now I've learned about mutating disappearing frogs, not exactly sure who Jude is. Can't understand why he didn't say anything. Frogs were his life. Wonder if he did tell me but I didn't hear. How would I have recognised his panic? What would he have said? That frogs are disappearing? But they weren't sure. They didn't know. Nothing was certain. Still isn't. For science, everything is a possibility, everything only a likelihood, more or less up to the latest theory.

The birds wait; queued up in trees, ready to take their splashy turn in the birdbath. Once there, families cluster around the edge. They sound like they argue about who should go next, chirping and squarking. Once in the water, they fling and splash in their determination to get totally wet. Heads down and wings arching, they whisk with brisk purpose. Both social and business in the bath.

Birdbath should be kept clean to avoid birds passing on mites and other, more terrifying for us humans, bird diseases. Shallow enough for the birds to be able to walk, placed on a pedestal high enough to prevent cat attack, and close to trees where the birds can escape to safety. Simone's cat, Nuri, used to be very interested in the birdbath when he visited, but that's all over now.

Stalk of birdbath is made from three concentric, bevelled-edge cylinders. Throw them on the wheel. They're large and squat at ground level, becoming slender as they rise to the bowl. A stake, driven into the earth, or a purpose-built stand, holds the three tubes steady. The bowl rests on the top cylinder with an indentation for added security. The whole conspires to make an unfolding, a four-part offering to nature.

The pedestal sections are part of a cone; in essence, one flared leg, although altered and shaped. The bowl is vaguely triangular to hint at the profile of Mount Baw Baw. Clay sprigs cover the surface of both bowl and pedestal. They are designed to imitate the warts of the Baw Baw frog. Glaze contains bone ash. Imperfections in finish look like motley frog skin.

Recent medical research has discovered certain frog skins can cure human infections like amphibian Band-Aids. Who knows where the next magical healing ingredient might be found? Could it be that the critically endangered Baw Baw frog has healing properties? It hides under rocks and logs near streams and sphagnum bogs. If this frog could be used to save lives, would humans try harder to save the species?

Underside of the birdbath is curdled creamy-yellow on brown, like the smooth belly and throat of the Baw Baw frog, *Philoria frosti*. The frog's habitat is threatened by a ski resort and climate change.

~~~~~

In Cambridge, we lived off-campus in a tiny flat. Jude commenced his doctorate research and, utilising some of his findings, had papers published in The Australian Scientific Journal. They served to remind his Australian colleagues he was still alive. In *Australian specimens in European museums: how and why they were collected*, he discussed the very frog I'd dissected in Biology One—the green and golden bell frog, *Litoria aurea*. Jude discovered that Charles Darwin himself had presented one of these frogs to the British Museum.

Cambridge is an otherworldly experience. The landscape, the buildings, the formalities are steeped in tradition, cut off from modern matters, its Puritanical history leading to purist thoughts.

Jude was perfectly capable of looking after himself and it seemed best to leave him to make the most of this opportunity. I couldn't sit around and twiddle my thumbs, so while Jude concentrated on academia, I sought my mud. I researched and visited pottery luminaries and offered to apprentice myself. I guess they'd call it 'work experience' now. Fortuitously, I met Bernard Leach's grandson, John, at a gallery and he invited me to meet the Leach family who were, of course, the great British pottery dynasty. I stayed with them in St Ives for three months. Mr Leach told me about the teachings of Soetsu Yanagi and *shibui*. In direct English translation *shibui* means astringent but in Japanese the concept means many things: profound, unassuming and quiet feeling.

Of course, I had read Mr Leach's, *A Potter's Book* when I was at East Sydney Tech but when I was there, in St Ives, looking at the kiln he'd built in the Japanese style and talking with him and the others in the studio I could see what he meant when he wrote, 'Enduring forms are full of quiet assurance' and 'Overstatement is worse than understatement'. On my return to Jude, I began to work out of a garage just around the corner in the thin lanes of Cambridge exploring the notions of *shibui* in my own Australian way.

The taste of Japan emanating from Mr Leach's work so whetted my appetite that I longed to experience that ancient tradition for myself. It took three years of scrimping and saving, but in April of 1965, I left Jude in the yellow sandstone of Cambridge and flew to Tokyo, a trip that was to be the highlight of my time away from Australia. The Leach family arranged for me to be met at Tokyo airport and billeted with families throughout my stay. The Tokyo Museum housed examples pottery of the Sung dynasty, the style I had seen in Melbourne previously. A single anonymous person utilising the knowledge of many generations builds each fine piece. There is great humility in subjugating one's own need to show off to the purpose of the utensil. A bowl is entirely and simply a bowl. It seems obvious to write this now but, standing in Tokyo, absorbing the quiet air of each piece, it was a revelation.

I returned to Cambridge with my head bubbling over with ideas and my hands itching to sink into clay. While Jude wrote and lectured, I set to work, and before long was turning out enough decent ware to find regular buyers in London.

Meanwhile, Jude climbed the academic ladder, specialising first in embryology, and then tending his growing interest in genetics which was all the rage in Cambridge after Watson, Crick and team discovered DNA. Jude published several papers. One, in published in Nature, titled *Adaptive evolutionary mechanisms in ranine development*, gained much attention and in 1968, as a Post-Doctoral Research Fellow, he gave a populist lecture at the Royal Society entitled *Cytoplasmic inheritance in an agricultural setting.* Although it made me proud to see him confidently talking about his studies and network-ing with academics and scientists from around the world, I'm afraid I understood little of what he was saying.

When I lost the baby, everything changed. Cambridge lost all colour. I had the miscarriage, not knowing I'd been pregnant, and was disappointed beyond understanding. Jude was solicitous and, as we imagined our lost little boy, agreed that we needed to get back to Australia and sunshine.

We bought a red Kombi van and made plans to drive across Europe, a trip we hoped would return adventure to our lives. We studied books, read maps and sought introductions to people who had made similar journeys. These adventurers and pilgrims gave us advice and warnings in equal measure. Trepidation grew in me but Jude insisted we remain calm. He didn't see why we should focus on possible dangers when we were about to learn so much about the world and all its cultures. We wanted to drive all the way to Austral-ia—well, as close as we could possibly get—seeing as much of Europe and the Middle East as practicable. Luckily, I'd just filled an order for Elizabeth David's kitchenware shop and that helped pay for our crazy journey home.

We drove through France and down to Naples to meet William before the three of us travelled to Positano together. William rented a villa with a magnificent view of the sea and the Amalfi coast. Jude and I were so pale and worn down by England, all we could do was lounge on our terrace, admire the view, sunbake, clink our glasses of chilled Trebbiano and dine on homemade spaghetti pomodoro, searing pizza marinara, and fresh black figs followed by copious quantities of Chianti Classico, green picante olives and thin, crisp grissini bread. We all drank far too much. William was getting over a love affair where he'd refused to convert. Given my history, I thought he'd given up too soon, he couldn't possibly have really loved her, and it was easy to become a Catholic. Of course, Jude and I were melancholy after the loss of our baby.

Our emotional fog lifted in Positano, such an unlikely growth of buildings and cliff and sea and such intensity of colour. The town was organic, as though the human constructions were lichen or fungus clinging in the cleft of the rock face. After a week of lying dormant we sprang up, ready to be tourists. William translated for us and we travelled the thin winding roads in the Kombi with no fear, searching for life, light and the sweet juice of the Sangiovese grape.

A highlight was a day spent wandering around Pompeii. I started on autopilot with a filthy hangover and sorrow over those thousands of wasted lives. Ironically, together with Positano energy, the coloured frescoes and statues lifted my spirits. The surviving pottery shards were of particular fascination—such magnificent deep-red slices of baked earth. I was inspired by their vitality. I sketched them, capturing designs I would utilise when I got home.

Our time on the Amalfi coast was marked by stimulation, motivation and fun. There were ceramicists to visit: wonderful plates, traditional patterns, and bright glazing. Everything was sensual: zesty limoncello, ripped basil, sweet glistening tomato, and soft, white mozzarella; the intense colours of bikinis on the beach, geometric umbrellas and gritty yellow sand; emotional vibrations of hysterical tenor arias of the chef in our favourite cafe. Overlaying everything, the drama of the bougainvillea: eruptions of violet, red sunbursts and copper fire shading walkways or clamouring up walls.

In my memories of our journey, our Great Adventure, Jude was smiling, his hands resting on the grey steering wheel of the Kombi. He wore a paisley scarf around his tanned neck and his lolloping yellow hair bounced down towards his shoulders. His black sunglasses reflected my sunglasses and white teeth.

We dropped William back in Naples and hit the long road (back to Australia!) ready for anything. We drove through Austria, Hungary, Romania and Bulgaria and into Turkey. We saw a lot of road and met many friendly and generous folk who entertained us. We camped where we could, kept to the road as much as possible, and discovered dust in the desert areas. We had to clean the engine filter every day and it was a battle to stay on the tar sealed road, as no one wanted their vehicle to land in up to two feet of dust on the roadside.

We were lucky; during the whole trip of six months we only had three punctures. We did, however, have some hair-raising escapes. For instance, as we approached the Khyber Pass we met a Swiss family who warned us about bandits. They'd been attacked and their van was pockmarked with bullet holes to prove it. They were very shaken and, last we saw, were off to buy a gun. We would never consider carrying a gun though we respected their experience might have given them just cause and set off warily up the precipitous road. Soon enough we noticed a small vehicle in front of us slowing down. It was impossible to pass. The ute had a tray at the back where about half a dozen cheerful young men sneered back at us. The vehicle slowed down even further and Jude grew exasperated. They clearly intended to invade the Kombi. We could not turn around; we couldn't go back, so Jude told me he was going to make a break for it and to hang on. As they grew slower and laughed more Jude planted his foot and overtook them on two wheels, half driving up the cliff. He'd turned into Mad Max but there was nothing else for it and it was only lucky the angle was not so extreme to cause the Kombi to fall back on them. The bandits were taken by surprise and we didn't bother to look behind us as we cleared out as quickly as we could. I thought Jude was a hero but then I'd always thought that.

We ate only what we saw prepared in front of us, boiled and peeled, but in Bombay (now it's Mumbai) Jude got sick. He suffered terribly with fever, vomiting and diarrhoea, possibly from bad ice in a drink, and we saw the end of the road. I sold the Kombi to an American ex-GI who wanted to drive to Goa. We flew out of India, Jude too weak to continue our heroic plan to drive towards Australia via Singapore.

Back in Sydney, just in time for the Vietnam moratorium, I discovered I was pregnant. Dad insisted we stay with him. He said he didn't enjoy rattling around the house in Greenwich by himself and made us believe he really wanted the company. We slotted back in as though we'd only been away a few weeks rather than six years. Jude contacted his academic colleagues in the hope of finding work and was glad to accept an associate professorship at Sydney University. I contended with a growing belly while trying to complete more and more orders on the wheel.

Our son, Peter, arrived on the 4th of September 1970 in the most straightforward and normal of births. Breastfeeding was another story. It was the days of four-hourly feeding. Although my breasts would became so swollen they'd involuntarily spurt milk, the staff at Royal North Shore had to obey their instructions and would take Peter from me. Swollen breasts turned into mastitis and by the time I left hospital, my milk supply was decreasing and Peter was going hungry. I couldn't wait to get home and disobey medical orders.

The idea of bottle-feeding seemed absurd to me having seen women around the world feeding calmly and easily. What was I doing wrong?

Sheryl encouraged me to attend a nearby mothers' group. It turned out to be a discussion group on breastfeeding and, though we didn't know it at the time, part of the embryonic Nursing Mothers' Association. We were encouraged to bring our babies and children to someone's home and talk about what it was like to feed and care for children and look after a house and feeding whenever the baby was hungry. At the very least, feeding on demand meant I didn't suffer from engorgement.

Being university holidays, Jude was able to take over cooking and cleaning duties for the first couple of weeks we were home. Dad was a great support too, preparing food for us after Jude returned to uni, never complaining when the baby woke him, and letting us sleep when Peter slept. Mum sent us a case of Verve Cliquot from wherever she was at the time. I was able to relax and feed Peter enough to build up supply again, learning from pamphlets from the La Leche League in America and new information from Nursing Mothers. It seemed common sense to me: women needed to share their experiences; we needed to live in a wider community; and we all needed help to raise our children.

Jude once told me that living with a baby in the house had given him an understanding of infinity. Some of our friends could not envisage infinity; they had to have a beginning and an end to time and space and clung to the notion of the Big Bang with vehemence. After Peter was born, Jude would ask people to imagine looking into a crying baby's face at three o'clock in the morning, to imagine the throbbing music helping the baby remember its time in the blood-pulsing womb. The Seekers' version of *The times they are a-changin'* had already worn thin and The Master's Apprentices were *Lighting a fire* for so long it burned into us the certain knowledge that this child would never stop. Crying. Red-in-the-face-crying. Little-body-arching-and-bending-crying. Loud crying. Ceaseless crying that claws deep into genetic survival guts and grabs and pulls at the very centre of a parent's being. Got the idea? That's infinity.

It seemed to me that every separate phase of the child's life went on forever. When chopping up fruit at kinder, it never ended; manning the sausage sizzle at cricket, it never ended; bringing cocoa late at night to support study for exams, it never ended; lying awake at night waiting for the sound of his car when he'd just got his licence and was out at a party, it never ended.

In hindsight, of course, it was not infinity at all. Once the child was grown, people would say wistful things like it goes so quickly or they grow up so fast and I would wish that baby back into my arms so my lips might twist the fine, fine hair, and nuzzle the scalp and breathe in that baby air... I suppose that's why they invented grandchildren.

I was breast-feeding in the days when it wasn't done. Not in public. You'd have to sit in the women's toilets and try to avoid hitting the baby's head on the toilet paper dispenser. With great daring, I would sneak the baby under my shirt in a quiet corner of the Argyle Art Centre. Another reason to be grateful to the Nursing Mothers, who suggested suitable places to feed and change babies in the city. Bit tricky for us new mums to burn our bras but there was still plenty of feminism in the Nursing Mothers!

It was, however, the time to be a potter. Everyone, in their flares and leather coats, bought pottery mugs, wine goblets, ashtrays and bread bins. I was busy and in love with my baby. We didn't have much money and we really wanted a home of our own.

Jude and I were still living with Dad and we felt it was getting too close. We needed to get out and live by ourselves. I'd told Jude I wanted a large family but didn't want to get pregnant until we'd saved enough to buy our own home. So I went to the doctor. I didn't trust the rhythm method, and neither did the doctor. He suggested a new option, the IUD. He said that nearly all the Catholic women he saw practised some kind of birth control. Glad to know I needed practice, I let him put a Dalkon shield in my uterus, despite the Pope having condemned artificial birth control in 1968. It wasn't as if we were using condoms. It was just until we became more settled and a bit more financial. We wanted to fulfil our Catholic duties. At least I did, but just not right there and then.

Jude was ambitious. He wanted academic tenure and the university bigwigs seemed to think he was suitable. He was keen to publish from Australia and was deeply involved in fieldwork, researching amphibian biology. After so much laboratory work in Cambridge, he really enjoyed camping, searching for and documenting different species. He and a colleague began work on a Field Guide to Australian Frogs and would travel most weekends and holidays to observe frogs and tadpoles in their natural habitats.

We moved to Glebe to be closer to the university. There were students and staff clustered around us now. There were urgent political discussions over bowls of steaming spaghetti and rough red flagon wine. It was time. Gough Whitlam became Australia's twenty-first Prime Minister on the fifth of December 1972 and change was in the air. Everyone smoked cigarettes. The seventies were defined by a stratus of tobacco haze in every room, over every barbecue, over entire Sydney suburbs and, it seemed, over the entire coastline of Australia.

After one field trip to Victoria with his students, Jude walked through our front door, his green tartan shirt stained with mud and torn at one shoulder. His eyes were serene and his arms reached for me even before he dropped his pack. His jeans were so filthy they felt like cardboard and his hair was wild. He scooped me into his wilderness smell of wood smoke blurred with foul, dirty man. The smell reminded me of putrid cheese the colour of his shirt. His eyes twinkled and he wouldn't let me go even though the front door stood open. He touched my face, kissed me, laughed because he knew his stubble scratched. He began to undo his shirt and I laughed, too. He began to move in the direction of the bedroom but I steered him instead towards the shower. We were both laughing in that daring, jeering, oh-ho-ho kind of way as I pushed him into the shower recess and turned on the taps even as I kissed him. The cold water flattened his hair over his eyes yet he wouldn't let me go as I tried to get the temperature warm enough. A bottle of shampoo leaned in the little wire basket hanging from the shower arm. I reached for it and before Jude could know, flipped the lid off, massaged a good dose of shampoo into his head and let a white froth of lavender run over his water-shine. I was soaked, his strong arms were out of his shirt, and his trousers were down around his knees.

I struggled away out of the shower because Jude was still wearing his boots and there was no way I'd have sex with him, not with his boots on, not to mention that rasping stubble on his chin. Jude just laughed and bent to take his boots off.

I became aware of the child who had woken and arrived in the foggy bathroom to find his daddy was home. Laughing with us, little Peter lugged Jude's wet and muddy boots into the hallway. I called after him to take them straight outside, went for extra towels to mop up the mess, taking Jude's stinky bush clothes with me.

It was only when Jude was drying himself that I noticed the grubby bandage on his knee. He told me that he'd fallen and twisted awkwardly. Knees work as shock absorbers but they don't like to be twisted. After removing the bandage, I rubbed liniment into both his knees and calves. His calves hung bulging from the sharp, shin tibia. Jude said they were really aching. It was not so much going up the mountain, he told me, it was coming down where it was so much easier to lose control.

When I developed a pelvic infection it was annoying. Just as I began to feel well again, the infection returned. I was very sick. The gynaecologist told me I wasn't the only one. The Dalkon shield was to blame. There was doubt at first, and then my dreams of a large family filtered away. I would be infertile. Empty. Futile. Me. Over.

The day the gynie told me, I ran. I ran through Glebe and Annandale and Camperdown. A dog jumped up at me and chased me. Groups of kids parted in front of me. Elderly ladies dragged their shopping trolleys out of my way. I ran until my shins were splintered. I ran until my knees were in agony. They had not absorbed the shock.

All that remained were other people's babies. There were prams and pushers everywhere. At the beach on bright sunny days when children shouted and pushed at each other in the shallows while the water lapped at my calves, my eyes blurred as if rain was falling. One day I threw up in the gutter outside a maternity shop. It was a heaving and outpouring of anger like a volcano. After that I started to grow numb. Perhaps I was turning to stone, like one of my pots, caught in the fire.

I worked and worked in my overcrowded studio amongst teapots, mugs and platters all splattered with clay slurry. I felt, in the distance, a growling argument between craftspeople, artists, ceramicists and funding bodies. I couldn't see what all the fuss was about. What difference did it make if the piece was about form or function? Why should that influence government funding? Is a thing made by an artist only art if it could not possibly be used to cook a casserole?

Strange that the search for essence and form should be happening at the same time as Picasso was expressing his disdain for function in art. When I went to Uji in Japan, I was shocked by their constant focus on purpose. Mr T. Matsubayashi, who built the Leach kiln in St Ives, came from Uji. He was part of the thirty-ninth generation of the Uji family of potters. Tradition and purpose minimise individual ego. In Japanese pottery, utility is the first principle of beauty—what Mr Leach's friend, Mr Yanagi, called *cha-no-yu*—whereas Picasso was thinking just the opposite.

~~~~~

Sydney's first Customs House, containing the Bond Store, was built in The Rocks, Australia's first suburb. It was a solid brick building with stout wooden doors and bars over dramatically arched windows. The NSW Government, in the shape of the Sydney Cove Redevelopment Authority, approved the creation of a centre for artists in 1970. That old Argyle Bond Store, once Tooth's Brewery, became the Argyle Arts Centre. It was a very exciting venture to find on my return to Australia and I was inspired by the energy of artists coming together in such a historic venue.

The Argyle Arts Centre received no subsidies—it had to survive on the proceeds of sales of arts and crafts. A well-regarded group of ceramicists displayed and sold their work in a venue called Ceramic Crafts. The group's leader, Des Howard, explained to me that he needed high quality domestic wares and decorative pieces at reasonable prices. As that was exactly what I had been making in Cambridge I was invited to join.

There was traditional art on the ground floor, a portrait artist and another gallery showing modern work on the top floor, and Mary Reiby's Parlour sold coffee and cake. Between the top and bottom floors, Argyle Arts Centre also attracted spinners and weavers, silver and gold workers, leatherworkers, copper workers and a candle maker.

All of those involved were excited by the vision of the Arts Centre with its great ironbark rafters, by our flared jeans, and by the bleeding colours of stained glass chunks. David Saunders, whose glasswork varied from delicate church windows to concrete abstract pieces, was on the top floor and I always enjoyed visiting his studio and listening to his Scots burr. Saunders loved to argue that he was not an artist, but an artist craftsman. I also conducted demonstrations on the kick wheel for Rocko Badolato, a master potter from Italy who ran a shop called Clay of the Earth.

Over the years, The Argyle Arts Centre became more and more commercial. Touristy and mass-produced work seemed the only way to pay the bills, and I stopped sending work there in the eighties.

Jude was spending more and more time at uni, while still going out on field trips and working on the guide. Peter started Prep at the local Catholic primary school, a Gothic place of dark-red brick and pointed roof. I was bringing in good money. It was very sad.

Chapter 5

Footrest stone

Achilles's mother, dipping him into the river Styx to give him extraordinary strength, had to hold him by some tiny handhold as if dipping a pot into glaze. She didn't have a glazing claw, so she held him by the back of his ankle.

It seems that everything has a vulnerable point, like the sacrificial fuse in an electrical circuit, when tested beyond endurance. Achilles's tendon became a weakness to exploit. A canary in a mine is a sacrificial device. Who can see the sacrifice frogs must make in anthropogenic climate change? Who is the weakest link?

~~~~~

Francis and Emma were shelling peas as we sat around my kitchen table. It was a sultry afternoon. The sliding doors were open to the roof garden. Leaves on the grapevine were edged with yellow and brown.

Simone called through the front door before she came in. The clouds lifted and light beamed into the flat. Francis kept on shelling but Emma leapt up and ran to grab her mum. Simone dropped the cat and hugged her child. The cat walked with stiff legs across the Persian carpets around the room and yowled.

Simone said, 'Hello, my darling poppets.'

'Mum! You're late.'

'Who are you? Mussolini?'

'What's that?'

'It's never-you-mind, Ms Know-it-all.'

It was clear that Simone had visited her place before picking up her children, having bought Nuri with her. Her blonde hair was smooth and lustrous and worn in a ponytail. Her face was clear and proud. It was a thin face, the bones a stark frame for her smooth skin canvas, full mouth, slender nose and sculpted eyebrows. Her eyes were startling, almost a violet iridescence—she might have been a model. In fact she had been, when the offer was good enough, until the profit margin on the other side of the camera became irresistible. Maybe it was the control that was irresistible.

Simone arrived at the table. Emma still clung to her mother's side. 'I don't know at all, that's why you have to tell me what a muscle-een is. Or I'll be ignorant. And you don't want that, do you, Simone?'

Simone rolled her eyes at me, then bent down and kissed Emma. 'Mussolini made the trains run on time.' She turned to her son. 'Hi, Francis. Okay?' She kissed him gently on the top of his head. 'Gorgeous. Glad to see you've put them both to work, Con.'

'Least they can do.'

'Actually, kids, do you think Connie's got some icy-poles in her freezer?'

'Luckily for you, I do. Can you reach the top shelf, Emma?'

'If I stand on a chair.' She reached for a chair and began to drag it over to the fridge. 'Then I can, easily.'

Francis pushed his chair back, 'I'll do it'.

'Thanks, darling,' said Simone. 'Is there something you can find to do in the other room?'

'I'll take my book outside. Thanks Connie,' said Francis, his icy-pole in one hand and Ivan Southall's *Ash Wednesday* in his other.

Emma followed, taking the icy-pole proffered by her brother saying, 'Can you read to me, Francis?'

Nuri stretched out on the rug in a sunny spot by the sliding glass doors.

'Simone? Wine? It's in the fridge. Help yourself.'

Simone and I sat at the kitchen bench. She pulled the cork on a bottle of Chardonnay and poured us each a glass. We raised our drinks to the murmur of Francis reading out in the roof garden and I continued to pod peas into the colander. 'Good idea those kids went away. We'll get more peas. Your Emma likes to chew on a pea. Only reason there's any in the colander at all is Francis.'

Simone appeared casual enough but her voice was tense when she asked, 'What do you know about her?'

I glanced up to make sure we were both talking about the same 'her'. 'Are we sure, then?'

'Sure about what? That his innocent children have reported to me that daddy's girlfriend likes lemon sorbet?'

'They actually used the word, "girlfriend"?'

'Does that matter?'

'Emma told me her name.'

'What?'

'Charlotte. She's called Charlotte.'

'Charlotte the harlot. Marvellous.' Simone loosened her strappy high heels and kicked them off across the room. One landed on Nuri's back. He howled and ran out to the garden.

'Oops! Sorry, Nureyev!' She stretched her feet as though doing exercises on a plane. She had hideous feet, having been a dancer. The toes were squashed together. They caused her serious pain. She rubbed them each in turn, grimacing a little, in between sips of sunny wine. 'How long have you known?'

'I don't know exactly what I'm supposed to know. Peter first dropped it. Intimated. Or something. He thinks something is going on. He's very vague. Not sure what she means to him.'

'Peter? He's met her?'

'I don't know. He saw them together at uni at the start of the year; it made him angry. That's all I know.'

'Peter? Saw them? Together? Doing what? Talking? More? What?'

I shrugged through her interrogation. She knew just as much as I did. All I could add was, 'Enough to get him worked up, whatever it was.'

Simone was on the warpath. She asked, 'Where is he?'

'Who?'

'Peter. Let's get him up here.' Simone moved to the phone.

'He'll still be at uni.'

She sat down again. Took a long drink, long enough to finish it. Looked at her empty glass and picked up the bottle. 'What the hell are we going to do?' She poured. A flash of sunlight reflected through the gold. Took a sip. I didn't have any answers. We pondered the condensation on the bottle.

I stretched out a finger to wipe a pattern into the water droplets gathered on the glass. 'Is there anything we can do?'

'Kill him?'

Didn't we laugh! Simone snorted wine from her nostrils and her eyes seemed full of glare. I got her a tissue.

She said, 'Is this what it was like for you? With Zita?'

'No. That was different.'

'And with me?'

'Different again.'

It's always been different and it's always seemed like betrayal.

~~~~~

Footrest is a simple, hollow, coiled pot. Use the extruder again. Giant garlic press with only one exit point. Collect a tray of smooth snake-coils. They rest on one another like turds. Blend each coil into next to make a strong wall. Use small-toothed cards to smooth surface. It becomes a shallow rectangular bowl. Leave for a couple of days to dry. As the first dries, build another and let that dry, too. Once both are the same texture, I join them, creating the rectangular boulder.

To emulate colours of the giant burrowing frog, spray footrest with differently coloured clay slips. One day, spray; the next day, polish; a layer each day for ten days; then fire.

Facts about frogs ground me. My only certainty is frog. The frog is endangered. The frog has become uncertain. Keep holding onto life, dear frog of slender limb and blinking eye. Keep on. Like me. One foot in front of the other. And then the next. One ceramic piece. And then the next.

Read about the giant burrowing frog, *Heleioporus australiacus*. Its back is dark and warty. This footstool is dark grey with yellow spots. The giant burrowing frog is listed as vulnerable. Its population is decreasing. As for so many other frogs, no one is sure why.

Although the footrest looks heavy, it is hollow. It looks old and worn. It looks like I feel… worn and heavy. Looks are deceiving, aren't they? For, like the footrest, I am simply empty.

~~~~~

It's difficult to pinpoint when a friendship has developed from a mere acquaintance to become a necessary part of life. It took an entire decade for the florist running the tiny shop at the top of Glebe Point Road to become such a friend. Initially, we would chat about my little indecisions of daffodils or violets or roses. When I mentioned I made vases, she offered to stock a small selection in her shop, for a reasonable commission, of course!

Our business relationship developed over cups of tea in the back of the florist shop together with the detritus of stems and leaves left after the flurry of bouquet making. Eventually, I invited her to share meals at our house. Zita was a powerful young woman with a sensible business brain and a large family of contacts who could help make anything happen. She had liquid, greenish-blue eyes and was never seen without mascara or a bright red lipstick. She loved to hug people. Zita was single, and according to her, all the men in Sydney were gay. What she really wanted, Zita told me, was a baby.

I could see Jude was attracted to Zita. There was calm in his eye when he talked to her such that I had not seen for years. Doing the dishes one night Jude and Zita laughed together in such a familiar way, that, after Zita had gone home, I suggested to Jude they go out, just the two of them. Jude demanded to know what I thought I was doing. I told him I wanted another baby, that I had always wanted a large family. He stared at me, saying nothing. I stared right back into his windswept blue eyes. He wanted another baby, too. I knew that. And Peter needed a sibling. Clearly, that wasn't going to happen. Not after my hysterectomy.

Oh God, this was wrong! I had disobeyed the church. I had brought this on myself, on our marriage. I had gone against all the teachings. Queenie would never forgive me. God would never forgive me. The church would never forgive me. I would never forgive myself. But I could do something to fix it. Zita would be for both of us. Zita was for our marriage, for our family and for our church. The last time I went to confession was before my marriage was annulled. I feel like I've been doing penance ever since.

~~~~~

Engrossed in books about frogs. I read that all frogs are cold-blooded (like Simone?). There are two families of frogs in Australia. The short-legged and warty myobrachids burrow. The hylids are climbers, like the green tree frogs. Hylids can grasp with their first and second fingers like a baby grasps a parent's hand. This is possibly why Jude loves them. Loved.

When he was a fresh-faced youth falling in love with frogs, I was falling in love with Jude. He talked about amphibians with excitement and passion and authority. I admired him. I was aroused by his enthusiasm. My mind drifts to him again and again. He'd be amazed I'm interested in frogs. Too late for him. It may even be too late for the frogs. Wish I could see him. Miss him.

Sometimes the giant burrowing frog is mistaken for a cane toad. Poor frog. But it doesn't have those evil glands behind its neck that the cane toad does. The male burrowing frogs often have black spines on their fingers to make sure they get good firm hold of those wriggling females.

~~~~~

Zita was a maternal figure even when I first met her. She appeared big, probably because she was loud and tended to the dramatic gesture, her Italian heritage, I suppose. During our little tea breaks in the back of the shop, Zita and I talked about everything. She was born in Leichhardt where her parents had a greengrocer shop. There were four children, the oldest a boy, then the three girls. Zita was the middle daughter and, growing up, had enjoyed working with her family, even as a small child, getting up early, going to the markets in her holidays and working in the shop after school. Her oldest brother was the natural heir to the throne, while her older sister married and fell pregnant as soon as she left school. Zita developed the flower side of the business once she had left school.

Once her older sister had had her first child, Zita's mum stopped introducing Zita to eligible bachelors (all invited to dinner under the most flimsy of pretexts) and no longer nagged her about getting married. But there were sickening arguments after she fell in love with a married man, so she went to work for one of her cousins who owned a florist shop in the city.

Realising that her life choices were now entirely up to her, Zita completed a business course and opened a little floristry in the popular shopping strip of Glebe. The married man, supporting her endeavours at that stage, lived nearby.

That modest shop became very popular. Zita initially took on a part-time assistant but within a year had need of two full-time employees. She became firm friends with a number of her regular customers and with other shopkeepers in the strip.

~~~~~

Jude and I talked about adoption. We talked about fostering. More talk. He said he loved me. I said I loved him. I said I understood he must want his own children and why not? He was still young. He could. I wanted to see more of his children. I always had. We discussed open marriages. They were all the rage. It wasn't for me, or for him. I wanted a closed marriage or nothing. I pointed out that Zita was a real Catholic. She was the daughter-in-law Queenie never had. Up in her heaven, Queenie would approve. She could rest in peace.

I told Jude I was giving him his freedom. I told him that I thought he should marry Zita and get on with having their large family. We cried together. We had lots of tearful sex together. Then Peter and I moved back to Dad's place while Jude stayed in Glebe and Zita moved in.

Luckily, no-fault divorces came through just in time and then; over the next eighteen months we went through the annulment process to satisfy the Church. Sheryl, together with Mum and Dad, struggled with the whole plan. They couldn't believe what I was doing. They went round and round. Marriage. Love. Families. Home. Babies. What was wrong with one child? Couldn't we have an open marriage? Could Zita? The cold hand of jealousy continued to squeeze my heart every time I breathed. But I was doing my duty.

This was the seventies. I told them I thought, as did the Catholic Church, that marriage was all about family and children, no matter how they spun it after Vatican II. Peter was my child—I loved him and so did Jude. While he had the chance to make more children, he should take it. It would give me the opportunity to be involved with his children, too. We would all have more family. I was confident Jude would not keep them away from me. It was going to be good for everyone.

No matter what I said back then, I believed, and still do, that humans mate for life. It was weakness perhaps, a girlish dream, head in clouds, making pencil marks on uni paper, my dreaming of Mrs Baldwin, Mrs Not-Her-Name, Mrs Her-Married-Name, Mrs Jude Baldwin. I would sit in lectures in a reverie of lacy whiteness, my dream dress, with family and friends surrounding me, upholding my happiness and joy; the rightness, the ribbons, the flowers and happily ever after. The love. The fitting. The husband and wife. Meant to be. For ever. Our marriage: my only marriage, my only husband. Unlike my parents' marriage, mine would last.

What was divorce to me? Nothing! It didn't count. Just legal humbug. What difference could legal jargon make to two souls destined for each other? I was married to Jude and always would be until death did us part. God knew what was in my heart despite what I told the marriage tribunal. I never imagined I was really annulling my marriage. How could something so real be made null? Just because a committee of celibate men signed off on a document didn't make it right.

~~~~~

In many fairy stories, frogs symbolise new life or transformation. In one story, a frog agrees to retrieve a princess's ball from the frog's pond on the condition she look after him and let him eat her food and sleep in her bed. The King agrees that she must keep the contract. After three days and nights of slimy horror, the Princess is amazed to discover that the frog has turned into a handsome prince. They marry and live happily forever and ever. That one just has to have been written by a man.

~~~~~

Jude transformed Zita's life. She bought out the married man who had been supporting her, taking over the business completely, and Jude moved into her flat. He used to joke he was becoming amphibious—because *amphi* meant double and *bios* meant life. Jude was indeed leading a double life: half on land with the clay, and half in water with the florist. He spent half his life with Peter and me, and half with Zita. We could never decide if he had become more highly evolved or taken a step backwards.

~~~~~

Humans walk on their entire feet, just like frogs. Birds and wolves walk on their toes. Cows and horses walk on tippy toes, their fingernails having evolved into hooves. Hard-hooved animals cause soil compaction in Australian farming land and in the native bush. Feral hard-hooved animals destroy riverbanks, pollute waterways, and deprive frogs of habitat.

And, of course, some people have feet of clay.

Chapter 6

Garden stools

Crouching in leaf litter behind the bushes in Cooper Park. Cold. Disorientated. Overwhelmed. Breath mulch-scented air with gasping breath. No memory of getting here. Last thing, working on garden stools in the studio. Don't know what time it is. Still daylight.

Hide behind a clump of desiccated Lilly Pilly trees as a man and a woman walk in my direction. They hold hands. Feel the clay on my own hands. Still damp. Can't have taken more than a quarter of an hour to get here. Understand it's time lost. Nestle behind the shrub, twigs scratching my scalp. Shaking my head. Can't afford to lose my sanity.

Life used to be so busy. Multi-tasking all the time. Children kept me focussed. Would turn from one to the other, planning ahead to transport each to class or sport or appointment or new shoes. They would run in and out of the studio. Each mother would voice their opinion. Arguments flared up on one side and then bubbled down just as another fight broke out between a different pair of mothers. Jude tried to play peacemaker as much as he could, which wasn't much. He would disappear and leave us women arguing. We had some humdingers over the years; like the one when I found it insulting that Zita felt she could tell Peter he should get a job even though he had exams coming up—she had no business overriding my parenting. Sometimes it seemed there would be no backing down but then there was food to prepare and someone to take to the dentist and someone to pick up or drop off, and everything would be forgotten in the demands of practicalities. Now all gone and it's just me.

The couple go past. I am safe. Undiscovered. Crawl down from the bush to the path and stand up. Brush the leaves from my shirt. Jude's shirt. If nothing else, I have survived. Move my feet along the path. Homeward. Ought to rest. Lightheaded. Will rest… after I've finished the garden stools.

Use slabs of terracotta. Cut out shapes before putting them together. Add sprig decoration. Thoughts of buttocks and seating bring the necessary curves into life. The stools have a greyish-brown surface with darker spotting. Like the back of the Mount Glorious torrent frog, *Taudactylus diurnus*, sometimes known as the day frog. There's an 'H' between the frog's shoulders. Not too difficult to distinguish the darker 'H' shape of colour over the curves of the stool. I'd call a pair of buttocks Mount Glorious any day, especially if they were Jude's.

~~~~~~

There was light drizzle on the day Jude married Zita. I drove to the church with Peter. We were running late and it was difficult to find a park. I found one eventually, further away than I would have liked, in the back streets. We walked briskly through the pale-grey concrete of Leichardt. The houses stood in neat rows with their manicured little gardens behind their tidy little fences. The only trees were spindly paper barks planted into holes along the concrete footpaths, there being no grass nature strips to spoil such order.

Peter was best man, entrusted with the ring and expected to present it at the appropriate time. He was not quite ten and, because he normally wore shorts, his hired suit transformed him. The long trousers made him look taller and the broad shoulders of the jacket made him look much older. He'd chosen a silver tie and matching pocket-handkerchief. He kept pulling the ring out to look at it. I warned him to be careful and keep it in his pocket.

I hurried along, anxious that Peter should arrive at the church on time to stand with his father before the bride got there. I glanced back to check he was keeping up, and saw him lying face down on the edge of the road with his arm down a drain.

I went back for him, heaved him up and, before I even began to berate him, he started to cry the snotty, messy tears of the almost adult. I began to cry, too. We cried in the snivelling rain of Leichhardt and we hugged and murmured things like, it's not an ending, it's a beginning. Then I lay on my front to see if I could reach the blasted thing, but the drain was too deep. Water came at me down the gutter. I got to my feet and cleaned us up as best as I could with a maternal tissue from my white handbag. Peter's face looked almost clean after I'd spat on the crumpled remnants and given him a good wipe. Luckily my dress was dark blue cotton that did not show the wet or it might have been a disaster. What am I saying? It was a disaster. Best men aged nearly ten don't lose wedding rings.

I stood beside the white sculpture of Dear Mother Mary outside St. Fiacre and took off my own ring. Zita would never notice. Peter was sworn to secrecy and it was unlikely Jude would suspect. So the second wife wore the first wife's ring, with the Church's blessing. Zita had her Catholic wedding, and it brought all her family together, beaming and crying, and forgiving Zita.

Jude's family, too, came laughing and sobbing and dealing out their memories like confetti. All the aunties and cousins avoided me like some kind of fungal disease. Azaria Chamberlain disappeared and the wedding party dissolved into passionate disputes about how much weight a dingo could carry and what evils a mother could possibly perpetrate on a baby. They never did find Azaria.

Like Azaria, *Taudactylus diurnus* hasn't been seen since Zita married Jude. The species is presumed extinct. It lived in the rainforests of coastal south Queensland, diving into streams when alarmed. It would cling to Glorious rocks in fast-flowing water until danger had passed. The last one clung to Jude. It was swept away by a torrent of dangers.

~~~~~

When Leaf was born sixteen years before, Zita was twenty-seven and Jude forty-one. My heart shattered every time I had the misfortune of seeing them. I wasn't sure how much longer I could maintain the thin façade of civility.

Jude called me after he and Zita had been at hospital the entire night and most of the day. He sounded exhausted. The baby, although only a couple of days late, was showing signs of distress and the obstetrician had recommended a caesarean. Of course I went. I left Peter with Dad. Both were worried for me. I tried to explain why I needed to be with my ex-husband while his new wife gave birth. How could I leave my Jude in such a state?

I met him in the waiting room just as he was about to accompany Zita into theatre. I told him I would wait. The next thing I knew he was shaking me awake. His rough face was shiny and sweaty and wet with tears. He had a new son. We cried together and our hug became something more than comforting. He kissed my forehead and with his hands on my temples, looked deep into my eyes and told me he loved me and always would. We melted together as though the previous years had been but a figment. I would always be his one true love.

Zita was okay, too. Sleeping in recovery. The baby was utterly perfect and unmarked, a beautiful child. He looked like Jude and like Peter. It was uncanny. Jude picked him up and stared into his solemn eyes. Then he gave the baby to me to hold. I loved him straight away. On that auspicious meeting I could clearly see his thoughtful centre. He was a serious soul. After all, he had responsibilities in life: he was the second first son.

I left Jude with Zita when she awoke and walked out of the hospital into the real world of traffic, frangipani trees and a passing father and daughter walking their two golden retrievers. Then I drove to the artificial world of the supermarket where the lights were too bright and the muzak too loud. I felt raw. I would never leave Zita and Jude's family. I belonged to them. I bought tiny clothes and flowers and returned to the hospital. By then, Zita's extended family had gathered and there was a great deal of laughing and crying and hugging and kissing going on in the hallway.

Vionella was Zita's best friend, a cousin she'd been to school with. Vionella was a beautiful woman, calm as the centre of a storm. She had married a greengrocer, though not one of Zita's clan. His name was Guido. He had a shop of his own nearby in Glebe, and had agreed to help manage Zita's floristry business for as long as it took Zita to get back on her feet.

I saw Jude's blue eyes turn to me through the throng of Italian merriment and knew my heart still belonged to him. When I reached Zita's bedside, the new mother was awake and weepy. I gave her the flowers, the little green suit and the singlets. She reached up and grasped my arm and I bent to let her kiss me. She did so several times, then whispered her thanks through sea-green tears. I knew exactly what she meant. I gave Jude the flowers and he wandered off to find a vase. The enormous bouquets, teddy bears and shiny balloons given by Zita's family swamped my paltry offerings.

A nurse, friendly and smiling, encouraged us to clear the room so Zita could feed her baby. Vionella and I shuffled the gang out towards the waiting room while Jude helped Zita sit up. Then he began to arrange her pillows. He used to do that for me.

The next day, Peter went on a school excursion to Taronga Zoo. Sydney had turned on her most dazzling March weather. The bright blue sky was high and still, and the water, seen through the trees and the designer viewfinders built into the walls and crevices of the zoo, was moving like a blue-and-white-flecked breathing tapestry. I had volunteered to be a mum on duty. Even though I hadn't slept, I reluctantly followed through on my promise to the teachers. I followed my little group of students as if in a daze.

The children had been given question sheets to answer about the animals. I simply allowed their discussions to flow around me.

Where did brown bears come from? What did chimpanzees like to eat? After a while of wandering unfocussed after my charges, I came to see baby animals everywhere we looked. I suppose Zita's baby made me sensitive. We'd already seen an enormous baby giraffe straddling an expanse of the bare giraffe enclosure and cute snow leopard cubs jumping around their mother; now we watched the chimpanzees, their tiny progeny cradled in wrinkly hands. A mother dangled her tiny babe by one arm as she swung it up to her chest to allow it to feed. Another ran across the enclosure with her baby swinging from her front. I sat down by the glass wall, fished out pen and pad from my bag and began to sketch the strength of a mother chimp's fingers. She looked directly into my eyes. She was a prisoner and, although she exuded sadness, I guessed she found peace in her baby. She had an air of acceptance though she was entirely without submission. I stayed with her for a while. She seemed to understand what I was going through. Chimpanzees have to deal with the rest of the harem, don't they, all those other mothers with their brats fathered by the Alpha male. She was a hairy beast.

I took Peter to visit Zita after the zoo. It was considerably out of our way. We were both tired and sunburnt, and I felt clumsy bringing the atmosphere of so much outdoors into the closed-in of the Royal Prince Alfred. Zita was asleep but her baby lay in the see-through crib wide-awake. I put my arm around Peter, who was still short enough and pliable enough to hug easily, and introduced him to his baby brother. Half-brother. Peter wanted to pick him up but I whispered that he would need maternal permission. Peter made a comparison to a little leaf, and that's when Zita opened her eyes, smiled, and thanked Peter for such a great name idea. Leaf.

I thought she was mad but could see straight away Peter's cheery grin and straightened spine—so why argue? Zita said of course that Peter could nurse him, so we sat the big brother in an armchair and I brought baby Leaf to him. I took a photo that Peter still has tucked into the side of his dressing table mirror: the fifth-grade boy, with socks around his ankles and solemn, proud face, holding a very pretty, serious baby he'd just named Leaf. Peter loves that boy. Maybe he reminds him of an autumn day at the zoo and baby chimpanzees.

When we came home to Greenwich, Peter was still overcome by the excitement of meeting his new brother. He was full of questions, wanting to know about his own birth. Luckily, that had been straightforward and ordinary, an event where I was still the expert. I got out our first baby photos and there we were, the three of us. Jude and I clutched the tiny, wrapped bundle that became Peter, cocooned against all prying lenses. We two adults were grinning, laughing, tired and untidy, looking into the camera with trust and love for the future. I tore my eyes away from that happy couple, stuck in the past like romantic fools, and rummaged through some of the other memorabilia I had stored. I found Peter's tiny shoes that had been amongst his first clothes from hospital. How incredibly small he had been.

Of course, I could glimpse the little baby in Peter's eleven-year-old face, traces of thousands of generations folded into the wrinkled newborn chimp who gradually puffed out into a fat little breastfed Buddha. The prepubescent angel was still a miniature old man somewhere in his makeup.

There was a knock at the door and there was Jude, really there, with a grin from ear to ear, saying he was incredibly pleased that Peter had named his second son, Leaf. Leaf, of all things!

Peter and Jude went out to fly the kite. I began to cry and couldn't stop until my sad sucking-in breathing brought on a bout of hiccups. I took my wet, swollen, snotty face to the bathroom and washed. Still hiccupping, I looked in the mirror. I knew I was lucky: I had a healthy son; I had a friend in my ex; I had an exhibition opening the following week. But I was falling apart.

Then Jude's face appeared in the mirror close behind me. He put his hands on my shoulders. I caught my breath. He looked at me in the mirror. I turned my face to his. I loved him still.

~~~~~

You can sit on one of these stools and take the weight off your feet. On a warm day, in the shade of the lemon tree, the clay is cool under your buttocks. The unripe lemons fall to the terracotta tiles and dry up.

If meditation were all it took to become enlightened, then frogs would be Buddhas.

~~~~~

'All the family? Sunday lunch? You want to bring her in front of everyone?' repeated Zita. 'You want to be like Simone?'

Jude shook his head. 'It's not like that. She's not Simone.'

Zita looked at me. 'I can't speak to him anymore.' She spun on her heels, picked up an old, cold, cup of coffee and flung it at Jude. The cup went over Jude's head but the coffee sprayed out in a spectacular arc, splattering him, the pale rug and the sheer curtains. She turned and marched out the door, slamming it after her.

The curtains billowed with the sudden pressure change. It was as if clouds were trying to get into the room. Brown sludge dripped down Jude's face. I left the mug on the floor.

Jude bent, as if he were carrying a weight across his back. His eyebrows tilted up, puzzled and anxious. Frown lines marked his forehead. After a tense silence he spoke. 'I don't think I can win, can I Connie? I've got students thinking it's the end of the world. Zita thinks it's the end of her world. There's no room for me. Where, Connie? Where am I supposed to be?'

'Are you saying Charlotte is Zita's fault, Jude? Simone's fault? My fault?'

'She's really not what you think.'

'Zita's right. You are stupid.'

Jude sat down at the kitchen bench, cradling his head in his hands.

I didn't slam the door when I left. Oh, but I wanted to.

Chapter 7

Bud vase

When Leaf was tiny, Zita would take him to her Glebe Point Road shop for a couple of hours a day. Even after waking for Leaf throughout the night, she'd breakfast with Jude every morning before at 6:30am. Then she'd pack her paperwork, dress, clothe and feed her baby, bundle the baby into the car, deal with peak hour traffic, and still be in control of her business. She was an eighties superwoman in shoulder pads. Although Guido helped out with buying flowers and with preparation of containers for weddings and other big events, Zita still retained responsibility for consultations and designs. It was her shop, she told me, and she needed to concentrate on it full-time because although there was no shortage of referrals from customers, the business was generating little profit. She knew it wasn't possible to maintain her level of effort; dealing with customers, planning for the future, event management, and coping with a baby was too much. Leaf was three months old when she weaned him. That's a lot of patience for Zita, for anyone really. Then he went into childcare.

One Friday she asked me to pick him up as she had some fancy wedding meeting she couldn't miss. The childcare centre, previously a large private home, had been purchased and labelled by a company that was starting to franchise childcare facilities. There were colourful designs of cute Australian film characters: Dinewan the emu, Tiddalick the giant frog, and Wahn the black crow, on the metal security fence. There was a circular driveway with ample parking for quick drop-offs and pick-ups. I parked and went through the entry gate, which had one of those childproof locks where you lift a latch before the gate will open. The gate clanged shut after me. I wondered about the effect this fortification might have on a child's mind, every day, reminded by this series of clangs and clicks.

There was an intercom next to the press-button security pad. I had to press a button and announce myself into a speaker grill. A distorted female voice hissed back that someone would be right with me. I waited. A lumpy young woman with black hair and pale brown roots opened the door and verified I was who I said I was by examining my driver's licence. Zita had informed the centre that I would be picking Leaf up. The woman—I hesitate to call her a slattern, though the stains down the front and sides of her ill-matching and tight-fitting tracksuit certainly marked her as her careless—led me into a dimly-lit foyer where the smell of old cooking was overwhelming. We passed through the kinder area with plastic toys scattered over the floor, though the children apparently liked watching TV best. A raucous advertisement was playing to a group of children sitting on the floor with their mouths hanging open.

We travelled through the toddler area. Apparently toddlers like TV, too, and afternoon cartoons blared out from the small screen. I could see a sandpit outside. The area around it was concrete. They had some trikes. I asked if the children could go out if they wanted. Dark-haired slattern said that they weren't allowed outside on this day because of the risk of sunburn. Then the smell hit me: a mixture of boiled cabbage, nappies and rotting old wood.

I followed Slattern across the room to an alcove where two girls were changing babies. As I drew closer, I could see that the babies were male. The girls were snickering. What could they possibly be finding so funny? Surely they weren't laughing about the size of the babies' penises?

Slattern told them that I was here to pick up Leaf. One of the girls, the one with spiky blonde hair, smiled at me. I was relieved to see her humanity and smiled back. She took me over to Leaf. I could see a line of cots in the adjoining room and asked her how many babies they had there? Normally, she said, there were a total of fifteen babies in the two rooms, with three childcare workers. I must have displayed my misgivings, and sighed. I could tell she didn't think it was adequate either.

Blondie showed me where Leaf's things were, then hurried off to another baby who was crying its little heart out. Leaf was in his cot, clothed, quiet and still. I gathered up his baby-bag and any other goods I thought might be his, strapped him into his capsule, carried him through the cooking fug, and waited until Slattern let us out again. It was fantastic to be in the fresh air. I packed Leaf into the car and drove him home to Greenwich. I gave him a bath straight away. He loved that, immersed in a warm bath with a droplet of lavender oil skimmed across the surface. He was a new, miniature version of Peter.

With Leaf secured into the baby capsule again, we drove to school and picked up number one son. During our afternoon tea, I asked Peter what he thought of us looking after Leaf while Zita went to work. Peter thought that would be cool, and had I checked out the latest Nintendo thing?

I told Zita that the baby-care place was no good. Not compared to me. I would look after Leaf because I'd always wanted lots of children and considered Leaf a part of my family. It would make me happy. It would make Peter happy. Zita would make me happy if she could do this small thing for me.

Zita agreed. She had a reputation in the wedding business to uphold. She needed to get back in the running. Guido didn't want to leave Vionella alone so often in the shop and Jude was away on a field trip for the next three days. As sure as frogs were frogs, Jude would be going away regularly until they'd finished the Field guide, and this would be a project years in the making. Zita couldn't afford to worry about her son but she insisted on paying me. Sure. Anything. I would agree to anything. I couldn't stand the thought of Leaf stuck in that dark environment, growing more still and placid, smelling that cooking smell all day every day, growing more separate, more alone, with the TV the only source of stimulation.

It was a bit of a drive from Glebe to Greenwich for Zita to drop the baby over in the mornings but as she was travelling anyway—to market or wedding or meeting—it didn't really matter. Sometimes I would have him overnight and sometimes Jude would bring Leaf himself. The flexibility made it work.

I suppose it was due to Zita's Italian blood that she never questioned my family urges. I certainly never did. I really believed the brothers were better brought up together. It was a thing of beauty to see Peter playing with Leaf. How concentrated and sweet is a twelve-year-old part-child, part-man as he builds a teetering marble run for a toddler's amusement?

~~~~~

Watch the bones through spy hole in the kiln. See faint arc of the pelvis turn orange-hot, over a thousand degrees. Wear armour of welding mask and gauntlet. Going into battle with a wild beast. Bones become ash. Never tried making bone china before. Brittle. Many imperfections.

The slender bud vase is cream. The pouched frog, *Assa darlingtoni*, has a cream abdomen with motley brown patches. Recently found in rainforests under rocks and logs. Doesn't need water to breed, which is possibly why it's survived.

Male stays close to the eggs. When they hatch he covers himself in the jelly left around the eggs. Tadpoles swim to him and jostle into his side pouches, although not every tad will make it into dad. Once tucked up safe and sound in their father's side, tadpoles metamorphose into froglets. Emerge from dad a couple of months later. Isn't it wonderful to see a father taking responsibility for his children?

Scientists speculate the amount of parental care is directly proportional to the number and the size of eggs laid: many small eggs, less parental care; few large eggs, more attentive parents. Just like humans.

Assa darlingtoni, also known as the hip-pocket frog or the marsupial frog is just the sort of frog I expect Jude to carry in his pocket and call darling.

Cannot tell where clay and I separate. Clay clumps are my fingers. We all rose from mud. We are still only mud. The mud grounds me. Return to my senses. Continue to work.

Bud vase takes on curves of the pelvis. Build seven but only two survive first firing and only one survives the last. It is very fragile indeed. As is reproduction; for frogs, that is. Humans are more successful, unless they leave it too late in life.

Jude would say that children are like tadpoles. He sees them as the second stage in the metamorphosis of humans into an adult form. That's if the zygote is the first stage. Who knows how many stages a human takes to mature? Perhaps some never make it to maturity. Perhaps some humans get stuck in a stage of development, never finding the stimulus to leave dad's pocket.

~~~~~

On April the ninth, 1983, Zita rang me just after school pick-up to tell me her second baby was about to be born. She'd told me many times before, after Leaf's awful labour, she had no desire to spread her legs for any golf-obsessed obstetrician. She wanted a midwife but the insurance was prohibitive, and having previously had an emergency Caesar, she was regarded with suspicion. Even so she managed to talk her way into the Paddington birthing centre at the Royal Women's Hospital, and I made preparations to look after Leaf. Zita would have preferred to have him with her, but she was concerned that seeing his mum in pain would frighten him. Jude was to ring us as soon as the baby was born so Leaf and Peter could be first in line to visit their new sibling. Our family was growing.

Zita's sister, Fiorella, dropped Leaf off in time for afternoon tea. I took him by the hand and we walked to Peter's room. Peter was at his desk doing his homework. Leaf climbed up onto his lap. Peter immediately dropped his pencil and grinned at the little fellow and gave him a hug. Leaf squirmed out of Peter's grasp, jumped down again and went straight to the basket of toys that Peter kept for him. I left them sorting through blocks, preparing to play that old favourite: build a tower, push it down, and laugh hysterically—big when you're two.

Dad was partial to a dry sherry before lunch. I went through to the sitting room with his tipple and found him slumped in his chair. I placed my palm against his forehead; it was cold. He wasn't asleep. I put the sherry down on the side table. The room was silent. Then a fly buzzed over by the window. I took Dad's hand. It was heavy and empty. I put his hand down again. How strange that death should accompany birth. A quake of sadness shook my body. Unbidden, my hand rose to my mouth. I sat on the arm of the chair and waited for my tremor to subside. It did not. I watched him not breathe.

My dad's name was John. He served with the RAAF in the Second World War, flying as a navigator with a bomber squadron based in southern Italy. I especially loved one photo of him on leave in Sydney that showed him handsome and square-cut in his uniform. Never particularly voluble about his war experience, he found his way back to earth in civilian life via landscape gardening. I was too young to remember him in any uniform but his pale green shorts and shirt.

Mum and Dad enjoyed a civilised life-style: she was away a good deal of the time, posted overseas by various magazines and papers, while Sheryl was his regular companion.

My mother, Lillian, had been a journalist in the days when a woman in the newsroom was a travesty of masculinity. She'd resisted all that race carnival hats describing and Vice Regal openings reporting and had become instead an investigative journalist with an interest in finance. She wrote a bestseller about women in business called *Keeping 'em in the air, not breaking 'em.* It did particularly well in the US. She said that Australians weren't ready for her.

When Dad died, Lillian was riddled with cancer, lying in a bed in a palliative care facility called Parkrest. She could not walk or dress herself but she would not give up breathing.

The tremor in me finally quelled and I found stable ground again. I turned myself back on. I had duties. I had to look after the boys. I stood up, took one last look at my bowed father, and began to move again, slowly. Things would never be the same again.

The two boys were clattering in the kitchen, spreading crackers with butter and vegemite and making worms by pressing the biscuits together. I let them be. I closed the door to the front room after me very quietly and rang Doctor Lewis. He came at once. He had seen our family all my life and was a good friend of John's. After seeing to Dad, he willingly agreed to explain the death to the boys and that kind people were coming to take the body away. The boys were subdued but went through to Peter's room to play. Doctor Lewis asked if I needed him to call anyone. I did not.

After the doctor, the funeral director arrived and was pleasant enough, and then, when they had taken Dad away, I decided to take the kids to see Lillian at Parkrest. I rang the Associate Charge Nurse and explained why we were coming in. I packed fruit and sandwiches and asked Peter to select books and toys to keep himself and Leaf amused.

There was a small garden area at Parkrest where the children could have a picnic supper. The residents were about to be put to bed for the night. It was quiet. I put the bag containing their amusements next to a wooden garden seat and went inside.

Lillian was sitting in an armchair next to her bed. The rolling table by her side held the remains of her dinner and a cup of tea from which a straw protruded. She concentrated, trying to get the straw into her mouth. Her hands were thin and the veins stuck out. I greeted her and she looked up at me, sideways, her head apparently too heavy for her spine stalk to hold it upright. The tea was steaming hot and she agreed it needed cooling. I made sure her straw was bent enough, picked up the water jug and put a splash of cold water into her tea. I sat down on the bed until she finished. Then, as calmly as I could I told her about Dad. I could not help weeping. I pulled a tissue from the box in her bedside cupboard.

We sat quietly for a while. Lillian pushed the table away and rose to her feet. She gripped my arms as she tried to stand. She gave two small nods of understanding and signalled with her eyes that she'd like to lie down. I turned back the pale green bed cover and helped her climb into the bed. Lillian lay on her side and brought her knees up. She shrank into the white sheets. Her hair faded into the pillows. She closed her eyes. I pulled the cover up to her shoulders.

I sat beside her. The sounds of the hospital came and went around us. After a minute or so, the AC appeared at the door, indicating we should talk in the corridor. I patted my mother on the hip and told her I'd be right outside. She remained silent and motionless. There was no indication she'd even heard or cared. The AC smiled at me reassuringly, expressed sympathy for our loss, and told me the boys were in the fishpond. She didn't seem unduly upset by this, but she exuded a nurses' calm authority, which clearly told me she expected I would do something about it.

I was never sure exactly how I got to the fishpond but I could hardly speak when I did get there. A nurse appeared with a couple of towels. Glancing up at the blank windows of the building, I saw a woman sagged in a wheelchair peering out at us. She smiled and waved cheerily. I ignored her. I gave Peter a towel and stripped Leaf before wrapping him in the other. Peter apologised profusely. He'd forgotten where they were. He just wanted to play with Leaf. Leaf was only two. They hadn't caught any fish.

Back in Lillian's room, even stories about the ones that got away didn't excite any interest. Lillian just lay there quietly, on her side. She wouldn't look at us so I ushered the boys outside to the corridor where they could sit and wait while I went in to see the AC in her office before I left. I didn't want my mother to give up. The AC nodded. She had a soft face, a fluffy face, and her body strained against her uniform. She'd been wearing that same uniform for a long time. I explained that we were waiting for news of a birth in the family and that my brother would be arriving soon from Hong Kong.

We all went to bed as soon as we got home. Around seven in the morning the phone rang, Jude announced the arrival of their baby daughter, Fern, and we all got up again. I loaded the kids into the car and drove through peak hour to Paddington. We found Zita in bed cuddling her baby, and Jude sitting beside them. Both parents looked exhausted.

Jude reported that it had been a peaceful birth. I was so grateful they'd waited before they rang and thanked them for their thoughtfulness. There was a blue birthing pool at the foot of the bed. It had been emptied, thank goodness, or I expect we could have seen more fishing from Leaf. Fern had been born in the pool. She had arrived in the world in the caul. She would never drown.

They did their best to smile for the photos. Leaf adored his new little sister straight away. I still have a photo of Peter holding newborn Fern with Leaf leaning on Peter's knee, looking in absolute amazement at the baby. Leaf needed to have a wee immediately after the camera snapped.

I left Peter and Leaf with Jude and drove back to my mother. The hospital had been trying to reach me. Lillian had fallen in the night and broken her pelvis. The break had involved the cancer in the bone. There was probably some bleeding. She could no longer sit up. They had given her pain relief and were debating surgery. She refused all food and drink.

I held my mother's hand. I tried very hard not to imagine the funeral director counting his blessings when I rang to tell him what was happening. I explained my brother was on his way from overseas and my sister had died twenty-five years ago.

Later, I explained to the curved lump under the pale green covers that I needed her to stay. We hadn't had enough time together. Lillian looked at me with wet eyes of great depth and, almost imperceptibly, shook her head. Two nurses came in and shooed me away. They told me to go home and get some sleep.

Jude brought Peter and Leaf home to Greenwich. They didn't stay long. I suspected that Jude was looking to offload them on to me. However, he must have seen I was far too tired to negotiate, and when I told him about Lillian, he packed some food and clothes and took the boys off again to his place to sleep. I slept for a few hours then went back to Parkrest in the late afternoon. Lillian was still in limbo. The Charge Nurse and I discussed hydration and feeding her, perhaps even intravenously, but decided that would be taking away her power. She had made her decision. She was sane. She had lived her life as she wanted, and would die in her own way. She would not be in pain.

~~~~~

All those done and dusted in the past faded and changed shape into Leaf and Fern after they grew and became teenagers. Once they cooked pizza in my rooftop kitchen on a late summer's night. The air was hot and still. The oven was on its highest setting. The fan was shifting hot air around the flat. It was stultifying.

Leaf spooned blood-red sauce over the uneven dough. He used the back of a big spoon to push it further over the white fleshy surface. He created a vortex.

Fern washed basil under the tap and then ripped the leaves into tiny shreds. She sprinkled green shards across the red sauce. Her fingernails turned green.

I handed Leaf the bowl of cheese I'd grated. He put far too much on top of the pizza. It tumbled off the sides of the dough like lava rolling from a volcano into the sea. There had been strong discussions about what needed to go onto the pizza. We decided less was more. I put the capsicum, mushrooms and salami away. They never even considered the broccoli. Not for an instant. And they wouldn't eat a salad. No way. I started cutting out the eyes of a pineapple to have later—not on the pizza—pineapple with ice cream for dessert.

Fern carefully put the pizza in the oven. 'If we were living in Brisbane we couldn't have pizza.'

'Huh?' said Leaf.

'There wouldn't be any power. We'd have to have salad.'

I said, 'If I lived in Brisbane I'd be happy to eat a salad.'

'Yes, but you wouldn't have a choice, not at the moment,' said Fern. 'They're having all these power failures.'

'What… blackouts?'

'Yes, bizarre, isn't it? They're talking about it at school. It's like the power stations can't cope with all the people or something.'

'Suppose everyone turned on their air-conditioners all at the same time?' Leaf stood in front of the fan and sang a long, lugubrious chopped-up note.

'Yes. And you wouldn't be able to do that.'

The fan chopped the ghost wail into staccato fragments. 'Let's move to Brisbane!' Still using the fan like a giant microphone, he sang, 'What will happen now?' He sounded like a dalek.

'I should think the oven is hot enough. Won't be long. You could probably set the table. Inside or outside?'

'No,' said the dalek, 'I meant with Dad's girlfriend.'

Leaf and Fern both stopped completely still and quiet and looked at me. I suppose I stopped too. There was an infinite silence when we all said nothing. The oven engine and the fan engine and the city engine continued, but we in the hot kitchen said nothing and did nothing.

I turned the pineapple around. I held it by the hard spiky leaves. The sweet acrid smell was overpowering. It looked like an oversized hand grenade.

Then Fern turned on the tap and began washing the tomato-sauce pot with extra energy. 'He'll forget us and go to live with her. Get the glasses, Leaf. I'll have water.'

'Who cares?'

She threw him the dishcloth. 'Shut up and clean up that cheese.'

The word 'girlfriend' ricocheted around my brain. Girlfriend? How did they know? What did they see? I got the broom out of the cupboard and considered how far to push this information spill. Would they clam up if they thought I was too interested? What was too interested? Could interested be unhealthy? I thought I might not get another opportunity to find out so, rushing in like a fool, I asked, 'What do you know of her?'

'We met her,' said Fern, still scrubbing red from the pot.

Is that so? I didn't know what to think. A jumble of questions formed a disorderly queue in my mind. How did they meet her? Why did they meet her? What the hell did Jude think he was doing? 'What' and 'When' pushed their way to the front of the queue.

'Couple of weeks ago.'

'Leaf, can you please not talk about it?' Fern said, then added, 'She seemed nice. That's all. Let's leave it.'

There. I knew they'd clam up.

'How can you say that? She's a home breaker. Connie should know everything.' Leaf smeared cheese into the bench top with a cloth. 'I don't know what she's doing with him. He's an old man. He makes me sick.'

The pineapple juice was sticky on my fingers. 'Do you know how old she is?'

Fern glanced up at me as she swung the pot onto the wooden draining rack. 'Mid-twenties? Older? She's kinda quiet, maybe because she wasn't expecting us.'

'Too right she wasn't expecting us. Neither was he. Selfish bastard. I'd never cheat on my wife. Never.'

Like father, like son. Jude was never going to cheat on me, either. Never. And now he had. Threefold, like the cock crowing in the distance. I could hear the frogs croaking in the park.

Damn. I cut myself. The blood stained the yellow of the pineapple in the sink. I waited until the water ran cold from the tap and washed my hands.

Fern gave me a paper towel and I pressed the cut closed.

'Maybe you should hold your hand up in the air.'

'Not that bad. Hey, Fern. Have you thought what you'd like for your birthday?'

Fern, wise woman already, looked at me with pity, knowing that her birthday wasn't for another month and it wasn't relevant, was it. I felt small and not very clever. My finger hurt and I tried not to weep like a little girl.

Leaf missed the point. 'Why won't anyone talk about her? Don't we have to face facts? Doesn't anyone want to do anything? Maybe we could put out a contract on her? Or something? She's going to ruin everything. Everything's fucked.'

I continued the failed policy of attempting to change the subject. 'I think we should eat outside. With candles?'

Fern opened the oven to look at the pizza. 'Almost ready.'

I was finding it difficult to breathe. I went out and threw a tablecloth over the full moon table. I could hear Fern inside. 'Can't you see how upset she is? Why can't you leave it alone? You're so boring.'

Leaf came out carrying some glasses. 'Sorry, Connie.'

'It's not your fault. I don't know the answers either.' He set the table in front of me. I could feel his confusion in the heat of the evening. I thought I'd better keep trying to improve things. 'I'm sorry, Leaf. I don't know what to say to you. You know that old saying, "Look after the little things and the big things will look after themselves"? Maybe that's all we can do. Enjoy our pizza and try to stay cool.'

'But that's not the way things work, is it? I mean, fuck, we're all worried about the little things and the big things are shit. Complete fucking disasters. This whole planet is going to turn into bare rock if those greedy economist politicians don't stop fucking around with their petty pathetic business bullshit.'

I wondered if I ought to correct his teenage language attitude. Then I thought, he's right. What can I say? The big things are stuffed. So let us concentrate on the small things crowding into my memory.

I remembered how years ago Peter and Leaf were such friends and then the new baby, Fern joined in. See how all three siblings would grow to rely upon each other in the future. See how well I got on with Zita. See how Jude looked after all his new family. See how my body still yearned for him.

~~~~~

Frogs have all their internal organs in one space, the coelom. Humans have three distinct cavities: the chest (protected by ribs), the abdomen and the pelvis. When you look at a frog skeleton you can see they have one wide, sacral vertebra but it does not bend round into a bowl like a human pelvis. Humans have evolved protection for their reproductive system.

~~~~~

I went to pick up my brother, Mark, from the swirl of the early-eighties Kingsford Smith airport. I picked up Peter and Leaf from Jude's place on my way across town. It was after the peak hour, thank goodness, and we managed the short trip in an easy half hour.

I hardly recognised Mark as he came through the door from customs amongst all those people kissing, embracing, posing with their cameras, laughing, greeting, crying…

As I stared, it was as if he came into focus. At first there had been an older man, fatter, better dressed, vaguely familiar, and then his cells seemed to morph into someone I knew. He stood out, strangely alone amongst the shifting crowds of cultures. In him I recognised my past, a boy in a man, my brother. More shocking to me was our father in the man. Our father was dead but he lived on in his son. Like my father, my brother had always had a merry face, until the Army hardened him. But now the rounder Mark burst into a watery grin as he lumbered over to hug me. Peter and Leaf stood, hand in hand, to one side, overwhelmed by the rush of travelling humanity, while I patted Mark on the back. Although we hugged, it seemed we were still far away from each other. Perhaps some distances cannot be covered by aeroplane.

Mark's only baggage was a leather carry-on bag so we made our way towards the car park. Once outside the emotional arena, I took a deep breath of Sydney mildness. Mark walked beside me but the boys, Leaf holding tightly to Peter's hand, went a few paces ahead. I had challenged Peter to remember where the car was and he only made one false move before leading us to the vehicle.

In the back of the car, Peter clicked Leaf into his car seat. I turned to ask my long-lost brother if he preferred to go home or to see his mother first. Mark looked at me, a mix of father, boy and strange man, and told me to go to Lillian. We negotiated the traffic simply, efficiently, while my memories took a less direct route.

I remembered Mark used to beat me at Monopoly (most of the time). I remembered he used to take me out rowing in the little dinghy he kept at the Greenwich Sailing Club. Every now and then I was allowed to take an oar and he would make me go round and round in circles for his amusement. I remembered we would climb the fig tree in the little park above the cliff, and I remembered the smell of the soft, salt air. I remembered, hot and sweaty-tired, walking home from school with him and William in the rain and how we'd ruin our school shoes in the gutter deluge.

How can a face be like a kaleidoscope? One moment his appearance would be strange to me, then the masks would shift again and there would be my little brother from the backyard as if it were yesterday.

Mark didn't bother making polite chat with the children. He gazed out of the car window at continually building Sydney, remarking on newness and replacement. Cranes dominated the horizon and we were stuck behind a cement truck for some time until it turned off into a building site. I supposed Hong Kong wasn't much different. He agreed, there was always building and redevelopment there, he said. Well, we were in the eighties after all, the age of developers and white shoes.

~~~~~

Arriving at Parkrest, I told the kids they didn't need to go fishing again… no, I meant it… and left them with books and chopped-up fruit in the garden.

Lillian was overtaken by medical supports now she had broken her hip. The room was cluttered with equipment—Parkrest was trying to avoid moving her to intensive care. Mark looked stricken as he saw his mother through the web of medical apparatus. At my suggestion, Mark moved to the other side of the bed so Lillian, if she were to open her eyes, might see him more easily. I joined their hands. Man and mother. Hers were hard, blanched and stringy with purple veins. His were tan and chubby with smooth, soft skin and a recent manicure. He was wearing a gold signet ring on his little finger but no wedding ring. I left them together and went to get Mark a cup of tea.

When I brought the tea back, the cup rattling in its saucer, I heard Mark singing, his voice rumbling like marbles rolling in a large drum: *her eyes they shone like the diamonds, you'd think she was queen of the land, and her hair hung over her shoulder, tied up with a black velvet band…*

Softly.

I didn't know the woman he was singing to. He clearly had a different mother to me.

I took Leaf and Peter home to Jude's new family and then, when I, the unencumbered daughter, returned to Parkrest, the AC with the fluffy face smiled sadly and shook her head. Lillian had died. I thought my mother would have known who did the singing. I imagined she had probably been waiting for Mark. I kept on walking to Lillian's room.

As I entered, Mark looked at me with such an expression of little boy lost. We stayed there, quietly, sitting next to her bed. She was still there, tranquil and soundless and not breathing. Her expression was free of pain for the first time in years.

I patted Mark on the arm and he burst into tears. They were harsh, barking tears. I put my arm around his shoulders. We were suddenly the older generation.

~~~~~

After Emma pulled the old phone off the wall in a tantrum, I purchased a new-style one. It was the late nineties and we were all getting them, those remote phones you could walk around with. Cordless. It was neatly in place, recharging, when it trilled at the same time as the knocking commenced on the door. I lay in bed and considered the dilemma: phone or door? I went for the door first and found Simone in some shimmery thing that could have passed for a nightie. Her face was red and screwed up in an unnatural way. This was unusual. Simone hated to frown. She thought it might cause wrinkles. It was difficult to believe she ever had any feelings. Her face was normally proud and smooth and still, like a beautiful dead woman.

Simone rushed through the door, waving her phone around and tapping at it ineffectively with the perfectly painted white edges of her pale-pink French nails. 'How do you turn this blasted thing off?' I grabbed her phone and pressed the hang-up button. Immediately my own phone fell silent. 'For your information, it's this button, right?' Simone nodded, didn't look where I was indicating and put her handset down on the hall table. She was distracted.

'You will remember that,' I continued, indicating her phone. 'Won't you, Simone?' I don't know why she'd got a cordless. She always had to make one of the kids use my phone to ring hers so she could locate it.

'You've got to help, darls. It's Francis. Poor kid's in agony. Probably appendicitis or something. He's all hot and yucky. Will you see him? I don't know what to do. I know I'm pathetic but he's just so sick.'

'Okay. I'll get my book and sit with Emma while you're out.'

'You go. You've been to the Children's before.'

'The Children's?'

'You can do it. Francis would prefer you.'

'Simone! This is your son we're talking about.' She looked at me blankly. I sighed. There was no point in arguing. She always got what she wanted. 'Okay, I'm not going to stand around and argue while his appendix explodes. I'll get dressed.'

'I'll get him ready for you.'

Typical Simone, I thought, as I rummaged in the washing basket for some clean-ish underpants. I pulled on bra, skirt and shirt and grabbed my wallet. I raced downstairs to find Simone's door open. Francis was trying to get dressed in the living room. His face was flushed, damp hair stuck to his forehead, and he was bent over and retching as he tried to pull his jeans on. 'Francis,' I said. 'Don't bother.' I went to his room and found his dressing gown. We left his jeans on the couch. 'Here you go, darling. Where's Mum?'

'Don't know.'

'Do you think you can walk?'

'Yes.'

'You head down to the car. Do you want a book? Sometimes they can keep you waiting.'

'No.'

That's when I realised he really must be sick. Francis was never without a book. I stuck my nose in Simone's sparkly room but there was no sign of glamour-puss. I called her name and heard a rustling from Emma's room. Simone scurried out. 'Don't wake Emma. You know what she's like if she doesn't get enough sleep.'

I stared at her in amazement. 'Simone. Can we focus, please? You might have a matter of life and death here. Emma will be fine.'

'Connie… please, darls…'

I didn't have time for her nonsense. 'Do you have Francis on your Medicare card? Are you insured? Paperwork?'

'Oh, yeah! Hang on.' She turned to go, then rushed back and hugged me, fast and firm. 'Thanks, darls; honestly, you're like my sister, really you are.'

Not like her sister, I mused. I'm a member of her harem. Her real sisters had nothing to do with Simone any more. 'I'll go and see how Francis is going.'

I caught up with the poor kid in the garage, bent over by the car door. He struggled upright, red in the face. I unlocked the car and said, 'It's going to be fine. You know how Peter had appendicitis when he was ten? You're much braver than he was.'

'It's not my appendix, Connie.' He gulped and wrenched the front passenger door open. He climbed up into the seat, leaving the door open as Simone could be heard calling behind us.

'Connie!' Simone rushed to Francis's side of the car. 'Here, darling. Here are the cards. And here's a bucket, just in case.' She looked over at me apologetically. 'He threw up before.' She shut the door and reached through the window to pat Francis on his chest. 'Mummy will come and see you as soon as she can, okay, sweets?' She stepped back from the car and said, 'I'm sorry to be such a pain, Con.'

As I pulled out of the driveway, I glanced in the rear vision mirror. Simone had already gone back inside.

There was little traffic and we made good time. Francis was quiet beside me except to say, 'She's scared of hospitals.'

'You are wise beyond your years, Francis Baldwin.'

'Thanks.'

'What's going on, Francis?'

'There's something wrong with my testicle. Mum just couldn't bring herself to say anything. You know what she's like.'

'I admire your sense. Maybe put that cool facecloth to use.'

When we got to triage, the nurse was matter of fact and sympathetic. She directed us to a cubicle. Poor kid was clearly in pain and the paediatrician didn't waste time ordering surgery.

~~~~~

Certain herbicides are known to affect frog testicles, causing them to shrink and lose function. Some male frogs develop ovaries and change sex completely when exposed to the chemicals. Females are not affected. There are many common chemicals, known as alkylphenolic surfactants, which are contained in detergents, paints, pesticides and personal care products. These are the hormone mimics or endocrine disrupting chemicals, a known cause of malfunction of frogs' testes.

Of course, frogs are tiny, frail creatures, very different to *homo sapiens*.

~~~~~

Mark and I went with the funeral director in his smart, up-to-the-minute eighties car. We sat in the back like children. I looked out the window. There were rain rivulets on the glass. Mark had taken my hand, I was not sure when. We were both sad. There's something suicidal about being alive. Who knows when life begins? It's obvious when it's over.

Two coffins stood shoulder to shoulder at the front of the church, one covered in tiger lilies, the other in banksias and leptospermum. Green carpet. Slippery wooden pews. High, patchwork windows with glowing glass and painted sad-face people. By force of habit, I looked around for Dad, but my glance slid beyond for he was not sitting up in church that day. He was lying in a box in the centre aisle next to his wife in her own wooden box. I put my arm around Peter and pulled him close. The child patted my arm gently. I was on shaky ground. There were ritual words and pleasantries. They played music. It really didn't matter yet everything mattered terribly. Lillian really did love Col Joye and the Joy Boys while John preferred Peter Sculthorpe.

My mother's friend wore a red jacket with gold buttons, a navy dress with white accents, and navy court shoes. She spoke of my mother's acerbic humour and her business acumen. She told that story of Lily burning holes in the boardroom table because she hated the new CEO. She told how Lillian loved men in suits who smelled of spicy, exotic flora. She described how Lillian would slide her arm through the man's, feeling his bicep strength and the quality of the wool, and promenade, laughing confidentially and gesticulating with her cigarette. She'd flick the butts away, the glowing embers spinning out into her future. The world was Lillian's and she knew it; she grabbed it and lit it and inhaled it down to the final gasp.

My father's friend, dressed in tones of earthy green, spoke about John's understanding of the elements—earth, rock, water and plants together in a system, connected, providing habitat and inviting vistas—and about John's legacy to Sydney's garden landscape. So many people, all with lovely things to say, and each parent with their separate friends. It seemed there was no one who knew them both, except Sheryl Richards and her son, William.

William had arrived home from Europe just in time for the funeral, just in time for the memories. He was born in January 1942, a few months after me. From as far back as I can remember, certainly from the time I started school at five, I'd spent more time at his house than at my own. His mum looked after me while my own mother Lived Life to the Full. Lillian was not a relaxed, motherly type. She would much rather travel to investigate business rumours and write daring exposés. This was highly peculiar behaviour for a woman in the forties and fifties. John got on with his landscaping business while Lillian never seemed to understand his quiet need for a wife. He would get home about six and Lillian might not be in Sydney, possibly not even in Australia. Sheryl would have popped a casserole in the oven and left a note on the kitchen table saying where the kids were. With her.

Sheryl mothered me; she was my mumsy mum.

Lillian was my birth mother, my going out mother, my successful career mother. She travelled throughout Europe, the USA, and Africa. She was a restless soul and a warrior with words. She would sit in her leather office chair with long legs crossed, smoking incessantly, poring over annual reports, urgently seeking answers on the telephone. She wanted to know who was boss, what was the bottom line and when it was happening? She knew who was who on what board of directors and snarled mouthfuls of smoke as she jeered about their trite sensibilities or lack of sophistication. She had financial acumen: she could pick out a flaw in an annual report that a bevy of crack accountants had gone to great lengths to hide, and her readers trusted her because of it.

She strode—no, she swaggered—a thin line between radical feminism, loving her own power and determination, and playing up to men, loving their power, especially when she was in Australia. She knew how the game was played and she'd stand, legs apart as though on board ship, and speak as if to a thousand people, perhaps holding an imaginary pipe, perhaps nodding to a contact, taking her time, knowing what she had to say really mattered to her audience. She liked nothing better than wearing a bikini and negotiating whilst staying in newly-developed Surfer's Paradise. She was made for the sixties; maybe she even helped make them the driving times they were.

It was Sheryl who was there, at home. Sheryl was the one who made sure I did my homework, made sure I was cleaned up and mercurochromed if I fell off my bike. Sheryl was the one who provided me with sanitary napkins and explained the facts of life, telling me she was so pleased to have the opportunity of seeing me grow up into a young woman. Sheryl explained that Mum loved me and that I was just as important as Lillian's career. I never believed it.

Sheryl was the one who taught me how to make Anzac biscuits, even forgiving the addition of excess salt in one particular batch, and she was the one who took me to the beach in summer. Took all of us, because William and Mark and Gracie were there, too.

William and I had always been best friends. We had baths together, made Christmas decorations together, listened to the radio together, painted pictures together, made landscapes for his model railway together and, if we fell over, we'd help each other up and keep right on going. Together.

Are my memories real or are they altered by the actual physical business of adult remembering? Could the brain's chemistry have distorted the electric imprint of those events? As I had been through the fire, could my brain have changed my perceptions of the past?

I do remember that Zita and Sheryl organised all the food and drink for the wake at my parents' house. The two women kept Leaf and Fern at home with them during the ceremony. I thought Sheryl should have been at the crematorium but she said she wanted to make sandwiches. She must have had her own way of saying goodbye to Dad.

William was put to work buttering bread as soon as he walked in. Peter was happy to join Zita, Sheryl and William in the kitchen away from the babble. All those people who'd shared some part of their lives with our parents swilled wine, pressed antipasto into their mouths, and babbled. Amazing how many of them still smoked. I asked them to go outside and they did, like lemmings, when I took all the ashtrays out.

Many of the visitors were shocked by the double funeral. Typical Lillian. When Malcolm Fraser orders up a double dissolution, Lillian does her best to oblige—double trouble for the undertakers.

They were so close, they all prattled. Were they? I didn't know what to believe anymore. I had a sense my parents were completely independent, that the kids were the only reason they came together at all. Mark agreed. Certainly, after Lillian was diagnosed with lung cancer, John came to support her more, taking her to treatments and washing her nightclothes. But people remembered their own versions; they rewrote the story as they thought it ought to have been. Who owns the correct memories? Is there such a thing as objective history? Not in that babble, there wasn't.

At Sheryl's suggestion, we scattered photo albums, scrapbooks, John's designs and other memorabilia on tables and shelves. People gazed at photos, smiled, frowned, sipped and guzzled, remembered and babbled some more. I remember a particular photo of my mother, thin as a rake, red miniskirt, huge rings on her fingers spiked out to jab her cigarette, pale pink lipstick: hard-hitting, dolly-bird journo chatting up the Prime Minister.

In another shot, she was outside the Royal North Shore Hospital at a grand event for the opening of a new wing; she was smoking. Poor Lillian. Always smoking. She hated it. Loved it and hated it, filled with vehement anger against herself, tobacco companies and the government for letting her become addicted. She couldn't help it. It was as much anger at what she saw as her own weakness as it was anger towards Big Tobacco.

John, I imagined, was her friend, as distinct from being partner or husband or lover. He was excited by his work and would spread his latest designs out on the table to show her: perhaps a fernery, perhaps a swimming pool disguised as a native rockery, or a curved driveway formally planted with eucalypts. Then he would take her back to Kingsford Smith airport and wave goodbye once more. Lillian was proud of John, admiring his sense of proportion and, most importantly, his honest acceptance of where he belonged.

Native garden design in the sixties was a weird novelty. John believed Australians had to acknowledge who they were, where they lived, and to that end he would drive his old Holden Ute out into the country, perhaps out past Dubbo or down to the Riverina, or up to Coonabarabran, looking for rocks and plants to suit particular sites. Forward thinking, he avoided doing damage, and, building on his desire to understand as much as possible, established one of the first indigenous nurseries in Sydney. He was one of the first to recognise city garden centres mining the wilderness couldn't go on unchecked, and urged government control over the transplanting of indigenous species. My father loved the earth. When we were children, John helped us make a miniature garden in a terracotta saucer. We filled it with dirt, added moss for lawn, mirror for pond, twig for tree. Dad helped us see the way things grew. He said that after that bloody war he wanted to have a bloody job where he was bloody well in charge and that it had better be bloody constructive.

Though there were plenty of photos of Dad with Mark and Gracie and I, none seemed to include Lillian, not even when we were babies. Maybe she outgrew us. Now, Sheryl and Dad, on the other hand, they were a team. They knew everything about us kids.

At my parents' wake, who should have drunk the most but Jude. He ended up completely sloshed. With Mark and William, that old comedy duo, he sat bleary late, long after the rest of the babble had gone. Sheryl swept up around them, hugged me too, before she escaped for Paddington.

Zita packed toddler Leaf into a warm jacket. She gathered their belongings together, forcefully. She threw a bottle into the nappy bag. She heaved the car carry-pod, in which baby Fern was sleeping, onto one hip. She was going now. She had babysick down one shoulder and toddler wee on her skirt. Zita looked at Jude, groggy and unfocussed as he lounged on the couch, yet another can of beer opened on the table in front of him. She took a deep, controlled breath. She looked undecided for a moment and then asked Jude politely if he was staying where he was? I suspected she did not want him to join her at all; she already had more than enough to carry. Luckily, Jude nodded his wobbly head. He had to stay with his old mates from China, his old china plates. How about a slow boat?

Zita gave an audible sigh before she marched out to the car. After she had gone, I went to bed but the three men kept me awake with their mumblings, shoutings and eruptions of laughter. I could hear them through two walls as they remembered when John sawed down the ornamental apple tree, which fell and smashed their fort. They remembered when Lillian was heavily into her futures phase and didn't sleep, her teeth yellow from coffee and nicotine, John fussing over her, still awake in the morning when they got ready for school. They remembered when John caught the boys trying to sell his old fishing gear to the second-hand shop.

Braving the cold, I wrapped myself in a blanket and went in to see them. I told them to keep it down because I didn't want them waking Peter. Jude posing drunken questions like, why not? He slurred that of course he could come in… he's my old mate, my old china plate. And on it went. I called them buffoons and they sniggered into their cleansing ales—oh, it's so good to see you old mate, old china…

They remembered everything, including the things they didn't know they knew to remember. Then, like bubbles in a stew just taken from the oven, they slowly stopped uttering, the final plops of dribbling interchange finishing with no rhythm or order. Sadly, the blissful silence lasted only seconds before the raucous snoring began.

~~~~~

I'd almost finished the magazines that included recipes and was about to focus on the travel publications when Jude turned up in the hospital waiting room. I dropped last year's Italian special of *Gourmet Traveller* and asked, 'Have you seen him?'

'He's in recovery.'

'Did they tell you anything?'

He looked around the waiting room. 'Where's Simone?'

I stared at him. Where did he think she was? He knew her. Simone wasn't the squeamish type. She was beyond squeamish. He must know that she was unlikely to be seen anywhere near a hospital. Instead of having a pointless discussion about her weaknesses, I asked, 'How is he?'

'He's going to be fine. Bit of a fright for everyone, though.' Jude sat down beside me. 'Thanks.'

'Mainly for him,' I said, acknowledging his gratitude with a shaky smile. 'Did they manage to salvage the family jewels?'

'The surgeon thinks they've saved the testicle. He said it will be functional but there might be problems with fertility later on. They've also put in a couple of stitches to stop the other one twisting.'

'Do they know what caused it?'

'Apparently, they don't really know what causes it. It's called testicular torsion,' he said. 'Sometimes it can run in the family.'

'Not my family. Yours?'

'Not that I've heard of.'

I looked at him, 'Maybe ask Stella; maybe she'd know.'

'As one of the guy siblings I should know, don't you think?'

I decided then I'd had enough. I left him on duty for Francis. Jude could be there for the kid when he woke up.

~~~~~

We were in the middle of an Indian summer. I stood on the roof, leaning my elbows on the perimeter wall, waiting for the sea breeze. The orange glow of the streetlights coloured the sky. Zita arrived with a bottle of Amaro in one hand, a plate under one arm and a paper bag of almond biscotti in her other hand. She fished out the two shot glasses she'd stashed in the bag, poured the wafers onto the plate and plonked everything on the table. As we sat down, she asked, 'Simone been in yet?' She scrunched the paper bag into a ball and put it on the seat beside her.

'Jude's taking her in tomorrow to pick him up.'

Zita shook her head. 'Sometimes I just don't believe her.' She poured the aperitif into the glasses. 'Explain this torsion thing to me? It's like blue balls or something is it?'

'More like black balls; the testicle twists and the cord and blood vessels get blocked. The testicle can die.'

Zita leaned forward. I could feel her concern even if I could not see her clearly in the dark. She exclaimed, 'Francis?'

'He's okay. They got to it in time. Apparently some guys have loose testicles. They're called bell clappers.'

'What?'

'Bell clappers,' I said. I couldn't help smiling and, I couldn't miss seeing her brilliant white teeth in the dim light, neither could she.

'Puts new meaning into going like the clappers, doesn't it?'

'It just means there can be excessive movement in the scrotum,' I said primly, trying not to laugh.

'I thought that was normal.'

'Some men have more swinging in the breeze than others, I suppose. Runs in the family… apparently.'

'Not our family,' said Zita.

'That's what I thought. But then, things change.'

'What?' She said, 'Like a mutation?'

'Oh, I wouldn't go that far.'

'But that's what happens, Constantia. Things go wrong. They mutate. Things become what they were never meant to be.'

I solved my restlessness by fetching a large candle in a bowl, to bring some light to the table. It was one of those so large that it needed three wicks. The candle was white and each wick had burned unevenly. I placed it in the middle of the table and lit it. The flames flickered as they caught, then burnt straight up into the still evening air. Their tall reach barely trembled.

As Zita sipped the bitter syrup, I saw she had wet track marks down her face. She had been crying. I reached out and touched her hand, only for a moment. When I took it away, she began to speak again.

'All my life,' she said, 'the next step has always been inevitable. You know what I mean? Not easy mind you, but obvious. When I left school it was obvious I would work in the shop with my parents. Then it became obvious I would take over responsibility for the flowers. Then I had to go to work with Vince, after… you know… and then, when you and I became friends, it seemed inevitable I would end up with Jude. And then, after Vionella died, it was important that I became independent, from both the church and the marriage. But now, nothing is obvious. I don't know what to do anymore.'

Zita dunked a shard of biscotti in her Amaro. The taste of Sicily was the burnt umber chocolate of broken dreams.

Chapter 8

Garden table

The finished chairs need a matching table. Imagine something that will withstand all weathers. Imagine sophisticated adults sitting there, enjoying warm evenings and alfresco living. Imagine I am in another life.

This table can support a cup of tea and a romantic novel. Or perhaps antipasto for two and a couple of glasses of sparkling wine. It might bear a potted plant. It has a quiet strength, though I don't advise jumping on it. The human spine is much like this table, just strong enough to carry the weight of a life.

When you look at a human back there's not that much to see of the spine. It is at the core of us. We rarely see an entire spine, unless it's made of plastic hanging outside the chiropractors, or fish, lying on the plate at a seafood restaurant.

The vertebrae are big bones, particularly in the lumbar region. Like removing blocks in a game of Jenga, if the wrong one is pulled out, you could just topple over.

As a spine is curved, so is this table. Stamping out the shapes from the sides is more than just lightening the weight of the walls. Each cutout shape looks like a vertebra. They fly around out of order, implying someone has fallen. If their bones are loose and scattered, the person must be lost.

Our top vertebra is called C1 or cervical one. It's also nick-named 'Atlas'. That's more like it, isn't it? The top of our spine holds up our head, our entire world.

~~~~~

Frogs were there at the beginning of life, when creatures first crept out of the primordial slime. Apparently the first frog fossil, *Triado-bactus,* was found in Madagascar. Scientists suspect it lived around 200 million years ago. It had a longer spine than modern frogs. It had sixteen vertebrae.

Australian frog fossils, found at Murgon in South East Queensland, are thought to be around 54 million years old. Modern frogs have nine vertebrae. The human backbone has twenty-four. Like humans, frogs don't have a tail. Instead, frogs have an urostyle, a kind of spiky bone. It could be evidence frogs once had tails of some sort. There are frogs in New Zealand, of the family *Leiopelma,* that have remnants of tail-wagging muscles.

Astounded to learn humans have been around for no more than one and a half million years. Modern humans are supposed to be less than two hundred thousand years old. Frogs have been on the planet for 53 million more years than us. It's irrefutable the frog is an incredible survivor. Up 'til now, of course. It's going to take more than backbone to save these creatures.

The giant barred frog, *Mixophyes iteratus,* is the largest of the ground frogs. It comes from shallow, rocky, mountain rainforest streams. It has gold eyes, like Guido. The tadpoles are gold. They are striped like a tiger to blend in with the rocks.

Glaze the table beige with a thin black stripe down the sides. The legs are also striped, like a cartoon prisoner. The table's surface is covered with variable dark-brown blotches.

You might find a giant barred river frog in northern New South Wales or in southern Queensland or you might not. *Mixophyes iteratus* is in danger. Who knows if it will ever be found again?

~~~~~

I saw them in the garage when I was on my way in to empty the kiln. Jude was helping Peter with the crumpled Datsun. They had rotated the tyres and were checking the air pressure. I watched them for a while. I wished these two men were all my family. I would die for them. That's when I remembered I lived in the real world. I left them to the tyres.

I was opening the kiln when Peter came in to the studio. I was pleased. This would be a chance to speak to him privately. I'd noticed he'd been morose and distracted, but by what? Perhaps he was having trouble with his students. I hoped his erstwhile girl-friend, Leela, hadn't resurfaced. I welcomed him in a jovial manner in hope of breaking his reserve. 'To what do I owe this honour?'

He did not return my merry greeting. Instead, he spoke quietly, 'Just looking for my spine.'

'What?' I thought it would take longer to get to the serious business but here we were straightaway. I gritted my teeth and prepared for the worst.

'You know, backbone. Courage. Got any lying about?'

I sent him a sympathetic look before I resumed working. Waiting for the real stuff.

He stood beside me and looked into the still-warm kiln. It was always suspenseful, unpacking a kiln. There were certain to be breakages but, just as likely, a glaze could turn out far better than expected. In this firing, my ceramic mother embraced her baby still. She was safe. I started unpacking the smaller pots stacked around her. Her glaze had fired a bit redder than I'd envisioned but it seemed solid enough. I looked forward to getting her out into the light of day, a family structure for a library. The architect who had commissioned me understood the library was for the family. We had also discussed the sad reality that sometimes a library was all the family someone might have.

'Nice work, Mum.' Then he turned away and walked around the workshop. He picked things up, dusted them down on his tee shirt emblazoned with, 'Radiators: *Feel the Heat*', then arranged them back on the shelf again. Without really looking at what he was doing, I said, 'Leave that alone.'

He turned to me, holding out a small sculpture in the palm of his hand. His light-shot eyes flashed like his father's. 'Can I have it?' It was an elongated bird, tiny like a blue wren. He stood there, holding it in his filthy hand, watching it as if the thing were alive.

'What for?'

'To give to someone. I'll pay.'

He certainly would pay. He'd pay in words. Words that would tell his mother what was going on. I felt smart-casual was the best way to eke out further information and continued to fossick in the kiln. 'Someone…?'

'Charlotte.'

I thought, 'Charlotte'? Oh, for goodness sake! Not *the* Charlotte? Charlotte the harlot? What the hell's going on here? When I spoke, I kept my voice cool and my hands busy taking plates from the kiln and stacking them on the bench. 'And which Charlotte would that be?'

'Charlotte Preece. I've known her for a while. Not well, you know. Just seeing her around. I think she's… lovely.'

'Lovely?'

'I saw her first, Mum.'

What's this son of mine been up to? After a long pause, I said, 'So, you saw her first. Then what happened?'

'Things developed.'

Developers develop. Photographs develop. People develop when they reach sexual maturity. People change when they develop. 'We are talking about *the* Charlotte?'

'Yeah. Only she's not…'

'Not what?'

'Not *the* Charlotte. She's not like… the enemy. She's just a ma-ture-age student, around my age. She's trying to get into medicine. She nursed someone through HIV AIDS. It changed her.'

Changed her? How? This sort of defence is not what a mother wants to hear. I am screaming to ask him, what sort of friend? What were you thinking? Did you have unprotected sex? Are you mad? But I ask none of these shrieking questions. I remain outwardly calm although I thought at the time I must go for a very long walk or else break something if he did not start offering more information. I act the very epitome of the very casual mother. Ruth Cracknel had nothing on me. 'Did you say, AIDS?'

'It was her brother. He left her some money so she can afford to study. She wants to help people but she's finding university difficult. She's delicate. Well, she's a carpenter and obviously not weak, but she's sensitive. Can't kill frogs, for instance.'

Strange. Very strange. A familiar story. Had it had been her fear of killing that attracted Jude? Why does it always come back to the frogs? I straightened up and looked directly at Peter. I said, 'She'd probably be good as a doctor. Do no harm. Isn't that the medical mantra?'

'She still has to get through Biology One.'

I returned to unpacking and stacking the plates. One was broken so I threw the pieces into the smash-palace box. 'What happened? When things... developed?'

'You won't believe it.' No, probably not. Peter said nothing more although he continued to roam around the room as though he had more on his mind. I waited, stacking bowls and plates onto the bench in an organised manner.

'She chucked me out,' he finally said. 'Threw my clothes out the window.'

'She what?'

'I confessed. Told her I was my father's son.'

He kept the little blue wren and I presumed he would give it to the girl. I remembered my own struggle with life and death and chloral hydrate. These were murky waters to say the least. What was the son doing, visiting his father's young lover... sorry, 'friend'? Without his clothes? AIDS, for fucks sake. I looked at him eye to eye. 'You'll do the right thing, Peter, you always do,' I said. Hoping I was right, and he was right. Set them free and watch them fly.

~~~~~

We table our cards. Table our problems. Once they're tabled, we have to deal with them. They're out in the open.

A human spine has the strength of a table. If we're on all fours, a human could become a table.

Stone strength from mud; the mud transformed by fire; metamorphosis in the kiln. It's only made from clay. It's not that strong. You could pound it into smithereens with a hammer.

Sit outside in the studio courtyard today. Stare at the three-panel bas-relief mural. Made it when we first moved here. Represents a goddess from Mesopotamia, Innana-Ishtar. She fell in love with a gardener. In the first panel she floats above him. She admires his work in the vegetable patch. She admires him. She longs for him. In the middle panel, she appears before him to reveal her love. He is so shocked he falls about in incredulity. She takes offence at his extreme reaction.

The final panel depicts his punishment. As retribution for his exaggerated negativity she turns him into a frog. I wish that could happen to me. As much as I seek my husband in the frogs I only find myself. How can I turn myself into a frog?

I'd have to find the right ingredients for the transformation. I'd have to learn about the alchemy of fire. I'd have to cause the metamorphosis from one form to another. I'd have to accept change. Understand that change does not come on demand. Inevitable but then, I fear change is only visible in hindsight.

The only thing I'm sure of in life is change. From the moment that first, chance bolt of lightning cracked into that accidental puddle of hydrogen, methane, ammonia, carbon monoxide and water, nothing has been more certain in my life than change. No matter what I've done to prevent it.

Our planet, and life forms, transform time and time again. Mammals were born only yesterday in the scheme of groaning time. Dinosaurs, the most successful of all long-term life, came and went. Humans, the newest of everything, are still evolving with each fresh generation and take a look what we've become! All billions and billions of us. In order to metamorphose into a frog, I have a feeling, right or wrong, I would have to go backward. So I trawl again through my memories, trying to find... I don't know... something.

~~~~~~

On the mildest of summer days, a kookaburra laughed at us from his perch high in a fig tree. A green ferry trundled towards Manly, surging on the water like a big old bus. A speedboat screamed and chattered as it bounced towards the city, and then Zita rose like Venus from the water. She was curvaceous in a navy one piece. Water cascaded over her shapely body, into her ample cleavage and down her rounded thighs, dimpled like soft ricotta. Jude stood in the shallows, watching her and then reaching out for her hand. The two of them, hand in hand, ran up the beach to me. Peter played with Leaf in the sand while I waited in the shade of a gum tree with baby Fern who lay asleep on her blanket spread out on the grass.

Zita smiled at Jude then peeled off her preposterous floral bathing cap—a joke gift from her husband—and shook out her dark hair. It tumbled to her shoulders. I watched and hated Jude's hand as it came around Zita's back... so intimate, such ownership. He had chosen the wrong person. I wanted his hand, so warm in muscle strength, on my back.

The Greenwich baths were small, a football field of seawater enclosed with a wire and white wooden fence. A list of rules was attached to the fence: no climbing, no running, no bombing. Life was ordered. We were safe. On the shore was a small playground with a swing and a seesaw, and crafty, arty strings of shells dripped from the kiosk like summer stalactites. Yachts were moored nearby, their ropes clicking against metal masts, and at the far side of the harbour, the re-discovered yuppie suburbs of Birchgrove and Balmain with a yacht-clustered marina near the Balmain Baths. To our right lay industrial Cockatoo Island with its cliff face and insipid buildings and to our left, the grey towering silhouette of the CBD, a mere ten minutes ferry ride away.

I remembered sailing to Balmain, in the beginning, trying to hang on to the sheet in the sailing dingy. I remembered when Jude asked me to marry him. Life really was plain sailing then. Waves were ebbing and flowing, ebbing and flowing…

In those days of the early eighties, I was practical and polite. I needed for us all to be close. I made sure we spent time with Leaf and Fern, knowing that Peter would benefit from a relationship with his half-siblings. While Jude was away at uni or in the field, I was happy to help Zita in whatever way I could. I avoided her temper and kept house for her, looked after shopping and cleaning, trying to make her life easier. In return, her family kept us supplied with gnocchi, lasagne and homemade sugo. We wouldn't starve. Not physically, anyway.

Twenty years had passed since I graduated from East Sydney Technical College in 1962. Like life itself, my work had evolved. There was growth and life and blood and energy, and the fire scarred us all.

~~~~~~

"Have nothing in your house you do not know to be useful or believe to be beautiful." I used to quote William Morris whenever I wrote an article for *Ceramics Today*. Over a hundred years ago, Morris declared that art was the expression of joy in our labours. Expression of joy! Morris was writing in 1882. He believed that having to work in poor conditions for less than a fair wage was no way for our fellow man to live. Why aren't people saying that now? What if, as William Morris suggested, we all use less stuff? The objects we do use could be made with hope, pleasure and a sustainable wage.

William Morris was a spokesperson for the arts and craft movement. So am I. Hope, pleasure and a sustainable wage. If everyone lived that way could the frogs be saved? Clay. Water. Fire. Frogs. These are my simplicities, my bare facts. Yet even they are filled with such complexity that a proper understanding cannot be achieved in a lifetime. Centuries of tradition have bequeathed us pure stoneware from the Song dynasty in China. You can see them down in the National Gallery in Melbourne—glistening bowls of breath-taking fragility—decorated with both chun and celadon glazes. These do not begin with an individual yet are made by a single person using their individual skill and drawing on the knowledge of generations of ancestors. The maker spins the bowl whilst sitting on the shoulders of the past. It is an infinite bowl.

With our post-industrial advances in technology, I imagine William Morris spinning in his grave. Spinning, spinning, then weaving a shroud for all humanity. His thoughts, over a hundred years old, are still relevant. Korea, now a bustling hot bed of tech development, was once the crucible of pottery. The first clay objects date back to the Ice Age. Prehistoric China, Japan and Africa all used clay for household items. Is it possible a potter used the shape of Helen of Troy's breast to mould a ceramic wine cup?

The Greek goddess, Athena, was the patron of pottery. The ancient Greeks looked at life differently from us modern go-getters. We face forwards, looking into the future with our unseen past trailing along behind us. The Greeks faced up to the past. They turned their backs to the future because it was impossible to see what was coming. I recommend it. The future keeps me upright. It pushes softly against my back. I can only see the past streaming out like the wake of a boat, like softly flapping flags, or Isadora Duncan's scarf.

Like rowers, the Greeks were content to face the opposite direction to where they were going. I too do not mind not knowing what is coming my way. I would rather not know. I would rather examine the streamers of yesteryear. My undulating past continues to flow like a comet's tail. What went before winds into itself. Memory colours events and juxtaposes episodes that are not related in time. It is a conglomerate of history.

Try to cushion yourself against the future. Regard your past with patience. It is a way of looking at a life. Hamlet says, 'What a piece of work is man'. Jesus says, 'Heaven is within'. The Old Testament assures us that man is made in God's image. If you want to get to know someone you must not rely on appearances. Beauty is more than skin deep. There's a lot more under the skin than is often imagined. A human is packed into a skeleton basket, squashed into fascia wrappings and full of miracle.

Looking deep into a human being isn't the best way to spend time with a loved one, but it is a way to say goodbye.

Chapter 9

Decanter

The decanter appears off balance and too slender. It is, in fact, grounded. It will not fall over unless pushed. Who would push such a thing?

When I throw the basic shape, the mouth is too thin to put my hand inside. Use a bottling tool, a hera, to push out the sides without stretching the opening too far. Once dried to leather-hard, take crescent slices from the sides. Ease the cut sides back together to make a shape like a fat boomerang, reminiscent of a liver.

The decanter is olive-brown. Down two sides are pale stripes accentuating dark bands. The dirty-white front is peppered with dark specks.

The colours are modelled on the tinker frog, *Taudactylus acutirostris*, also known as the sharp-snouted torrent frog. What better frog for a decanter? The sound of bottles and empty vessels, tink, tink, tinkling. The top of the frog's limbs are striped. Copy the stripes to highlight the pointed neck of the decanter. Tinker frog hails from the rainforest, a place of damp and rot.

I learned to make delicate sake jugs and cups during the study trip to Seto in Japan. They were profitable. Graduated to wine decanters as a result of our stay in Italy.

A decanter can hold more liquid than a little sake bottle. This decanter has to contain an entire liver. Make five at the outset. Two explode in the process. One cracks.

Dry pancreas, gallbladder and liver overnight in the kiln before grinding. Mix the meaty chunks into the clay as grog. Wedge clay for a long time. Want to remove air bubbles. Run it through pug mill for good measure.

The liver is the largest gland in the human body. It's the second largest organ after the skin. A liver normally weighs about one and a half kilos. It's a chemical factory known as the immortal organ. The Greeks must have known about its ability to regenerate. They gave us Prometheus who had to suffer his liver being eaten by an eagle every day only to have it regrow overnight. Every new day, Prometheus endured the same, though brand-new, agony. Know how he feels.

~~~~~

Back when Mark and I sat across from the lawyer in an office seemingly coated with Venetian blinds, I felt a strange emptiness. I had lost both parents. I felt cut adrift.

The lawyer of the thousand Venetians, that someone else kept clean for him, sat in his darkened office. He leaned forward into his hands, balancing his chin, asking if we knew that our mother was a wealthy woman. Mark and I looked at each other uneasily. Was she? The lawyer told us that oh, yes, yes, very wealthy indeed, at least on paper.

I hadn't been expecting anything. Lillian had intimated when I married a Catholic that I was out of my mind and out of her will. Now it seemed she had not followed through with her threat. Unlike her.

We were stunned as the lawyer read through Lillian's portfolio. He suggested we take copies and study them, perhaps get advice. He could recommend a financial advisor.

Mark bent over, examined the carpet, exhaled and shook his head. He muttered under his breath. He said he'd known our mother had played the market to some extent but hadn't imagined the magnitude of her success. All that money! She'd never splashed out when she'd visited Mark in Hong Kong. He was hurt. He said it was his area of expertise yet she never once asked him for advice. He felt belittled. I patted him on the back, believing that Mark had never asked Lillian for advice, either. But I didn't say that. And it was not the time to mention she'd bought Jude and I tickets to England as a wedding present. Perhaps she'd done something similar for Mark. I let sleeping gifts lie.

The solicitor asked his girl to bring tea for us. I was dazed. The carpet was the same green as the carpet in the crematorium chapel.

Mark wanted to take a taxi to the airport by himself but Peter was keen to see the planes, so I drove him in the evening sparkle light. It was easier to find a car park this time and the low-flying planes ushered Mark, Peter and I into the check-in area. Mark was quickly through formalities, as he had no luggage. Clumps of people stuck together in the bar. We spent our final half hour together in an alcove amongst clumps and agreed to speak soon, Mark and I, of course we would. We were all that was left of our family now. I wished he could stay longer. He said he had regrets but he was keen to get back to his life in Hong Kong. I asked about where he lived and if he lived alone, but he was cagey. I'm not even sure if he had a girlfriend or a cat or... I was left wondering. We walked to the departure gate and he turned and waved as he went through the doors into Departures. Goodbye, my baby brother. Peter looked at me with an adult, worried expression. I reassured him that I was feeling fine and we went home together.

Later, as the only adult left in the family home to clean up, I was licensed to snoop. I didn't pry into everything all at once. The desk was filled with manila folders. I would take one folder at a time, after Peter was asleep or at Jude's place for the weekend, and open them out onto the dining table. It took a couple of months to sort through the entire desk, to which I had never before been invited. Dad, who had little financial aptitude, had been responsible for the legal and financial side of their lives ever since Lillian had gone into hospital. I found property certificates, legal letters, letters from the accountants, unpaid bills, menus and programs for *Giselle* and *The Pyjama Game*—all mixed up together.

It appeared my parents had their house in joint ownership but Lillian had investments in her own name in Australia, the United States and Japan. She started her portfolio when I was born. I suppose that in those days she wouldn't have been able to show up at a newspaper office pregnant, or even with a baby, so Lillian had looked to the share market as an alternative way of keeping herself amused. That was where her maternal instinct had been focused: her portfolio was her baby.

Two months after the funeral, in a hissing long-distance phone call from Hong Kong, Mark said he agreed with my analysis of the investments and was happy to take half of the shares and all of the family home as his inheritance. As well as shares, my share included a rundown, Art Deco, three-storey block of flats overlooking Cooper Park. Its name was *Bindiwurra*.

The real estate agent managing *Bindiwurra* told me that during the Second World War, Japanese submarines had fired upon Cooper Park. They were apparently aiming for the Rose Bay flying-boat base. I was a month old and safe on the other side of the harbour. My mother, bored to tears at home and keeping an eye on the property market, decided that picking up a block of flats on cheap, frightened land would be just the thing to lift her spirits.

As the years passed, Lillian may have forgotten she owned *Bindiwurra*, the agent quietly dealing with any issues and funnelling her broker trouble-free rents. The tenants must have been uncomplaining types because not much maintenance was ever done, that's for sure. Perhaps she had other properties and didn't need to call in the profit. She must have been paying hectic taxes. I would have to rationalise quickly.

Cooper Park turned out to be an oasis in a steep cleft between Bondi, Bondi Junction, Bellevue Hill and Edgecliff. Little paths led over bridges and rain shelters in the style of Taronga Zoo's old sculptural, concrete structures. Large trees, including *Angophoras*, peppermint gums and grey gums, rose around the slopes while scentless rosewoods, figs and shiny-leaved lilly pillies grew in the gully. Tennis courts were surrounded by lush greenery on all sides, birds chirruped and water tinkled in the creek. It was a forgotten land, a crack in the designer flow of the Eastern Suburbs.

Just the idea of owning *Bindiwurra* lifted my spirits. This would be an opportunity to have my dream family home. I hoped my child, my husband, his second wife and their two children would all come to live here. I gave thanks to Lillian.

~~~~~

The pancreas, tucked under the stomach and connected to the liver, is the second largest gland in the body. Known as the sweetbreads.

Hard to survive a liver transplant, whether as donor or recipient. Hard to survive with a failing liver. Alcohol is a powerful corrosive in Western society. At least in the people I know.

The liver acts in much the same way in both frog and human, extracting toxins from the blood. When frogs go into torpor, or hibernate, their livers create glucose to lower their freezing point—a sort of frog anti-freeze.

Simone included the total liver cleansing diet amongst her many fads. Allen Ginsberg died of liver cancer. Livers are necessary for life. Apparently they are nice fried together with bacon. So are sweetbreads. The pancreas contains the Islets of Langerhans, home of insulin. Zita's favourite food is chicken liver paté. Foie gras is the liver resulting from the forced stuffing of a duck for human pleasure. I am vegetarian. Thank goodness they invented baked beans. I eat baked beans again and again. I cling to facts about frogs to keep my brain alive.

Liver is the Anglo Saxon word for the seat of life.

~~~~~

The phone rang. It was Jude, wanting to see me. Could I come down to his place? The bedsit, not Simone's flat.

When I went in, Zita was sitting at the table with a cup of tea. The window was open and a cool zephyr shifted on my skin.

Jude said, 'Would you like something to drink?'

'Sure,' I said. 'I'd better go for a chamomile.'

'Nothing stronger?'

'No, thanks.' I sat down. Zita looked tired but had put on extra make-up and appeared to be making an effort not to scream.

'Simone's at the herbalist,' Jude explained, offering me a mug and sitting down opposite. I could tell at first sniff he'd given me peppermint tea.

'A herbalist? What would you want from a herbalist?' said Zita.

'What's the difference between a herbalist and a naturopath?' asked Jude.

'Is that a joke?' asked Zita, with no hint of humour.

'There's a difference?' I asked.

When Simone appeared, glowing and glamorous as usual, we put the question to her. Simone tossed her ponytail before she answered. 'The herbalist I see is a man trained in China who also practises acupuncture. He's been working on my blood, clearing it of toxins. The Chinese have been studying health and medicine a lot longer than Western naturopaths. Plus, I think Westerners are very controlled by the big herb companies. But it's all a matter of trust, isn't it?'

'I wouldn't go near any of them,' said Zita.

'You wanted a green tea?' asked Jude, and he did put a green tea in front of Simone. Just what she wanted, without even her asking! She looked radiant. I might have looked radiant, too, if I'd got what I wanted. I sipped my unwanted peppermint without complaint.

I found our mugs very interesting. They were mine, made in white clay, with a slight hourglass figure. I remembered the handles giving me trouble until I got the knack of pulling them into that

119

strange angle. The blue splash was a wild attempt to emulate Brett Whiteley's ultramarine in unpredictable glaze. The result was not near enough for anyone to notice.

Simone leaned towards me and whispered, 'It's like a marriage guidance session.' Everyone else had fallen silent and she may as well have shouted it.

Zita laughed a little too loudly and added, her voice a little too strident, revealing how agitated she felt, 'Imagine if we all turned up to marriage guidance. We'd have to guide the poor counsellor.'

I could tell she was feeling the ground had shifted under her feet because that's what I was feeling. I tried to show my empathy by agreeing with her and offered a weak joke, 'I'd rather go to a naturopath'.

Zita and I leaned and bumped our shoulders together, sharing a sympathetic grimace.

Jude didn't tap his spoon on the cup, that would have been too much, but I could tell he would have liked a formal way of starting his little speech. He cleared his throat before thanking us for being there. He was formal. 'I wanted to tell you there's no need for panic. There is no girlfriend. No one has to move out. We can all go on as before. Okay?' There was a silence as we took this in. Then, we all spoke at once.

'But who is Charlotte?'

'What about Charlotte?'

'What have you done with Charlotte?'

Jude looked irritated. 'Charlotte's a student I was helping. She's returning to education after a break, she needed more support than some of the other mature-age students.'

'Is that what you call it? Support?'

'Come on! Use your brains. There are laws about students and teachers. I'd be mad to touch her.'

'It's the kids,' said Simone.

Zita agreed. 'What were you doing, introducing her to the kids?'

'I would have liked you all to meet her,' said Jude. 'But it's really not what you think.'

'Did she drop you?' asked Zita.

'For God's sake, no... no one got dropped. You wouldn't let me get a word in the other day. Okay, it did get complicated for a while but it's not now. Things are simple. They're better off the way they were. Aren't they?'

'Are you going to do it again?'

'No! No, I'm not. I'm really sorry everything got confused. I didn't mean to hurt anyone. There are no secrets. There's nothing to hide. It's working, isn't it? I see the kids. We all help each other. I help you. You help me. That's the way it should be, yes?'

We three women exchanged glances. I thought our arrangement was best for the children and assumed Simone and Zita thought so, too. But we couldn't go backwards. No one ever could. It was unclear what lay ahead of us all.

The air was growing colder. As I left, I shut the window.

~~~~~

When I first walked through the front door of *Bindiwurra*, way back in '83, I felt as though I was coming home. She was dilapidated, for sure. There was no denying the dark, the dirty smell or the grime, but there was no damp, thank goodness—she was filthy but not rotten.

The Art Deco block of flats crouched on the side of a hill overlooking the valley of Cooper Park. Northern walls seemed perilously close to the edge of the cliff but she clung on. To me, *Bindiwurra* looked like a castle—my castle. The building's overall shape was squat and strong and claimed the air. There were three floors: each curvaceous with its own veranda bending around views of green treetops and acres of sky. There were racing stripes horizontally along each level, a *linea nigra* repeated in darker decorative brickwork. Geometric groups of four dark bricks created a kind of zip along the sides of the verandas punctuation by a jaunty trilogy of stripe at each beginning and end.

Her name, *Bindiwurra*, was painted in gold on black tiles set into a short wall curved around the driveway like a tail, and repeated on tiles embedded in the wall by the main entrance. Outside was a mess with junk scattered everywhere: newspapers, filthy mattresses, milk crates. A ratty cat slunk away between a heap of cardboard boxes as I approached a rust-bucket Holden with a pattern of *Save the Franklin* stickers on the windscreen. As I walked down the driveway into the garaging area, I could see that with a rearrangement, a little building, there would be a studio. I nodded, pleased with my mother, as I moved around the clutter. It would work. It really would.

The agent, wearing a prominent gold power tie with his black suit and shiny shoes, came in behind me, shaking his head. He was sorry the place was in such a state. He didn't know how it had come to this. I didn't bother talking to him. I wasn't in the mood for excuses. I went up the stairs to the top floor. There was a thick layer of dust and litter. But I was thrilled with the potential. It was undeniable, *Bindiwurra* did have good bones.

It was a sunny winter's day outside but we couldn't have known in the gloom of the stairwell. It wasn't until the agent unlocked the door to the single apartment on the upper level that we were almost blinded with the sunlight flooding the first room. Walls and ceiling were painted white, a couch and easy chair were red with a black coffee table between. As the agent and I moved through the flat, I could see the harbour in tantalizing ricochet glimpses through the dense green of Cooper Park. This flat would have to be mine! I could hardly wait to evict the current tenant. The power!

As the agent explained the terms of the lease we moved downstairs to inspect the two smaller apartments on the second floor. The smell of old frying was here. The curtains were drawn in the first two-bedroom apartment. When we opened them we could see the place was dirty and littered with empty beer cans and pornographic magazines. The second, used only for storage, was filled with boxes, camping gear and broken bikes.

Down on the first floor, two cats sunned themselves in the hallway. They barely twitched a whisker as I followed the agent past them. He knocked on the door and introduced me to the woman who answered it. She explained her friend was still asleep. She worked as a night duty nurse. We promised not to disturb her and could see the shape of the two-bedroom apartment, which was clean but untidy with a large pile of unironed washing near a washing basket, without prying into her bedroom. In the bedsit at the end of the hall were three more straggly cats and an elderly woman who had just been to the hairdressers. She became upset and tried to call the police until the agent pulled out identification and let her telephone the manager of the real estate agency. All these vulnerable humans would have to find somewhere else to live and I didn't care!

I left the agent at the front door step and set off up the hill to Bellevue Park. As I walked and admired the trees and view, I considered *Bindiwurra*. The place was certainly habitable; it just needed work getting rid of the debris and the smell of cats. I stood at the top of Bellevue Park and looked over the harbour glistening before me, a *belle vue*.

~~~~~

Taudactylus acutirostris is critically endangered. The tink, tink, tink of the sharp-snouted day frog may be fading out...

Clap, everyone! Clap! If you believe in frogs, then clap! Clap harder!

Chapter 10

Breadbin

Once I had a ceramic bread crock in my kitchen. It was as round as a barrel. I found the lid too heavy to lift for my early morning toast activities. Given Sydney's humidity, I could never keep the mould out of it. I gave it to Sheryl. I think it's in the courtyard at the gallery. She kept goldfish in it. William has probably cleaned it out and sent it to the tip by now. I sold quite a few in the seventies.

I felt the fear even before Jude and I were married. It seems obvious now. I was scared he'd leave. Scared the whole thing would come crashing down, imploding and annihilating me. Where would I go? What would I do? I couldn't survive on my own. I just couldn't.

Then again, I'm not dead yet.

~~~~~

In the sixties, happily travelling, making charming mugs and soup bowls, I became a wife and a mother. In the seventies it all changed and I became the first wife. It takes a second wife to make a first. I had to make it work. I had to keep my family together.

I knew I had only to convince Zita. I expected Jude would fall in with whatever she thought best—he generally did. I decided to take us to Cooper Park for a picnic. I packed Leaf and Fern into the car while Peter was at school. We picked up Zita from her Glebe Point Road shop and headed across the city.

By her reddened eyes and blotchy nose, I could see that Zita had been crying. My heart went out to her. I had no idea what was going on. But I would wait until we were settled in the park before saying anything. Sometimes, I have to admire my self-control.

We wandered past the tennis courts to the picnic table near the little creek. Leaf stumbled about exploring while Fern lay on the rug gurgling and trying to eat leaves. Chubby fingers would reach out and grab a handful of greenery and one of us would dislodge the pasture and give her the blue crocodile or the green teething ring. She'd shove that into her mouth with one hand and then, fascinated, reach for the grass again. Dribble coated her hands as she crushed stalks and raised them toward her wet, gummy mouth.

Without preamble, Zita announced that her friend Vionella had been diagnosed with aggressive breast cancer and had only months to live. The air whooshed out of my lungs as I remembered my own mother's descent into the sufferings of lung cancer. Vionella didn't deserve that.

Zita was furious. Vionella was only thirty. How could such a life, such a good life, be cut so short? What sort of God took the best people from the earth and left only the suffering behind? The worst aspect was that Vionella had just discovered she was pregnant. She would not consider an abortion so medical staff could not proceed with potentially life-saving chemotherapy. Guido and she had been trying for a baby for over ten years. Vionella was filled with determination to proceed with the pregnancy even though it was unlikely that either mother or child could survive. It would be God's will.

Zita couldn't believe she would have to say goodbye to her dearest friend. The priest had been well meaning but insulting, the church's decrees not helping either Zita or Guido in their anger. Guido could not accept that Vionella was dying. He wanted a cure. He was desperate. He thought God should be sorry.

As she spoke, Zita's eyes continually filled, she sighed and hiccupped, and her breath came in little gasping puffs. Sucking in small steps of air, preparatory to a long, falling sigh, she tried to get Leaf to eat another piece of rock melon.

Sunlight dappled over her distraught face and the creek trickled away the time. It was as though we were trapped in her grief, petrified in amber anguish-light. She was supposed to have her best friend all her life. Of the things Zita had counted on, Vionella was the most important. Vionella was an anchor, even more so than Zita's mother's continual disapproval.

We stared at the toddler engrossed in piling up sticks to make a huge fire. Leaf was particularly interested in fire fighting at that time, and his absorption was perhaps an escape from Zita's emotion. During a lull in her outpouring, I told her about my inheritance on the hill. Zita was happy to be distracted so we packed up the picnic to go and look at it. We carried the children for the five-minute walk, then we stood in the valley below and looked up at *Bindiwurra*.

The air was filled with the rustling of insects and the motion of wind through leaves. *Bindiwurra* gleamed in the sunshine. She looked expectant. It felt like she was waiting for us. I had already started eviction proceedings for all the residents. Once they were gone we would clean up the place. I had so many ideas for my studio I knew I wouldn't be able to fit everything in. There'd be three good-size apartments for our own use and two small bedsits for renting out. I hoped Zita didn't mind, I wanted the top apartment but the other two bigger flats were liveable, too. *Bindiwurra* was close to the city, close to schools and shops. She had to agree, there was much to commend living in this area.

Zita raised heavy eyes to my castle. She sighed. Every breath she took seemed to diminish her. She agreed she could see the potential. She didn't need to return to work immediately so we took a drive around Bondi Junction and down Bellevue Road to Double Bay—also known as Double Pay because it was supposed to be the most expensive place to shop in Sydney.

I wondered if she would consider, if and when she were to move with me to *Bindiwurra*, could she move her business closer? She shrugged and nodded. With an arch of her eyebrows and some upward pressure from her bottom lip, she thought it might be possible but I could tell her heart wasn't in it. We parked the car and put Leaf in his pusher. Zita carried Fern in her baby car capsule. We walked around the shops with narrowed eyes contemplating the area's potential. There was much to be said for a wedding specialist sprouting in Double Bay. More research was needed but at first glance there didn't seem to be a comparable florist along the village-esque laneways.

We chose the Cosmopolitan cafe for cappucinos and sat outside on the terrace, a great place to people watch. An elderly couple sat at the table next to us. The woman, decked out in a thick mask of makeup, took a bite of her large cream cake, which left her with streaks of cream across her face. She had a great deal of difficulty wiping the cream without removing large swipes of foundation. It wasn't long before she'd finished the bun and left the table, carrying her makeup case, presumably destined for heavy repair work.

Four bedraggled student types sat clustered around a table clos-est to the kitchen. They wore jeans, sweatshirts and old dirty train-ers. One stirred her cappuccino slowly, eating the froth caked with sugar, while the others smoked and talked quietly.

In extreme contrast, three women dressed like Madonna—tight minis, high hair and pointy shoes—with logos on their handbags sat at another table. One had an apricot Toy poodle tied to her chair. The poodle had been recently clipped and sported a pink bow on the top of her head. A young man with long hair, a flouncy shirt like a romantic poet, and pointy, leather boots flopping loose at the ankle, joined them. As his hair covered his eyes, I presume it was accidental when he stood on the poodle. The dog squealed, the women shrieked at the sound of the dog's pain and then the four of them lit up cigarettes to get over the shock.

While Leaf toyed with a babycino and Fern slept in her carry-cot, Zita told me that was that. She would not have any more children. She wanted to spend time with Vionella before she died. She took a sip of cold water and watched my reaction with her deep-aqua eyes. I told her I would be happy to look after the children while Jude was away. She wouldn't have to cope alone.

Zita meant something more conclusive. She meant forever. She was finished being the perfect Catholic wife. She could not do it anymore. She said that she'd always been wary of the dogma that her parents spent so much time defending and now, with the official church response to Vionella's diagnosis, Zita wanted to make the most of her life… and that meant her business. She liked the idea of me being a silent partner and buying into a shop, but Guido had warned her about the costs of maintenance on buildings. She thought it might be more cost-effective simply renting and spending more on fit-out and stock.

Zita believed something had to give. It was a good time to think of a move, a new shop, and she could see Cooper Park being a great opportunity for the children. Whatever occurred, she would not be living as Jude's wife. She took off her wedding ring and handed it to me. It seemed she had always known it was mine. While I considered the circle in my hand, and all that the ring symbolised, Zita asked if I could possibly take Leaf and Fern home now and drop her at Edgecliff station on the way?

Of course we could, so we stopped by the bus station, watching her wounded heaviness getting out of the car. This was not right; this was not how I wanted our family to start afresh in our own block of flats, our own estate where there would be plenty of room for us all. I took a deep breath while Zita kissed her children, shut the door, and turned away.

The black spray graffiti on the side of the Edgecliff bus station screamed, *OH YOKO*.

~~~~~

Is it ironic that I find solace in frogs? More than just solace, I relate to them. Maybe I'm disappearing too. The northern gastric-brooding frog, *Rheobatrachus vitellinus*, made Queensland's rainforest creeks its home. The frog brooded its young in gastric juices. Before it became extinct.

Jude believed the mother frog actually swallowed her babies. She looked after them in her gut. Stomach acids don't burn through stomachs, human or frog, because the cells in the lining of the stomach exude a mucus to neutralise the acid. Production of hydrochloric acid in the gastric-brooding frog's stomach would have been turned off by prostaglandin in the jelly surrounding the eggs. Possibly, the mother might have digested a couple of babies in the process of the acid turning off, but then again, she needed to keep up her strength.

The sturdy, stone breadbin harbours yeast, full of life, in its cool belly. Pale brown with dark streaks. Has a whitish abdomen like the gastric-brooding frog. The frog had yellow flares on its limbs. The yellow brings to mind the flames of the kiln and of the baker's oven.

Frog stomachs work in exactly the same way as human stomachs. Do I have the stomach to continue? Now that I've started, there's nothing else to do but to carry on. Like digestion, the process is inevitable.

People with strong stomachs can eat anything. People with weak stomachs had better remember to peel or boil, especially when traveling. Delhi belly or Montezuma's revenge can be harsh. Poor Jude nearly died in India.

Jude was much happier with plain food. His mother, Queenie, and his Aunty Nesta, brought him up after falling wool bales on the wharf had crushed his dad. There were three older surviving siblings and three younger, of whom only Stella returned from her Overseas Experience before getting married. The rest of them were scattered over the globe. There was no fuss in Queenie's kitchen, just good, solid meals of meat and three veg. It was a special occasion if there was bread and butter pudding. Who could have predicted that Jude's simple life would become so complicated?

~~~~~

Not strong anymore. Tire lifting such weights. Won't be making things this size again. Forgotten how much work it could be. If I make a mistake, things could easily get out of control. Can't countenance an accident. Getting weak. Can't stomach horror films. Can't stomach torture. Can't stomach adultery.

Is not a husband innocent until proven guilty? Is that applicable to the first time only? If a man cheats on his third wife, is he not also cheating on his first and second wives?

~~~~~

As pre-arranged, Simone dropped Emma off at my flat one morning. Simone must have sensed the cold snap in the air. She had changed from her Sydney-summer-whites to Sydney-winter-black. It was a smart little suit with a tailored jacket cut smoothly down to the waist then flared out with a jaunty peplum. The skirt length was just on the knee, showing her tanned, smooth calves to perfection. She was wearing a glinting, golden anklet and high-heel mules. I supposed she worked in bare feet. I wouldn't have been able to walk in those shoes much less run about taking snaps. Her glossy ponytail swung as she handed Emma her backpack and bent down to kiss her.

Simone had no time for coffee; she was running late. Emma and I had planned a Cooper Park picnic and a hit of tennis if a court was available. Emma wandered into the laundry to find the racquets. Simone gestured me out into the hall for adult privacy. 'Have you seen a white station-wagon up the street? Or somewhere near here?'

'A white station-wagon is not an uncommon vehicle, Simone.'

'But this one... man inside, sunglasses, watching?'

'Obviously you've seen it, or you wouldn't be asking.'

'At least three times now, maybe more! He was parked across the road yesterday when I was leaving, then I saw him again in Newtown. Gave me the serious creeps.'

'You think he's following you?'

'Drama queen, aren't I?' She laughed but she didn't find it funny. 'Probably all in my imagination, which is why I thought I'd ask you. Because if you think I'm nuts, then I can forget about it.'

'Do you think he's there now?' We went out onto the roof. 'Hang on,' I remembered my telescope and ran back in to fetch it.

On my return to the roof, Simone was jumping with excitement. Her dancer's body wriggled with tension and her black peplum bounced as she pointed out a white station-wagon parked a little way up the road.

'Give it here!' She grabbed the scope out of my hands and looked through the eyepiece. She shook with frustration, 'Quick! Quick! How do you focus this thing?' Given that she was jittering around as if she was wearing her jazz shoes, I relieved her of the telescope and turned it to the vehicle. The number plate was obscured by another vehicle. There appeared to be a man in the driver's seat.

When I reported, she shrieked, 'It's the same one! Got to be! That guy, the way he's sitting, make a note of him, Connie. Have you got a camera?'

'Simone. A photo is not going to help at this distance. It's a white car…'

Maybe I sounded just a little bit too sceptical because Simone abruptly changed the subject.

'When did you get a telescope?'

'Years ago. Jude gave it to me.'

'Our Jude? Who never gives presents? That Jude?'

'Years ago. When things were different.'

'Hey, darls, your birthday's coming up!'

'I'm not expecting anything from him.' I don't know why I kept talking to her as if she would understand but I did. 'Do you?'

Some of the brilliance faded from her eyes. 'No, probably not.'

Jude had given me the telescope just before he'd gone on a research trip. That way, when he was camping in the mountains, we could look out into the same space and see the same stars and fall into the universe as though we were together.

~~~~~

Climbing kilns of Japan illustrate digestion. Fire burns for days. Heat spreads through a succession of small chambers built into and rising up the hill. Astonishing amount of wood is ingested to keep the fire burning. The heat is intense, dark and smoky. Sweat flows from the workers. Fire is a hungry dragon. There is great respect for the fire-breathing monster. Finally, as the kiln cools, thousands of pots disgorge from the belly of the beast.

Kiln is a place of magic. Fire will test faith of the potter and it will test mettle of the clay. Many types of kiln: large, small, walk-ins and test ovens. Lift the lid of something that looks like a washing machine and pull out a shiny waterproof utensil that was soft mud only hours before the generous application of heat.

Like a stomach, the kiln applies heat and transforms the contents. Digestion changes food into ever-smaller particles until they can be absorbed in seven metres of gut and transformed into energy for use by the body.

Kiln exchanges energy, making one element, earth, undergo great elemental exposure to fire, thereby forming rock and glass. Elemental.

~~~~~

I couldn't talk to Jude about Zita, or my wedding ring, because he was away. So I went back to Glebe to plead with her instead. I helped her bath the kids, I read to them and turned out the lights on their soapy-smelling forms tucked up safely in their beds.

I couldn't lose that. I couldn't lose those long eyelashes resting on those smooth, plump cheeks. The sweet smell of a sleeping baby with her little face nested in her hand: that tiny button nose breathing in and breathing out; tiny form in shadows, rising up and sinking down, snuffling, turning over—life in warmth.

When the kids were quiet, Zita and I slumped at her kitchen table, each of us with a glass of sweet Botrytis Riesling and a slice of lemon tart. I said all those things about staying together for the sake of the children. I told Zita she had to try. I reassured her it would all be so much easier when we were living at Cooper Park. I had thought it out: we would provide Jude with his own separate apartment. It would be a bedsit, an oversized den, a bachelor pad.

Zita told me Vionella was fading fast, turning into an angel right in front of them. She could not believe how quickly Vionella was losing her battle and was finding this hard to live with. Despite her grief, she agreed to think about Jude and consider my ideas. Then she left to sit with Vionella, to give Guido some respite throughout the long night vigil.

It was very early the next morning, a Saturday, when Leaf, Fern and Peter joined me in the big bed in Zita's blue and green bedroom. When we were all tucked in and comfortabubble, we giggled over *The Muddle-Headed Wombat* as we took turns reading about Wombat and Tabby and Mouse and their adorabubble adventures.

How I loved these children! I loved their soft bodies and the smell of their hair. I loved their earnest faces when they had something important to tell me. I loved the little clothes, the dungarees, and the baggy shorts that present their endearing legs thrust into chunky sandals. I loved their teeth and their lack of teeth. I loved their hats that shaded chubby cheeks. I loved their mouths, especially when covered with tomato sauce or avocado or a great big chuckle.

~~~~~

On another day as I cleaned up after dinner, I noticed that even though I'd vacuumed, glitter was still in evidence. Emma had been making presents for her mother. I was exhausted after looking after her, providing for her craft projects and negotiating all day. I couldn't wait for the school holidays to end.

Full of the worries of adulthood, Peter arrived with a bottle of 'good news' Chardonnay for my birthday. He insisted it would not keep and found corkscrew and glasses in quick succession. 'Never mind the dishes,' he said, so I sipped the lemony coolness as I leaned on the kitchen bench and stared out the window. The tops of the deep-green trees in Cooper Park were touched with the orange glow of late afternoon.

Peter also brought with him a bulging manila envelope. From the apologetic look on his face it didn't contain anything pleasant. I prodded it with a finger as it lay there unexplained. 'For me?'

'That's the bad news. Sorry.' He pulled the envelope open and poured the contents onto the bench. A cascade of shards was all that remained of my little ceramic bird.

'Charlotte?' I asked.

'*The* Charlotte, you mean.'

'So she didn't like it?'

'Could you fix it?'

What did he want me to fix? His hurt? Some things adult children are supposed to take care of by themselves. 'I think it's beyond my help.'

I'm sorry.' Using his hand, he swept the pieces back into the envelope and dropped it into the bin.

We refilled our glasses and went out into the autumnal air. The lemon leaves were turning yellow, in need of nourishment. Peter stared at his glass. He ran his finger around the edge of the condensation, drew patterns through the chill droplets. 'I thought all you had to do was want, and be there, and prove your love. Be steadfast and loyal and reliable and your dream would come true.'

Love? He loved this Charlotte?

'That sounds like a good start,' I said tentatively, knowing that when a mother starts wanting to deliver a lecture, that's the very time she should shut up. But it's so difficult!

'She doesn't want anything to do with me.'

'Give her time.'

'It's been months.'

'It might take years.'

'Meaning maybe never.'

Yeah, well. Sometimes you can't have the one you're with. I should know. Come on, my son, ask your mother that old chestnut about how she manages to live with your father when he doesn't even notice her? 'Aren't there any other girls in the world?'

'Not any more.'

Is this because of his father? Is his relationship so screwed up he only wants a woman his father has rejected? 'What do you want me to do?'

'Talk to her?'

'I might make it worse.'

'You might just save me five years. Who knows?'

It's not fair. I wanted my son to be at peace with his studies, with his band, with his love life, and now this cheap little girl had wrapped his heart around her stone-cold vengeance. I could make him a new ceramic bird but it would never fly.

In China, frog meat was known as heavenly chicken because people thought that frogspawn fell from heaven. Maybe Charlotte thought the bird was a frog.

My son was a grown man and should have been able to look after his own girlfriend. But it seemed not and I hated seeing how he was diminished by her loss. I could not stand to see his sadness. When he gave me her address in Bronte, much against my better judgement, I couldn't turn him down. He was my only son. I left it a couple of days and then jumped into my wretched old Volvo and dropped in unannounced. It was a compact cottage nestled in the hills above the beach. It looked away from the sea, in good order and appeared freshly painted: white with slate-grey trim. A large wintering coral tree reached through the entire front garden. I knocked on the fly-screen and waited. Then, just as I'd begun to think no one was at home, a woman around my age opened the front door. We considered each other through the fine wire mesh. She was slim, fit and tanned with friendly, wrinkled skin and warm, brown eyes. She wore tailored trousers with a cotton shirt in orange tones. I asked, 'Is Charlotte at home?'

The woman paused before replying. 'I'm her mother. Can I help you?'

'I'm also a mother,' I said. 'Of a son.'

'Ah,' she said. 'Does your son happen to be a friend of my daughter?'

Without too much ado, she went in for her handbag and we came to be sitting at a café at Bronte Beach thawing in the warm June weather. Her name was Sarah... Sarah Preece. She had just started yoga classes in an old church hall, visible from where we sat. 'I love it. I'm able to think again.'

'I'm hopeless!' I told her. 'I fall over even in the simplest pose!' I stirred my cappuccino froth and continued, 'My son asked me to talk to Charlotte...'

She spoke over me at once. 'I am glad. I've been so worried about her. Especially as it seems she's going to drop out of university. I have no idea how best to help her.'

'She's your only child?'

'Her brother died last year.'

'My son did tell me. I'm sorry.'

'My husband died in a car crash before Charlotte was born. I had to bring up the two children by myself. I didn't want Charlotte to have to go through that.'

'No, of course not.'

'My family are from Adelaide. They helped as much as they could but my husband's family is here and I didn't want to take the children away from their grandparents. They missed their son, too.'

'Family...' I agreed with her, '... is so important.'

'Only thing that matters, in the end.'

We had forged a relationship without any comprehension of our children's connection.

'My son's name is Peter.'

She frowned for a moment before speaking. 'I don't know a Peter, she's never mentioned him, but then again, I'm not allowed to let anyone in—no one, old friends or new. She won't let me talk with them if they do come to the door or ring up. I have to tell them to go away.'

'You let me in.'

'You're another mother. Of a son… and I wanted to know…'

'… and his father is Charlotte's lecturer in Biology—Jude Baldwin.'

'I haven't heard her speak of either of them, I'm afraid. She refuses to discuss who might be responsible. No names, no pack drill.'

'Responsible?'

Sarah looked at me quizzically. 'For her pregnancy.'

'Charlotte is pregnant?'

'You didn't know?'

'No! I did not know.' Well, I thought, that is quite a development. Seemed like there would be a lot to talk about with Ms Sarah Preece, mother like me. 'Another coffee?'

We walked across the park sipping our coffees from polystyrene cups. Children chattered in the playground and a tumble of playgroup-sized kids wheeled on trikes around the playground bike paths. We walked towards the beach and then along the coastal pathway, watching waves crash over the rocks and wispy brushstroke clouds paint themselves over the blue. There was much to discuss: many interesting questions with few answers.

'I don't know what Charlotte is to Jude,' I said, 'but I do know that Peter is obsessed with her. Besotted. He's tried to see her but Charlotte has rebuffed him at every turn.'

'In a way,' said Sarah, 'this gives me some idea, which is better than none.'

'I can understand, I think. It's not something I'd like bandied about if I were her.'

'What was your son thinking? And your husband?'

'He's not my husband, thank you. He's my ex-husband. And I am ashamed of both of them.'

'Men!' Sarah shook her head in that time-honoured woman's way.

'Men!' I agreed. I asked, 'How pregnant is she?'

'Just over four months now, too late for an abortion, not that she'd ever consider one. She has no idea how she's going to support herself and the baby, so I'm putting my place on the market. I'll move over here… couldn't think of a better place for children. I'll find a job closer.'

Behind us, in the playground, a toddler fell off her trike and started wailing. Her mum, carrying a baby wrapped in a pink rug, picked up the trike and rubbed the bruised knee, all the while continuing to chat to her friend. Sarah and I shared a wry smile. Parenting was best done in a group and it was a great environment here.

We continued along the coastal path, leaving the park behind us. Man has pinioned the fenced concrete walkway into the side of the cliff and so far the sea has only toyed with it. Sydneysiders know full-well how easily the sea can uprise and rip tiny fences away, how the force of tides and winds many miles away can power an irresistible insurgence. Vulnerable as a couple of ants, we walked beside this torrent of energy and talked about our own children and their new lives. The air tasted of misty salt and the seagulls cried and argued.

Sarah resumed her anxious frown and said, 'I've told her it would be easier if she comes clean… that she would feel better if she talks about it.'

'If she doesn't,' I said, 'May I propose we keep in contact?'

She stared at me for a moment before looking away to the horizon. She muttered, 'I hate secrets.'

'It's not ideal,' I agreed. 'Put it this way: is it possible to ask them in such a way that we don't do ourselves out of a communication channel?'

We walked up past the bogey hole and past the swimming baths built into the rocks. We sat on a bench beneath the bulbous cliff face whose upsurges of brown, beige and sandstone swirled and blended like ancient waves set in a memory. There were smooth bowls of hollow next to rough outcrops of outreaching and the cliff was as powerful as the water, only still. We were stuck between a rock and the hard, cruel might of the ocean. I preferred the security of the concrete to the wild rock edge; Sarah seemed to relish the emerald breakers pounding into the rocks. Out towards the horizon, the sea mist rose above the surf and turned the air faint like a Lloyd Rees painting. Surfer seals dotted the water.

'They're not really kids, are they,' Sarah pointed out as the wind whipped her hair around her face.

'I can't blame them. Youth and indiscretion go hand in hand, don't they? If only Jude wasn't involved. That's what I find so inexplicable. Wonder if a paternity test would tell us anything?'

We both shuddered and looked out to sea. Sarah nodded. 'You might be a grandmother as well. We ought to stick together, at least until we know more.'

I wondered aloud, 'Does Charlotte have a right to privacy now there's another life involved?'

Sarah considered that and added, 'Does the unborn child have rights?'

Everywhere we looked, far out to the ocean blue, there was yet another question. I answered by saying, 'Does the child have a right to a father?'

Sarah looked at me seriously. 'Which father?'

I wanted to press into the cliff face behind us. I wanted to melt into the coffee-chocolate gelato swirls of rock and disappear. I wanted to curl up into those smooth hollows and weathered curves of sandstone and be no more.

Brain coordinates vomiting. Abdominal wall and diaphragm contract together to squeeze stomach. Some jockeys hit themselves in their solar plexus to make themselves vomit. Bulimia is a beautiful necessity for the middle classes and was too for Romans in their purpose-built vomitaria.

Both *Rheobatrachus vitellinus* and *R. silus*, the southern gastric-brooding frog, have gone from their entire known range. No herpetologist has seen a gastric-brooding frog since Zita handed me her wedding ring.

~~~~~

A couple of days after meeting Sarah, I completed packing an order into boxes: a set of bowls this time. I had an appointment with my dealer the next day and felt virtuous for having prepared the required delicate basins ahead of time. As due reward for my diligence, I took a cup of jasmine tea out to the roof garden. It was quiet and cool. I had on a jacket, so was warm enough. I contemplated the treetops. I watched the Manly ferry cross the harbour and I looked far past where the horizon might be, beyond the Heads, across the ocean into a distance that I could not possibly see.

It was true that I'd occasionally thought of myself as a grandmother, especially with Simone's children, particularly Emma; they were so much younger than my own offspring. I did think, sometimes, I was too old for this, and was glad to give them back at the end of the day. How would I feel if the baby I held was my own son's child?

As I pondered this, enjoying the warmth of the mug of jasmine tea, Fern appeared beside me. She looked deeply into my face. Her features gave the impression of melting and smearing together. Her eyelids drooped and her mouth was slack and she smelled of alcohol. She swayed a little but kept on staring. Though her appearance alarmed me, I remained outwardly calm. Not that she would have noticed. I asked her, 'What's happening, Fern?'

'Mum's out. Film Festival. You'd… better come.' She took my hand and tugged, none too gently. I rose to my feet, set down my cup, grabbed my granny feelings and held on tight.

Fern took me down to Zita's flat, still clinging to my hand like a wobbling two-year-old child. I could hear Leaf before I could smell him. I'm not big on vomiting and I could see Fern was even less of a fan. There was vomit on the floor in the living room and before we got too much further, I realised I had best deal with this by myself.

'Fern? Okay?' She nodded, her head moving in slow motion. 'Can you stay in my spare room tonight?'

'Great idea'. She swayed only a little and nodded again.

'There's a spare toothbrush in the cupboard under the bathroom sink.'

'I know.'

'You know where the clean towels are?'

'Yup.'

'Have a shower and drink lots of water.'

'I can do that.'

'Great. Sleep well, darling.' I looked down at our hands stuck together. She smiled and loosened her grasp. I gathered face cloths and towels from Zita's linen cupboard and went to meet my groaning young friend. He was spewing horribly into the toilet. I kept up a running commentary to give us both strength. 'Are you going to be sick again? It's better if you are. Let's get you into the shower. Doesn't matter. Who cares if I get wet? Thank you. It's okay. Yes, I'm sorry he's not here. I'd like you to vomit on him, too. He is a shit, you're quite right. Can't change Jude. Only one person in the world you can change. No, it's you. You're the only person you can change. The world will be fine. There is hope. Some people do care, Jude amongst them. They do. That's a bit of water over your head. Yes, you do need it and shampoo as well. That's better. What were you drinking? Never mind, let's get you dry. Come on, try drinking some water. It might make you… There you go, you made it. Try again.'

Finally, Leaf was dryish and rehydrated-ish and asleep in his bed. I cleaned up the vomit over the bathroom floor, the living room carpet and down the hallway. He must have had an episode of the *Exorcist* spinning head for there was nothing on the hallway floor. It was all on the walls and it was not green and it did not include carrots. Spirits stink to high heaven.

Here comes the next generation.

Chapter 11

Fountain

As Zita and Simone prepared to move they hired skip after skip to take away their junk. Found myself joining in even though I had no thought of moving then. We sorted. We scrubbed. We prepared for Zita's wedding to Guido. Everything was cleaned and tidied. Everything would look just perfect on the day.

Now, I can't stop thinking. I think. I am. My brain ferments. Brain throws out memory after memory. Bubbling reminiscences rise and pop day and night. Like air bubbles in clay, I have to press them out before I explode. There is so much more to do.

Time for the mental bonfire. Throw my belongings out on the lawn, sort them, toss what's not needed, dust what is, and straighten up the shelves.

That's how kidneys work. They take everything out of the blood, sort it through, chuck out waste and put all the good stuff back in the system.

Sometimes fate sorts it out for you. Makes sure you get what you deserve. Other times, it's not fair. You don't deserve that loss, or that win. Up to me, now. Decide for myself. Whether I deserve what I got.

Often hear that without trust, love is nothing. Maybe it does all boil down to trust. Let's face it: we had a lot of boiling to do last winter. The Sydney Water Corporation detected parasites in our supply. Citizens were asked to boil water for at least a minute before drinking it or even washing their hands. Here we were, living in one of the wealthiest cities in the world and we could no longer trust our water system. If our treated water could be contaminated, how would it feel to be a frog? Frogs have no filtration plant. Frogs must suffer all the chemicals and bacteria and bacteria in the world. They do not suffer lightly. It is a matter of life and death.

~~~~~

I was standing at my kitchen table, filling containers with cooled, boiled water, when Simone opened the front door and strolled in saying, 'Why have you got the curtains shut?'

'Bit cold.'

'It's a cave in here!' She marched over to the window and hauled open the curtains. An insipid light insinuated into the fug. I was not in the mood. 'I'm rather busy, Simone.'

'Really?' Nothing would stop her. Did she even draw breath? 'Have you got any of that Ural stuff?'

'Huh!' Ural? All I could think of was mountains. But no, she was in the valleys.

'You know, darls, that UTI stuff you dissolve in water that tastes like piss.'

I looked at her for the first time—this week, anyway. It was true; she didn't look well. She'd chosen some dingle-dangle diamanté earrings, possibly to cheer herself up—I wanted to put my dark glasses on. 'You haven't been drinking the water?'

'No, no, no, not diarrhoea! Urinary tract. It's a different thing.'

'Honeymooners disease?'

'I wish. Just agony!'

'I'll look.' I went into the bathroom and shouted from there. 'You know Louise Hay, don't you?'

'I've heard of her… bit spooky, isn't she?'

I looked amongst old packets of aspirins, sunscreens, joint and muscle creams as I shouted through the wall. 'She thinks people get urinary tract infections because they're pissed off.'

'She's got that right and a half.' Simone spat the words. 'So pissed off! I've just had this utter bitch pig-dog marketing cow asking me all these personal questions about my relationships. If I hadn't taken my evening primrose oil this morning like a good girl I would have bloody decked her. As it was I had to chuck her out. She didn't make it up here?'

'No pig-dog cows here.'

'Utter, utter cow. And bloody, bloody Jude. Never want to see him again, either. Took Frances out to see some sculpture in the Biennale but thought Emma was too young to go. Now I've got to drag her along with me to the chemist.'

I didn't believe Simone for a moment. She did have a tendency to play the drama queen. Of course she wanted to see Jude again. She depended on Jude. 'I'll pop down and visit her while you go.'

'Thanks, darls, that would be great. Do you need anything?'

Do I? What could I possibly need?

~~~~~

Jude's morning urinations were prodigious, like a full bucket of water poured into the bowl. Always neat, never spilled. I guess Queenie had made sure her boys were as fastidious about hygiene as she was. Maybe that's what led them into science—trying to understand what she was on about.

After his morning bladder relief, Jude might pop back into bed, snuggling, and offer me a lovely massage. Just like that? Higher, perhaps? Lower? Much lower? His hands on my flesh… us together as if we would never be apart. I missed Jude's body and it was far more than missing his body, it felt like some part of me was gone, leaving only an ache…

I could no more imagine taking him back from Simone, from Zita, or even from Charlotte if it had to come to that, than bungee-jump off the Australia Square tower. Yet sometimes, fleetingly, I would give anything for a quiet morning massage, just one more time.

It was not to be. I had given him up. I knew I was doing the right thing. When I'm on my deathbed I will have no regrets. It was for the good of the family. I could have seen Jude every day if I'd wanted but I didn't need to make any confusing demands on him.

~~~~~

Peter had gone out with his spotty friends to celebrate the end of his school life. I bought a bottle of champagne on impulse. It was time to use it so I rang Jude and he was there and agreed I could pop down for a moment. I stood in front of the mirror and smiled honestly to myself before gathering up my bravery and gold foil-wrapped bottle and marching out.

Jude opened his door, frowning, thinking about something other than whoever was at the door, still with red pen in hand. He looked at me vaguely and gestured me inside. There were stacks of papers all over the table. He was marking. I offered the bottle. He looked at it, and then at me, intently. He searched for my agenda, shrugged slightly, then went into the kitchen and returned with two glasses. He frowned as he twisted the bottle to extract the cork as quietly as he could. The frown continued as he poured. I took a glass and raised it to our child. Yes, to Peter.

Our son had survived his school years and so had we. In glowing terms we discussed our boy and then Jude asked if I knew that Zita didn't want any more children? I said I was aware and had been since we moved in. He told me he loved babies. He really wanted another one, another brother or sister for Peter, Leaf and Fern. I wasn't surprised. After all, so did I.

Jude showed me an article that had recently appeared in the *Good Weekend Magazine*. I was impressed. The article, complemented by a number of photographs, was about his journeys with Frog-watch. I congratulated him. He asked me what I thought of the main photo.

It was an astounding shot. Jude lay on his back in a shallow mountain stream, light pouring in through the surrounding sparse trees and pooling on him. His hair was wet-plastered to his head. His windswept eyes, straight up to camera, were inviting, shining, ecstatic. A happy, male Ophelia. The lively, bubble-filled water laid white strokes of verve over his face. The river rocks were mossy at the edges and dazzling dark-wet in the running water. There was a hint of frost or snow on the ground. Half of Jude was dressed in a workmanlike manner, prepared for the outdoors: sturdy boots, moleskin trousers. The other half was less sensible: torso bare, hands crossed at the waist in a strange imitation of death. Three tiny torrent frogs were ranged across his chest, each with their little X marked backs visible. He wore them like medals or like a necklace. XXX. Three kisses.

I asked him who had taken the picture. He told me about Simone. He thought I would like her. She'd suggested he lie on the wet suit to avoid rock rash. She used to be a dancer. She was fun. Fun!

I asked Jude if he'd given any thought to a graduation present for his first son. He drained his glass and told me he would now. He gestured apologetically toward the stack of papers. He smiled at me as I took the hint, rose and moved towards the door. He laughed, saying if he didn't know better he might have thought I was trying to seduce him.

Longing punched through my shock and transferred angrily to embarrassment. I turned back and grabbed the champagne bottle. When I got home I drank the rest of the bubbles but all my mouth tasted was chagrin. I'd wanted to celebrate our success as parents, to congratulate each other on a job well done. But he was busy, wasn't he? Busy with his marking and his new girlfriend, the fun photographer.

I slid away from asking what I really wanted. It wasn't possible to contemplate.

~~~~~

With memories bubbling up, fountains and springs and fresh clean water are an obvious analogy. Sydney is such a town for fountains; they're everywhere. Jude's next memorial is a fountain.

The Tank Stream fountain near Circular Quay is an eerie monument to Sydney's first polluted water. After the white settlers arrived, how long did it take to clog the stream with rubbish, offal and excrement? Weeks? Months? The Tank Stream fountain features still-life possums, lizards and, of course, frogs, all gone from there in real life. The frozen creatures appear careless as sculptured water swirls around them.

With its kitsch colours flaring through the spray, the El Alamein dandelion is a giant bauble, the vulgar hub of the Kings Cross whirlpool.

Apollo, god of sun, light and truth, stands at the top of the Archibald fountain in Hyde Park. He wears a peacock tail of water spray and stretches out his right arm to beam on the grubby, hot-summer-city humans. Below him are representations of Diana the warrior, of Theseus slaying the Minotaur, and of a young man with a sheep and a goat. Water sprays out of the mouths of turtles.

The Tidal Cascades in corporate Darling Harbour is a lying down fountain. Water trickles over a double spiral of diverse surfaces, taking a journey into angles of no retreat.

My fountain celebrates all those little boys squirting the world with their penis hoses. The kidney is a filtration system, the bladder stores the water and the boys soon learn to hose.

~~~~~

Vionella died in April 1986. Zita rang to tell me she'd died at three-thirty in the morning but Guido hadn't let her know until daybreak. She had managed to get Leaf to school and Fern to kinder but… I didn't let her ask… I jumped right in. Of course I'd look after the kids while she stayed with Guido and the family. I did the pick up after kinder and school and let Peter make his own way home. The four of us stayed indoors, quietly concentrating on homework. Kindergarten child Fern was able to build her own marble run by then. We cooked a couple of cheese and spinach pies and ate one with salad and bread. The uneaten pie went into Zita's fridge for later.

After dinner we sat on the couch, not knowing what to do. Vionella had been a major support in Zita's life: from her difficult growth away from her parents, through setting up her florist business in Glebe, and then when she moved to the eastern suburbs with Jude and the kids. Leaf and Fern knew Guido well—he'd helped with some of the bigger weddings and the kids had seen him buying for the shop—but they were bemused by the extent of their mother's grief over Vionella. They hadn't really known their mother's friend at all.

I tried to explain that Vionella was like Zita's sister. I found myself telling them about Gracie… Gracie, forever fifteen. It was terrifying to lose a sister, I told them. I reflected that we'd had no time to prepare for such bereavement. It was so quick in Gracie's case.

When Gracie died in 1958, my parents faded from my life just as William did. They faded away. Mark and I were left to get on with our own lives. I knew how much William had loved Grace. He was bereft.

It happened on a chilly, spring day. There'd been a storm the night before and we'd worried about possible fallen branches over the track but nothing would dissuade Dad from going ahead with this long-planned bush walk to Burning Palms in the Royal National Park. There were six of us altogether: Dad, Sheryl, William, Mark, Gracie and I. Dad complaining, whenever someone would listen, how difficult it was to organise everyone into one place. In the event, the walk in had been easy, the track clear and the sky free from rain. When we arrived in the bay, we'd flung ourselves on the sand and admired the lonely stretch of beach. We'd eaten lunch and rested before the galloping began.

The sea was grey-mottled and heaving, the beach clotted with seaweed and rubbish. The sun sparkles made the water seem harmless but in reality it lay coiled and breathing, waiting, like a great, slate serpent. There was running and shoving and panting and pushing as the game of football progressed. Each time the ball ploughed into the water, a wave would snap it back within easy reach. In the end though, the water grabbed the ball and kept it.

It was so riotously disappointing. We all lined the cold water's edge and hooted as the ball floated away. I was bending over trying to catch delighted breath as Gracie cheerfully bounced into the water. We were laughing, saying it was too cold, she was mad, she'd freeze… come on Gracie, come back in now, Gracie… come back, Grace, come back…

We were all strong swimmers. One thing Dad had insisted on: Lane Cove pool at least once a week every summer. Floundering that first length of the pool when we were learning, splashing and gasping, and as the years passed; swimming more and more every summer, sunburn-peel laced over our noses and shoulders. All that swimming should have made a difference but it didn't.

It was winter and there we were on the beach, giggling, puffed, red faces, growing colder. Our understanding clarifying as we watched Gracie get further out, see her lift her knees high and see her turn to take the explosion of surf breaking on her back. Straightway, without respite, the roaring waves kept pounding in, stronger, more frequent, and blasted her from our sight. Our knowledge congealing into that's it, the joke's over, and colder and shivering and concern rising and alarm surfacing. She rose almost immediately, laughing, wiping her wet hair out of her eyes but she couldn't keep upright, she jumped and leaned, trying to keep on her feet and it took no time at all for Gracie to wave before she was gone. One hand, pale, contrasted with the grey granite wall of water that swept her away. One white hand, left like an x-ray against the water, faded until there was just grey, undulating heaving as far as the eye could see.

We screamed. Dad rushed into the surge. We all called to her: Grace! Gracie! Angular sharp shouts crossing over each other, weaving a net of cries. Gracie! Wading out into the cold, slam waves. Shouting again. Dad's arms fluttered this way and that and his legs splashed and we were transfixed. Horror mingled with disbelief; the fierce, grey water pulverised the sand. We watched the horizon stretch out until we could look no more. I cried and Mark leapt and floundered out to Dad who had turned to cold, stone rock. Terrified Dad would get swept away too, we both clung to him, watching the waves, watching the water, but there was no sign, no flash of any colour except grey churn and spume. We would have to get help. Sheryl and William set off in the direction of the car while we watched the shore.

They searched for days. Maybe a Chinese submarine took her.

It was a red ball. We never saw it again.

~~~~~

Frogs excrete nitrogen in two ways. As tadpoles they merely excrete ammonia—a compound of nitrogen and hydrogen—into the water. The adult frog produces urea: a mix of nitrogen, hydrogen, carbon and water. Same as humans.

Fish don't have kidneys. Palaeontologists thought the earliest fish must have lived in fresh water rivers and lakes before they ventured out into the salty seas.

Frogs and humans have kidneys. Both species crawled out of the salty ocean bog. Frogs were first, by a long way. Humans can't win that race.

Humans just keep pissing in their own nest.

~~~~~

Leaning one elbow on the ramparts of my roof garden, I ate my muesli in the weak, winter sun, and perused the neighbourhood. I noticed Simone's white station-wagon parked across the road again. I didn't pause to think, which I admit was foolhardy. I just reacted.

I marched downstairs, crossed the road, went up to the driver's window, and rapped on the glass. He was a middle-aged man with greying hair and a gut divided into straining segments by his seat belt. He started to yabber into the mouthpiece connected to his mobile phone; yabbering and staring straight ahead. I continued rapping until he looked at me. He shook his head and his telephone debate got even hotter. I rapped on the window again. The window went down. He shouted into the phone, 'Hang on a minute mate... sorry about this.' He glared at me. 'What do you think you're doing?'

'Talking to you, young man.' He perhaps half a dozen years younger than me but I was grabbing all the gravitas I could; I had accosted a total stranger for very little reason. He might have a wrench under his seat but having gone this far, I figured I'd better find out what I could.

'I'm in the middle of a business call. Can you please leave?' he blustered.

I stared at him. Oh, really! Did he think I came down in the last shower? I persevered. 'I believe you've been following my friend and I want to know why?'

'For Pete's sake, lady, buzz off. I've a meeting round the corner in five minutes. I've got nothing to do with your friend unless she's knows something about a shipment from Spain tomorrow?' He wound up the window and continued yabbering into his phone as though there really were someone on the other end.

That was interesting. I crossed the road and watched him. He yammered on for a bit, then turned on the engine and drove off without looking back. Make your defence look like an attack, eh? I hadn't told him my friend was a 'she'.

Whoever he was, I guessed we wouldn't be seeing him again and for this I was grateful. It wasn't in my nature to be confrontational. I'm sure that sort of behaviour could get a person into trouble.

~~~~~

Jude's fountain has three wheel-thrown cylinders and three bowls such as Goldilocks might have found in the house of the Three Bears. Each is altered, bent and carved.

The water spits up in a bubbling-shoot to fill the smallest, top bowl and cascades into the deepest part of the middle bowl. The water swirls to find the lowest point to tumble into the bottom pool, the reservoir pond supplying the pump. The pump drives the water up to the top bowl, and so it goes, down and round, like a marble run.

Although the bowls are concentric, each is twisted to allow water to flow from the pouring lip in a mini torrent. The bowls look like kidney dishes.

The movement of liquid captivates. Make a series of test shapes and play in the children's blue shell pool in the courtyard. Run the hose stream into and over different planes and angles. Hypnotise myself with fluid turbulence.

Colouring for the fountain reflects the browns and yellows of the Eungella torrent frog, *Taudactylus eungellensis*. Pale, smooth front and an X-shaped dark mark on its back. There's the X, in the top bowl. The frog's arms and legs have faint bars echoed on the outside of the bowls. They are striped like old mattresses.

Torrent frog tucks into crevices of waterfalls, surviving always in a torrent of water. In biologists' jargon, it is critically endangered.

Taudactylus eungellensis makes me think of that band, Not Drowning, Waving, because the tiny creatures tend to wave rather than call. Presumably they can't be heard over the roar of the water. Jude didn't think they possessed a vocal sac because he'd seen them waving and hopping in a gymnastic display to get another frog's attention. But the frogs do make sounds. They've been recorded making a soft, clucking noise. How cute is that little, round, yellow, disappearing frog!

You can just wave it goodbye.

~~~~~

Happy, brilliantly happy; following the sound of childish laughter in a land of verdant pastoral beauty. Gently rolling hills meet blue timeless sky in a symphony of balance. I am beautiful in a gossamer gown that floats in the gentle breeze. A butterfly flutters past. Everywhere I look, bees, beetles and birds bumble through the air. My family meanders ahead of me: Jude and Peter; Zita, Leaf and Fern; Simone, Francis and Emma. They laugh and wave to me, encourage me to keep up. I wave back, cheerful, and walk a little faster. Can't seem to catch them. Soon they are out of sight.

Heading uphill. An easy slope. No exertion required. Relaxed. Almost in ecstasy. Enormous flowers and vibrant fruits framed by heart-shaped leaves are shining in the sun. A liquid honey-fall is golden and unctuous, flowing into a creek of milk and bubbles. A wonderful melody fills my mind.

I walk and sing and sway to inner music. Out of breath. Amused to find I am walking a tightrope. It's becoming more difficult to keep my balance. My abdomen clutches with alarm. The ground is far beneath me. My arms are full with two giggling, chubby babies, and then awfully, terribly, the very land cleaves and uprises in front of me.

Sway on the tightrope, dropping one baby, then the second. They fall, screaming, into a bottomless crevasse that crashes open around me. Grapple for balance. Devastated by the grinding moan of the very earth itself.

The earthquake rearranges the ground as if it were tissue paper. Fall down, twisting and turning and grabbing, clawing at the air. I am ground into the earth. The tremor shakes plates of rock, which groan together and drive me further down into the dirt. My face is filled with mire. Boulders crush my worm-like body. My eyes are closed by the weight of filth. My head is thrust down by an on-slaught of mud and stones. My mouth is wrenched open and filled with gravel and I cannot and I am not...

~~~~~

Wake in the chair in front of the flickering computer. Crash into consciousness. Rub eyes. Shake head. Try to find the edge of reality.

Type everything, urgently blinking, into the bright screen. Must record this ordeal. Discipline it. Bring it to heel, so I can breathe calmly again. Once the nightmare is recounted I stand and stare out the window. Stare into the dark. Try to make sense of the earthquake. Need to urinate. Walk to the bathroom and sit on the cool, plastic seat in the dark. I let go.

A year can be continuous, unchanging, blending into the next year and the year after that with barely a bump—or it can be cataclysmic. The year after Gracie drowned I met Jude, and William left for the States. Cataclysmic! That same year I dropped out of uni and went to East Sydney Tech. Over the next twenty years or more, William only returned to Sydney for brief visits: twice for Christmas, a couple of times over the English summer breaks, and once for his mother's sixtieth birthday.

Now, I look back on this last year. Jude and Peter both met Charlotte. The Sydney Water Corporation fell apart. It has been another cataclysm for our family. It took only twelve months but everything that had gone before, for the last two decades, was lost, fallen like frangipani petals now decomposing to slime on concrete. This last year had been a catastrophe.

~~~~~

Kidneys are greyish brown. They vary from the swimming pool design to a sort of bean shape. They filter waste products from blood using a basic unit called a glomerulus. When I email this information to Francis, he replies he thought Glomerulus was one of the guys in *Lord of the Rings*. Two tubes called ureters carry urine to the bladder for storage. The bladder swells up until it's time for a wee. It's a complicated, conscious business. Learning to control a bladder is harder to learn than walking.

~~~~~

Jude told us that Simone was 'fun', and we surmised that he loved her, or thought he did… if there's any difference. Jude's bedsit was on the same floor as Zita's apartment. To all intents and purposes he was still the kids' Dad, still around to pick them up from school and muck in at the working-bee on Sunday mornings, but he was no longer Zita's husband.

One nippy, spring day, Jude invited Simone for lunch. One look at this frail, worried little creature covered in make-up, *Choose Life* tee shirt and Lurex tights, and Zita and I, whispering together, couldn't understand what Jude was thinking. Simone looked like a child herself.

Peter hated her on sight and was nastily teenage and unpleasant. I ordered him to have an early night and we left to have a private discussion in his room. By the time I got back from grounding him, Zita and her two kids had finished the washing-up and were putting everything away. Jude had already left to take Simone home. Zita muttered things like *wrapped around her little finger, we should name this place Brady Bunch Balconies,* and *did we really want to live in a harem?* That was the first mention of the *harem* word, but it wasn't going to be the last.

It takes three wives to make a harem. At least three.

Chapter 12

Garden lantern

The man that married me was about to get married again, for the third time. It was May 1986. Zita and I took enormous pleasure chanting *Marry in the Month of May and you will surely rue the day*, but not in front of the children. Or Simone. Or Jude, for that matter. The invitation was slick and desktop published. Both of his previous wives and all of his children were invited to the nuptials. Zita and I had discussed our misgivings about this whirlwind romance. It had happened so quickly. We could see that Jude was involved but we couldn't see that he was exactly happy. He was proud to walk beside Simone, he liked her, but she was all over him. She draped herself physically on him when they sat together. She leaned on him emotionally as well. She wanted him to make all the decisions: where they would live; what she would wear to the wedding; the menu selections. It was disturbing, and Zita and I agreed we dreaded the changes this wedding might bring to our lives.

Zita arrived to pick us up. She was frazzled. At my front door, she pushed Leaf and Fern in at me then ran to the bathroom. She'd come from the venue. Everything was ready. She thought the flowers looked good—not her best effort—but good. She'd used a lot of candles. She'd given them the flowers as a wedding present. Jude had tried to give her some money. Really, couldn't he just be gracious and accept her gift? She'd insisted and he had no choice in the end, apparently. Normally a small wedding like this wouldn't faze her, but it seemed that marrying off her ex-husband to a blonde floozy was more than she could cope with. I knew how she must have felt. We wore shoulder-pads, high hair and gaudy lipstick, hoping like hell it would make us stronger. Peter played Donkey Kong incessantly and Leaf and Fern were too small to argue.

After she'd done up her seat belt, Zita snapped a small tablet in half and popped one portion in her mouth. She held the other half in front of my face as if she were offering a sugar cube to a horse. She told me it was only Valium and would kick in just about the time we would need it. She was grinning. Hey, we both grew up in the sixties. What harm could it do? We found a parking space near the Bayswater Brasserie. Things were running smoothly for this, the third wedding, the only one where Jude was not a Catholic.

Zita and I slumped down in our seats as the celebrant, and the drugs, kicked into action. With lighted candles on every surface, I perceived a luminescent floral musical and prepared to enjoy myself. Simone looked lovely in a sort of shapeless sack thing that appeared to have had a chalice full of sequins poured over it. Zita and I were clandestine. We whispered to each other: Simone would look lovely in a shower curtain; you would look fat, Zita; you would, too, Connie. It was a meltdown. Hilarious. We slumped and sniggered, fatties forever together, quietly wittering… *and you will surely rue the day.*

Zita was still in mourning for Vionella. Her parents, avoiding the irony, came to take the kids so Zita could relax and enjoy the party. Even Peter was happy to leave his father's wedding and go with Leaf and Fern's grandparents. As for Zita and me, we were happy drinking Jude's champagne at the Brasserie and to make exhibitions of ourselves in the Cross as we tried to flag a taxi home. I simply would not let Zita go to the All Nations Club. It was too late. She wanted another drink. We had to think of the kids. The cabs were all full. It was a dump. We never get a night out. Come on, Zita. Just for tonight. We were not that drunk, surely. We were. We had to draw the line somewhere. We went home.

All those weddings—I thought he should have got better at it, not worse.

~~~~~

My early lanterns were made for flex and bulb and switching on. Now I prefer those tea-light candles, or a citronella candle to freak out the mozzies. If the candles are in the centre of the lamp, in its heart, they will burn steadily for the length of the barbecue. Candle-light throws a romantic glow. The lantern is best down amongst the pots and plants, looking alive.

I want to illustrate that love is light. The shapes are unambiguous hearts. The light is steady. Protected in the heart of the little pagoda. Love heart cutouts are twee. The glaze shines with orange heat-light.

The children call them 'love hearts' now, not plain old beating hearts, but love hearts. Why do they need to be qualified? Is it not obvious heart signifies love? Isn't love heart a tautology? Oh, this younger generation! Oh, evolution! What an unnecessary adaptation love heart is.

When I find it unbearable to think of Jude, I think of frogs. Got a garage full of ceramics and I'm making more each day. Can't stop. All I do. At my wit's end and look like it, too. At the supermarket accidentally glimpse my reflection in a window. I'd been avoiding it. Today I look. I see myself. My hair is shocked. Completely grey. Disgusted. My eyes are panda shadows. Sick of myself. Sick at heart. My hands are turned to clay. Would have to improve my health and appearance if I want to live in the normal world. Then I ask myself, what does it matter? What can I do but keep working? Keep doing. That is all I am.

Why does love lie in the heart? Is it the seminal gush of life it-self, the determining push into the future? If there is no circulation, is love possible? We know life is no longer viable.

I know love doesn't stop because one heart stops. But I do not know what will happen when my heart halts for good.

I think that love lies beyond muscle and platelets and ventricles. Love is light. I miss Sheryl so much I want to talk to her. I get in the car and drive to South Head cemetery. I sit on the grass between the graves. It's just been mowed. Her ashes are squeezed into her family plot with a multitude of relatives. They lie in the shadow of the tall, white lighthouse. I can still feel love. I watch sails bright against the blue, deep sea. The light is intensely vibrant. The brilliance almost hurts.

I tried to rescue everybody. Who can rescue me?

~~~~~

I struck the ball, a safe forehand, directly at him. 'Jude,' I said. 'I've something to tell you.'

He hit the ball straight back to me to return the favour, making it an easy forehand. It had been raining. There was a smell of damp mulch and growth. An orange sunset gleamed in the tops of the gum trees.

We were on a tennis court in Cooper Park, surrounded by leafy safety. The tension was still there, piled high around my shoulders, even after thrashing the ball for twenty minutes. So much for exercise releasing stress, I was just getting tired. I missed.

'Yeah?' Jude prepared to serve again.

'Charlotte. Your friend.'

'What about her?' He threw the ball high.

'She's pregnant.'

His cracking serve went wild. 'Ah.' He turned away to pick up fallen balls.

I waited while he retrieved half a dozen tennis balls and packed them, one by one, into their tin cylinder. When he'd finished, he turned to me and said, 'I'll have to see her.'

What possible good could a visit from an aging academic do? I waited for a moment before hitting back with, 'Will she want to see you?'

A look of such wounded surprise I was almost sorry for him. 'She'll need my help.'

I wasn't sorry for him. 'But you said she was your student and you'd be a fool to touch her...'

'I was.'

Jude smartly zipped the pieces of my heart into his sports bag and strode away in his big, white, sports shoes.

A willy-willy raised a spiral of leaves to chase him across the tennis court.

~~~~~

Garden lantern is a stocky shape. Built in slabs. Cut out the heart shapes with an old cookie cutter. Fire the heart in the centre of the lantern. Lid is fired separately.

The iris in the eyes of some frogs can be the shape of a triangle, a star or even a heart.

~~~~~

Simone moved in and immediately announced she was pregnant. Jude, stud man, was over the moon. Jude and Simone then relocated to the second floor apartment and Simone put up her shingle as a portrait photographer.

The baby, whom they named Francis, was born six weeks prematurely. He was a big baby even so and Simone was probably fortunate that she didn't go full term. Jude was away on a field trip but when he returned... what fanfare, what excitement! It was difficult for the first two wives to share his thrill. I tried, but Zita kept in the background as much as possible—didn't you, judgmental woman?

Francis had blond feathery hair and serious grey eyes. Jude loved him with an unreasonable passion. Perhaps it was because Simone was so keen to set up her darkroom and snap as many portraits as she could find sitters, that Jude became the responsible one. He was often to be found wearing Francis in a sling, marching around Bellevue Hill, Double Bay and Bondi. He would visit the priest at Holy Cross for cups of tea and discussions about lapsed Catholics.

Zita had been my friend but Simone never made the grade. Sorry, but she felt like an interloper to me. I could find no comfort in our relationship. Before Francis's first birthday, Simone announced she was pregnant again. She was now much happier and fleshier than the fawning, scrawny waif that Jude had dragged in. Simone now glowed with health and sometimes positively smouldered with potency. So I was shocked when she lost the baby. Her parents arrived from Melbourne to take care of her. We all pitched in to look after Francis. We grew used to the harem jokes. And no, we weren't morons either.

~~~~~

The red and yellow mountain frog, *Philoria kundagungan*, is presumed to be in decline. Its back can be red, black or yellow. There's a black stripe from each nostril, through the eye to the shoulder. It's a smooth-skinned frog, just like a heart is smooth.

Kundagungan is an Aboriginal word meaning 'mountain'. Maybe this frog should have been called the land rights frog.

Human heart is about the size of a fist. Weighs about half a kilo and consists of two pumps. The heart pumps oxygenated blood from lungs around itself before sending blood on to the rest of the body. Heart will always feed itself first, like a parent using emergency oxygen on an aeroplane. (Always fit the oxygen mask to yourself before assisting anyone in your care.) Similarly, when body goes into shock, it shuts down from the outside in, conserving and protecting the heart.

Two blood types, red and blue, should never mix unless you are a fish or a human foetus. A baby receives oxygen from the mother. It's not until birth, when the child takes its first breath through its own nose or smacked-open mouth, that the two pumps need to operate separately.

Human heart has four chambers. The frog has only three, missing out on one lower chamber. As a result, the two blood types are continually in the same chamber. They do not mix because of the direction of the current. In contrast, humans have evolved to protect their own oxygen.

Fertile land is said to be in good heart.

Frogs have always been associated with fertility. The goddess, Heqet, was the ancient Egyptian protector of new-borns. She had a frog's head. Egyptian women used to wear amulets shaped like frogs, or stamped with a frog's image, for protection when giving birth.

Inspired by those ancient Eygptian days, I once made similar amulets for sale in hippy gift shops. That frog amulet was a nice little earner, thank you very much.

Fertility is obviously connected to the heart. There's a very good reason for Cupid to be depicted as a baby. That's because babies decide who their parents will be. Ask parents who've been on the pill, who've used condoms, who may have seen their baby with an IUD embedded in its head; they've all tried very hard not to get pregnant. Ask them: where did their children come from?

It's not just the woman and her attendants present at a birth. There's another player. The baby. Consider the standing reflex. Babies have no need of a standing reflex. Why on earth would they need to stand? For goodness sake! That's a pushing reflex, for pushing themselves out of the womb. An eject button.

The most dangerous journey is the first one; down the birth canal. Why wouldn't babies play a part in their own destiny? A few might lie there and let birth happen around them, but why? Babies are causation. They are active and pushy. Cupids, all of them. It is their birthday, after all. They want to get out and be the present.

The heart is central to a human chest, as if we were lettuces. The left ventricle is stronger and larger than the right, having to pump blood through the entire body. The left lung is smaller because the heart leans to the left.

Under Montezuma, the Aztecs sacrificed enemy soldiers and offered their hearts to the gods. Which, as God is supposed to live in our hearts, seems redundant.

~~~~~

From the beginning, Peter assumed the role of protector of Francis. It made no difference to him that Simone was Francis's mother. Peter had no time for Simone. If he saw her coming he would leave, taking Francis with him.

The new baby, Emma, slowed Simone down. Never was there such a demanding child. Emma did not want to be born in the first place. She clung on in the womb, was posterior, and must have caused considerable pain as she arrived, late and induced. I'm sorry to say, she remained a pain in the posterior. She hardly ever slept and, when she was awake, was always hungry.

After Francis, the angel, Simone was in shock. She was lucky she had Zita and me to provide for her. We took turns cooking dinner and did her shopping for the first six weeks of the baby. It was hard for Jude to take more time off and Simone couldn't get out of bed in the early days. I would take the children whenever I could. Still, Emma ruled the roost. She was going to be something, that girl, and as the years passed, I was more and more inclined to think that particular something would be trouble.

Simone hated breastfeeding. She told me she hated feeling like a beast in the fields. Her body was light, airy, used to be blown around the stage like a bit of dandelion fluff. Her life was about public admiration and Art. How could she sit in a chair with her body tired, bulging and drooping while a froglike creature sucked the life out of her? She fed Francis for nearly six weeks, which for her, was an achievement. With Emma, she stopped trying after a couple of days and went straight to formula. Zita and I couldn't understand how Simone could regard the whole process of measuring and heating formula and cleaning bottles as easier than sticking bub on breast. But there we were, cows in the paddock. Moo.

Simone was desperate to get work. She paid me money to babysit, to measure out the formula, and to heat and clean bottles while she changed lenses and snapped up and coming actors. Francis was now in kinder, Leaf and Fern were in primary school, and Peter was at uni.

Simone also needed space. She told me she could not cope with Emma. In hindsight, perhaps she suffered some degree of post-natal depression. Perhaps she really couldn't cope. Perhaps it was hormones. But whatever the cause, I truly believe that Simone could not stand being alone with that child. Not only did she put the baby in the front room so that she and Jude could get some sleep, but when Francis had gone to school she would seek me out for a chat. Or she would leave Emma with me while she disappeared for the day. I disliked being taken for granted. We argued. After some tension she took Emma to coffee with her and let the childless dancers dandle her baby. Nearly every day she would attempt some kind of escape.

Despite the trials of Emma, Simone always appeared beautifully groomed. Jude looked dishevelled in comparison though I'm sure he made an effort. He was proud of Simone. He finally had a trophy wife. Not his fault the other wives didn't think much of the trophy. But we all tried to live happily ever after, didn't we, Zita?

Simone was the scintillating party girl and not even two small children could shake her style. She loved first nights at the ballet and at Sydney Dance Company. She began to garner some respect for her dance photography. She was invited to be part of a successful group exhibition, 'Dance Alive!', all *en pointe*, leap, fabric drape and double-entendre. As a result of the positive buzz around her work, Sydney Dance commissioned her to do a calendar. My personal favourite was Mr March's, *Present Arms!*

Zita had long been displaying my vases in her shop when she started using them at weddings and other functions. Apart from large arrangements for the front tables of events, she also commissioned two-dozen bowls to use as centrepieces. These attracted positive comment, inquiries and a number of profitable sales. Interest from punters increased and we came to realise our work was indeed complementary. We pondered how we might best capitalise on our professional relationship.

~ ~ ~ ~ ~

It was opening night of the *Dance Alive!* exhibition at the Australian Centre for Photography. Zita and I clutched our glasses of torpid bubbly and wove a curvilinear path through the most expressive, arm-waving, lip-hugging, hat-wearing group of people we'd ever seen. The work of six photographers was on display. Each had been given open access to Sydney Dance and invited to photograph whatever took their fancy.

Some of the shots were taken during performance or rehearsal, some were portraits of dancers at rest and, I had to admit, Simone's photos were rather good. They were largely close-up, atmospheric shots: the overworked foot in the grubby, broken-down pointe shoe, the shoe's ribbon unfurling; a hand, veins obvious, resting on a sweaty, leotard hip; a hand glued to an inner thigh, taking the weight. Possibly because she'd been a dancer, Simone knew where to direct the viewer. She'd managed to capture energy as though the camera was part of the action. The photos were very inviting.

I caught Zita's eye. We had one of those are-you-thinking-what-I'm-thinking? moments. Standing amongst the mass of gabbling sinews and Darlings and Luvvies, we agreed that photography was the missing piece in our triumvirate puzzle. We would offer Simone a job taking photos of Zita's flowers in my vases. Not that night, obviously, because she was far too star-struck, but another night, Simone could to talk to us ordinary beings in a dimmer environment.

Simone agreed to photograph a vase full of gerberas and another smaller one of David Austen roses. Once. To see how it went.

Initially we used the shots on Zita's business cards, made little gift cards to sell and, after a number of enquiries, asked Simone to enlarge three of the prints that we especially liked. One was an extreme close-up of a gerbera, the second a spray of blowsy roses, and finally, a fully-laden vase—you could almost smell the blooms. We framed them and hung them on the walls of the shop. A Double Pay dame came in, dressed in tennis gear, and bought all three for her shack at Palm Beach. Simone reprinted. They sold. The next printing sold, too. She printed other shots of the gerberas and they sold.

I mentioned Simone's success to Sheryl Richards during lunch at the Gallery one day. The numbers impressed Sheryl, and later, seeing the work for herself, was impressed by that, too. Sheryl phoned me the day after she'd been in to the shop. She wanted to get the three of us together to discuss a possible exhibition at Catalina Galleries: three wives, three different pursuits and, she certainly hoped, three bankable biddies.

It was so much easier for Sheryl to come over to the three of us, so we met at Simone's shiny flat. Simone made us green tea and we sipped from my delicate porcelain cups. We sat in four, squat, white chairs with bold primary colour cushions, around a fat, square white coffee table streaked with a spilled array of proof sheets and ribbons of coloured light.

Simone's sitting room faced east and it sparkled in the morning sun. A year or so previously, she'd found a box of broken chandelier pieces in an op shop, brought them home, and given them all a good clean. The clear crystal shapes, gnawed diamonds and glimmering beads, were strung above the windows. They caught the sunlight and splintered it into rainbows. Each of us sat in our own random splotch of vibrancy as though on stage with a mad lighting designer in the bio box. There were times I had to bring my sunglasses down from the top of my head to prevent a migraine from developing.

Sheryl looked at us over the top of a sheaf of proof sheets as if she were holding a rather good poker hand. She asked what we imagined might make a good exhibition? This from a gallery owner with artists lined up for the next three years. She dealt in a small, profitable stable of collectable names. She had artists coming in with portfolios every week. She could afford to be choosy.

My heart sank when Zita described the forest she envisioned: something that wouldn't be out of place at Canberra's Floriade. She wanted to bring in potted trees. She wanted fountains. She wanted aroma. She wanted mist. She wanted colour, texture and showers of tiny, tiny blossoms in unexpected places.

Simone was chafing at the bit to deliver her vision. She wanted space. She wanted room to move. She wanted light and shadow. And me? I wanted the earth.

Sheryl took it all in wearing her cute little Mona Lisa smile. She thought for a moment and then explained she didn't think one exhibition was going to cut it, was it? We exchanged determined looks, preparing to do battle. I could see the hackles rise on Simone, because she was so thin, while Zita was sucking in air, preparing to spit out a deluge. Sheryl intervened in the nick of time.

Sheryl exclaimed it was all going to be so much fun. We're not going to do one show. We're going to do three! We all murmured our surprise while Sheryl continued with her genius plan that would have each of us direct a show, and she just couldn't wait to get going. She raised her glass and proposed a toast: to The Baldwin Girls!

The WHAT? Oh, no way would we be called that. Eeeew-yoooooh! Each of us lowered our glasses and protested. That's when the argument really started. The Baldwin Winners? The Baldwin Wives? The Baldwin Marriage? Three Wives and a Frog?

Chapter 13

Ashtray

Keep breathing. Life. Air. Oxygen. Sometimes, drowning means water blocks the airway and prevents air travelling into the lungs.

The distinction between drowning in saltwater (where the salt in the lungs extracts water from the blood) and fresh water (which invades the lungs and blood to paralyse the circulatory system) made no difference to Gracie at all.

~~~~~

It was one of Sydney's best days on our traditional September picnic. There were still puffs of yellow on the acacia branches and the birds trilled as though their lives depended on it. For many years, spring found us out in Cooper Park for a combined celebration of the birthdays of Jude, Peter and Francis. This was a beautiful Sunday afternoon: fresh air, family, and our traditional, mad, ramshackle game of cricket.

Guido looked impeccable. As he bowled to Leaf, a gold chain bounced and glinted around his neck, just visible under the collar of his cream polo shirt. The battered old cricket ball trickled off Leaf's bat. Fern picked it up and flung it back to the bowler with ease. Guido caught it and grinned. 'Well done, my dear.'

Fern grinned with delight. I suspected she was unused to praise. She looked alert, prepared to impress Guido again if she could.

Simone picked at the skin on her arms and adjusted her straps to give her shoulders an even chance at a tan.

Jude was batting with Leaf and they laughed and egged each other on, bats stretched out towards the crease before they turned for just one more run. Leaf smacked the side of his shoe with the bat as he waited for the next delivery. When the next ball came he hammered it away with vehemence. The ball flew towards the stone steps heading up the hill and disappeared. Emma ran her hardest all the way to the edge of the park in a vain bid to retrieve it. Guido jogged closer to Emma as she fumbled around in the long grass. She found the ball, threw it to Guido and the game continued.

I was preoccupied with Jude. Even as I watched the children, involved in the game in their individual ways, I knew where Jude was at every moment. I was conscious of his energy, his inclusiveness and his own awareness of the kids. I was finding it hard to forgive him, though Lord knows I tried. My falafel roll sat in my stomach as though I'd swallowed the cricket ball. I was finding it difficult to breathe.

I wandered over to Francis. He was reading a crumpled newspaper. He'd probably found it in a bin or somewhere. It was a replacement for the book we'd confiscated so he could better focus on the game. I asked him, 'Not anticipating any big catches today, then?'

'If anything looks like coming my way, I'll be ready.'

'Don't doubt it. What are you reading about?'

'The gas explosion. Melbourne's been cut off. Makes you think, don't you think?'

'I think.' I smiled at him. 'At least, I think I think.'

Suddenly the others were all shouting at us as the ball swooshed out of the perfect spring firmament and landed fair and square in Francis's hand. Francis grinned and raised his index finger to the sky. 'Who wants it?' He laughed.

Jude, his bat on the ground at his feet, was bent over, hands on knees, gasping for breath. He'd been caught out.

~~~~~

Remember when we all used to smoke tobacco? There was a cloud around each individual at the Royal George, a personal smokescreen. I make an ashtray for Jude even though he never did smoke, just held a cigarette to feel part of the gang.

The tray is grey-brown with hints of silver and red-brown. These are the colours of the tapping green-eyed frog, *Litoria genimaculata*. I imagine tapping ash from the cigarette and my green eyes weeping, irritated by the nauseous smoke.

~~~~~

I drove Peter to Camp Cove, a tiny suburban beach. We bought a lemonade iceblock each, just as we had done many times over the last twenty-seven years, and strolled along the track to South Head. We took the track down to the water level and clambered to the seaside over the boulders. I clung to the rock while Peter gazed out into the ocean-wide horizon. I told him that Charlotte was pregnant.

The inevitable white waves overturned and smashed into the rocks. A vibrant blue sky heaved over us and the thunderous sea enveloped his shock. It seemed like rotten luck. The one time they were together, their impatient need for one another, their complacency, their youth: all combined in a time of fecundity to create a new life, a new Cupid. Or was it fate?

Such an accident was out of character for this careful, organised, studious young man. He was not impetuous until he met Charlotte, and she had brought him undone.

'She'll have to see me now,' he said.

No, she does not, I thought, but said nothing because mothers are supposed to be supportive and he mightn't have heard me over the crashing of the waves.

~~~~~

Emotions make a life worth living—a mere thought, a wisp of a smell, a colour, a drift of a texture—can all trigger an emotion. Emotions cause decisions. The choices we make are informed by how we feel. Everything we do is shadowed by the past.

Logic, knowledge and past experiences are imbued with attached emotions. Unconsciously, each step is guided by our emotions. Breathe deeply. It will help you through the motions. If you take quick, sharp, shallow breaths you might be overwhelmed.

The first time I slept with Jude was our wedding night. I'm sure I didn't sleep at all. I just lay awake and watched him breathing. That was all I needed, just the simple elements: air in and air out of lungs... and love.

Once a first wife, always a first wife. Even when faced with a third. What happens when there's a fourth? I'm still number one.

Then again, I feel fear. Try to talk myself out of it. Ask myself, what's to be frightened of? Sometimes I answer, plenty. Other times I know there's nothing but fear itself. But then I wonder, what of all those people who appear to lead interesting lives untroubled by anything more than eating or what's on TV or planning their next festivity? When do they panic, suck air into their short-changed lungs, hurting as air rasps past raw tubes? All those people in the supermarket where I scuttled like a rat last night—what do they fear? What do they guess? How dare they look at me?

~~~~~

In her chair by the botanic gardens, Mrs Macquarie envisioned Sydney with two chains of parkland around the harbour. The populace would be free to walk the length of the shoreline and enjoy picnics right to the water's edge. All the way around the harbour! Imagine that. Of course, that dream vanished when rich ex-convicts claimed their personal piece of the water and enclosed their own stretch of coast. That was the beginning of modern town planning, still under the control of wealthy ex-cons today. It's impossible to walk around the harbour's edge due to private jetties, boathouses and large barbed wire covered barriers. Governor Macquarie himself had many a grand plan for Sydney town and look what happened. Developers!

There are still parks—the city's lungs—thanks to the builders' union that protected Centennial Park with green bans. And today there's a growing recognition that past compromise between developers and breathing space was weighted on the side of concrete. I hope Sydney's focus on the fresh millennium and upcoming Olympics will encourage planners to connect more with the city's lungs, though I have no great expectations.

Like developers, frogs take in air through their nostrils; the air flows down the windpipe and into a pair of lungs. The frog has no ribs or diaphragm to suck and push. The frog can also breathe through its skin. When a frog is submerged, it absorbs oxygen directly from water. Because the frog's skin is permeable it can absorb all sorts of things. Unfortunately.

A study quoted in *Declines and disappearances* examines mutations in frogs. The study suggests the appearance of frogs with only one leg, or no legs, or twisted arms or other hideous deformity, is due to the effect of parasites. *Cryptosporidium* and *Giardia* are parasites. They're the bugs that caused the Sydney Water Corporation to issue a 'boil water' alert. Like frogs, then, humans are vulnerable to parasites in their water. Unlike frogs, humans can boil their water. If we get too hot, will we jump in time?

Breathing. Concentrate on breathing. Breathing is a reliable sign of life. Our lungs look like inverted bunches of broccoli. They continually suck in and blow out with the aid of our ribs. The lungs are an exchange system. A mixture of gases rushes into our lungs, then rushes out, with good oxygen absorbed and carbon dioxide heaved out.

The red blood cells rub up against the walls of the alveoli. They grab oxygen and turn bright red for all they are worth. It's such a no-big-deal-thing—taking a breath, the diaphragm pulling down to inflate and pushing up to exhale—we don't even know we are doing it. Until it comes to an end. Then we miss it. Or we might if we were conscious.

I imagine Jude must have felt like a miner with a canary. Frogs and canaries are sentient beings. They're known as sentinel species. They stand guard, keeping watch for us. As if they care.

As frogs disappear, or rather, as their habitat shrinks, ecologists and biologists have evolved into early warning systems, blinking and waving. They are taken almost as seriously as that old TV robot— *Warning, warning, Will Robinson*—or Cassandra, or any other doom-laden foreteller. Their funding is cut. Their research is directed from above. Their results are harnessed to fit the bill.

You might think about those scientists' published articles, opinion pieces, or their letters to the editor for a moment. Should the common person take them seriously? Scientists have done some terrible things in the past, creating weapons of mass destruction, environmentally destructive pesticides and those non-biodegradable plastics now filling the Pacific whirlpool and the guts of baby albatross. What do those scientists know? Why should we listen to them now? What if they have results that spell out dire predictions for the future of frogs… and for the future of human beings?

Can we do anything about it? What should we do? Order a new car? The status quo is not frightened by dire predictions. They believe the market will cure all society's ills. They hope their shares will grant them a fat dividend. Then we can carry on as normal with our easy, wasteful lives. Unless we're refugees. Their life isn't quite so easy and they have nowhere else to go. Like frogs with no habitat. Are frogs refugees? Who will be the next refugees?

There are big differences between frogs, humans and canaries. When a canary is about to take a fresh breath, it empties its lungs. The next breath in for that little canary is all new, all-powerful, and if there is dangerous gas in the mine, it's all over.

Our lungs don't empty with each breath out. So we humans, our lungs possibly holding some of the very first gas we ever inhaled, have time to escape the mine.

A frog, however, has permeable skin as well as lung sacs. Its vulnerability is not just in one breath. The frog absorbs chemicals from every direction.

Even though humans might not notice the frog showing deformities on metamorphosis or disappearing from its range, or even silently going extinct, we are all in the same mine together. Humans must continue living on Earth because we haven't yet built a colony on Mars for us to pollute. We can't get out of the mine, and according to biologists and climate scientists, we will eventually run out of oxygen. Frogs can't get out of the mine we call Earth either, and, unlike most humans, can't afford bunkers and protective clothing. When do we start to care?

Homo sapiens doesn't seem to be concerned about frogs. We seem to accept a percentage of deformities resulting from herbicides and pesticides as a matter of course. Consider the amount of chemicals that are manufactured. Consider the shareholders that need that manufacture to continue. Where do the chemicals end up? It is acceptable. Our society regards it as normal for both frogs and humans to hang in the balance between marketing chemicals and survival of the fittest.

The lack of action must have been frustrating for Jude. I think it suffocated him.

Chapter 14

Party platter

Struggle to remember where the slab roller is hidden in the work-shop. Find it after a search under piles of cardboard and old plaster moulds. Clean roller. Oil it. I am an industry again.

Slab roller is like a giant pasta maker or old-fashioned mangle. Roll out a thick piece of clay paste. The clay is mixed with bone ash and with dried, ground flesh. Pale and not very plastic. I fight to lift one side and flick it, like a heavy, wet towel. After a couple of attempts the clay flares out into a driftwood curve. Rest the slab in the dent in a pillowcase filled with vermiculite. As usual, make three platters because if they don't break as they're made, they might break in the kiln. If they survive the kiln, then who knows what else might go wrong? Things do go wrong. Transport, packaging, display; anything could happen. We all need to imagine the possibili-ties.

~~~~~

The skin on Jude's shoulders and upper arms was exposed to Bondi sun, Glebe market glare, and the stinging lack of ozone as he went in search of the tiny corroboree frog in mountain peat moss and bog.

Jude's arms could lift piles of notes from his field trips as lightly as one of my pots, as tightly as he could hold me in his arms. He would help me transfer my pieces to the kiln or turn a pot out of a mould. He carried the shopping home in the early days when we didn't have a car. We'd heave the bags off the ferry and up the hill. In blue working singlet, his biceps would roll and his underarms were delicious, hiding pale, curved tendril hair wet with sweat.

Jude loved a party. He would chop up roast chicken, array the pieces on a party platter, surround them with cherry tomatoes and parsley, and proudly bear the platter out to the gathering. He would demand help to clear a space on the table and orchestrate cries of admiration. He would prop at the nearest fireplace with a glass of something fizzy and tend to an attractive woman nearby with fascination in eye. He would lean back when he laughed, then warm to her again, incline toward her, as if mesmerised. I would move to him and ask, please, if he could give me a hand, and yes, of course he would, then ever so apologetically he'd nod to the pretty face and follow me, placing his arm around my shoulders, beaming down at me with complete trust and honesty.

Then Jude would lift another platter, of salad perhaps, and bear it out, demanding a new opening be cleared for this masterpiece, and he would wave one arm in the air and call upon us to raise our glasses and toast the chef and organiser of this party—hasn't she provided us with plenty and isn't she beautiful?—and he would look at me like a breath of fresh air and they would cry out, happy feast day, Jude, come on, you've done enough work now, come and talk, and he would look askance at my apron, putting his arms around my waist and smiling into my eyes as he undid the strings in the most impossible, unseen way. Then he'd press a glass of rosé into my hand and it was cool and his arm was around my shoulders and it fit.

~~~~~

The black and yellow of the corroboree frog (*Pseudophryen corroboree*) inspires a vibrant clash over the surface of the platter. Not quite stripes, the bands of yellow and black suggest an electric maze or labyrinthine route map. The underside of the platter, like the frog's underbelly, is pale yellow.

A corroboree is a gathering. For thousands of years Aboriginals gathered on Mount Kosciuszko to hunt clouds of protein-rich Bogong moths. During the summer breeding season the feasts turned into parties and the backing band would be the mating calls of corroboree frogs.

In these urban days the moths' brown-fur flutter sweeps through Sydney more or less every spring, clustering onto roadside callistemon bushes and choking careless people surprised by their flighty mass.

The corroboree frog is critically endangered. Cattle farming, ski resorts and warming temperatures in the mountains lead scientists to believe their corroboree is all but over. What meaning does 'critically endangered' have? How hard do those words have to be? Where has their bite gone? CRITICAL. What does that mean to you?

Further north, in the lands of vineyards and asparagus farms, up near Mudgee, my friend Janet lives on her family property. She's a potter. We met at the Argyle Arts Centre in the seventies. She's dedicated one particular kiln to salt glazing. It's a wonderful cavern. The ceiling of the kiln, being used in such a violent way, is covered in a magical, glass gleam.

When it's time to glaze, I take the platters up to Janet's place. Like witches in the night, we throw handfuls of salt into the heat. The engulfing flames lick out trying to escape the kiln, trying to eat us. The chemical-synthesis fireworks distort the glaze into an orange-peel surface. The salt glaze gives the platter a froggy, warty skin. It is superficial.

Janet worries about me. She makes me breakfast the next day as we wait for the kiln to cool. We sit next to each other at the table. She pats my hand. She suggests I stay longer. She thinks I look tired. She thinks I need looking after. I say I can't stay. I don't tell her it's because it's such hard work to appear normal. I can't accept her concern. I feel my mask slipping. She must guess. I make a good show of reassuring her. I get away without breaking down in front of her. She insists I come back very soon. I need looking after. Of course I'll come back, I tell her, of course I will. Perhaps I will. Perhaps I won't.

It's raining on the drive back to Sydney. I pull over to the side of the road as the water pelts down. The window wipers fight to keep the windscreen clear. They swipe through an onslaught. Repetitive, mechanical battle; backwards and forwards, lambasting the water. Turn the engine off. The rain clatters onto the car. Crack into a thousand pieces. After some time, I cannot say how long, I pull myself together. Must get back to my work, to my job, to my purpose in life: to the frogs, to my mud, to my man, to my strange, ceramic golem in several pieces. The rain stops. Get out of the car and climb over a fence. Walk into a paddock and trip over. Fall down a gentle hill. Unharmed. The ground is cushioned with long, damp grass. Lie still. My back grows wet. The sky is a grey ceiling. The clouds curdle. When I start to shiver, stand and climb back up the hill. My feet slip at every second step.

The car starts easily and I pull onto the road. Before I know it, I'm back in Sydney with its overwhelming traffic and lights and movement and colour. Cannot wait to get back to the clay. Back to the quiet. Back to my memories.

~~~~~

As the harem grew into itself, or rather, we grew into a harem, Simone came to rely on us more and more: for babysitting; for advice about eating vegetables and getting rid of lice; and as a sounding board for all the myriad drama-ettes a mother needs to discuss. We were there for her with Francis when he was a baby, and even more so now with Emma. We were our own mothers group.

With Zita a florist and Simone a photographer, eventually it dawned that we typified marriage: photography, flowers and containers. I represented women in marriage as containers of the future of the human race. (Before anatomists knew better, wombs were supposed to jump around in a woman's body like a toad, giving rise to hysteria. Modern science may have tethered the uterus to its home, but wombs are still regarded much like toads: unseen, dark, damp.)

Simone had worked at a few weddings—by then, photography had become almost as important to the ritual as the ring—and Zita's floristry business was focused on weddings. Also, on a personal note, we had all married the same man.

Marriage became the theme of the Catalina exhibitions. Simone would art-direct the first exhibition. I began to see the sense in Sheryl's plan: she would only need to negotiate with one of us at a time.

Zita and I were disappointed with the first proof sheet of Simone's work. The photos were the same, ordinary, studio compositions that we could use in the shop—nothing special. We talked about it as the children ran around Parsley Bay one day. Parsley Bay was an inlet in the harbour, a netted miniature beach set into parklands in Vaucluse, near South Head. A graceful, pedestrian-only suspension bridge spanned the inlet. There were large fig trees bordering the lawn giving it a feeling of enclosure.

Leaf and his mate, Jim, were sitting apart from us, chowing down on enormous hamburgers from the kiosk after burning up fuel in a very splashy swimming race. Fern had gone exploring with Francis, looking for Eastern water dragons in the caves around the park. Emma puddled around at the water's edge, building sandcastles and pouring water over them. We three mums sat on the grass watching her, Simone indulgently but Zita and I more warily as we had known Emma to throw water on more than just sandcastles.

I told Simone that if we were going to work collectively, we needed to be more creative. After all, our main bond was certainly due to creation. I wanted to push the boundaries of what a vase could be. Zita took her inspiration from these clay forms, responding with perhaps a single dramatic spray of flat white orchid, a thin swirl of twisted willow, or blocks of packed fruit or vegetables. Ironically, it was the branches of chillies, clumps of artichokes and stacks of asparagus that helped to make Zita's name in the wedding industry. In contrast, the larger pots staggered under a cornucopia of Victorian flowers piled in and fired off in a blaze of colour.

This was our chance to break into Big Art. Catalina Gallery was no humdrum, outer-suburban wallpaper shop. This was an opportunity. I reminded Simone that Sheryl had taken artists all over the world. Only the year before she'd shown a collection in New York that had introduced two Australians into the art scene there with a bang. Our show could also be a stepping-stone to something big. There was a very real possibility of not only domestic success, but also overseas exposure, if not sales. We expected Simone to look deeper.

Simone leant forward, her eyes starry and calculating, her mouth slack, and her fingers tapping impatiently on her knees. She admitted she hadn't seen the possibilities that way. She would look at it again. She explained that she trusted our work and relied on the pieces and arrangements to speak for themselves. We told her she was in danger of verging into chocolate-box territory. Zita and I wanted more than a passport photo. We wanted her to find a new way of looking. Simone was offended. How dare we? Chocolate box! What did we know about photography? She tried to resign. We had to talk her back, flattering her, cajoling, while we rolled our eyes behind her back. Of course we couldn't do without her, she was the light of our lives. Ha.

After that Parsley Bay discussion, Simone seemed driven by the need to prove herself. She wanted to find a new vision, one distinguished by textural expression: blast-crazed ceramic, fragile petal, soft-curled leaf. She tested and experimented until her depth of field became mysterious, often using the morning in her studio to get particular clarity in the foreground while the background swirled into painterly mist. The images ranged from garish Georgia O'Keeffe homages to sly, black and white Mappelthorpe ideals.

Our first exhibition caused significant buzz. We'd been able to milk some friendly publicity in the weekend papers because of our unusual living arrangements—not many harems in the eastern suburbs in 1996; not that we knew of, anyway. 'The Three of Us' in the *Sydney Morning Herald* told of the three wives living in an artistic harem. The article got a great response, though not all of it entirely positive. A letter to the gallery berated us for living in sin. Someone else commented to my dealer that we were disgusting and warned that the children would all grow up warped. But most people were polite about it, at least to my face.

Simone named the show *The Light of the Common Day,* from the Wordsworth poem, *Intimations of Immortality.* She said she chose this title because of another quote in the same work that Zita would just have to use: *Splendour in the grass and glory in the flower.* Also, the poem itself is about glimpses of heaven in childhood, which is at the core of marriage, isn't it?

At least, that's what Simone said.

~~~~~

Both frog and man have one bone, the humerus, connecting elbow to shoulder. The humerus is wrapped in the long, strong biceps and triceps muscles. The shoulder is made up of three bones: humerus, clavicle and scapula. Human clavicles and scapulas (possibly divine but definitely not frog) are often found in reliquaries. The clavicle, or collarbone (you can easily see Simone's), is the longest horizontal bone in the body. The scapula, or shoulder blade, is the thin, triangular one historically used for scraping leather.

~~~~~

Peter leaned against the outside studio wall. I was cleaning the kiln, scraping glaze drips from the shelves. Listening to him complaining. 'She won't have anything to do with me. Her mother's standing guard like a dragon.'

'What do you expect?'

'She can't deny me my rights.'

'Your rights?'

'Fathers have rights. I am the father, after all.'

'Are you?' Scrape, scrape, scrape...

'I told you. We had unprotected sex, five months ago. You know all this. I told you what happened, for God's sake.'

'What got you into this in the first place?' Scrape, scrape, scrape, sweep, sweep, sweep, tidy, tidy, tidy…

He quietly suggested, 'We could have a test.'

'A test?' This surprised me. I had thought of it before, but dismissed it as too melodramatic. I echoed him: 'You want a paternity test against your own father? Would that work?' He shrugged. We both knew his options were limited.

'How else can I get through to her?' There was no answer to his question. We both knew that.

'I didn't get past her mother, either,' I admitted.

Peter dragged an old bar stool over nearer to me. He sat with one foot on the ground, ready to run. 'She seems nice… the mother.'

I took pity on him and volunteered some information. 'Your dragon's name is Sarah. She's done it hard, bringing up two kids all by herself. She knows what it's going to be like for Charlotte. At least I had Zita and Simone.'

'Zita and Simone?' Peter frowned. 'You think they helped?'

'We've been a family, haven't we?'

'We've been a joke.'

I glared at him. How could he think that? He'd always had someone to talk to, someone to share things with, someone to look out for him. I'd given him a support network that would extend into his life forever. I thought to argue with him, but perhaps this wasn't the time. I changed the subject. 'You lied to her.'

'I can't imagine a future without her. I can't think of anything but her. How am I supposed to work when I'm so fucking distracted?'

'Peter, you're an adult. Talk to someone. A doctor. A counsellor. The university must have someone. You want me to find someone for you?'

'You think I'm sick.'

'You seduced your father's girlfriend.'

'I saw her first.'

'Like a bird pretending to have a broken wing.'

'What?'

'Trying to lure the predator away from the nest. But who were you protecting?'

Peter leapt to his feet, knocking the stool over. 'Grant me some respect would you, please?' He picked up the stool and looked in all directions as he struggled to contain his temper. Perhaps he was counting to ten. He placed the stool carefully back on its feet. He leaned his forearms on the stool, making a plank, looking down at the seat. Maybe I'd gone too far. Then he said, 'Could you imagine this might just be about me? What I want? Maybe Charlotte has nothing to do with you and nothing at all to do with Dad. Maybe I just wanted her to see me... *me*... for what I am. Without any broken wing family crap. Maybe I just want her for herself.'

~~~~~

The Light of the Common Day went ahead as planned. We only had three days to hang the exhibition. I repainted the wooden stands for the arrangements of pottery and flowers while Simone negotiated with Sheryl as to the best position for each of her prints. Simone had decided not to frame the work, printing them instead on gorgeous art paper and pinning them up like a collection of large rectangular insects. Sheryl was unhappy with the holes in her wall but conceded Simone's instinct was correct. The images themselves were brilliant: filled with tension and lit dramatically. As well as several sculptures, Simone selected sixteen vases, each slender and pale, each reaching to a different height; displayed together in clumps like a coral garden.

Zita provided sparse foliage for the vases: grey-green eucalyptus, dark acacia, and spikey bottlebrush. The few blooms she chose were displayed individually. In an alcove by the front door she built a trellis of invisible fishing line. Therein she tied dozens of tiny test-tubes in which she nestled a train of running postman and glossy Sturt's pea flowers—bright-red, sculptural, exotic forms trailing down to the ground.

Sheryl's lighting consultant worked magic, striking light into the arrangements, bringing them into relief, picking out the forms and leaving the edges of the rooms in shadow. All I had to do was deliver, not break anything, and leave, while Zita had the final touches, as her ingredients would need to be replaced every two or three days; arranging stalks and blooms, just so.

We opened on a Wednesday evening, hoping for reviews in the major weekend papers. Catalina Gallery looked brilliant. The gallery doors were open to the dusk and excited chatter, clinking glasses and brightly lit merriment poured into the street.

As soon as people arrived, even before they tucked into cheesy nibbles and sluiced back icy, pale Hawkes Bay sauvingon blanc or darkest shiraz from Mudgee, Sheryl was consulting the receipt book in her office. As a gift to Sheryl, Zita had constructed a lavish arrangement of flat hot-house orchids that rose around Sheryl's desk like enormous butterflies. Seated there, Sheryl looked like she was the centrepiece of an Art Deco embellishment. I have to admit, I stayed hidden with her in the office most of the night, not really enjoying the babble of excitement amongst the many guests. Sheryl barely had time to notice, however, as she dashed in and out so many times to place a red spot on a sold piece. In the end she gave the packet to each buyer. They could put their own spot on the wall so she could stay and deal with the next customer.

I sold all my vases and two of the sculptures. All of Simone's work was sold, with multiple prints ordered for several of her photographs. The buyers seemed thrilled with their purchases, for I saw many a proud photograph being taken as happy customers affixed their red spots to the wall. Sheryl, although calm and busi-ness-like on the surface, seemed to be enjoying herself immensely. There was nothing like a successful exhibition to bring the gallery and Sheryl to life. This was the culmination of her dreams; happy people excited about making things and paying her for it!

We closed the door on the last of the guests, around ten o'clock, and Jude popped the cork on a bottle of champagne. He said that Peter and the kids couldn't understand why we were not singing and dancing. The three of us took the glasses he passed to us, and I proposed a toast to Sheryl, thanking her for her enormous trust and support. Then we all took a large swig and then found a place to sit. We were stuffed, that's why, after being on our feet all night talking with enthusiastic punters. All we wanted to do was get our shoes off!

We were all so awake and excited and each of us had stories to tell about different things people had said to us and what the reviewers might or might not have seen or done that it wasn't long before another bottle was called for and another...

It was when she went to get the third bottle of Veuve Cliquot that Sheryl fell on the floor of her kitchen. It was almost a joke until she didn't get up.

Jude called an ambulance and waited outside to usher the ambos inside. I travelled in the back of the ambulance with Sheryl. Zita and Simone stayed behind in the gallery to clean up. When she got to hospital they kept her there. She underwent a series of tests. On day four they found a brain tumour. There was no time to lose.

~~~~~

The freckly skin on Jude's arm grew thinner over time and the dusting of hairs grew coarser. It became looser, crepeier, and there were moles and marks that slightly enlarged or darkened. There isn't a time when you notice gradual changes. You only notice when things will never be the same. You'll notice when he's dead.

Jude would rest his arm across the back of the couch when watching *The Curiosity Show* with Peter. The two of them would find balsa wood, cork, string and plastic bottle or whatever it was that week. They would joke about the show's catch cry: always ask Mum first!

~~~~~

Forearms are often exposed to the air. In fencing, they are target for the épée. When a warm understanding is reached, an aged auntie will grab you by the forearm and give you a gentle pat, just to stay in contact. Many of the plaster casts of corpses in Pompeii show humans shielding their faces with their forearms.

The two long bones, radius and ulna, sound like names of great aunts. More tea, Ulna? Don't mind if I do, thank you, Radius. Very kind.

These bones cross over each other as the arm rotates. No other bones in the body do this.

The single bone in the frog forearm is called the radio ulna. Not a tea drinker, I think. More an FM station for the lost and lonely… like me… like the last, lost frogs. Tuning into Radio Ulna now.

~~~~~

A piercing, childish shriek, 'I wanted to be a butterfly!'

I said, 'But darling…'

'I look like a rabbit!' Emma was very excited. She had on a new party dress, all frills and pink froth. She sported a new sparkly headband. Tears spurted from her eyes. Simone and Fairy Chi Chi both reached out a hand to her as she wriggled beside me on my couch.

'You look adorable.'

'No, don't smudge it…'

'Sweetheart…'

'Oh, dear…'

Emma plunged her face into my shoulder and rubbed. The boundary had been crossed. Emma rubbed her face and eyes until, when she sat up, the entire make-up was blurred into smears of brown. Simone went into helpless mode, raising both hands, shaking her head and rolling her wide-open eyes, and left me to deal with her daughter. How unfair was that? Would I have done that if I'd thought of it first? Fairy Chi Chi also escaped. She went back to painting little Miranda's face, smiling in a lovely, interested way with her head tilted to one side as she listened to the latest gossip about the Spice Girls in the queue of girls, concentrating on the task in hand. Survival of the fairy.

Simone smiled a brilliant smile at another little girl, bent down to her ear level, and murmured, 'How pretty you look.'

It was Emma's sixth birthday and she was having a fairy party in my flat. We were supposed to be in the park but rain stopped play. A neon-pink cake emitted Grrl Power on a party platter on the kitchen bench.

The sky was ominous. Mashed, swirling clouds were grey and lowering. Earlier rain had left puddles gleaming over the roof, reflecting the leaden atmosphere.

I took Emma to my room and wiped her face with a wet cloth. I paused to rinse out the cloth and before I could stop her, she dried her face on an embroidered handtowel that had belonged to my grandmother. Oh, well, Granny never liked those towels much. I rubbed her face gently with cleanser as she continued to wail, 'Fairy Chi Chi sucks.'

'Okay, Emma, stay here and think about what you want from this party. There's no reason why you can't have fun. The other girls are.'

'I'm not.'

'Stay here quietly, then. I'll find you a book to read.'

'Daddy would get me another face.'

'Daddy's not here yet.'

'He will be.'

'You could be very polite and ask Fairy Chi Chi for another make-up, but what will you do if you don't like the new one?'

'Chantelle's is better than mine.'

'You looked nicer than Chantelle before you rubbed your face on my shirt.'

'I didn't do it on purpose.'

'You're too big to behave like this. You need to calm down. If the wind changes...'

'What?'

'They say that when the wind changes, your face stays that way. I have to tell you, your face looks pretty crabby right now.'

'What?'

'I suppose when things change, that means time passes. If you're always wearing the same grumpy face, frowning and sneering at life, it becomes the face you wear, over time. You've seen old, wrinkly people with sad, cross faces haven't you?'

'Yes. You.'

'Thanks.' I took a deep breath.

Simone twinkled around the door. 'It's time for pass-the-parcel.'

'Yay!' Emma rushed out to join her friends, Simone lighting the way. I took a deep breath and followed.

Leaf and Fern had been roped in to help. Leaf turned up the music. He made disgusting retching faces at me. I hoped the wind wouldn't change. Fern had given Emma *In Deep* by Tina Arena and now they were *Burning* up their lives. The little girls shook and shimmied and stamped and wound their bodies round. Remember go-go dancing? The Pony was never like this. These little girls were modern Spiced-up grrls.

Once the girls were seated, the music began again and an enormous parcel moved around the circle of pink flowers and flounces. Everywhere it stopped, a gift went to the unwrapper. No waiting for one central prize for this young crowd. Leaf had to judge who already had a present when he stopped the music. Fern had a list. She ticked off each present-ed girl's name as she gyrated to the music. Girls eyed each other's loot carefully. Is her paint box better than my bracelet?

Strangely, Emma was calm. The glint of greed was absent from her birthday-crazed eyes. I stood beside Simone and congratulated her on Emma's impeccable behaviour. Simone beamed back at me.

'Oh, I knew there'd be problems, so I bought two of everything. I gave them to her yesterday when I was making up the parcel.'

'Simone, there are ten other children here!'

'That's right. Emma's got each of those prizes already. What's wrong, darls? You've got that face on.'

'Don't you think you might be pandering to her a little too much?'

'You don't have to live with her. More champagne?'

'Absolutely.'

Fairy Chi Chi made sure all the girls had been made up. Emma was finally satisfied with her new face, a glittering butterfly flitting over her left cheek. Then Fairy Chi Chi had them sit in a circle while she told them a story. It was about a fairy who had lost her magic wand. 'It was in a room, just like this one… in fact, I think it just might have been here. It really looks familiar. I'm certain of it. What do you think, girls? It must be here.' She looked around suggestively. 'Where could that magic wand possibly be?'

Suddenly, eleven pink little girls were blown like fluff to all the corners of my flat. They tossed aside cushions and flung open cupboards, with me running around amongst them as if I were the ball in a pinball game. In a bid to expand the search for the wand, Emma slid open the doors to the roof garden and led a pack of fairy-floss children screaming outside.

Jude chose that moment to open the front door and enter the commotion, causing great gusts of wind to swell into the cross draft. Pieces of pass-the-parcel wrapping paper whirled and flapped through the air. I shrieked and ran to call the girls inside. Once they were back, wet, bedraggled and only slightly hysterical, we were all grateful to slide the doors shut again.

Only two children fell over in their patent leather shoes and frilly socks. We dabbed Mercurochrome on one girl's elbow while the other girl required only soothing words. No one I talked to actually saw Emma push her. The strap of her handbag was broken but that would be an easy fix.

Once we had the children sitting in front of Fairy Chi Chi, the magic wand was produced and presented to the birthday girl. Fairy Chi Chi was delighted to declare the fairy birthday feasting open.

Outside, the rain was blown sideways and the trees in the park bent in the wind, arching over, silvery undersides twisting far, reaching out for... balance?

Jude carried the party platter to the table. Emma was thrilled to see him and demanded her present immediately. Jude, charming as usual, hugged her tightly and said he'd rather give it to her later when all the children had gone home.

Fairy Chi Chi packed away her make-up kit and made good her escape back to the lowly land where poor acting students live. We needed to fire up the cake but I couldn't find matches. No one smoked anymore. I popped down to Zita's flat thinking she'd have some—each of us had keys to the other flats.

I surprised them. I hadn't been able to find Zita at first. I called out, I know I did, but not hearing any answer, just came on into the flat. I could hear water and, thinking Leaf might be up to one of his tricks, tapped on the door. Still hearing no answer, I bowled right into the bathroom and there they were, in the shower together, hair soaking wet, and kissing. They looked at me, wet rabbits caught in a searchlight. We were all snagged in time. I gasped and felt like my eyes were going to break out of their sockets. My outer Judy Davis smiled and waved as I turned to go, but inwardly I was shocked and swearing. How long had this been going on? I wondered. Where might it be going, and how would it affect us all? Guido wouldn't want Zita to stay with us. Soon she'd be moving on, wouldn't she? How could I bear it?

Jude should have had some matches. He was in charge of the barbecue. He should attend to this. Jude was good at blowing things out.

~~~~~

If you've ever had a fall from your bike, like William did when he was eleven and broke his radius, you'll remember how you put your hands out in front to take the impact. Humans have evolved two bones in the forearm in case they fall forward. The forearm is doubly strong to take the weight. Apart from Kermit, frogs don't tend to ride bikes.

~~~~~

The Three Sisters at Katoomba are big, sharp rocks. They are a tourist attraction. They prise open the sky as Blue Mountain tourists sprinkle litter around the lookout. The story goes they are supposed to be three sisters who were promised by their clan to marry three brothers. There was a war. In order to protect the girls their father turned them into stone until he returned from battle. He never did get back. The girls never did marry anyone. At least they had a simple life. The three women Jude married managed to become more complicated with every minute of every day.

~~~~~

Our second exhibition at the Catalina Gallery, *The Splendour in the Grass, the Glory of the Flower,* sold out on opening night. Even as we rearranged the photos in the last minutes before we officially opened the doors, people were writing cheques in Sheryl's office. Luckily, she had a spare packet of red dots in her stationery supplies.

Zita found a blue-leaf eucalyptus that smelled of hot days, and the air filled with conversational babble that lifted and floated and drifted into the streets of Five Ways. The exhibition wandered through extremes of vegetation and foliage such as had never been seen in the David Jones foyer, much less in a little gallery in Paddo. The atmosphere was giddy with fragrance and conversation and with the delicious smells of mini pizza from Donatello's catering.

I had been playing with contrasts, particularly in size, and found a way to make huge vases and, at the other side of the scale, tiny, tiny pieces just big enough for one delicate antenna stalk bearing the architectural seed head of a native grass.

Simone's photographs were, again, astonishing celebrations of light and shadow, colour and transparency.

Sheryl brought another bottle of champagne back to her office to share with us and ripped off the foil. As she eased out the cork, a shadow of pain crossed her face, a shadow that did not fade with the pop of release.

I took the bottle from her and poured gushing fears into all our glasses. Sheryl leaned back in her chair. She sighed and rubbed her forehead. Simone massaged her poor ballet-scarred feet and even Zita slipped off her sensible shoes with a sigh of relief.

Sheryl took a long drink of her *méthode champenoise*. She spoke to the piles of receipts and cheques on her desk. Although she had never enjoyed such a triumphant opening night as this one, selling everything that could be sold, she had no choice: she would have to close the gallery.

We would not be able to proceed with the third exhibition, which was to have been my moment in the sun. And Sheryl would not be able to proceed with her life.

Brought low by Sheryl's announcement, a tremor ran up my spine when I realised William would have to come home. I would see you again, William.

Chapter 15

Teacups

It had been chilly for late October. It was 1998. I was in the kitchen making a tomato sandwich for my lunch. Up until today, it had been cloudy and cold for the last few days; people were commenting that it felt like winter had come back. Today the wind had dropped and the sun was making a weak effort to shine.

The knife wasn't sharp enough and tomato squished all over the board. I heard a tentative knock at the front door. I opened it to find Jude there, smiling. I did not want to welcome him, yet I did not want to refuse him anything. I felt at peace and devastated at the same time. It was as if we were in the eye of the storm. There had been much before this and perhaps the worst was yet to come. 'You lose your key?'

'No, no, I've got it.' He dangled a set of keys in the air. 'I generally do knock. When I do my laundry, for instance. But you never seem to be home.'

'Okay.' I opened the door wider and showed him inside. 'I believe you.' I didn't see any bundle of laundry, so I looked the silent question at him: why are you here?

'I'm going to take the kids to the Festival of the Winds at Bondi. Want to come? See some kites?'

'Thank you, but I've work to do.' I went to open the door for him. 'Hope you get some wind.'

He shrugged, as if he'd been expecting I wouldn't go, adding, 'And there's this.' He held out a small, black, plastic pot containing a winter-bare stick of frangipani. 'You have a better home for it?'

I nodded and led him through the rooms to the roof garden. There was a place for his gift on the ceramic table outside my bedroom window. The poor little plant would need re-potting. I looked out over the park to the harbour towards Manly. There was a wind starting to shift the trees. It looked like the kites might get some air after all. I was waiting for him to explain himself. He took his time. He came to stand beside me. We both leaned our elbows on the rampart wall. Then casually, it came. 'I've been thinking. Maybe she should come here… Charlotte.'

I'm sure my face would have betrayed my shock but Jude was looking out to distant horizons. I echoed, 'Charlotte?'

'Part of the family.' He was relentless. He spoke nothing but common sense. 'Another baby.'

I dithered around in my mind for something noncommittal to say. I thought of Jude and Charlotte together and the feeling of impending doom deepened in me. 'Have you asked her?'

'I wanted to speak to you first.'

'Get permission?' I turned and took a few steps, encouraging him back inside. I didn't want to even think about this. A fourth wife? That would be at least one too many. My mind went blank. Get some space. Be gone you ex-husband, you. He looked like he was reluctant to move from the terrace. I stood in the doorway of my flat and looked out at him. I frowned at him and then thought of his mother. 'Superstitious?'

He looked at me then, 'What?'

'Have to sit down for the count of ten before you leave a house by the same door you came in by? You know. Your mother.'

'Oh, Queenie. All her rules.' He came past me into the living room, perched on the side of the armchair, and counted quickly to ten. I followed him into the room and watched him, waiting for him to get up and get going. Then he said, 'Remember? We wanted them, didn't we? All the children. We wanted a gang of them. We wanted to be surrounded by them.'

I closed my eyes, shutting him out. I took a deep breath and tried to paste on a happy face. When I felt in control again I opened my eyes and said, 'You're so obliging.' I'm sure he would not have noticed anything amiss.

He moved towards the front door. 'I'd do anything for you, Constance.'

'Enjoy the kites.'

He turned in the doorway. I couldn't remember the last time he had looked at me as if he'd really seen me. He leaned over and kissed me on the cheek. It was uncomfortable. I felt embarrassed and belittled.

After he'd gone, I went to the roof garden and picked up the frangipani. I noticed now that the roots had grown through the base of the pot; they looked like the fingers on a corpse.

Home. I'll make it a home.

~~~~~

In my memories lie his hands. Hands: so full of bones, so muscular, so necessary. His hands held the frogs with hands just like ours, only jelly. His hands caressed Francis's hair. His hands soothed the Band-Aid over the graze. His hands held the cup. His hands were tanned deep brown. His hands on mine. His hands waving… waving me goodbye.

In one bright, blue, sunny memory, tiny blonde filaments glitter over the back of Jude's hand. He wears a wedding ring. My ring to him. Or was it? Maybe it was later. Too many wedding rings, too many weddings.

He had strong hands with long fingers. Expressive hands. He moved them through the air in mild, curving gestures as he spoke. The base of his thumb was round and fleshy. There was a mole on the back of his right hand and a dusting of freckles over both. His fingernails were oval and ingrained with riverbank mud. The nails were hard and their half-moons clearly defined.

Jude could be exquisitely gentle and the frog in the palm of his hand lay quietly bloodlike in its flesh-nest. The soft padding of his palm smoothed over the surface of my skin.

What memories they are! They are not mine to enter and dispose of at will. They are not under my control. These memories rise up unbidden, chaotic and inescapable. I serve my memories. They are instructing me. How I wish I could compose them as if they were clay. I could make sense of our lives by sculpting and shaping. But these memories are not clay and they will not be told. Not properly. I am doing my damndest. Do you believe me?

~~~~~

One afternoon, as 1998 ran down and turned into summer, I saw Jude in the fruit and vegetable shop at Edgecliff station. I watched him as he contemplated a pile of bananas. He picked up a clump of three and placed them into the shop's basket he carried. I was beside him before he saw me. I said, 'I thought you didn't like bananas.'

'I don't.' He must have understood my unspoken question because he added, 'Francis does.'

'What will you do? About Charlotte?'

'I don't know. She won't speak to me. But if that's my child...'

'It might not be.'

He frowned at me—a sidelong glance as if to ask what the hell would I know—and walked across the shop to a stack of avocados. He picked one up, assessing it. We felt a train wallop into the tunnel below, pushing the air through the building, before we heard it. Jude replaced the avocado and picked up another, cradling the deep-green fruit in his hand. 'I really do want another child.' He looked directly at me. 'There's nothing more important, is there? A new life?'

I couldn't help thinking we weren't doing so well with the lives we were responsible for already. 'What are you telling Simone?'

'If I tell her, it's over.'

If? What did he mean, if? There was a choice?

~~~~~

Like cartoon characters or puppets, frogs have only four fingers on each hand. The true thumb is lost. Some frogs may have a rudimentary thumb bone called a prepollex. Francis, what do you say to that? Another lost character from *The Lord of the Rings*? Are you loyal, Prepollex? Can Prepollex be trusted?

Male frogs develop nuptial pads on their fingers. These pads act like little bits of Velcro, enabling the frog to get a better grip, either near the female's armpits or around her waist, depending on how he prefers his amplexus. After mating season the frog will shed his nuptial pads with the rest of his skin, which he'll eat, and then he'll be a bachelor again.

Hands holding teacups need opposable thumbs. Teacups are built to be held, but not by frogs. Cups with handles must be held between fingers and thumbs. These little cups are fragile, made from bone china. Almost conical, with turned-out lip, they're coloured like the rock frog, *Cophixalus saxatilis*, brown with irregular, darker markings. Base of cup and centre of saucers are creamy white, with some dark spots—like the frog's belly.

An example of a creature evolving to fit a very particular habitat, this frog lives in warm, humid cracks in Black Mountain. Black Mountain is a pile of tumbled granite boulders in Far North Queensland. The frog's hands are not webbed—these frogs are rock climbers, not swimmers. Also known as the boulder frog, or rock dwelling elegant, this microhylid is notable for the discs on the end of its long fingers.

Attempt to find an approximation of the frog's colours with each glaze, but unpredictable ingredients, the temperature of the kiln, and the oxygen level in the smoke conspire to wreak havoc.

I suppose a tadpole might be surprised to find itself a frog. Transformation doesn't necessarily mean improvement. Which way lies progress then?

~~~~~

Some days in the studio are better than others. Some days find a rhythm. Once, years ago, having made twenty-odd pots and lined them up beside me in tidy rows, a sense of achievement hummed as the electric wheel groaned on and on. That's the secret to productivity: keep the metallic gnawing going until you've covered the bench in product.

I had collected this particular clay over a weekend with Leah, a pottery colleague, at Wisemans Ferry on the Hawkesbury River. Both of us agreed there's something extremely satisfying about making products from clay self sourced and we looked forward to the outing. Even though Hawkesbury is a sandstone ridge, there is clay down by that river in some localised deposits of shale. A local farmer had told her about good quality clay on his land. He directed us to a cracked clay bed, not far from the river. It was a hot day and the gum trees were heavy with oil. The air was thick and still. We shoveled pieces of the cracked dry surface that had once been wet and slick. We half-filled a couple of twenty-gallon drums already balanced in the back of my old Volvo. Filthy car already, potential resale wasn't improved by the exercise. We also loaded up some drums on the back of her ute.

When I got home to Sydney, I flooded the drums with water for a couple of days. Using an old, beaten up electric paint mixer, I stirred up the clay into slip. Then I used a jug to decant the slip through my excellent fly-screen sieve. Once the organic matter and stones were out of the clay, I built ingots the same size and shape so I could run a series of tests on the flexibility and the fire-ability of the material. The clay was gritty but smooth enough to warrant further work. I never added much other types of clay to it. The sand in it gave it bones.

In pre-industrial landscapes, from Denmark to Indonesia to South America, men were excluded from such work. Women were in charge of gathering the raw material, for it was only they who knew where clay was to be found. They would approach the quarry with respect and religious ceremony. Fertility rites, sculpting earth gods and even eating the clay were among the business of women. They would have rituals for digging and for transporting and for transforming.

My Hawkesbury clay did seem somehow special. I made half a kilo or so into a ball, threw it, and centred the clay on the wheel's spinning circle. I pulled the body up. My hands were covered in slip, the surface of the clay slick and shiny. The finger grooves slid beneath my skin and the clay form came into being, as the twenty before it had. I turned the edge over, the lip forming easily.

As my thumb bent into the shape, the roughness of the clay under the surface-slide pushed me back. Perhaps it was the form caused by the inherent sand ingredients of the clay. Perhaps those tiny bacteria combined to have some life force. However it occurred, the clay's behaviour was an epiphany. It seemed that the clay had its own strength. Suddenly I knew the clay was alive and knew where it wanted to be. I had foolishly thought I was the one in control. But it had been Mother Earth guiding my hand and giving me breath all my working life. It is Gaia who senses the form that ought to find the fire. It is she who has the power.

This made me remember my discussions with Father Brian. Sometimes the potter's resolve is not enough. The child will become what it will and not what the parent moulds. I wish I could remind Father Brian that some things are beyond God's control. By now, perhaps, Father Brian already knows. Perhaps he is an angel on a cloud. Perhaps God has already explained all the secrets. What can he know? Can he see everything? Can he see what I'm doing? What must he think of me now? It's a long way up to the clouds.

You'd think the Sky God and the Earth Mother could get it together after all this time, wouldn't you? What's keeping them apart?

~~~~~

I absent-mindedly spooned the chocolate from the top of my cappuccino, the spoon shaking in my uncertain hand. The cup was white with a green stripe and then a red stripe. The afternoon sun toasted the hard streets of Leichardt with a yellow tinge.

Guido filled his well-tailored suit, his shoulders broad and powerful. His lion mane of hair swept back from his face accenting his cheekbones and glamour jaw. Though I had known him for years I still felt inadequate, my feet slimy in my sandals. He was too big for his cream, plastic chair. He seemed to fold himself down into it. Always graceful, even in discomfort, he put his sunglasses and mobile phone next to the ashtray. Bar Italia was not crowded at this time of the afternoon and its empty, brittle surfaces made the place ring loud with every plate and cup that made contact.

Guido put his tiny espresso cup down in its tiny saucer, his manicured fingers shining. 'You weren't just passing.' He smiled at me, showing his teeth, but the smile did not reach his eyes.

Of course I had made a special trip. He knew everything, or gave that impression. I cowered from his judgement. I could never keep up with him. 'I wasn't exactly passing on the spur of the moment, and it's none of my business really, but...'

He bowed to me. I couldn't tell if he was being gracious or sarcastic. 'Thank you for recognising that, Connie.'

'I wanted to say...' I felt slimy all over as I tried to construct a sentence under his scrutiny. 'I just think the kids are better off in our extended family, where people are looking out for them all the time...'

A man in a dark business-suit pressed his hairy hand to Guido's shoulder as he was leaving the café. 'Guido! See you later?'

'Of course, Pietro, wouldn't miss it for the world.' Guido nodded and saluted the man. 'Ciao, Pietro. Ciao, ciao.' He turned back to me. 'My cousin. Having a party for my auntie tonight. She's turning seventy. You want to come? Zita and the kids will be there, of course.'

I avoided his gaze and looked anywhere but at him. A noticeboard by the door bristled with posters for concerts, exhibitions, bands and Radio 2SER. There was a flyer for a concert by *The Cafe at the Gate of Salvation* gospel choir. I wondered if I would go. No, the date had passed; I had missed it. I still needed Salvation though. The floor had assorted chunks of marble set into a pale-green, granite bedrock. The chunks were an assortment of black, grey, creamy swirl, reddish waves and human flesh. It was crazy paving.

'Guido, you know I love those kids. They've been happy living as one family... they really have.'

Guido took a little sip from his tiny cup then put it back down on its tiny saucer. He looked directly at me. 'Have you?' The gold bracelet on his arm coruscated blasts of yellow brilliance into my eyes. 'Is this the way a woman should live? Hoping for a glance once in a while from the man she loves? Maybe you are the one fooling yourself. No, my dear, please don't take umbrage. You remind me of a cat with all its hair standing on end.'

I'd had no plan except that Guido would listen to me and would understand. It seemed obvious to me that they should stay at *Bindiwurra*; it was the best place for them. But now, on the edge of the precipice, I could see I had made a mistake. I had no business being here. Yet I could not back down. I would look ridiculous. I had to make some kind of last stand. Somehow I had to bluster on through. I had so much to lose. I was fighting for my family.

I sipped my bitter coffee and tried to gather courage from its froth. I put the cup back down on the saucer, trying to be quiet in that place of hard clattering surfaces, and leaned back into the plastic chair. I took one more deep breath before sallying forth over the abyss. 'I'm not sure where Vionella fits in with all of this?'

Guido's eyes flamed. 'Vionella? She is the best of all of us. She can never grow old. Vionella lives on in our hearts. Safe. No one can touch Vionella. Don't you worry about her, Constantia. She's the least of our worries. We, however, we who are left behind, we have to look at our lives as they will be from now on. We have to imagine the future. Things can improve, you must understand this. I am a man. Zita is a woman... a beautiful woman. I love her. And more than that, we make good business sense together. You know I love those kids. I worry about them. Leaf is drinking. Fern thinks only about animals. What kind of life do they have without a father? And, tell me, what kind of life do you have, Connie?'

'I don't need a shoulder to cry on, Guido.' He smiled at me with such empathy, as if he knew what I needed... and it was more than just a shoulder. But something in me kept insisting. I couldn't give in so easily. I had so much to lose. What makes us humans keep trying to stay the same? Why can't we accept change?

I fired one last salvo before I slunk off in shame, sliding in my sweaty sandals. 'The kids are comfortable where they are, in familiar surroundings, where they've been since they were little.'

Guido picked up his espresso, took a sip and then set the cup back down. He was careful. He looked up at me. He put the full force of his righteous anger into his narrowed eyes. He waited, as if he were trying to contain his anger, before he spoke quietly and clearly. 'You want I should ask you for permission? Is that it?'

I looked away, not wanting him to know he'd hit home. My temperature rose with shame. I didn't know what to say. Tears liquefied my vision. How could I have dared to invade this good man's space? What was I thinking? I bit the inside of my bottom lip. Hard.

Plates and glasses hit the marble surfaces at the bar far too loudly and the coffee machine hissed like a wild beast tricked into a trap of its own making.

'Constantia, I'd like your permission... it would delight me of course, but it would be meaningless... you understand? We will live as a family without it. So, why not stay friends, my dear? Another cappuccino?'

I couldn't stay. I rose to my slippery feet, flapped for my hand-bag and my sunglasses and dropped them. I was awkward, so apologetic, so off-beam, so unnecessary. He remained steady, quiet, not standing as I gathered my shrapnel together. A casual salute, 'Ciao, Connie. Ciao, ciao. See you soon. At the wedding, I suppose.'

'Guido, you won't...?'

'Tell Zita? But I already did, my dear.' He picked up his phone and smiled pleasantly at me. 'I already did.'

~~~~~

At Paddington market, a palm reader told me I would have only one child but two husbands. Two major loves. She pointed to my fingerprints. Told me that Chinese legal systems had been using fingerprints as identification for thousands of years. The loop and the whorl are always different. Inspired, I went on to do a series of fingerprint plates and platters. All different, each with their own distinctive loops and whorls.

Could both my husbands be in my one Jude? One in the formal marriage and the next in the recovery? Or, almost unthinkable, is there someone else for me in the future? All I feel now is unbearable loss. Grow weary of work, of clay, of memories, but there is nothing else to cling to. Try to find new memories in frogs, but these memories slip away even as I become aware of them. Cannot rely on the frogs. No one can rely on frogs and it's not their fault. Frogs are unreliable.

~~~~~

Once upon a time a city frog went to visit a country frog. On the way the city frog saw a cow and was impressed. When he arrived at the damp, dark cave where the country frog lived, he explained to the country frog that he had just seen an enormous animal. The country frog asked, 'How big?' and the city frog puffed himself up and stretched out his arms and spread his fingers wide and said, 'This big!'

The country frog said, 'How big?'

And the city frog puffed himself up and stretched himself out even more and said, 'This big!'

And the country frog smiled and said, 'How big?'

And the city frog puffed out and stretched up, and exploded.

~~~~~

Jude's hands used to hold mine but now the gorgeous thrill of his bones, covered by silken-skin and cushion strength, is lost to me. My heart feels squeezed by his hands so capable but now so wrinkled in the long bath of my own terrible grief.

~~~~~

William did return to nurse his mother. I went to see him whenever I could. It was as though we'd never been apart. Except that we didn't know in any detail what each had been doing for the last thirty years. Sheryl grew weak very quickly.

~~~~~

The water is heating up all around us. Will we recognise what is happening? Will we be able to jump out before we are boiled?

Chapter 16

Bowl

Work with the drag of the wheel, not against it. Physical, hard work, particularly when centring the clay. Lean into it. It is a forceful balance. Not throwing. More like growing. Especially when turning out twenty in one sitting.

Potter's body has to stay grounded. The wheel turns and the clay lies in the centre of the metal circle. Gentle laying on of hands is not enough. Rib cage behind elbows reinforces the arms. Exert extra power on the clay to keep it in very middle of the wheel. Must not wobble. Unless that's the desired effect, when, of course, off-centre is the perfect place. Potter must be in control of the work either way. Push clay down and pull up and shape with one hand curved and the other straight. Keep within boundaries of the clay. Pull cylinder up and then either hook in top or push in and hook out to make a bowl. Respect the clay. It can collapse if too wet or too thin or not wedged enough.

Prefer working with softer clay and slower wheel than when I was younger. More fluidity perhaps? Practice. The only way to find out. Leave to dry for a day or two, maybe even a week, depending on weather. When leather-hard, turn over. Moisten the work and apply a sharp tool to define surface. Make a flat standing base.

Design edge for the foot of the bowl. The base is the boundary and stability of the piece. Base must balance form of bowl. Base defines essence of form. Base is grace note.

Are you thinking when you meditate? Do you meditate when you make a pot? Is pottery meditation? Is meditation hypnotic? Is pottery thinking? I cannot divide myself from clay—it is so much of my personality. It is all I have left.

~~~~~

I paid brief but daily visits to William as he nursed Sheryl in her final days. I took him food while the palliative care nurses looked after Sheryl. They insisted he step out with me for a walk and he equally resisted. He did not want to leave his mother in case she called or wanted him for something. He needed her to know he would do anything for her.

The day he opened the door to reveal only silence, I was not prepared and I knew, without him telling me, that Sheryl had gone.

As I walked into the vacant room, William told me that the funeral directors had taken her body away the night before. He hadn't wanted the nurse to call anyone. Not yet. His eyes were hazy and he was unshaven. Like a caged tiger he paced between the walls of the empty gallery, the footfalls apparently putting him into a trance. He told me he'd always hoped for a miracle. Ridiculous, he knew, she would never recover from this brain tumour. She'd just kept slipping away. But he couldn't help it, he just kept hoping. He'd been away for so long he wanted her to stay, he wanted to look after her, and most of all, he wanted to cure her, to make everything better. He wanted to make amends for his continual absence but now it was too late.

In answer to the funeral director's inquiries, all William had to say was that his mother wasn't much for religion. Then the funeral director had suggested some sort of wake or gathering at the gallery. William was pleased by the idea. Zita could handle the flowers perhaps. Sheryl's friends from the art community—they'd help, wouldn't they? Did I know of a band? There would need to be music.

The gallery was stuffy and smelled of sickness, of chemicals, disinfectant and faeces. The blinds were closed and the hospital bed stood in the middle of the polished floor. The walls were hung with Sydney artists, both from Catalina books and old stock. In one corner stood a trio of differently-sized pots, while a jagged sculpture covered in tiny mosaics stood in another.

William told me that Sheryl had loved the idea of moving down here to the gallery. Here, in the main space she had envisioned and then developed over the course of thirty years, she knew who she was, even though at the end she was unconscious for much of the time. She had thought of herself, William said, as her own performance art, loving the idea of the stained sheets and muck of her death being admired and examined for meaning. He felt she needed to see her things around her: the pots and the paintings, all the art that became her way of life. He had carried and fetched and arranged each item to her specification.

William stood in the darkened gallery, the devoted son who had given his all but too late. He was grizzled and weather-beaten, training for and running marathons had kept him wiry. Sheryl had been so proud of every marathon. She kept me up to date with her hardworking son. Who would let me know where he was now?

I encouraged him upstairs to the flat and into the shower, and suggested he shave. I washed dishes and found spaghetti, garlic, olive oil, dried chilli flakes, and parsley from the window box. William said he wasn't hungry but eventually he ate a few mouthfuls of pasta washed down with a glass of Shiraz. His eyes brimmed over and he wept. I held his hand.

Once William had regained some composure, we talked. We spoke of all manner of things. He told me that after Gracie's death he hadn't known what to do with himself. But none of us could. Whilst he and Mark had stuck together like glue, cycling around the North Shore and hanging out at the rowing club after school,

William felt I'd become distant when I went off to university, all blue stockings and serious. Then he remembered how reluctantly I had gone with him to his school formal—he was a friend of my kid brother and by then I was in love with a frog killer.

We had danced together, laughing, cheek-to-cheek at the end of the night, William's nose bumping into mine. I thought he'd been in love with Gracie; I thought he was imagining Gracie, slow dancing with Gracie right there in his arms. I'd been shocked when he tried to kiss me.

But it never had been about Gracie, William told me in the flat above the gallery with the blood of Shiraz on his lips. The sun had gone down and we sat side by side at the kitchen bench not wanting to turn on the light. It had always been about me. William had always intended to ask me to the formal. It had always been me he had wanted to kiss. At that time, for me, it was about Jude. Any moment for William and I, our possibility, for whatever that might've been, had been lost.

The night was closing in, much like our memories and misalignment. The streetlight came in to the room. I poured William another glass of wine. William revealed that he hadn't known what to do when I had come home from university full of Jude this, Jude that, Jude everything to me. If I was young and impressionable, William was moreso. For his last couple of years of school, there was an expectation he would go to the States and then to Italy to meet his father's family. His next few years were already planned and now, because of Jude, William would only come back to Australia to visit. He could not countenance living in the same city as Jude and me until now, when his mother needed him desperately. Until his mother died.

I'd had no idea. William was my other brother, my old bath-time pal: together we played cowboys and Indians, *Shintaro* and knife-throw steps; we smoked cigarettes under the house; he'd been my pirate mate, my cubby-building accomplice, and we'd even learned the twist together. But he had not been in love with my little sister, a love I had believed in all my life. There was nothing I could say or do... I felt overwhelmed and could only stare. William Richards was in love with me and had been for fifty years.

I stood and picked up his glass and a bowl preparatory to doing the dishes. He rose and stood beside me and gently, very gently, took the bowl and put it, gently, very gently, on the table. He put his hand on mine and slowly ran his fingers over my hand until he held it warmly, then very gently lifted our joined hands to his mouth. Very softly he ran my thumb over his lips.

William's eyes watched me carefully. They were sad eyes. Slowly he brought our joined hands down and let go, only to bring his hand to my cheek, softly. He held my neck with one hand and my cheek with the other and quietly, gently, drew my head to his and laid his lips on mine. I closed my eyes. He was warm and lovely... oh so lovely.

I had to go. My glasses were fogged.

He asked if I knew how long he'd wanted to do that. I told him, William, I just can't, it is all too much. I told him I was sorry, I was confused, too full with... and William said, Jude. And I said, no, it wasn't him, but William said it was Jude, Jude said William. And he was right... it was Jude.

William asked if I'd ever thought that I might have been wrong? I smiled, told him that, well, maybe, now and then... it was possible that I'd been wrong.

I left William in his flat and rushed home to the safety of my rooftop overlooking the harbour and the park, a place where I could be alone and there were no surprises.

No surprises... if only that were true.

From that day onwards, life has been full of surprises.

~~~~~

Simone went out for her birthday. She was a Scorpio. I was the babysitter. The kids and I had negotiated to hang out in sparkle palace rather than have a sleepover at my place. We had cottage pie for dinner, even though it had been a warm November day, and then Emma had a bath. Frances ploughed through his homework. He had to read *The Gathering* for school and he didn't like it. 'It's hard to get too worried about The Dark in Sydney,' he said. I could see his point. Sydney was just too bright and brash to worry about any old evil Occult lurking about under things. What evil there was, devils, demons and damnation, was hanging out in Kings Cross for everyone to see and their names were Poverty, Greed and Addiction, not Satan.

Emma wanted to read *Isabella's Bed* to me, Alison Lester's book about a grandmother. As I sat on the side of her bed and listened to her, Emma interrupted the story to say to me, 'You could be my grandmother.'

'I could be, my friend, but I'm not. Queenie was your grandmother. She would have liked you.'

'Really?'

'Yes. She liked decisive people.'

After they'd gone to bed, I did the dishes then sank down into the couch to relax with a grim, British murder on the telly. I moved the cushion a bit to get the scratchy sequins away from my arm and that's when I found it: a blood-brown copy of a selected Wordsworth. It was well loved, with a loose binding and some dog eared pages and it wafted fragrance of aged book as I turned the pages. It may well have been a school textbook, so I wasn't surprised when I found, in arduous, bouncing, dark-old ink, complete with blotches, the following instruction: 'If this book should chance to roam, box its ears and send it home.' Underneath was the signature, *R. Luxford*.

And on the next page, in light blue ink: 'To my divine Simone, the epitome of romance, forever yours, Rufus.'

I stared at these beautifully penned words and then flicked through the pages, reading a verse here and there. When I found 'Intimations of immortality from recollections of early childhood', I read the ode again, this time more seriously, realising this was the source of Simone's inspiration for the titles of our exhibitions. I read and wondered, 'Whither is fled the visionary gleam? Where is it now, the glory and the dream?' And it seemed…

I had to shut my eyes…

Just for a moment…

~~~~~

Suddenly the room was filled with noise and light and perfume. Simone was back from her party and had turned on the lights. She was radiant. I'd never seen her glowing like this. 'Connie! Connie! You're not going to believe this!'

Probably not. I blinked, blinded and confused.

'Wait, wait,' said she as she flung herself around the flat in a swirl of perfume, shoes divested, scarf slipped over the back of a chair, glinting titanium earrings tossed onto the bench. 'Champagne! We must have champagne! I have some. I'm sure there's a bottle in here. Wait, wait, wait…' Simone opened the fridge and crouched down in her backless, glittering gown, looking behind and shoving aside half-eaten yogurt pots and jars of sweet chilli sauce. There was a bottle in there and she grabbed it. 'Fantastic.'

I disentangled myself from the couch, feeling achy and old compared to Simone's lithe luminosity. All in a blear I stumbled into the bathroom and splashed my face with cold water. By the time I returned, she'd poured the bubbly into two glasses. Wordsworth had disappeared.

I was able to tell her, 'The children are sleeping.' Not that she needed reassuring, way up there on cloud nine.

'Of course they are; thanks, darls, never thought they wouldn't be. Don't know what I'd do without you. Couldn't manage at all. You're such a treasure! I don't deserve you. Anyway, darling, you will not believe this. I don't believe it yet I know it's true.' She hoisted her glass into the air between us and chorused, 'Here's to me! My birthday!' She took a long draft from the glass, leaned on the kitchen bench, and from her shiny mouth bubbled an unstoppable froth of words. 'It was Rufus, Rufus, all this time. Where I've been tonight. He's been following me. Oh, not him exactly, this private detective… who would have imagined? Little old me? Followed by a private dick, just like in some novel.'

'The guy in the station wagon?'

'That's right!' She frothed some more: 'I forgot I told you. Yes, isn't it amazing? He was working for Rufus all along. Can you imagine? A detective! After me! Rufus couldn't find me after I left London… you know I ran away from the company, don't you? Anyway, Rufus hired this agency. He said he'd been looking for me ever since I disappeared. I never thought he would. Now he wants to see more of me… of all of us. I just can't believe it. He wants my family. He's a dream come true.' She twirled with glee, wine slopping over the edge of the crystal tulip as she bumped into the kitchen bench.

My heart started to creak as much as my old back, and my fizzy wine tasted sour.

Simone blithered on. 'He gave me this. Look! He remembered my birthday which, I have to tell you, is a lot more than Jude did.' With her ballet dancer's grace, she held out her arms in an attitude for me to admire. 'What do you think? Isn't it precious?'

There, on her wrist, was an elegant bracelet of gold and jade, the palest fog of the lightest, mountain-mist jade. It did look precious.

'I can't think straight. It's all so new. I want to do the right thing for everyone, but for him to come after me, after all those things we said. Blissful. I couldn't have a better birthday.'

I drank the flirty bubbles and gasped at her effrontery. For God's sake, where did that put the last twelve years in her life? In all our lives?

~~~~~

Bowl's pattern is from the holy cross toad, *Notaden bennettii*, also known as the Catholic toad. It has a round body and a warty skin. Pale bronze with paler beige circle on back with a pattern of black rings centred with black, white, red and yellow spots forming a distinctive cross shape. Not often seen above ground. One of those frogs that buries itself for survival until the next rains give rise to stories of rebirth and resurrection.

When the holy cross toad is annoyed, its skin secretes a poison now being investigated for medical use as glue—sticking bone to bone, tendon to bone—a miracle of medical togetherness.

Of course, whereas the toad is convex, the bowl is concave and the cross pattern sinks in rather than rises to the heavens. The bowl is symbolic of the skull, and crucifixion is all in the mind.

~~~~~

Continue my research on Jude's computer. I read a story about the earthly Buddha. A shepherd stops to listen to the enlightened teacher. The shepherd leans his hands on his wooden staff planted into the ground. The staff sinks deeper as the shepherd becomes more entranced by the ideas he is hearing. Eventually the staff presses into a frog that happens to be buried there. The staff carries the sound of the Buddha's words into the frog. The punctured frog does not try to escape because it is transfixed, listening to the beauty of the teaching. Because the frog did not complain as it died, it was reborn into the world of the gods and became Lord Indra.

~~~~~

The Bondi Junction office had only one small window, through which I could see a beige wall perhaps five metres away. I sat in an uncomfortable, rickety chair, presumably designed to ensure that clients did not stay long. The detective sat on the other side of the desk, shuffling through papers. He had intense eyes the colour of cow dung. Once he stopped riffling through papers, he was business-like as he pried into my life, a sort of personal affairs dentist. His facial expression teetered between avuncular concern and retail relish.

Privately, I renamed him Mr Banksia. The detective's thick hair was greying and it stuck up all over his head like an old cone on a banksia tree. His shoulders were sprinkled with flaky bark skin and he had enormous pores on his face, particularly on his bulbous nose. His ancestors might well have been big, bad Banksia men. His body was packed into a nut-brown suit. He'd buttoned the jacket, perhaps only recently, and it stretched across his belly so tightly that he seemed to be divided into seedy segments.

After Mr Banksia had extracted the relevant information, he seemed disappointed, as though I'd confessed to over-indulging on fizzy drinks and sweets. That would explain the cavities but I wanted to know how much the work was going to cost, and if it would hurt.

'Summing up then, if I may, you know for certain that he's been looking for her for the last ten years and that he's from England. That's the sum total of it all? Is that right?' Then his face suddenly sharpened. 'What do you reckon? Could there be another agenda?'

Oh, for God's sake, I thought. I've just been telling you that. What am I paying you for? Of course there's another bloody agenda. 'Yes.'

His beady eyes switched to alert and he leaned forward. He was onto something. 'And what do you reckon that might be?'

'That is precisely why I am paying you: to find out what is going on between Simone and Rufus. Okay? Exactly who is this Rufus Luxford? What's his background? What does he intend? That's what I want to know,' I said.

'Right.' He nodded, frowning. 'Maybe she's got something on him.'

'Maybe, considering she's a photographer,' I said. 'Negatives?'

'Negatives… right! That's a starting point. She just might know where the treasure's buried. Righty-o, Mrs Baldwin. *Mrs Baldwin.*' His eyes twinkled with extra relish. 'That's funny, isn't it? How many Mrs Baldwins are there?'

I didn't find it funny. 'I'm the only one… in this family. The others went back to their maiden names. Well, Simone hyphenated and Queenie, his mother, was always Queenie. Never Mrs Baldwin. At least not to me.'

'Is that right?' The relish dropped from Banksia man's face. He became serious, rose from his chair with purpose and offered me his hand. The palm was not hairy, but it was oily. 'I'll be in contact within the week. By then I reckon I'll have some preliminary findings and an idea on how to proceed. Alrighty?'

'And an estimate of costs?'

'Indeed, Mrs Baldwin, indeed. A quote, so to speak.'

'You will keep out of sight?' I asked, knowing that if Simone was to find out, I could kiss those kids goodbye for infinity and beyond.

'Mrs Baldwin, you don't need to worry about us. We're not known for our indiscretion. In fact, we're hardly known at all, and that's our selling point. You know what I mean?'

'I think I do. I think we have a very big worry right here. I mean this very, very, seriously. I want you to remain a figment of my imagination. Do you understand me?'

The big, bad Banksia man nodded and lowered his eyes to his desk. He picked up his pen and twisted it between his hands. It made him look thoughtful. But looking thoughtful and actually thinking are two quite different things.

~~~~~

Many facts give me comfort. Byron used to drink blood from a skull and he wasn't Robinson Crusoe. Poor skeletons used to lose their heads to many a grave robber seeking the curative benefits of drinking from the skull. The death's head, mounted over crossed femurs, symbolises pirates and warns of poison. Skulls line the catacombs under Paris. Skulls were stuck on pikes on the roof of the Traitors Gate at the Tower of London. When first squashed through the vagina into life, a skull has three soft spots, the fontanelle. A skull is not just one bone but a jigsaw puzzle that offers strength by juxtaposition. Gradually the skull grows and hardens. We all harden up eventually.

~~~~~

It was not such a long way but it was an uphill walk and we'd agreed I'd chauffeur the kids home from the pool because it was such a hot day. I couldn't see Fern anywhere in the water but Leaf was on the pontoon in the middle of the water. He was shiny and scrawny with board shorts barely clinging to his hipbones and in the midst of a clump of other shiny young guys. They looked like a jamboree of sea lions. I waved to him with generous sweeps of my arms. Leaf returned my large gesture with the smallest lift of his forefinger like a country driver passing another on a remote country highway. Thus acknowledged, I wandered over to the café to purchase a lemon fizzy drink and the *Herald*. I was fighting a headache and rubbed my temples hard. I found a patch of shade on the grass, placed the paper open on my lap, sipped from the straw in the bottle and slumped. I thought I might read the paper but I was content to stare about me.

Summer shone its beacon hard into the Redleaf Pool that afternoon. The pool was a beautiful fenced-in piece of harbour in the middle of Double Bay marina life. Metal bars between wharf legs held up a wooden walkway. The white fence, together with its apron walkway, went all around a white, pipe-edged, semi-circle of safety and kept toothy sea-creatures away from flimsy, human frames. The harbour water lay in front of us, while the land rising beside the bay was dotted with buildings, predominantly blocks of flats, built into the hillsides; patterned, rectangular boxes like tessellations in an Imants Tillers painting.

A green and cream ferry trawled away from the city, a smudge of exhaust trailing above it. White triangle yachts, yellow water-taxis and noisy powerboats criss-crossed their wakes across the water. From above came the clatter of a helicopter and the drone of a small plane, puncturing the boisterous whip-crack of teenage hilarity. Under these percussions, the sound of the waves rolling into shore was repetitive to the extent of being hypnotic and also emphatic, like the flicking of a bed sheet into submission before the folding.

Fern appeared beside me wearing a broad smile. Her wet hair was smoothed back, her face was shining happy, and she smelt of sweet apple shampoo. I rifled through my purse and found five dollars to give her. Just then, Leaf, Dan, Jim and Stammas arrived up so I turned out the purse's lining for the scrapings, a few silver coins.

The kids headed off to the café arguing over the flavour of milkshake they could all cope with, and then Fern was back. She plonked down on the grass with a bottle of fizzy lemonade. I shut the paper and smiled at her. She smiled back then turned to watch the passing human parade. We hadn't spoken for a while so I took the opportunity. 'You looking forward to it?'

Fern seemed lost in a blissed-out, après-swim plus too-much-sun hypnosis. 'Huh?'

'You know, the wedding... moving out.'

'It's a pain moving,' Fern said, 'but it's not like we're going to the end of the world. It's Haberfield, land of Sulfaros! You got to love Sulfaros. Remember? Where we got those almond biscuits.'

'Yes. Delicious.' It was difficult to sound sincere.

'So cool. And Pasticceria Papa!'

'You're telling me you're moving to Haberfield because of the cake shops?'

'Why not? You've had that baked ricotta cheesecake?'

'I've had the cheesecake.'

'That cinnamon and sugar on the pastry top? How yum is that? I love Haberfield! And it's not like we have to move schools or anything drastic. And I get to take Nuri. You know Simone's given him to me? Isn't that excellent?'

'Nureyev is the lucky one.' Then I couldn't help myself; I had to know. I asked her, 'What do you think about your mum and Guido?'

'Yeah, that's cool.' She looked at me, suddenly alert, the après-swim dropping and a daughter's protective instinct kicking in. 'Isn't it?'

'Of course, everyone should be allowed to find their happiness, but...'

'But what?'

'I worry about Vionella.'

'Vionella? Why?'

'Well, Vionella and Guido were...'

'She died, Connie... ages ago.'

'But she's never far from the surface, is she? Maybe it's more to do with her than them. Know what I mean?'

'No. Not at all. Mum's happy. She deserves to be happy. What's up with that? I'm going to help her choose shoes and jewellery and do her hair on the big day and wish her love and loads of luck. Aren't you, Connie? Don't you want to help her, too?'

'Of course I do. But what about you? You don't need to be moved across town, especially at your age.'

'Connie, I'm fourteen. I'm not a child.'

'Exactly the age where you need stability. You've got exams coming up and all that academic stress...'

'We've got Mum, Connie. She's stable. I don't know what you're trying to do but please stop?' She stood up. 'I'd better get Leaf.'

I watched her go to her brother and his friends. Something leaden was growing in my head. They were leaving me and they didn't care. I would have to get that through my thick skull. That something leaden was probably my just desserts.

~~~~~

Find out a skull missing its mandible is called a cranium. Burn and crush into ash. A cranium is a bowl, holding the slurry of grey brain matter safe. A cranium holds the windows to the soul. Cranium is the carrier of the mind. Skulls can get fractured. Can get shaken and cause concussion of the brain. Not percussion, although vocal skills could not resonate without a skull. Rather, it is those sinuses, huge in an elephant or giraffe, which help to keep our heads light. As time goes on I feel more and more light-headed. Skulls can be unearthed to tell forensic stories. Skulls are meaningless unless attached to a life.

~~~~~

Never wanted to be present at the birth of any of Jude's children... other than Peter's, of course. The name Peter means rock or stone. Even in the process of giving birth I was creating stoneware. Peter is not, however, a rock. He is an all too fallible human being. He is finding out what being a father really means. And so it goes, onwards and forever, the tragedy of continual human reproduction: endless, endless babies and not enough death.

~~~~~

Electricity, chemical reactions, everything, truly everything that has ever gone into it, are the things that make a brain. Incredible percentage of what we become is learned when we are babies. In order for babies to understand other humans, and to walk, speak and cope with the business of digestion, babies have to develop their brains.

Babies and little children obviously need food, security and comfort. And without doubt they need stimulation of their brains. Almost all the human brain has unfurled by the age of seven. Yet it is during this early childhood period that parents think it's okay to leave their munchkins with someone else, someone paid just a few dollars an hour, in the hope they will motivate their child together with nine other infants they must look after. This is the future of our society. This is how we develop our citizens. Desirable, cheap childcare may have unforeseen consequences.

In the brain, neurons fire off and information pathways develop, form a groove or are pruned. It matters, grey matter. It is the future of our species and it's still largely unexplored. The last frontier may well be the frontal lobe. Maybe we should take better care of it in its infancy?

~~~~~

I concentrated on my new sculpture, a woman bending over backwards. She formed a bridge over a small child who was curled into a foetal position.

Zita appeared at the studio door. Her black hair was whipped into a frenzy. 'Constantia, you'd better see this.'

'What?'

'On the TV. They're bombing Baghdad.'

She left. I stared at my clay. I did know. I had turned the radio off after they started broadcasting Operation Desert Fox. I found it too harrowing. We were all aware of Clinton's posturing around Iraq's supposed weapons of mass destruction but he'd managed to avoid violence until now. I covered the human bridge with wet towels and plastic sheeting and washed my hands. I grabbed my Aristophanes hand cream to take with me.

I massaged my dry fingers as I sat in Zita's apartment watching a lethal fireworks display unfold on CNN. Fern turned a worried face towards her mum. 'What if they hit some biological weapon?'

'They're going for a whole lot more than that,' said Leaf. 'They're bombing police and airfields and heaps of stuff.'

'But what if they release some germ?'

'It's got more to do with Monica than Saddam,' said Zita.

A green flare streaked across the television screen. It was the same green as the curtains in Zita's bedroom.

'You don't believe Saddam Hussein has weapons of mass destruction?' I asked her.

'Clearly, Clinton would rather be seen as a big, powerful warlord than the lying, semen-spilling arsehole that he is.'

'Warlords are not arseholes?'

'I'm not American. Of course they're arseholes.'

'Poor civilians,' said Fern, watching eerie explosions rock the once beautiful city. They looked like fireworks flashing over Disney castle.

'They're not aiming for civilians,' said Leaf.

'Politicians never do,' said Zita.

'Is this going to be another world war?' Fern asked. She turned her frowning, worried face in my direction.

'I really hope not,' I said.

'But we can't tell,' said Leaf. 'It could be. It could be World War III and we wouldn't have a choice, would we? We'd have to live with whatever the big, rich, fat-cat politicians decide is the best way to save their bogus skins, wouldn't we?'

'We've got to hope,' said Fern. 'That's what we've got. We've got hope.'

I reassured them. 'They're not going to destroy the whole place. Did you hear Madeleine Albright say they were degrading Iraq's ability to manufacture weapons of mass destruction?'

'When Clinton was already degrading himself,' said Zita.

We watched the television in sadness. Leaf said, 'Why do people make stupid promises they can't keep?'

Zita and I exchanged a shrug. What could we say? We couldn't lie to them, could we? That would make us as bad as Clinton and he'd just been impeached by the House of Representatives for lying about making love to Monica. As if that would change the way a man ran a country.

~~~~~

Wordsworth had an illegitimate child, Caroline, born in France in 1792. Because of the Reign of Terror in the 1790s, Wordsworth was forced to return to England shortly after the birth and did not see his daughter again for nearly ten years. Meanwhile, he married and had another family.

Rufus was born in the Lake District and grew up with the ghost of Wordsworth, even following him to Cambridge. Was Simone simply remembering Rufus as we devised the exhibition titles? Or was she issuing a call for help? A signal from afar?

Had they been kept apart because of the Reign of Terror, or was that yet to come?

Terror. Where does that come from? Catastrophe? Critical endangerment? Cataclysms? Whoever holds the terror makes the rules.

Chapter 17

Wind chimes

I went to see Jude in the Biology Department. Standing at his open office door, I could see he was immersed in a document displayed on his computer monitor. His hands grasped through his hair. He frowned as he scrolled. He shook his head as if in disbelief. When I tapped on the door, he looked up, turned his head towards the sound, but did not appear to see me. It took time for him to focus on my presence, as if he were surfacing from diving in a deep lake. He looked as if he were unsuccessfully clinging to a thought.

I said, 'We need to talk.' He appeared bemused, perhaps wondering why I was here, what I could possibly want to talk about.

Then he held up his hand and nodded a silent agreement. 'Not here.' He picked up his keys and wallet. 'We'll walk. I need some air anyway.'

We went outside into the rumble of university traffic. A plastic bag filled with breeze sailed skittishly along the road, lifted, then soared up and over a building. We rambled around the uni talking about Christmas and Balmain and Queenie. She'd always been there for her kids in that tiny house. She'd be the first to yell or hit out with a wooden spoon if they ate all the bread while she wasn't looking or if they came home drunk, but she loved them all. She'd lie down and die for them and that's what she did in the end. I told him, 'I'm worried.'

'Aren't you always?'

'About the kids.'

'You must have known it wouldn't last, Connie,' he said. 'You're too romantic.'

'What's romantic about it? It's practical. The kids need to be together. They need to grow up with their brothers and sisters… and their father.' I looked at him sidelong as we walked. He was focused on the footpath in front of him.

After a minute he glanced up at me, then looked down again. 'They have. They do know me. And each other. They are grown-up, Connie.'

'Not Emma. Not Francis. Not Leaf or Fern, actually. They all need you.'

'The mothers have lives of their own. You know that, Con. I can't be a husband to either of them, much less you.'

'You are husband to me.'

'Oh, Connie, for God's sake, you wouldn't let me. We've been divorced for more than twenty years. Our marriage no longer exists. Not in law, not in the eyes of the church… nowhere. I've been a father to your child and that's about as far as I go with you women. I'm no good at supporting any of you. You don't need me. I'm not allowed to love any of you. What's the point, Connie? Tell me that.'

'Please, Jude,' I said. 'Can't you talk to them?'

'What the hell do you think they want to hear? "Zita, come on love. Stay. For the good of the kids." Is that what you want me to say? And, "You too, Simone. It's for the kids' sake." Oh, yes, I can see them agreeing straightaway.'

'They might. There's a chance. Have you ever asked?'

Jude came to a stop, turned to me and said, in a deeper, searching voice, 'Do we know they're definite? Both of them?' He looked around the quadrangle, as if he'd heard something that interested him. Perhaps it was echoes from 1960 he heard—philosophy students arguing about the lack of freedom in the patriarchal capitalist systems imposed on their lives. He knew as well as I that Zita and Simone were as much a part of our family as Peter.

'Yes,' I said, 'it's definite.'

Jude stuck out his bottom lip as he considered this. 'Listen, Connie. This is what I believe. People have to do what they can to grab any bit of happiness. You know that. You're the one who's been telling me that for years. It's your reasoning. I listened to you then because I promised to love and honour you all the days of my life and you know I always will.'

'You're not helping. Can't you at least make an effort? Talk to Simone?'

'If you love someone, set them free.'

'Oh, you are maddening…'

'It's what you always told me.'

'Maybe there are different kinds of love.'

'You! It's you.' Pointing at me. 'You're the one who doesn't want to let the kids go.'

He didn't understand. 'Jude, face facts. He's British. You'll have to travel to bloody England to see them.'

'So I'll travel to bloody old England. Maybe we'll cut a deal. Maybe he can send them over for holidays or something. I'm no gaoler, Connie. They have to do what they need to do.'

'But what about the kids?'

'They're not babies.'

'Is that what this is all about? Babies? Maybe you should stop and have a long, hard think about Charlotte's baby.'

'What are you saying?'

'Maybe things are more complicated than you know.'

'Things couldn't possibly be more complicated.' He paused for a moment before asking again. 'Could they?'

'Maybe your children have formed their own opinions about your choices, about your life. Maybe they are more proactive than you think. Maybe one of your children has upset your little applecart and tipped it right over.'

I had said too much. I wished I could vacuum those stupid words right back inside.

Jude stared at me. I turned and walked away, leaving him standing in the quad. He called to me but I kept walking, really quickly. Then I broke into a run.

~~~~~

The Wallam froglet, *Crinia tinnula,* is a tiny pale creature. It's found in acid paperbark swamps. It has a white back with black flecks. Belly is white on light brown with darker splotches. There's a line of white specks down the middle of its throat. This frog is also called the tinkling froglet. It has a call that sounds like a small bell tinkling. If you believe in frogs, then clap your hands! Clap, why don't you?

Want wind chimes to tinkle. Pottery chimes can sound more like clacking as they blow against each other. Don't want clacking. Each part of the chime is a long thin curl, twisted and strange, like a John Olsen squiggle. Each has a different tone.

Treat the clay as if making multi-coloured toffees in Brighton Rock. Cut a slice from a slab of layered, coloured clays. Flick the slice and roll it again into thin sheets. Cut and alter the final shape by hand.

Each different form is a challenge. Dredge my memories for ways to make these things. All the processes, everything I've ever tried, I've resurrected. My career is encapsulated in this collection. I farewell my own work history as the pieces gather together. My understanding of pottery culminates in this studio. All my working knowledge of clay is here.

~~~~~

The strange shell-shape of a human ear seems implausible. How can it capture noise? Compared to the ears of a bat or a dog, human wrinkled flabs lie flat against our head. How do we ever hear anything?

The human ear contains our smallest bones. The bones of the tinkling froglet are even smaller.

I decorate each Olsen-esque strip with clay slip. Each clay squiggle has a line of white dots down the middle like a tinkling froglet.

Do frogs have ears? Mostly. Wallum froglets have ears or they wouldn't bother tinkling at each other, would they?

Frogs don't have an external ear. Their eardrums are fully exposed and smooth. A frog's eardrum is called a tympanum and is located just behind each eye. Each species of frog has a different size, shape and placement of the tympanum.

Earless frogs are not deaf. According to his notes, Jude assumes the bones in the skull must transmit sound by resonance.

Humans have evolved deep protection for hearing. But do we listen?

~~~~~

When Fern did a talk about animal rights at school, her classmates were horrified. She told them what happened to horses when they'd finished their limited racing careers, how pigs were bred, and where chickens were kept. The kids begged her, saying things like, *don't tell me*, and *I don't want to have to think about it*. They all said they didn't want to hear any more about experimental animals, shark fins or dog fighting.

When there's something rotten in the state of Denmark, it stems from poison in the ear of a king.

Jude used to listen to me. Back in the day.

~~~~~

Peter came early to help. He handed me his present, which was wrapped in pink tissue paper, before he'd even got in the door. I kissed him and said, 'Merry Christmas, darling.'

In an effort to make the place look festive, I'd thrown tinsel over the olive tree and brought out all the kids' early pottery efforts. Some of them dated way back, even to Peter's first attempts. There were little monsters and trees and fighting machines and indeterminable blobs all shiny with glaze arranged around the roof garden in nooks and crannies, in circles and one after the other in long trains. There was history there, a ceramic story of families born, blended and raised together.

I opened the champers and half-filled two flutes. 'To us.'

'Merry Christmas,' he said, and we raised our glasses.

The champagne was ridiculously expensive but delicious... light, fragrant and tasting of toast. The tiny bubbles winked hysterically at the brim as they expired. 'Doesn't get much better than this, does it darling?'

'Mum. You do realise? This will be the last...'

'Not now, darling. Can we try to get through the day without analysing the future?'

Peter's present to me was a set of Egyptian cotton pillowslips, which I loved. My present to Peter was socks—because I'm a mother—and a new watch that could be taken to depths of a hundred feet.

'But I don't dive,' he said.

'Not yet. But you never know.'

We put nibbles in little bowls, laid out Christmassy table napkins, and arranged the presents. It was companionable. It would never be like this again. It would be our last Christmas together. I took another swig of blissful Champagne. I thought I'd better make the most of it.

~~~~~

Did I abandon them? No, no, I reassure myself. It was them. They left me. It was Simone: she went first. Then Zita: she's the one I miss the most. She's supposed to be my friend. She's not even phoned though she still lives in the same city. I dare not call her. I have not spoken to her kids for fear they would think me trying to influence them. Why can't she call me? Why can't she let me know those past few years were not a figment? Why? When I thought she was my sister! Why has she left me so alone? Why? Why, God? Why have you abandoned me?

Crumple onto the studio floor. Lie in the clay dust. Everything settles. The whirling slows. Everything is still. I see under the bench. See dust. See chunks of clay. Stone settles in my gut. There is a piece of cloth. It is his white handkerchief. It is scrunched into a ball. I must have dropped it. Lie with the ground cool under my cheek. Lie curled into foetus shape. Lie still. Lie stagnant. Fade away.

I hear a car pull up. The cogs of my brain whir. My eyes widen. I am awake. I drive to the front of my brain. I drive to the front of my optic nerve. My gut tightens. My back energises. I am standing. I have sprung to my feet. I'm not sure how long it took. Feels like no time. I can move again after weeks of sluggish drag. Am spritely. Slap on a smile… try it on for size. Been a long time since I've smiled. Move the smile around my mouth. Mouth is dry. Teeth stick to the inside of the smile. Does not feel real. Go quickly out of the studio. I see. I know. Do not have to look. Check mentally with my super-efficient, whirring brain. What is visible on the bench? Nothing is obvious. Nothing recognisable. My heartbeat is strong, fast.

Move out through the doorway. See Peter. He's getting out of his car. He slams the door and looks around to see me and my smile is real. He looks dishevelled. Feel relieved to see the muddleheaded wombat. He must be. He is sleep-deprived with that new baby. He is bleary. He hugs me. He is tall. We stand in embrace. I rest there. I think he is resting, too. We lean together for strength. He laughs and picks some clay from my hair. He needs some clothes. We will go to his flat. I feel like I've been given a reprieve. I've been so careless. I've had no need to care. So he's not forgotten me although his main purpose is to gather clothes to take back to Charlotte's place. He makes me tea. In his small bathroom I wash the clay from my hands and face. The flat smells musty. The shower curtain is mouldy.

I open the window. We both want fresh air. We've been missing the air. We bring our tea out to the sunshine. We sit on stools in the driveway. I feel myself relaxing in the warm light. He tells me about Betty—she is adorable, growing, putting on weight. She knows him. She smiles at him. I should come and see them. They should bring her to see me. I will go there. I say I will. I want to see her. Soon. I ask about Charlotte—she is well, manages to sleep. Peter will have to go back to work soon. They've been so lucky to have this first three months together. He loves them. He feels at home there. He presses me to make a date; to come and see them all. I will. I should. I say I have to check my calendar. I sit in the sun outside his door while he packs shirts into a bag marked with the insignia of his university. Then he leaves. After I have finished waving and the car is gone, I know I cannot give up. I give up giving up. I get back to work. Soon there is clay on my hands again.

~~~~~

In ancient Egypt, a ram-headed god called Khum made pottery on a wheel. He made the world. He made the gods and then he made humans. He used the fertile soil of the Nile.

The potter god, Khum, moulded the body and soul of children before birth. He was the husband of Hequet, the frog goddess, who gave children the breath of life.

In my own life, the frog must represent Jude. Perhaps that's why he had such a strong urge to reproduce. Clearly then, in parallel, I am the potter god. Here we are again with strange echoes from mythology weaving through our lives.

Frogs and fecundity, babies and tadpoles: connections now severed as the quantity of humans overtakes and surpasses all other living things. Is that what is meant by the human race? We're winning. God save us.

~~~~~

We made a small shopping troupe down to the fish market. Francis was aware of everything—every colour, every smell, and the cacophony of it all. He moved toward things as he became aware of them, while Emma clung to my side, affronted by that same palette of sense bombardment.

232

The wet, busy sounds of the harbour slapped under the wharf, ice dropped with industrial crashes, and male-shouting sales energy refracted off the metallic fish gleaming under white lights. Everything mixed together with a strident yell of odours. I found prawns and oysters and then peeled Emma from my side to get her to focus on what I had to say. 'Are you ready for fish and chips, or shall we sushi?'

'No!' shouted Emma as if in distress. 'No! Please, Connie. We have to go. We'll be late to meet Mummy and Rufus and you know she doesn't like it if we're late.'

Sadly for Emma, Francis was already eyeing off chips, so Emma had to sulk. She tagged along while we gathered sustenance from the food and drink providers and sat down outside on the only available table. It was wobbly so I wedged a folded-up napkin under one of the grubby legs. I had a coffee with a heart shape swirled on top, while they crunched chips and the seagulls counted the moments. 'What about Rufus?' I asked them.

'He's giving me a pony,' announced Emma, matter-of-factly.

'He is not! You're making that up.' Francis stood, wandered toward the water, looking out, perhaps to the horizon, perhaps to the future, perhaps wanting to leave Sydney as soon as possible.

'He is so too. What would you know? You just go along with everyone.' Francis kept his back towards Emma. She gave up trying to reach him so she turned back to me. 'I'll be going to a really good school where we don't have to wear uniforms, just really nice clothes, and Rufus said he'll buy us anything we need and then I'll go to finishing school so I can speak French and German and be really rich and have lots of friends…'

'Wouldn't you rather stay here?' I asked.

'Oh, I don't think so.' She slung her hair with a thrilling air of importance. 'I mean, for instance, would I still get a pony?'

'I don't know about a pony but at least you'd still have your friends. Chantelle? Miranda?'

'I don't really like those girls anymore. All they think about is themselves.'

'What do you think about Simone and Rufus?'

'Actually, they're a bit annoying because they only talk to each other and it's difficult for them to understand I have needs as well. I mean, if I don't get enough attention I might have to behave badly in order for them to take notice of me.'

Such guile took me aback, even from Emma. I spooned the rest of my latte from the polystyrene cup. Francis, having finished his chips, came back to sit at the table and looked at me with an eerie intensity. 'But you'll write, won't you?'

I smiled at him. 'Of course.'

'There are lots of ways we can keep in touch, Connie. The world is getting smaller. You could get a computer. Peter could help you with the technology: email and messaging and Skype. You could do it.'

'I'm not worried about technology, Francis, I'm worried about you. I'm worried about your family. I want to see you as you grow up. I don't know what sort of life you'll be living in London; I can't imagine it.'

Emma wiped her mouth carefully with a paper napkin, pursing her lips into an adult lipstick moue. 'Perhaps you'll forget us. I think I might be too busy to think about you much.'

Francis said, 'Emma! That's a nasty thing to say.'

'Don't worry, Francis. She doesn't know what she's saying.'

'Oh, yes I do, and I know you're trying to make us upset with Rufus so it will be more difficult for Mummy.'

'That's not right…'

'It is, and Mummy said she can't wait to get out of your clutches.'

Francis said, 'Emma!' He sounded shocked that the girl could be so transgressive, more shocked than I was!

I said, 'Did she?'

'Yes. She thinks you're an old maid grieving over a dead man.'

'Emma! Shut up, why don't you?'

'Because I'm saying the truth. That's all. Connie knows that, don't you, Connie? She wants to know the truth about Mummy and Rufus and I'm telling her, just like she wants.'

The sun crashed into smithereens over the surface of the harbour. I reached for my sunglasses. Just what I wanted. Be careful. What I wished for. My polarised sunglasses were useless. Piercing water-reflected light lacerated me.

Chapter 18

Oil burner

It was a little after ten on a Wednesday night. I was cleaning my teeth in the bathroom when I thought I heard a polite knock at the door. I stood, uncertain for a moment, looking at myself in the mirror. I was frothing at the mouth. But there it was again so I went to the door and there was Fern. She appeared sober—her eyes were bright and her posture straight—but there was no getting away from the fantastic fragrance surrounding her. It was like a force field. More than an aura, the mishmash of odours gave the impression that a bull had crashed through a perfume shop and rushed in through my door. She smelt incredible. Despite the pungency of my toothpaste foam, her reek was thick enough to chew. 'Here for a shower?'

'If you can cope with it,' she said. 'I won't stay long.'

'Sure,' I said and gestured her inside to the kitchen. Then I went to spit and rinse. Back in the kitchen, I turned on the light over the stove. 'Hot chocolate?'

'You just brushed your teeth.'

'For you.'

'Not if you're not.'

'I'll have a peppermint tea. So, tell me; what's the smell?'

'Emma.'

'What now?'

'She mixed up Simone's perfumes in a plastic cup. The place stinks.'

'So do you!'

'Thanks.' Fern rolled her eyes. 'Simone is going to kill her.'

'She might not mind.'

'Because of lovey-dovey Rufus?'

'Maybe.'

'Why can't Francis look after her?'

'He does, but as you know, Emma can be a handful at the best of times. Nice to share the burden, don't you think?' I opened the cupboard and found a packet of chocolate digestive biscuits, well within the use-by-date. 'Hungry?'

Fern took the biscuits. I considered putting them on a plate but it was too late for formalities. She said, 'Couldn't they just stay in and watch a video for once?'

I smiled at her. If only everyone did what we wanted. I finished stirring hot milk into Fern's mug, she took the armchair, and I rearranged the cushions on the couch. I dunked a peppermint teabag in my mug, leaving it there until it became toothpaste strong.

Fern ripped open the biscuit packet with her teeth and took three before offering the packet to me. I waved it away. 'Pretty good training, babysitting.'

'What for? Torture?' We both laughed.

'Does your school teach parenting?'

'We have Health, but that's mainly about sex and drugs.'

'Handy information.'

'Yeah, know your product.'

'What I meant was, most of you girls will eventually have children.'

There was that roll of the eyes again. 'I guess so.'

'What better training than babysitting?'

'It's not the same. I'm not going to have an Emma.'

'You're half-sisters. You do share the same genes.'

'Don't remind me.'

'I was in the supermarket queue once encouraging Leaf and Peter to stay with me—which they didn't want to do—and to help unpack and stop fighting over the chips. You were sitting in the trolley crying because I wouldn't buy the sweets at the counter. The woman standing behind us reassured me. She told me you just have to keep doing head counts. I asked her how many kids she had. She said, "Twelve!"'

'OMG! Twelve! What a nightmare!'

'I said, "You have to be a saint." She said, "No, it's easy. The big ones look after the little ones."'

'Until one gets run over or something!'

'Peter used to look after you,' I reminded her. 'I loved having you around when you were little. Some women do. Love it. Children. Some women just drift into it and try to cope. But I'll tell you something for nothing: I think there are some women who should never have kids.'

'And some men.'

'True enough. Some people are just miserable. Hate every minute. What do you think? Do you want kids?'

'I'm too young. I don't want to think about it.'

'Don't let motherhood creep up on you. Make the choices early. Actually, what am I saying? Look at me! Nothing ever goes the way I plan.'

Fern rose and came to sit beside me on the couch. She patted me gently on the arm. She brought the chocolate biscuits with her. The smell of perfume-chaos was overwhelming.

'Don't listen to me babble on. I don't have all the answers, Fern.'

'But you do have the problems.' That was funny, but as our chuckles faded, I began to think about the family splitting up, the children leaving me.

'Sometimes I think that maybe I'm the problem,' I said.

Fern shook her head and smiled at me. 'You're not a problem. I'm the one who stinks. You know what? I think I'd better go hop in the shower.'

I didn't argue. She really did smell. That Emma! Mixing up trouble in a plastic cup.

~~~~~

Then, because time always passes, New Year's Eve collapsed upon us. We were soon to be in the last year of the nineties… the penultimate year. A new millennium was approaching. The gathering dusk felt warm and oppressive. Although Prince had the song of the moment, Leaf had recently discovered ACDC and we were *Burning Alive*, again and again.

I had sparklers for everyone. We'd planned a mini New Year celebration for Emma, fearing her temper would not be improved by having to wait till midnight to see fireworks. Simone planned to put her to bed about ten.

Farewell to 1998 and on with the New Year, the last of this millennium. Peter was strung out on tenterhooks, maybe concerned with the impending baby, whilst Jude looked haunted, possibly by Charlotte or, more likely I now realised, by millions of dying frogs.

Guido and Zita calmly arranged antipasto platters and chatted about their new living arrangements. Fern played an animal card-game with Emma. Francis was inside, reading *Tomorrow when the war began*. Jude talked family catch-up with his sister, Stella, by the olive tree. I don't think he mentioned Charlotte. Some things the rest of his family didn't need to know. I put a bowl of guacamole next to the corn chips on the table. 'Anything I can do?' Jude asked.

I shook my head. 'All done, I think.'

Emma appeared in the doorway just as Leaf and ACDC encouraged us to believe *This house is on fire*. 'I think I should have my sparklers if you don't mind, Connie. It's nearly time for me to go to bed.'

I raised my palms in supplication as ACDC continued their on-slaught on my eardrums. Fern's face brightened as though she had been waiting for the merest reason to argue with Leaf. She went into combat mode, insisting on listening to *Change* by Marcia Hines. Leaf held a Radio Birdman CD over her head. Even though I agreed with Fern that none of us needed to hear *Burn my eye* again for a while, I didn't want to hang around to debate the matter.

I held my glass tightly. It was more than a premonition. I felt afraid. Was it too much champagne? Everyone chatted and blurred and moved too fast. I'd never be able to keep up. I went to the kitchen in search of matches. After the shock of finding Zita and Guido, I'd made sure to pick some up from the supermarket this time. I knew exactly where they would be, on the kitchen bench and I moved confidently to fetch them. But I should have learned by now. For there in the kitchen were Simone and Rufus, intertwined. Is this why matches were tied up with matchmaking?

Rufus was a big, handsome, sandy-haired fellow. He might have been a rugby player with that thick neck and tall arrogance. I knew he was a specialist in skin disorders. His hand lay firm on Simone's shoulder and his present of the gold and jade bracelet glinted on her wrist. Rufus stroked her hair and turned her face towards him for a kiss. Sensing public interest, she lightly shook him off. No kissing in front of the family. She flashed me an amused glance and steered him out towards the roof garden.

I took the matches from the bench and went back outside to give the youngsters a few sparklers to start them off. Fern and Leaf had discovered years before that when you pressed two sparklers together, they fused and burned from the middle out, leading to the creation of interesting shapes.

The kids clustered together and found primal energy in fire. They laughed as their sparklers became a fizz of white heat, then they carved out their names in the darkness. They smiled as they stared out into the light, their bright-edged faces carved like new moons.

Standing behind Simone and Rufus, Jude watched his children cavorting. Rufus put an arm around Simone solicitously and the light flickered across Jude's face. He watched as Emma cried out, 'Look at me!' He watched Francis collect dead sparkler sticks and place them in the bucket of Bondi Beach sand. Jude turned his attention to Rufus and Simone. I couldn't begin to guess what he was feeling. His face was blank as another man separated him from his children and he could do nothing about it. I felt pity for him yet was surprised at his apparent acquiescence.

When I think back, Jude had shown no concern when his wives witnessed each replace the next in the list of serial monogamy, so perhaps he found some justice in the rebalance. I could not see it. This was different. The wives had worked together, in the same place, to make a family, whereas this new man would take our children away. Our tribe would be broken up. How was that constructive?

Jude might have had similar thoughts, yet watched impassively. I wanted him to do something... anything. I willed it. I pushed my extrasensory perception out through the smell of burnt sparkler and imagined him acting to protect his children. Could he fight Rufus? Duelling was out of the question, sadly, and I couldn't imagine Jude getting drunk and pushing the ex-rugby player around. Peter was a lawyer. Jude could get advice. Couldn't he refuse to sign their passport applications? Couldn't he at least argue with the man? He did nothing.

Simone took Emma's hand when the sparklers had run out and kissed her on the top of her head. She said, 'Say good-night to everyone, darling, and Happy New Year.' Emma obliged, going to each of us in turn and parroting, 'Happy New Year'.

When Emma came to Jude, he got down on his knees and hugged her. 'Happy New Year, my darling girl, and very, very good luck for the future.'

Surprisingly, Emma kissed her dad politely on the cheek, perhaps overwhelmed by his emotion, or perhaps Simone had bribed her with a pony, or a trip to Disneyland, or tickets to the circus, or some preciousness beyond my imagination. Then Emma followed her mother obediently downstairs. Rufus joined them.

Jude turned to Francis and put his hand on the boy's head. 'Don't think I'll be able to do that next year, mate... you'll be too tall.' Of course he wouldn't be able to. Francis wouldn't be in the same country.

Jude smoothed the curly hair from Francis' face then bent to kiss him on both cheeks. Straightening again, he said, 'Happy New Year, Mate.'

Francis replied, 'Happy New Year, Dad.'

I gave Francis a spare packet of sparklers that Emma hadn't needed to know about. Leaf and Fern joined him in fusing and burning, testing how many they could combine in one flame, deliberate care in their actions, childish delight barely concealed by teenage superiority. The year before, Leaf had manufactured sparkler bombs for his own entertainment and to raise our blood pressure. I didn't think he would do that again but one could never be sure where the next impulse would take that young Leaf.

I leaned against the rampart wall as if we were on board a ship. I closed my eyes and let the sea breeze and the sound of the park leaves in the wind conspire with my fantasy. I wasn't going anywhere. When I opened my eyes I found myself hidden by the large pots of lemon and olive trees, I watched the treetops glisten with reflected light while half keeping an eye on the sparkler experiments. The air smelled of gunpowder.

Simone arrived back on the roof, her green and gold Wonder Woman armband glittering. She poured another glass of champagne and raised the tulip to Jude, a cheeky twinkle in her eye and a sideways tilt to her head. Jude put his hand on her elbow and steered her closer to the wall, nearer my hideout. Did he realise I was there? Had he received the message I'd sent by ESP? They spoke intently. I hoped I was about to witness some action. Here we go... he's going to insist those kids stay in the country. Good on him.

Simone removed her elbow from his control but turned to listen. He said quietly, 'You do know what you're doing?'

'Jude, come on!' Simone grinned at him. 'It's a party. Relax for once in your life. Can we talk about this later?'

'She's my kid, Simone.'

'He's just reading her a story. I think you should calm down.'

'Simone, have you decided or not?'

'Are you inquiring about my intentions, or Rufus's?'

'I'm hoping for a straight answer.'

'That's the problem.' She laughed. 'There are no straight answers... you know that. It's been complicated for years, ever since you first met me.' Her hands told the dance of her story. 'Hasn't it all been higgledy-piggledy like a bird's nest? We're all stuck full of sticks and twigs, bits of wool and hair, strings and feathers and old chocolate wrappers! I don't know what's going to happen any more than the next person. I know what I hope might happen.' Simone stared blandly at Jude and added, 'But I've been disappointed before.'

He looked at her intently, as if struggling to understand. 'I always tried to make you...'

'Don't say, happy.' Her voice hardened. 'I couldn't stand it.'

'Maybe not, but I did try to look after you and the babies.'

'Yes! Yes, of course you did. I was grateful, you know that. But things have to change.' She took a deep breath. 'Jude, there are things...'

Jude said harshly, 'I don't want to hear any more.' Then, perhaps fearing a confession, his tone became placating. 'Simone...' He paused. They stared at each other, both with more to say, apparently about to reveal something. It was hard to tell if neither wanted to say goodbye or if they simply didn't want to burn bridges. This was surprising. There seemed to be more between them than I had believed possible. Then Jude said, in a rush, perhaps to prevent any unbearable revelations, 'I hope your resolutions come true this year.'

'So do I. Have you made any?'

'I just want to be a better father.'

'Lovely.' Simone smiled, the spell broken. 'I'll go see what's happening.'

'Let me.'

'No, Jude, I'll go.' She went back into the flat and Jude stared after her. So, there had been no action. My ESP had not reached him.

A breeze ruffled Jude's hair. The light glinted off his skull. I could see skin under his thinning hair. I'd never seen that before.

After the official Sydney Harbour fireworks had drifted away, we returned to our real lives. 1999 was nearly an hour old when Rufus brought in another pile of plates and cutlery and balanced them precariously by the sink. 'Anything to go out?'

I looked up at him from the suds. 'I think there's enough food out there for the moment.'

'What about a dry tea-towel?' He found one even as he spoke and we stood, companionably, me with my hands in the sink, he with his gold cufflinks glaring rather too orange next to the yellow wattle emblems on the tea-towel. 'Are you going to be all right now, Connie?' he asked.

I laughed at him, in shallow party mode. 'Awright? As in 'awright, sheila?'

He frowned, terribly British. 'I beg your pardon?'

I no longer felt in party mode. I tried to cover my discomfort. 'Just an Aussie expression. Sorry. You heard of Strine? As in Australian slang?'

Rufus looked at me as if I'd spoken to him in Mandarin or turned into a King Parrot. There was no trace of understanding in his expression.

I continued, trying to cover my discomfort, 'No? Ah, well… yes, I'm okay. You?'

Rufus was essential, clipped, and straightforward. Serious. 'You didn't trust her, to start with.'

Too right I didn't trust Simone when I first met her, and now I trusted her even less. As Rufus appeared to be in love with her, I decided the less I said the better. 'No.'

'That explains it, then.' He seemed relieved. 'Do you now?'

Nope! I wasn't going to discuss her. I said, 'Could you pass me those plates, please?' and indicated by inclining my head which plates I meant.

As he picked up the stack and loaded them into the sink, he said, 'You don't wear gloves?'

'No.' I looked at him, bemused that a man could care about dishpan hands. Then I remembered the detective's report. 'Is that the dermatologist in you?'

'Can't help it, I'm afraid.'

Changing the subject, again using information supplied by the Big Bad Banksia man, I said, 'I suppose you can support them in the manner in which Simone...'

'... has become accustomed? Indeed, as you very well know.'

I realised how he knew. 'Your hired gun spotted my hired gun?'

'Same outfit, more money.'

'Bastard!'

'I would have told you. You only had to ask. Come and visit, Connie. Meet my wife. You'll like her.'

'I only wanted...'

'Yar?'

'For them to be safe.'

'Same here.'

'Do you have to take them?'

'Yar, Connie, I really do. My work is in London. I'm needed there. The children will like it, honestly they will. I promise to do my utmost to make sure they settle quickly and lead fulfilling lives.'

'Can't you just take Simone?'

'Do you really think that's possible?' He looked at me seriously, considering my suggestion. Then he decided. 'Unthinkable.' He turned and leaned against the bench, tea-towel forgotten. He was so obviously making an effort—taking the time to befriend me, taking me into his confidence—I felt quite touched. 'I want a family around me, Connie. More than I can say. I knew she was pregnant when she left England, but I simply couldn't cope with that sort of responsibility then. I was in love with a beautiful ballerina, the toast of the ballet world. We went to opening nights, to clubs and soirées and we had our photographs in *Tatler* and *Hello!* It was all tremendous fun. Babies didn't fit into all that. Then Simone disappeared, Lady Diana crashed; everything crashed. The social world simply didn't whirl anymore. I found solace with Beth, who became my wife. When it became clear she could not have a child, she took on more duties in Parliament. She was never at home any more and I became a widower to politics. So when I read of your exhibition, I guessed Simone must be here. Who else would use Wordsworth in this day and age? Who else would know of Wordsworth's child? I had to find her, Connie. I had to have my family with me. Surely you of all people must understand that?'

I was completely confused. Simone, pregnant when she left England? She'd had one miscarriage; maybe she'd had another. What had Wordsworth got to do with it? I suppose I should've stopped scrubbing the lasagne dish and charged in with more questions, but I couldn't cope with the information and didn't want it to be my business anyway. So I had nothing further to say to him. I was busy, cleaning up, when he left the kitchen. The water in the sink was greasy and there were no bubbles left.

~~~~~

More than a year before all that, we had been together at Sheryl's funeral. William requested that everyone wear purple at the wake. Zita went out of her way to find purple vegetation and flowers of all kinds. Clusters of New Zealand flax speared up from pots by the door; centrepieces on tables erupted with the daisy shapes of asters; the cone heads of *Echinacea* mingled with ethereal anemones, from palest lilac to deepest violet. There was a wonderful arrangement of purple smoke tree interspersed with fluffy heads of purple fountain grass.

The bright light from the gallery spilled onto the street. A floaty jazz combo coloured the air and people mingled, chattering and sipping their wine or lattes as they remembered good and bad times in Sheryl's Catalina Gallery.

There were speeches and readings. I read Sheryl's favourite poem, *Warning*, by Jenny Joseph, 'When I am an old woman I shall wear purple' but Sheryl, of course, had always worn black and silver. I spoke about her smooth hair always neat in a chignon and her beloved poodles, Turner and Rothko, who would trot along behind her wherever she went. William, wearing an elegant Armani suit (or so Zita told me), delivered a eulogy of sorts, and it was a revelation to most of the audience. As I listened to the story of her life, I could not help but reflect that human beings change so many times during their lives; so many stages we go through, so many transformations—we are always in flux.

Sheryl had been a school child, a daughter, a student, and the betrothed of an American serviceman. Her ex-husband—William's dad, Mike—sent a huge wreath of bright carnations. One of her brothers, Aubrey, presumably there to support William, tended rather to sit and sniff in a corner and drink whisky.

Sheryl came to Greenwich with her parents in her childhood. She was the baby of four children and always wanted to be an artist. She loved sketching, particularly landscapes. The Second World War saw her volunteer for the Red Cross, where she met Mike Richards, a pilot in the night raider Catalina flying boats in the Pacific war theatre. She was captivated by his love of art and on his days off they would wander through the New South Wales Gallery. There were parties and much fun because in those difficult times they were sure everyone was off to the war to die. The two lovers married in a rush before Mike was called back overseas.

Most people I spoke to afterwards didn't know about Sheryl's whirlwind romance and marriage. When William described how

Sheryl had actually boarded the ship taking the other war brides and their babies to America but had escaped down the gangplank at the last minute, his audience gasped. Sheryl, he said, had not been able to leave her mother to care alone for the old curmudgeon; her father, a shell-shocked amputee from the First World War.

William remembered when he was nine years old, asking Sheryl about his dad. She recognised he needed to know about his father. She'd expected it. She told him everything she could, showed him photos and eventually he wrote to him in New York. Following in his own father's footsteps, Mike had become an importer of Italian items; food, furniture and ceramics. He had remarried by then and had two children, a boy and a girl.

Mike and his wife travelled to Sydney in 1956 to introduce their children to William, their half brother, who was fourteen at the time. The kids all wanted to be part of the same family and his wife agreed. Mike invited William to come over to New York when he'd finished school and check out what it was like being an American and see if he liked the family business. Then he sent him to Italy, to Roma, to live with his own parents for a year or two. It was here William's fascination with art grew and he decided to study art history. Mike financed his studies while William lived in Rome and took on his doctorate in Naples. William never came home.

Mike didn't want Sheryl to think he'd stolen her kid away. He knew how much of her life she'd put into raising William and caring for her parents. When he heard that she was studying art history, and interested in buying a gallery, he offered financial assistance. She refused a gift but agreed to a business deal with him as silent partner. Mike saw her independence as reflective of the way she parented William all by herself. Sheryl named the gallery 'Catalina' because of him, and they'd remained good friends.

And so it was that Sheryl became not only my familiar neighbour, but my proper mother, and finally a grand dame of the arts.

William, spoke then of his indecision. He wanted Sheryl's gallery to continue but could not decide how best to go about it. He had an on-going art history business investigating disputed provenances with offices in London and New York and was not sure if he would employ a manager for the gallery or return to Sydney to run Catalina himself.

Later, as William mingled effortlessly with artists, dealers, potential customers and friends alike, I found it difficult to take my eyes from him. I began to feel like a stalker, so turned my attention to my family. Peter and Leela were filling glasses while Leaf, Fern and Francis carried trays of nibbles. Emma clung to Jude.

Although a sad occasion, Simone and I floated through Sheryl's funeral supported, and a little embarrassed, by the hubbub of interest generated by our two exhibitions. It seemed our work was garnering more attention than the event warranted, but as our work had been Sheryl's passion, too, we agreed to talk about it. It seemed as though none of us—florist, photographer or ceramicist—would ever be out of work again.

A lull in questions about our next exhibition gave me a moment to watch my family moving around the gallery. What did Shakespeare give us? Seven ages? I amused myself seeing my loved ones as the seven ages of women. Emma, the baby, insisted on dressing herself and on this occasion had chosen bright purple trousers and frilly skirt. Sheryl would have cheered.

Fern, now a young lady, was not sure at first how to handle the flirting young art students who gathered around her tray of mini bruschetta like bees around orange blossom. But, as the evening wore on, she seemed to grow more comfortable with their attentions and responded with a sashay here and a spicy look there.

Simone strode up to Jude. He'd been holding her handbag while she visited the bathroom to check on her radiance. I don't remember him ever doing that for me. Mind you, I'd never owned a teeny, tiny, ridiculous, spangly thing like that. She kissed him on the lips, lingering and teasing just a bit about his man-bag before she took the bag upon her own arm, removed a small wad of business cards from it and, leaving Jude, handed one to a man in a business suit before moving on, strategically working the room, flashing her pearly whites and thrusting cards at whomever would take one. I thought she was carrying the business aspect too far. What did she think it was, a bloody conference? I felt like stuffing her business cards down her neck.

Zita, her clothes stretched tightly across her abundant chest, was hiding in the kitchen. She was checking out food supplies and making sure rosé decanters were full while giving the children advice about loading trays with tiny spanakopita triangles and mini pizzas.

Then there was me, watching them all through heavy-lensed glasses. Wearing a once-smart cotton dress that was getting a bit too tight around the tummy and a bit loose around the boobs. And finally, there was Sheryl. Sheryl, who died in oblivion. She died in the gallery, of course, nursed faithfully by her son, but she was certainly unconscious.

I took William to the airport the next day. We were polite but we were late, so there was no time for in-depth discussions. We embraced at the entry to Customs but I turned my head when he bent to kiss me. He kissed my cheek. He whispered that he would be back. I held his hand just a moment too long.

When I got home I took off my rings and put them on the window-dow ledge above the sink. I put the plug in place, turned on the hot tap and squirted in lemon-scented dishwashing liquid. I put last night's wine glass, my overnight water glass and my morning juice glass into the sink. I plunged bare hands into lemon soapsuds. The water was too hot and the tiny bubbles burst against my skin. Then, one by one, I curled the glasses around under the running tap and laid them on the wooden drying rack. The glass glinted in the afternoon sun. Water dripped down the edge of the glasses in staccato rivulets. Steel puddles gleamed on the benchtop. The sunshine washed over sink and bench. The window framed a pale glow of wispy clouds. The clouds drifted across the harbour, cast shadows on the treetops, and sprinkled silver over the dark-green leaves.

What does a living frog smell like? Scientists have sniffed vanilla and onion on American frog skins. There's an Australian frog that smells of mustard.

Although frogs breathe mainly through their skin, they do have two nostrils. They are open to the air unless the frog is submerged. A frog's sense of smell is monitored by the front part of the brain, which is also the biggest part. Smell must be particularly important to a frog.

I wonder which object could best celebrate the sensation of nostrils? How best to illustrate the odour of clay?

The advent of the oil burner, a common item in many shops and homes these days, brings tea-light candles into the supermarket and aromatherapy into business. How strange that we should be affected by lavender and bergamot burning in a little cup. Can our mood really be altered by aroma? Some oil burners are stymied by the use of cheap oils. Horrible stuff containing only the barest amount of essence, coats the bottom of the bowl, only industrial cleaner will remove it. As with so many things, it's worth seeking the good oil.

This particular oil burner is not *shibui* at all. It proclaims its vibrancy. Motivated by Art Deco, the folds blend into the sides. The water-holding frog, *Cyclorana platycephala*—pale green racing stripe down the green-brown back, and grainy-white front—inspires the colour.

Water-holding frog is a desert burrowing frog. Squirms into sand backwards. An outer layer of skin protects body from loss of moisture. The back feet are fully webbed. Body expects to encounter water sooner or later. Above ground the frogs absorb water through their skin. Then, in times of need, buried, they store it in their bladders and in pockets around their body.

Normally, the frog's skin would be shed but in times of drought and long burial, builds up until it becomes a hard cocoon. The water-holding frog can stay underground in baked clay for as long as two years. Thirsty Aboriginal travellers might dig up the frog, give it a gentle squeeze, have a drink, and let the frog go unharmed. The water smells fresh.

No one knows how many water-holding frogs are left in existence. Could be thousands hidden in the deserts. That's unlikely but no one can get funding to study them. Jude was encouraging one of his students to take them on, but without success.

If a frog dies in the desert does anyone hear it croak? If there are no frogs left out there, will travellers die of thirst?

Like an oil burner, *Cyclorana platycephala* needs water to survive. Without water, the burner bowl overheats, cracks and breaks.

Essences brought to the baby Jesus included scent as valuable as gold, as I'm sure Chanel would tell you. At the end of the *Camino di Santiago* pilgrimage, in the Cathedral of Saint James, Jude and I watched as the huge incense burner swung the length of the church to cover the stink of unwashed pilgrims. We were not pilgrims then. Just observers. Now I am a pilgrim. I am searching for the way. I know I must keep on. Will I know when I get there? I can only hope.

We don't think about smells, unless they are particularly odious or particularly magnificent: pheromones that bring people together, chemical reactions in mingled sweat, ownership of an armpit, nostrils flaring in desire, all operate under our conscious radar.

~~~~~

Emma sat in my lap. She was smearing avocado over a rice cake with an old round-ended knife. Sun shone on this hot day as we clustered together in the shade of an old Moreton Bay fig at Nielson Park. Those of us fresh from swimming wore our hair plastered dark to our heads. The taste of salt water dribbled into each mouthful we ate. Our togs were last year's and comfy.

Fat, yellowed leaves and small, pithy, oval figs lay on the sandy soil. The figs, hard and knobbly under our picnic rug, smelled of white, sour-sweet sap. The coolness of thick leaves arched overhead. The sun radiated over the harbour's grey-green waters and the froth-tipped waves rippled into the shore of Shark Bay. There was a skin of sand over the rock wall by the beach edge. The mostly submerged net fence around the swimming area was defining and reassuring. The bushland over on the North side was friendly and green, lapping the harbour edge. A kaleidoscope of colours ranged around the parkland: grass, boats, towels, togs, skin, flags and wrappers.

The melee of colours coalesced into the arrival of Simone, who jogged up to our picnic wearing a bright pink-and-blue Lycra gym outfit; she looked frighteningly like Olivia Newton-John. Emma jumped up and ran to Simone who picked her up. Emma, her long legs dangling down like a foal's, snuggled adoringly into her mother. Simone sagged quickly. 'Oh darling, you're getting far too big for this.' She put her child down, but Emma stayed near as Simone arranged herself on the picnic rug.

Simone leaned forward and selected a grape. She examined it in detail, then returned it to the plastic container. She picked over the grapes, rejecting those she found suspect and taking only the perfect ones. I supposed if she was only going to eat a few things in her life, they had better be the best on offer.

Emma draped over her mother's knee, but Simone boosted her away, saying, 'Darls, honestly! It's too hot.'

Emma pouted for a moment, then reached for the peanut butter and a rice cake.

While Emma laid too much peanut butter over the rice cake, Simone continued her inspection of the food and drinks laid out on the rug. 'Ooooh, what have we here?' I suppose she found the containers filled with Anzac biscuits, apples, grapes and melon slices all too prosaic for she took nothing for herself. 'Aren't we all so lucky. I hope they've thanked you, Connie?' Simone twinkled round at us all.

'They've been great,' I said. 'They're always great.'

'It's been a godsend… honestly, darls. You're so fabulous. I can't thank you enough. There's still so much to organise. And the school holidays! Oh… my… God! Nothing's open. Still haven't heard about Emma's passport… it's been a nightmare. And I really wanted to go to *Symphony under the Stars* tonight. I've ordered a hamper. Thank heavens Rufus is so patient. He's being an angel and the kids just love him.' She beamed around at her children. 'Don't you darlings?'

Francis stood up and looked towards the beach. Simone watched him. Fern noticed Simone's shrewd appraisal of her son. She put down her rice cake and said, 'Time for a swim. Emma, are you coming?'

Emma grabbed a handful of Anzac biscuits and jumped up. 'Let's go!' Francis remembered their hats and they all ran off to the water.

'Stay where you can see us,' I shouted.

'Don't worry, Con,' Fern shouted back, apparently taking her carer's duties seriously. I watched them run; healthy, tanned and slender, across the park to the beach. Fern and Francis jumped down from the top of the seawall to the sand but Emma, ignoring their outstretched arms, walked calmly down the sandstone steps, self contained and self absorbed. The older kids waited for Emma, then they ran and splashed into the water together. The waves were insignificant and they sat in the water and rolled, laughing.

'Do you think it was something I said?' Simone asked, peeling the skin from a juicy, green grape. 'Francis can be a bit… well… too sensitive for his own good. Probably puberty or something embarrassing.'

'Simone,' I said. 'Do you have to?'

'Have to what? Oh, you don't mean… come on, Connie, don't you go making a fuss as well.'

'As well as who?'

'Silly old Jude, of course. But darls, you know what it's like. They want to be with Rufus now.'

What was this? I considered her carefully made-up face, gold knot earrings, and her hairstreaks waved in expensive neglect. Did she really think she could swap men without consequence? Did she really believe that fathers could disappear and reappear—completely different actors, like a soap opera star's fictional plastic surgery after a fictional crocodile incident—and no one would mind?

'Couldn't he move here? That would be less disruptive, wouldn't it?'

'They're big enough. In fact, they'll blossom. The experience will expand their minds. It's going to be a great adventure. You'll see, darls. You'll come and visit and see the museums and art galleries with them. It's going to be marvellous.'

It was an opportunity, I could see that, but the children didn't need the Grand Tour, they needed their family. She was talking like a travel agent, not like a mother. I tried to avoid judgment clouding my voice when I said, 'I don't know if that's enough.'

'Of course it's enough. What's not enough? What more do children want? Me? Money? Security? Education? Culture? International travel…'

'Their father?'

She flashed me a stunning smile. 'You don't know how right you are. That's exactly what they need. Each of them need to know their father.' She spoke as if with obvious import, with neon lettering hung out over the beach, flashing, but I still couldn't understand her.

'And their father will be in Sydney?' I said.

'And Emma will always stay in contact with him.'

Emma. Why did she only mention Emma? Had she just phrased herself badly? She had, of course, but that wasn't because she'd forgotten. I reminded her anyway, because I'm the helpful one, 'And Francis.'

As if brushing aside a mosquito, she said, 'Yes, yes. Francis.'

There was something funny going on. Her voice was as brittle as her split ends. Her peroxide ways were showing.

'Simone? What do you mean?'

Simone was losing patience with me. 'Oh Connie! For God's sake, work it out.'

The sun glazed the wavelets crunching sand at the shore. The children rolled around at the water's edge and I worried about sunburn. When did they last put on sunscreen? I stood up and held a hand over my eyes. I couldn't see them. Tears made me blind.

I picked up a roll of paper towel, ripped off a square and blew my nose. Elegant indeed. Words spilled out. 'I remember when you moved in. You were so desperate, weren't you? Looking for a bunch of suckers. Wanting security and a family and a nest for your cuckoo's egg.'

'Hey, that's Francis you're talking about.' Simone laughed. It was not a humorous laugh. Nothing I could say would make a dent in her. She was immune and radiated confidence as she explained. 'Actually, darl, I was only looking for one sucker. The rest of you were unexpected, a mad, extra crowd coming along for the ride. And why not?' She laughed again. 'You understand, Connie, probably better than most. What difference does it make who the father is? They just do their one happy act and off they skip, mission accomplished, off to their shiny careers without a backward glance, without a doubt, without an emotional claw stuck into their bleeding maternal heart. Worrying all the time: is baby safe? Dry? Fed? Cream on the rash? Not drugged? Not dropped? It's impossible to do by yourself, isn't it? How much happier is it for a bunch of single mums to work together sharing the load? It might have been a deception to start with, Connie, but I pulled my weight. I helped you with your clay deliveries and your close-up photos; and what about our exhibitions? Of course it was your turn next but with Sheryl, who knew? You're okay. You've got plenty of work. It's not like you've wasted time, Connie. None of us have. Don't blame me. It doesn't matter how it came to be.'

It did matter, now it wasn't going to be any more. But I said nothing. I just packed up the picnic. It was over.

~~~~~

Have to keep going. All I can do. Eaten through Jude's larder although cannot bear to sit down to eat from a plate. Fork the beans straight out of the tin, standing up at the sink. Think I've lost weight. Can feel my hipbones for the first time in years.

Telephone rings when visiting my flat to do laundry. Unexpected sound shocks me. Stare at the phone. Ringing seems insistent. Habit overcomes my reluctance and I answer. It's William. So pleased to catch me at last. Chats on and on. Adamant I join him for dinner. I refuse. I hang up. He rings again. I have to go out with him or he'll come round to see me. I can't have that. He wonders why I am so secretive. He is persistent. I understand he will not give up. I explain it will have to be an early night.

Have a shower before I go. Dress as if I were a normal woman. The old blue dress hangs on me. Put on makeup. Drive down to Watson's Bay. He is waiting in the front room when I walk into the pub. He looks tired but when he smiles at me, oh dear, he looks happy. I try to look ordinary, as if I'm living a normal life. Go through the motions of common decency and communication. He hugs me and double air-kisses my face as if still in Europe. I smile. Even laugh. Wonder if there have been any marathons recently. Tells me he is very excited about the host city marathon coming up in April. It follows the Olympic course and even though there isn't to be a Canberra marathon this year, Sydney will more than make up for it. He is looking around him as he talks. He almost sniffs the air. He suggests we go to Doyles, as the pub does not impress him. Watson's Bay still feels like a fishing town, with the little houses and thin curving streets, even though Doyles is the last fish stall there. Walk along the concrete beachside path, staring out over the harbour, looking at the water-taxis and the hydrofoil coming in through the heads.

Seated at Doyles, laugh about the most expensive fish and chips in the world. Haven't been here for ages; just the same. He orders a bottle of Marlborough Sauvingon Blanc. Cold, yellow light swirls in the glass as the waiter pours. Sun sets and the place fills with chattering people wearing sunglasses on their heads. William puts on his Doyles bib and dribbles tartare sauce over his calamari. What do William and I talk about? Can't remember. Let's see.

William tells me about Catalina's renovations. Filled with stories about plumbers and builders holding up schedules. He is keen to know how I am coping. Must be a big change for me, with everyone away. Do I feel abandoned? Should he come and stay? I am frozen with horror at his kind suggestion. He leans back and changes the subject. Perhaps he talks about the food. Offers more wine? I cannot focus. His lips continue to move. His ideas echo in my mind. Stay? In my flat? I don't even live there now. I am nested inside Jude's place. To live with William would be impossible. How things have changed.

~~~~~

I was wedging clay when the phone rang. I let it go through to the answer machine. It's best to grow the rhythm needed to fold the clay again and again into the wheel of turns, to ease out the air and heft it, compounding and pressing again and again until the work is complete and the wedged clay is orderly, creased and compact; a wheel of clay.

'You've reached Constance Sonnenberg. I'm sorry I can't take your call right now. Please leave a message after the tone.' Awful. My voice was so stilted and awkward. After the beep, Peter's voice came on the line. He sounded breathless. 'Mum! Pick up. Please! I know you're there...'

I grabbed the phone with mucky hands. 'I'm here.'

'Thank God. Charlotte's waters have broken. Sarah's out. I'll take her to the birthing centre. Can you meet us there?'

I put plastic wrap over the clay and locked the studio. I dumped my work clothes in the laundry, took a quick shower, scrabbled around for something clean to wear and drove to the birthing centre. It was only a short trip over to Paddington from Bellevue Hill and the traffic behaved itself. Of course, then I faced the ubiquitous challenge of finding a parking space in the tiny back-streets of Paddo. I drove around the one-way alleys and lanes growing annoyed. Charlotte would have had the baby by the time I got there. Perhaps it wasn't Jude or Peter's kid. Perhaps it would be born so obviously another's child, with white blonde or coal black hair or...

I managed to jam the Volvo in between a Pajero and a Merc with the barest of bumps on each. I hurried to the hospital, avoiding the remarkable amount of dog excreta along the footpath.

The sallow-faced woman at the reception desk was in confab with two other women, one of whom wore a spotless, white turban. She told me the room number without any interest as to who I was. I was expecting an interrogation; to have to explain our rather complicated arrangement, and was relieved as I walked down the corridor, all too aware of the smell of cleaning products.

The door was just open enough for me to stick my nose around the corner. I could see Charlotte, balancing her weighty belly, on the edge of the bed. Peter was helping her out of a chunky hand-knitted cardigan, though why she was wearing a cardigan in this weather, I didn't know. Under the wool, she wore a simple blue cotton sleeve-less dress. The room itself was much like you'd find in a rural motel, but with medical touches like the oxygen valve and the yellow sharps container.

I stood outside the door, undecided. Should I would knock, or not? I was becoming less certain that I had anything to do here. Surely this moment belonged to these two young people? Charlotte sighed as her body tensed. She drew in a sharp breath through a scowl and gripped my son's arm; he didn't flinch. He stood there, concerned, focussed on her, *en garde*. How strange it is that giving birth is such a solitary experience yet there she was, hanging on. Keeping a hold on the outside world. Keeping a hold on my son. So this was Charlotte. *The* Charlotte.

I must say I was surprised. She was not what I had imagined. Charlotte the harlot was a solid woman. Well, after Simone, skittish thoroughbred, it was difficult to predict what Jude's 'type' would be. Charlotte's hands appeared strong as they clung onto Peter's arm.

The veins were distinct and the knuckles were white. She wore no jewellery or nail polish. She had soft looking brown skin over toned arms. After all, she was a carpenter. Her long, thick, reddish-blonde hair was restrained into a single plait that reached halfway down her back. Judging from her now stretched grimace, this baby was in a hurry to be born.

I was on the verge of leaving when Peter looked up and caught my eye. The look of gratitude on his face thrilled me. Any doubts disappeared. Of course I would help him, my own son; how could I not?

Charlotte released her grip on Peter and pushed him aside. 'Go find my mother.'

'Okay. Anything else?'

She bent forward to suck in more air. 'I need my mum.'

Peter beckoned me in. 'Charlotte, this is Connie. She'll help.'

I stepped into the room; what else was I to do? When I came to stand next to Peter, Charlotte looked at me with as much pleasure as if I were a cane toad come to visit. Maybe she was right.

'Hello,' I said to both of them and, in a quiet aside, asked Peter, 'Where's the midwife?'

Peter sighed. 'Changeover. Won't be long.'

'Good,' I said.

'Hurry,' said Charlotte, and the way they smiled at each other gave me hope. She liked him. That was plain to see. That was a start. That was something.

Charlotte's eyes were hazel: electric flashes of green spearing through brown. I didn't know what to say to her and she was preoccupied with her inner life.

'Would you like a cup of tea?' I asked, as Jude closed the door behind him. I was thinking: boil kettle, find spare towels, ingest anti-oxidants, save the brain, keep busy, busy, busy…

'That would be…' she began, but I could see another wave flowed through her and she succumbed to the pain.

I never wanted to be there when Jude's children were born. But the birth of Peter's child? Could I be there for that?

Into the sounds of the hospital—the banging of doors, the wheeling of trolleys, the far-off bells and buzzers, the walking of staff and the murmuring of worried families—Charlotte heaved herself up from the edge of the bed and shuffled around the room. She was apparently having pains that caught up with her and threw her off balance. I went to put my arm around her; she stopped moving and held on, gasping for breath, as another wave of tension surged through her body. She was being driven by that primal energy: the forces of earth and rock, of blood and bone, of her body opening and widening. As I watched her internal journey, I was plunged back into memories of my own birthing experience. Then Charlotte pushed me away and continued to move around the perimeter of the room. I wondered for a moment whose child she carried, then realised I should be doing more than stare. 'Cup of tea?' I asked.

'No!' she said. She had no time for petty drinks. Then she grunted from the ground up. Her face stretched into an involuntary mask like those worn by fierce warriors in Japanese *noh* plays. With one hand I took hold of her left arm and with the other, rubbed the base of her spine. Her breathing became a little slower and less erratic, but she continued to stumble around the room with me following. 'Are you sure I can't get you anything? Check on the midwife?'

'Don't go.'

'I'm sorry.'

'Not your fault.' I supported her when she wobbled and I listened as she opened up. I guessed that was the right thing to do. 'It's my fault. There's no denying that. All my fault. Even my mother is treating me like an idiot,' she said. Charlotte paused to suck in air. 'She's right. She should treat me like an idiot. I am an idiot. Unbelievable idiot! What could I do? Innocent. Stupid. Naïve. You know how dumb I was? Sucked in by my biology professor. That's how

261

dumb. And I am a mature age student. Mature age doesn't give you maturity, that's for sure. He was kind and I was pathetic. Dumb! Dumb! Dumb!'

Charlotte leaned against the wall by the door and panted. 'It wasn't his fault. My fault. Hadn't recovered after my brother died. Too soon to go back to school. Thought I was super-human or something. Needed to get into something new, something challenging.' She burst into laughter and began moving again. She slowed and propped against the wall by the window. 'Boy, did I get a challenge!' She leaned into the wall, then bumped her head against it, hard. 'God I feel so stupid. How bloody fucking ridiculous.' She bumped her head again for punctuation. 'Never crossed my mind I'd get pregnant. How feeble is that!'

Again she moved her heavy body, seeming to shift almost without volition, across the room until she found a chair to grip. She held tight and said, 'All we thought of was dying. For so long. So consumed by death... with David.' She waited, bent over, slightly swaying and then clenching, the tension rising through her body. 'So careful with Jude. Nice to be looked after, and then... that bastard son of his. What an idiot I've been.' Another surge of pain must have overwhelmed her, for she threw her head back and howled. She cried, 'How fucked off. Ashamed. Bloody despairing...' She marched around the room, on parade. 'All I wanted was an abortion. Should have been aborted myself, come to that. My mother's the idiot. Must tell her. Left it too late. Up shit creek.' She slowed and pressed her back into the wall by the bed, rolling her head against the hard surface. 'Been looking forward to having a baby, don't worry about that. Looking after him, taking care of my baby. I think he's a boy. Perhaps a baby will make David's death easier to bear, not that I've told Mum that; maybe I will one day. Maybe I'll call the baby 'David' and he can take on the giants. And win. Maybe that's going too far.'

As I listened to her speech full of effort, I searched the room for something practical that I could do. I saw the sink and water glasses. I rinsed a glass and half-filled it. I brought it to her and placed it in her hand. The other hand pressed into the wall as she took a sip. She returned the glass to me without acknowledgment and again began to waddle through the room like one of the brown bears in Taronga Zoo—heavy, hopeless, bouncing from the boundaries—though now it seemed she was getting tired: she looked pale and her voice was becoming softer. Then she stumbled, enough to cause her to lurch onto the bed where she sat for a while, rocking as the strain ricocheted through her body.

'I should never have had sex with the prof. Not my type. I liked him but not like that. Not like a lover. An older man? Father figure? Pathetic! See? An idiot. I never knew my dad. Car crash.' She was matter of fact, no need for emotion now. 'And Mum… she can't do everything. Although she does… try to do everything.' A trickle of tears ran down her face. 'Don't know why we ever… I felt so low. He comforted me. Said he wanted to help, make me feel better. Maybe he can't read women very well, I don't know. Maybe he was trying to make me feel wanted or interesting. Maybe he was trying to be wanted or interesting himself. Maybe I was the one comforting him. Fuck, I don't know! Maybe he's just a randy bastard. But I did enjoy being his friend.' She took the cold facecloth I offered. Her hair had escaped from its plait and wet tendrils stuck to her face. 'I wanted him to be happy.'

Sometimes she roared. Other times she whispered. It was a strange soliloquy. One I both wanted to hear, yet really didn't want to know at all. It was as though words were escaping out of her with the baby. I didn't know what to say and it didn't matter anyway—she only wanted me to listen. But I did feel I was invading her privacy, and Jude's and Peter's. Did Charlotte even know who I was? I waited for a time to tell her, I watched for an opportunity; I was alert, really I was, but there never was a time.

'But his son, Peter, Peter Baldwin, my Peter,' she continued, almost dreaming now. 'It was lust and fire and something else. Something right and obvious and meaningful… and a lie. A complete and utter lie. When he told me who he was—a total fucking prick, a devious shit, a complete and utter fucking arsehole—oh, how dare he! Fucking me so that his father would come home—such unbelievable, mutant thinking. As if the father had anything to do with his old mother anyway. It's all to do with those other women. How the fuck do they cope trapped in the same place? Imprisoned. I'd die. Where does it leave them? In the rubbish? All the same? What price individuality? And if Jude tells me one more time he wants me to go and live in that hellhole with those witches, he can go jump off The Gap. No! No, I'll throw him off. Can you imagine? All happy harems together? The audacity of it! Makes my skin crawl. Obscene. Revolting. Putrid. Idiot. What you deserve.'

I felt humbled by her experience, yet here was Charlotte, talking about my loved ones and my support network as though they were crap. But we're not like that. We're not. All our children have been loved and cleaned and fed and educated, and have grown up with their siblings. How could that be wrong? I wanted to rupture her ranting and tell her the truth, but suddenly Peter and Sarah were in the room with us. I acknowledged Sarah with a silent nod.

Sarah took up position beside her daughter, putting her arms around her and giving her support. Charlotte's face reddened and her mouth made the shape of an 'O' as she leaned into her mother. Sarah looked gratitude and gravity to me, then said, 'Thanks, Connie. We'll let you know how we get on.' She rubbed Charlotte's back. I was dismissed.

Peter took my arm. 'Come on, let's go.'

Outside in the corridor the air-conditioning was working over-time. It was freezing. After the stifling heat of Charlotte's room, the hall was like the Antarctic. At the far end of the corridor was a silhouette picked out in clumsy hospital lighting. The figure drew closer and became Jude. Peter dropped my arm and walked towards his dad. He and Peter walked towards each other like two gunfight-ers at high noon. The atmosphere became electric; a father and son face-off. I was too tired to laugh. I was too numb to cry.

Peter was a man now. There was no doubt he was more than Jude's equal. Although Jude was fit, his shape was beginning to stoop and his youthful jeans were loose in the wrong places. They stood two body lengths apart and stared at each other, hands by their sides as though on holsters.

That it should have come to this, a fight between the two men I loved best; the very two who should be working together to keep our family intact, who should be planning the education of a grand-child; that these two should be pumping and chesty towards each other caused my heart to hammer dread through my guts.

In a very quiet voice, Peter said, 'I don't think she needs to see you.'

Jude took a menacing step forward and whispered, 'You can't stop me.'

'Jude, please, there's no call for this; let's go...'

'No, Connie. If she's having my child...'

'She's not,' said Peter.

'You can't know that.'

'She told me. Look at you. You're too old for her. How could she possibly love an old man like you, Dad?' Peter piled hatred into the word 'Dad'. He made his father sound like the worst kind of deserter, the most malicious traitor, or the vilest child molester. Dad.

Jude rallied. He brought all his paternal superiority into play. 'You can't understand. It's a serious responsibility to bring another life into this world. You have to be prepared to look after the child until it can stand on its own two feet and look after itself.'

'Who the fuck do you think you are?'

'Whoa, boy...' said Jude, but there was nothing that could stop our son now.

'Don't be so fucking patronising. Don't understand? I've had the best teacher in the world. I know all there is to know about fatherhood. I've been watching you all my life. Do you really think you know what you're doing? You? Crawling from woman to woman, searching for... what? Your own self? Your youth? You're

265

pathetic. You have no idea what love is. You only want someone to care for so they'll look up to you, and you will be the big, strong, macho head of the family.'

The air sang with testosterone. The two men seemed to grow bigger and I shrank, cowering, against the wall.

'I want another chance, Peter.'

'How many chances do you get? You couldn't even stay with my mother.'

'But I did.'

'Sure you did. In a fucking harem so you could keep your whores as well.'

Jude jerked his arm back and let loose a punch full into Peter's face. Peter toppled backwards, blood spilling from his nose as he lay sprawled on the floor. Vengeance burned in his eyes as he looked up at his father. I could see he was restraining himself; I could feel his fight, see he was trying to stop his instinctive retaliation.

Jude, rubbing his knuckles, took a step backwards. I supposed he was feeling shame and shock at his own violence. I presumed he didn't know the battle continued on in his son.

I felt sick but crouched down to grab Peter, possibly hold him back. I'm not sure what I thought I could do; perhaps somehow I could give him the strength to give up the fight. With my hand on his shoulder, I could feel his tension, the potential energy strung back, primed to fire off a massive salvo that might inflict some real damage.

Jude offered his handkerchief. I pressed it to Peter's face and Peter held it to his nose. Then I straightened up and stared at my ex-husband. Jude looked bemused. His face was pale. He opened his mouth to speak, glistening saliva strung thinly between his teeth, but I forestalled him. 'Go home, Jude.'

Jude took a small step backwards and watched as Peter pushed himself to his feet. I attempted to put an arm around his waist but he brushed it away. 'I'm okay, Mum,' he said.

'Are you sure?'

'Just tell him to keep away from her.'

'You got it.'

Peter went back down the corridor to the men's toilets. The door snicked shut behind him. I turned to find Jude frowning at me. 'Got what?'

'Jude, what the hell do you think you're doing?'

'No, Connie. What are you doing?'

'Trying to protect your son. Trying to protect your dignity.'

'You've got no idea, Constance. No idea at all.' Jude turned away. I watched him walk down the corridor, away from Charlotte's room. He walked slowly and did not turn back. He seemed to carry a feeling of resignation rather than failure. I watched until he went through the doors and into the outside world. Suddenly I was weak and shaking. An orderly stared at me, concerned, and a fat woman in a green tartan dressing-gown looked away as I caught her eye. I could hear Charlotte screaming.

Chapter 19

Candlestick

When God made Adam from clay and Eve from the rib, did He think women would sculpt the children? Or is God still in charge of sculpture? Rwandan women used to leave bowls of water handy at night so God could get on with his pottery business of shaping their babies. Who is shaping babies now? Can we focus on quality rather than quantity, please?

~~~~~

I knew Jude wasn't there but for some reason I could not stop knocking on his door. With each rap of my knuckles my inner questions became more urgent. Why wasn't he there? Where was he? How dare he not be there? I'd told him to go home, yet he hadn't. I couldn't work it out. Perhaps he was just not answering. But why wouldn't he want to see me? I hoped he had not gone to Simone. She had the power to devastate him more than he knew. I didn't want him to be hurt like that. Or did I? I kept knocking for far longer than was reasonable. He was not at home to me.

Eventually I went along the hall to Zita's. She opened the door. She was dressed for work in old jeans and a stained sweatshirt. Her hair was even more dishevelled than usual. 'Come in, Constantia darling.' She looked at me and raised an eyebrow. Her expression became concerned, she tilted her head and her eyes grew more intent. 'Are you okay?'

'Give me something to do.'

She looked at me, frowning, then practicality took over. 'Try these mugs. Here's some butcher's paper.'

I wrapped a mug while she turned her concern back to getting plates out of the kitchen cupboards. I popped my first wrap into the nest of other wrapped objects in the crockery box. 'Have you got...?'

'Have I got what? I got plenty. I got everything. I got way too much. Guido's already got tons. Look at all this stuff! The kids and I have been taking stuff over to Guido's for ages, and there's still more junk.'

'Zita, I was wondering... about the furniture.'

She barely paused as she wrapped. 'Auctioneer. Next month. I'm going to organise storage until they want to put it in the showroom.'

'Can I make an offer? Only I was thinking of trying for the furnished market. Then, maybe if the right tenant turns up...'

'Connie! You're not thinking...'

'I don't know what I'm thinking. Maybe put *Bindiwurra* on the market...'

'Good idea.'

'You think? I'm still undecided. I might stay or, maybe go away...' I shrugged. 'I only know things have to change.'

'I thought she might move in.'

'She's in labour.' I told her about Peter and Jude. 'It's a disaster.'

Zita watched me cry then found a pile of grubby paper towels. We had a hug. I had a good nose blow and then got wrapping again while we waited for the kettle to boil.

'When does she go?'

'Simone? Not soon enough.'

'What's she done now?'

'You don't want to know. Why don't you just use newspaper?'

'Because you have to wash everything after you've unwrapped; this way there's no staining with the printers' ink.'

'She's saying Frances isn't Jude's.' I reached for another piece of paper. 'She came out with it. Point blank. I couldn't believe it. I still can't believe it. I can't believe her.' I saw Zita's lips tighten but that was her only reaction. I thought she was being defensive. 'I told you, you wouldn't want to know.'

'This isn't a big surprise to me.' Zita stopped wrapping and turned to face me. 'Does that mean…' She hesitated. 'Rufus?'

'Apparently. She kept saying things like the children have a right to know their father and I thought she meant Jude. At first.'

'We always did think…'

'Yes, that he was big for his age…'

'And we often thought…'

'He was too good to be true…' I nodded with her.

'And we probably never…'

'Would have said it…'

'No,' said Zita. 'But we both thought it. You did, didn't you?'

'I'd never have believed it if I'd actually said it. That would have meant she was just out to hook up with any old guy for some pathetic idea of respectability—and that is beyond my comprehension. It's so unfair on Jude.'

'Are you crazy? Would you please stop worrying about Jude for once! Constantia, please! It wasn't Jude who looked after Frances. It was you! You and me. Come on… please, Connie. It always comes back to Jude with you. You have to stop. He's not good for you. Please tell me you can let him go. I'd love you to find happiness, some other love. Why can't you do that?'

'I've tried, Zita. I really have.'

'You don't try. There are other men.'

'Where?'

'You're blind. Why? Because of some duty thing?'

'I don't know. I just can't.'

'You can. You have to live your life. You're a gravedigger, you know?'

'I can't talk about him like this, behind his back.' I turned to the packing case, resting my hand on the cool butcher's paper, clicking through the gears into practical groove again before wrapping another mug.

Zita couldn't help herself. 'Please, Connie. I've got to say this. You have to move on. Face facts. We're all leaving. You've got to get on and find a future, a man or a plan or a career change or travel or something... please, I worry so much...'

'There's no need. I've got work. I'm fine. No, not so fine, but only because of bitch-face Simone; it's all her fault. What are we going to do about those children?'

Zita picked up a plate. 'Does he know?'

'Jude? Not sure.'

'Who's going to tell him?'

'Not me.'

'She's the one who's got to tell him.' Zita finished wrapping her pile of plates and closed the lid on the box. 'Before she goes.' She grabbed the packing tape and unrolled it fast across the top of the cardboard with a screech. 'What about Francis? Does he know?'

'Oh Jesus, she's such a fucking slut. Sorry, Zita, but I can't believe she'd go on letting everyone believe this, and then, when everyone's all set, go and pull out the truth, just to hurt Jude.'

'And Francis.'

'She's unbelievable.'

'I'd like to kill her.' Zita spoke remarkably calmly, as though she were making a comment about the supply of cardboard boxes. There was no doubting she was sincere.

I wrapped a cup and then a dose of ice slid down my spine, the reverse of a hot flush, and with added nausea. I envisaged Zita carrying out her threat. I had seen her panic and kill a blue-tongued lizard once with a broom. With a cold hard jolt of realisation, I thought she may even be able to complete the objective. I watched her whip together a cardboard box. She was strong. She could have contacts. And there was something about Guido: the gold ring; the implied power in his physicality; the way he knew everyone in the Italian community. Was she joking? I really couldn't tell. 'For God's sake, Zita, you wouldn't.'

Zita smiled at me reassuringly and said, 'It's too far to grey old England with our little Francis.' She deftly flicked out the flat cardboard to form a box, then burst forth with another suggestion: 'Kidnap him!' A screech of tape and she finished another box and slid it across the floor. 'Why not? She'd never miss him.' She flicked open another flat box.

'Rufus would.'

'Someone has to look after the children, no matter who the bloody parents are.' More screech of tape. Another finished box dropped to the floor. 'I'm so pleased she won't be at my wedding.'

I shook my head and said, 'Simone's a fucking bitch and I hope I never have the bad luck to see her again. To be really awful, I'm not going to miss Emma all that much, either. Wonder who *her* father is?' Zita screamed at that.

The kettle was boiling at last. It screamed and we screamed and laughed and cried again, too. I had packed all the cups.

~~~~~

The candlestick is my last ever piece of pottery. It's a twisted collection of three orange-brown shapely limbs. *Nyctimystes dayi* is commonly called the lace-eyed tree frog or lacelid. Lustre glaze on the surface of the candlestick provides a weird gleam, like the surface of an eye.

The frog's eye cannot change its focus. Frogs can't see stationary objects; they can only focus on moving things. Frogs can see above and around them with their bulging eyes—handy for a sentinel species always on watch for potential predators.

Possibly because most frogs don't have tongues, frogs can use their eyes to assist swallowing. When frogs close their eyes they draw them into their sockets and down into their mouths. The eye presses on the roof of the mouth as the frog blinks, helping to push food down the gullet. I wonder if they can watch their food go down as they stuff themselves?

The outer eyelids don't move but there's a third eyelid called the nictitating membrane. The lacelid has a distinct pattern of veins on its lower lid. It has huge eyes making it unbelievably cute and, as usual with my choice of frog, it's endangered. I must be attracted to danger.

Who knows how long these creatures will grace the earth?

I will never turn on the kiln again. After I empty it for the last time, I dismantle it. What choice do I have?

Things have to change.

~~~~~

A United Airlines plane took off in the distance while a smaller craft taxied across the concourse like a toy. Heavily loaded baggage carts delivered their cargo to conveyer belts leading into the body of the waiting planes. An Air New Zealand jet was closest to our window. The Qantas jumbo Simone intended for her family was next in line, the red kangaroo already leaping away on the plane's tail.

Zita, Fern and I shared a booth with Simone and Rufus in the International Departures bar. The carpet was red with a black and brown swirl sliding through the room. The aroma of stale beer was strong even though it was just turning seven in the morning. The people at the next table were walled in with piled up glasses and empty plates. Discarded pieces of newspaper fanned around their habitat.

Rufus returned with coffees and hot chocolates on a tray. We faced the window; the continual action entrancing. I tried to shut Simone's voice out but it was impossible. Rufus smiled at Simone indulgently and sipped his tea as she prattled on and on about their planned stopover, a week at the Mandarin in Bangkok, '... so Rufus can really get to know the kids... really spend time with them.'

'And his money,' muttered Zita. I was too nervous to smile. My mask seemed to be slipping and I was getting tired just holding my mouth shut.

Half a dozen garish game booths lined the wall by the entrance to the bar. Leaf stood at one holding a large plastic gun and focussing along its barrel. He shot things on the screen with silent intent. Peter assisted, feeding in gold coins as required. He'd been staying over at Charlotte's helping with baby Betty—she hadn't got the hang of sleeping yet so Peter looked as tired as any new father might. Fern was chatting to Francis about Morris Gleitzman's book, *The other facts of life*. She'd bought it for him to read on the flight. Emma was clinging with one hand to her sparkly bag and with the other to her glittering mother. 'It's boarding!' she said in her spoilt-child imperious tones. 'We should go now, Simone.'

Simone laughed, showing her teeth. She reminded me of a neighing horse. I thought of offering her a carrot. She smiled at Rufus. 'Time gentleman, please.' When she laughed again I swear it was a whinny. Rufus smiled back at his blonde pony and patted her on the shoulder. Good horsey. They began gathering up their cameras and duty free goods and carry-on bags, and their coats for the cold winter in England—all the material goods they could get away with taking on board.

I went to Francis and slipped my arm through his. My mind was filled with his name: Francis, Francis, Francis... please stay, Francis. Suddenly I couldn't see and I blinked, blinked hard, and said, 'Daft old biddy,' then laughed and hugged him. 'Right, let's go,' I said, leading him out of the bar and into the airport corridor, moving fast, bending towards him, murmuring my question to him. 'Where to?'

'Connie, you know I'm going to London.'

'We can go anywhere you like, Francis.' I urged him on.

Francis was not so keen. He held me back, saying, 'I thought of running away but I'm under-age. She'll just make me go back.'

'We'll stop them.'

We passed Ken Done, the Body Shop and the newsagency. We followed builders' signs and kept to the safe walkways, for renovations and rebuilding was taking place throughout the airport. Sydney was improving herself for the Olympics. From the moment they touched down at Kingsford Smith, athletes would be getting a welcome they were never likely to forget.

'They won't let you, Connie. Mum's got it all organised. You know what she's like.'

Then we ran into a breath of grave-cold air. It was Jude. 'Where do you think you're going?' he said. He was chilly.

I did not want to stay and chat. 'Home,' I said, and walked around him and led Francis away towards the check-in area.

Jude called after us, 'Is that right, Francis?'

We kept walking. Francis put up more resistance as he began to realise I was not joking.

I felt a hand on my shoulder, stopping me. Jude had followed us. I shrugged him away but he put both hands on my shoulders and turned me round to face him. 'Better head back to Departures.'

Francis pulled his arm away from mine. 'Back to Departures, Connie.'

I think I was crying. My face was wet, anyway. I wiped away the tears as I pleaded with Jude. 'He doesn't want to go. He can stay with me. Or with you.'

'Connie.'

'Yes, Jude?' I held Francis by the hand now. I looked at his hand and patted it. I grabbed his other hand and held both tightly in mine. I did not want to let him go. I did not want to let him out of the country. I did not want to let him out of my sight.

'I have to go, Connie,' Francis said, and wriggled his hands free. 'Mum will seriously go off if we're late.'

Jude wrapped his arms around me, held me tight to his chest, and whispered in my ear. His breath was cool. His lips stuck to my hair. 'Connie, don't be stupid. Do you really want his last memory of you to be like this?'

Then he drew away from me; Simone was there, and she was angry. 'I might have known you'd try that.' She seized Francis's arm. 'You must be stark raving mad. To steal my child, to hire a private detective, to put up with this man for years... mad!'

She marched away, dragging Francis with her, spitting words over her shoulder. 'You're sick! Depraved! Psychotic!' Her back was straight and her ballet-trained torso strong; her ponytail swished from side to side, standing straight out from the force of her movement as she turned a corner. However forceful her movement, she still managed to look as if she were gliding compared with poor Francis, an adolescent beanpole teetering beside her. He, apparently resigned to his fate, looked back at me apologetically.

I followed them. I was still trying to think of something that might stop Simone in her tracks. I could hardly bear to see Francis dragged along like that, just a few metres ahead of me.

Jude fell in beside me. 'What private detective?'

I tried to explain but we were walking too fast. My eyes were blurred and my nose was clogged. I couldn't get enough air into my mouth. I tried to answer him. 'I just wanted to be sure...'

Simone snapped back as she clacked along. '... sure you're a nosey, controlling bitch? We're sure of that already.'

'But can't you see?' I tried to communicate with Simone. 'Did you ever think he might have a record or he might be—'

'And what did you find out?' snarled Simone. 'That he's got a wife and she can't have children... is that it? Well, I've been down that old familiar path before so it makes absolutely no difference at all to me.'

'What about her?'

'Who?'

'The wife.'

Simone stopped, released Francis, and swung around to face me. Leaning forward, she exploded. 'It's what she wants. She's the one behind it. She's encouraged Rufus all along. It makes her happy to make Rufus happy.' Simone's blonde hair started to escape from its smooth, shiny ponytail and her mouth opened wide with red lip-ribbons of shining, shrieking shame. 'You should recognise that. You think you know all about sacrifice. Well, she's doing it for real. She's really left him. She's not clinging on like a leech, like some kind of fat intestinal worm. She's free. Why aren't you, Connie? Why can't you just dry up and drop off?'

Simone grabbed Francis's arm again and resumed the march, alternately dragging the boy and pushing him before her like a prisoner, clicking her high heels on the glassy floor. With staccato machine-gun raps, she shattered my family—clack, clack, clack, clack, clack...

Waiting at the entry to Customs, Rufus stood with one hand on Emma's shoulder, keeping her steady for Simone's return. Simone flustered back towards them and pushed Francis forward to Rufus. 'Come on, let's get the hell out of here.'

I came up to them and said to Rufus in the most friendly tone I could muster, 'So, Rufus, how are your balls hanging?'

Rufus, the very essence of a mild-mannered Englishman, looked alarmed. 'I beg your pardon?'

'Would you happen to have bell-clapper testicles in your family?'

Rufus rallied and opened his mouth, about to speak. But Simone contained more venom and more speed. 'Really, Connie,' she hissed, 'this isn't the time.'

'When, Simone?' I asked. 'When is the time? When were you thinking of telling them? You haven't told either of them yet, have you?'

'You stupid bitch!' She was on the attack. 'What the hell are you blabbing on about now? You should be in an institution, really you should.'

'When are you telling Jude?' I asked again. Jude straightened up beside me. I could feel the increased tension build through his body.

'He already knows.' She turned to Jude. 'You must have guessed.'

Jude frowned at her. 'What are you talking about?'

'Francis, of course,' said Simone's slashing red lips. 'He's Rufus's child. Which is why we have to go.' Simone turned, gathered her little family up and began to herd them towards the entry to Departures.

Rufus stayed quite still, as though he couldn't quite believe what he'd just heard. 'Simone! You said—' said Rufus, looking around him apologetically. 'I thought they knew.'

Simone didn't look at him as she embraced Emma and kept on going. 'Well, they didn't. We'll sort all this out later.'

I said, 'You'll have to, you selfish cow, because you hurt them.'

Simone spun on her needle-thin heels. 'You're the selfish cow,' she shrieked. 'You're the one who told them. It wouldn't have cost you anything to keep your big fat crone mouth shut, you piece of shit. God, I hope I never have to see you again.' She turned back to her children. 'Come on, let's go.'

Jude stood there like a lost man.

Francis broke away from the group and ran up to Jude. 'It doesn't matter, Dad.' He put his arms around Jude's shoulders and hugged him urgently. 'I'll visit. Soon as I can.'

I was allowed to hug Francis, too, though both Simone and Rufus hovered near him. 'I'm sorry, darling. I only did it because I love you so much and I hate lies. I just hate them.'

'I know,' Francis said. 'I'll email Dad...' and here he looked deliberately at Jude, '... as soon as we get to an Internet café.' He turned back to me. 'Connie, please, please get a computer. It's not that difficult. You can do it. You have to. Dad...' again the look at Jude, '... will give you my email.'

I would. I would do anything to keep in contact. I told him so and hugged him again.

Zita, Leaf, Fern and Peter took turns hugging Francis. Then each said goodbye to Simone. It was a final farewell.

I gave Emma an awkward hug, awkward because she was short and I did not bend as well I used to. She endured it politely, not responding in the slightest, her arms just hanging by her sides. I said, 'I'll expect a postcard, at least.'

'If I can find one, Connie.' She turned to Jude.

They had to pry Emma out of Jude's arms, and then Simone, quicksilver and laughing with anticipated freedom, took her children away from us. They disappeared into the customs hall. Those of us left behind turned slowly to look at each other.

Jude looked desiccated. His face had sunk back into the sinuses of his skull. His skin vacuumed back to the bones. He had become weightless and restless, continually in motion. His eyes could not fix on anything. He glanced over at the newsagency then flicked his eyes back to the children, then to Zita and then over to the souvenir shop.

I took him by the hand and we became two zombies drifting, lightheaded and aimless, through the rackety shopping mall. The air filled with the babble of humanity in migration, the crashing of suitcases into the conveyer belts of airline purpose, and the wheeling of little trolleys dragged behind clickety-clackety heels on endless, shiny, airport surfaces. Incomprehensible languages, children crying, and peals of laughter added to the cacophony as we wandered. Jude was the eye of the storm, quiet, confused, not knowing what direction to take, while all around him a tempest whirled and jangled.

Zita took control and guided us back to the cars. Peter drove Jude home to Zita's flat, and Zita drove Fern, Leaf and me back to Bellevue Hill. She had more packing to do and thought Jude would be better with her, doing something useful.

I went straight up to Simone's flat. It was completely empty. Even the darkroom had been stripped, with windows letting in light after years of photographic gloom. There was nothing left. Even Nuri had gone to his new hunting grounds in Haberfield. Simone had had professional cleaners in and they'd been professional to a fault. There was no evidence of her family at all. I sniffed the air, searching for a hint of Francis, even of Emma, but there was nothing... just the odour of Vim, corrosive and cleansing.

The sun glinted, tossed from leaf to leaf in the park. It was very, very quiet.

~~~~~

Email Francis about Zonule of Zinn. Ask him to tell me what he thought it might be before he looks it up. He said it sounds like a computer game or a book by Emily Rodda. Then he googled it and discovered the Zonule of Zinn is a line of suspensory ligaments in the human eye. Who names these things? After dissection and purpose definition, the naming must occur. A lacelid is exactly that. An eyelid made of lace. But a Zonule of Zinn?

Eyelids wipe the eye clear of foreign bodies and smooth tears over the cornea. Frogs have a second eyelid. Does that mean frogs have more tears?

~~~~~

The day of Zita and Guido's wedding was aureate—a wonderful, perfect, Sydney afternoon. Slivers of cloud etched delicate-thin over a deep expanse of blue.

My friend Zita wore a sleeveless Marilyn Monroe-style pleated dress that flowed around her like a river. She stood glowing, Guido her proud lion beside her: a regal just-married couple. For once, it had been Jude's turn to watch as one of his wives found happiness with another.

The kissing and farewells had simmered down and that traditional moment in the wedding ritual had arrived. The bridal bouquet was Zita's crowning glory: sprays of tiny yellow orchids, a weaving of golden roses, and miniature, buttery lilies embellished with a flourish of starry, tinsel ribbon. As Zita raised this wonder on high, it caught the glare of the sun and coruscated. I turned to look at the baby slung on Peter's chest, worried: was Betty getting sunburned? I remembered Simone had left some of Emma's baby clothes in storage in the garage. There could well be a sunhat there. Suddenly I was standing in the glare of a spotlight. Time stood still and a cacophony of calls rang through the air.

'Connie!'

'Watch out!'

'Constantia!'

'Heads!'

'Constance!'

Gold summer Sydney air, light sea-breezes stirring now as I spun back to see the joyful wedding faces and was struck full in the face by a crackling bunch of gold. You no-good, scheming, best friend of mine, I thought, but still found the strength to laugh at Zita. Then I caught Jude's eye; he was frowning.

I held that bouquet, straightened my glasses and grinned at the cameras, drawing on my inner Dame Edna. All around me were friends and family. As I looked from one beloved face to another, I felt the power of ancestry and history. Some echo of school Shakespeare pushed into consciousness and I reconsidered the seven ages of women in my life.

I saw the mewling baby Betty in her father's arms. I remembered Emma, the shining-faced schoolgirl, and Fern the young lover. I thought of Simone the warrior at the airport. I understood that Charlotte, who had fought for her independence and won, now took Simone's place—she would have to graduate to the justice role. And Zita would be the pantaloon. It was up to me, senior citizen—though tending to second childhood in this eventful history—now atop the pyramid. My only way forward was down.

~~~~~

I learn more. Australian frogs have been in existence for around 54 million years. In other places, recognisable frog fossils have been found dating back 200 million years. Now, a third of all frog species in the world are facing extinction. The rest are struggling to survive.

Frogs are masters of metamorphosis. They've survived extreme changes over millions of years. But not all frogs can happily dwell in a toilet.

~~~~~

Around six o'clock one summer's morning when the air was clear and the sky already bright blue, I heard a light knock on the front door. When I opened it I fancied I could smell the salt in the air. It was Jude, smiling around his eyes, and leaning casually against the doorframe. 'Just heading down to Bondi. Want to come?'

Because of Grace, the beach held bad memories for me. I tended to avoid even thinking of the sea and rarely visited the coast at all. But I was caught in Jude's blond-sunlit eyelashes, the light in his sky-blue eyes. I couldn't say no. 'I'll just…' I indicated my pyjamas.

He nodded. 'I'll wait in the car…'

I managed to find my togs, change and fling a sulu around me in double-quick time. I grabbed a towel, sandals and hurried downstairs. I found Jude behind the wheel of his battered old Jeep. I hopped into the passenger seat, slamming the old door to make sure it stayed shut. Some things don't change. The noise of the engine prevented conversation. The warm air flashed through the vehicle and whipped my hair.

Jude parked facing the water at the northern end of the beach. We left our stuff in the car. He called to me over the roof of the vehicle. 'You running?'

'Not bloody likely!'

He laughed, locked the car, stretched and jogged away.

I meandered across the lawn and down the steps to the sand.

The few people dotting the beach at this early hour came in all shapes and sizes: a large-bellied, deeply-tanned man in an orange towelling hat, a couple of pale girls wearing floral bikinis—perhaps British backpackers—and further away, three tanned men wearing black Speedos and wreathed in gold chains. Two older women in bike shorts and tee shirts walked with purpose, leaning forward, swinging their arms, letting the air envelop them as they discussed something very important indeed and he said and she said…

Surfers still waxing their boards cast long shadows over the rutted sand. At the far end of the long water-curve, waiting surfers were dark shapes in the water. Closer to me, a lone fisherman's strong, brown feet grew into the sand like tree roots. Up by the pavilion, a red tractor raked the sand. It rumbled along towards the Icebergs Club. The sand was combed clean where it had been, pockmarked and littered where it had yet to travel.

The sea-air was gentle, the sun only just warming up. The water was a rolling patchwork of green and blue and aqua with hints of grey where it touched the sky. The breakers were long, hooked scythes that swept across the bay and rolled their sharpness over and over into the sand with a hiss.

Salt tanged my tongue as I walked along the wave line, swinging my arms. Further and further, I strode along the water's edge, exercising my knobbly legs like some bloated, retired racehorse that had been fortunate to avoid the knackery.

I stopped and faced the horizon. I walked into the waves. The sea was open and wide, uncontrolled and wild. I was transfixed by the edge of the world. I was tempted to keep on walking, deeper, past my knees, past my waist, over my head.

Gracie had plunged into the water and never come out. Perhaps she had been the lucky one. I told her I wished her well. I forgave her. Even though she'd left us too soon, I forgave her. I communed with my long-dead sister and the sun glinted and the sea-wind swirled around me. It was not cold. It was as if I were the same temperature as the elements around me. I dipped into the water as though baptising myself. I lay down. I was submerged. I swam and then floated. As I rinsed in the water, I forgave Zita. When I stood up again I felt clean. I felt renewed and powerful. I rinsed my hair back from my face. I wiped the water from my eyes.

I sought out the region called the horizon where the sea became the sky. The sunlight was orange-warm and glowed. I forgave Simone. My heart lifted and I was seduced by the regular, soft crashing of water weights around me. I could go on. I did have a future. For the first time in many years I felt independent, free and vital. I took a deep breath and returned to the sure safety of the beach and continued along the curve of the edge of the sea.

A seagull ran across the sand in front of me then wheeled up into the breeze, describing a perfect arc over the beach.

Jude came up beside me. He must have been back to the car for he held out a kite—a green and yellow arrowhead. It was made of plastic and had strings attached at two corners. I took it and he backed away, unwinding the strings. He was tanned and freckled with crinkly eyes saying yes, yes, yes to me. 'Okay?'

'Absolutely.' He couldn't know that I was reborn in the waters of Bondi Beach. He didn't know that I had been washed clean and was freshly alive. I studied him as he retreated, tied to me with string. I saw Jude in a new light.

'Let go,' he called.

The kite lifted from my hands and soared skywards. Jude juggled the control strings and the kite began to jive, skittering, jittering and scaring the seagulls. The wind was not strong and the kite began to sag, dip and dive, and finally to fall.

I picked up the kite and brushed the sand from it. Jude rewound the strings and came to where I stood. He took the kite from me, and, wordlessly wanting to extend our visit to the sea, we sat down together on the sand, close but not touching. The sand was gritty, morning-cold. The water side of the horizon shimmered. He rested his hands on the kite. He looked out to the sea. I followed his gaze and a tall man walked swiftly beside the white curl of the beachside, across my field of vision. Jude said, 'I'm going away.'

I turned to watch him, still feeling the exhilaration of my baptism, letting his words sink in. He was leaving me. Again. Then they would all have left. I would be alone. My body felt alive and tingling. Anything was possible. The seagulls were laughing.

'I'm setting up a sabbatical, but first, and immediately, I'm taking indefinite leave without pay.'

'When will you be back?'

'Don't know. There's been so much…'

'Yes.' There certainly had been.

'It's made me realise: I've just let things happen; it's as though I've been coasting.'

I frowned at him. This was a new story. 'What do you mean exactly, coasting?'

'I've only just worked this out. It's still new thinking, not clear yet, but it's about being me, making decisions, for me.'

I looked at him sidelong. This wasn't making any sense. Hadn't it always been about him? He didn't take his eyes from the sea as he continued. 'Clearly, I chose to work in biology. I chose you, obviously, and we got married. But everything that's happened since, I didn't choose. It wasn't me. Hasn't been for years. I've just gone along with you, and then Zita; then Simone properly duped me. I was happy enough to just do what all of you required; and with the children, that was probably the right thing.'

I was listening to this, trying hard not to judge him. It was exceedingly difficult. So I asked him, 'How do you explain Charlotte?'

'Charlotte,' he echoed. He did have the grace to glance at me then. Momentarily, before dragging his eyes back to the water and the heaving infinity of it all, he did look repentant. 'I'm sorry about Charlotte. And what that did to Peter. I've told him that.'

'You chose her.'

'She reminded me of you.'

I tried not to laugh. I continued to stare out to the ocean gleam as he collected his thoughts. He went on. 'It's as though, subconsciously, I was trying to take control again. I chose you, Connie. Charlotte, well, she was so needy it was hardly a choice. She needed help; academically, emotionally…'

So vague. I wanted nuts and bolts. I wanted to know where I stood. I interrupted, 'She couldn't kill frogs.'

He looked at me quickly, apparently surprised I knew this and had no hesitation in agreeing with me, 'Like you. Yes.'

'You fixed her?'

'Fixed. What an idea. I couldn't fix anyone. I was trying to help. I know it wasn't right. I could have lost my job. Maybe that's what I wanted.'

'You've fired yourself.'

Again, he agreed with me. 'I got complacent. Must have to make a slip-up like that.'

'Slip-up?'

'It was a mistake, Connie. Don't you feel the world speeding up? How easy it is to fall?' The sea continued to move restlessly. The breaking waves marked time, crashing like the slow motion tick of a giant clock.

I breathed in the salt air and saw clearly in the morning light. For just one moment life was straightforward. But all too soon the moment was broken.

Jude turned his gaze to the horizon again, and so did I. With a fresh wave of energy he continued, 'And you have no idea what it's like now, at the university,' he continued. 'Fighting an uphill battle. It's wrong, Connie. I've sat through meeting after meeting, so many damn meetings, about academic standards, funding shortages, student numbers, bottom lines, applications, satisfying funding requirements, all without resorting to bald-faced lying. It's a war between the needs of business and the imperatives of education. It's just not me. I'm not about marketing. I'm not about management. I have to do something to save myself while I still have some research skills left. Herps all over the world are trying to solve this thing with frogs; trying to let people know... popularise frogs or something, anything, to get the public to influence their politicians. It's a mess. Scientists aren't trained to do PR, for God's sake. There's a guy researching frog declines in the States. I need to get over there, see if I can help. This planet, covered in humans... I don't know what we're looking at. If frogs can't survive...'

My bum felt cold. The sand was hard and wet. I had listened to him in silence and with growing anger. I thought he was making excuses. I said to the sea, 'I don't believe you.'

'What?'

'You say you just went along with everything Zita and I wanted. You say you were coasting. But you can't just deal yourself out like that. You were a player. You've been there all along. You've made decisions. You're perfectly capable of standing up for yourself. You're the one you're trying to make happy. You see what you want to see and you believe what you want to believe. I think you're living in a bubble.'

'I'm living in a bubble?'

'Yes, you are. That's what it looks like to me.'

'What about you, Connie? Are you so perfect?'

I stared out to the primordial sea. That place where the sea meets the sky has been the same for billions of years. My hands lay on grains of sand. Countless grains. How much did our tawdry little lives count for in the end? The billions of little human lives dotted all over the planet?

The words poured out of me, joining the tide, all beyond my control. 'Simone was right. I am a controlling bitch. The kids knew I wanted them to turn against her. And then Guido told Zita I went to see him. The kids really like him no matter what I think, and now they've left me and will probably never speak to me again.'

'You know they will. Francis said he would.'

'Doesn't matter what you think, does it, because you're going away, too.'

'Connie, they've gone for themselves. People are like trains: they get coupled together to travel to the same destination for a while, then one will detach and sit in a siding while the other travels on...'

'Get covered in graffiti...'

'You can't spend your life waiting to be hauled. Don't look outside yourself for impetus. Once you understand *you're* the engine, you can go wherever you like.'

'Nice analogy, but doesn't get us very far.' I stood up and brushed off the sand.

Jude rose, too, and faced me, still distant. 'You're the one who drove everything, Connie. You're the one who called it quits because you couldn't have more children. You're the one who found Zita. It was you, Connie. Not her. I always wanted...'

'What have you always wanted that you haven't had? You've had a great life. You've had a life the envy of most blokes I know.'

Suddenly Jude's tone changed. There was a passion in his voice I'd rarely heard. 'I've lived like we're the endangered ones. Trying desperately to father more children for the survival of the species. If you asked them, I don't for a moment think that any modern Catholic believes we should breed enough worshipers to suffocate the planet, because that would mean the destruction of all God's creation. When God said we should have dominion over every creeping thing, do you think He meant we should destroy them? Make every creeping thing extinct? How much respect for His work—His diversity—is that?'

Of course. All things bright and beautiful. I didn't want to have to think about that environmentalist nonsense. Not now. I didn't want to hear it. No one wants to have to think about this stuff. I attempted a joke to change the subject. 'Aren't you preaching to the converted here?'

He nodded in agreement and smiled politely. 'My mother haunts me. What can I say?'

'She haunts me too.'

'I wish we hadn't annulled...' If he could have sucked the words back in I think he would have. He looked at me quickly and there was a pause but the waves kept rolling in, the clouds stayed stuck to the sky, and the Earth kept on turning.

I said, 'So do I.'

'We did have a marriage.'

'We did,' I agreed. I longed for the past. I longed for him.

'Do we? Still?'

'Uncoupled trains.' I smiled at him. I was happy to leave it there, happy that we'd had this conversation, like the old days, honest at last.

He looked at me. He was serious. There was a crease between his eyebrows, a single crease that had become deeper over the years. I wanted to smooth it out. 'Just love, Con. That's enough, isn't it? Love?'

'Is it because I'm the only one left?'

He sighed. He seemed exasperated. 'It's always been you, Connie. You've insisted I'd be better with someone else and I've never wanted to argue. But it's not what I thought then and it's not what I want now. Please don't turn me away. We've wasted so much time. Will you come with me? To Minnesota? It would be a fresh start.'

I had been reborn in the surf. I knew what I wanted. I didn't need to say it. He understood. We turned from the sea, not touching, not smiling, and walked back to the car. Finally, I knew where I was going. And I couldn't wait to get there.

~~~~~

Brains constantly distort what we see. We use memories to assist our imagination in describing to our brain what is out there. We see remarkably little. Vision is a two-way street with massive amounts of stored information going backwards and forwards in our brains. Visual memories inform perception. Seeing is only another form of dreaming.

The brain is a dreaming machine. The brain is modulated by the senses. The eyes inform the brain. Can you believe your own eyes?

We create our own private universe, our own reality. That's my problem. I imagined we were all one big happy family, when of course we weren't.

~~~~~

There it was again, the slippery surface wetness, creamy sliding with strength underneath; fullness of form and weight, dryness below, surface slickness. The strength knew where it belonged; the knowledge was in the mud. The shape existed before it was there. The hand pushed into it and was answered firmly by force of skin that gave and answered. The hand was like wind over the water's edge. It touched and left no trace, yet the pattern accumulated. There was more, achingly, as surface tension eased sweetly. Curled into spine strength, the shape of joy rose into the fabric of breathing. The sliding, gliding together, the making of shapes, the finding of breath, breathing more shapely, more in tune, more high tensile, more dreaming of becoming. The answering knowledge of life and certainty grabbed attention and let go as clay dissolved into slip and liquefied, smoothly and velvety soft like a cloud, like a wisp, like a secret, and then melted and found weight and physical strength endured.

Grounded and recovered, we bound together like a pot on the wheel. We needed to drag wire between surfaces stuck fast with wet suction to separate, to break us jagged apart.

But this time the weight stayed and was boundless and heavy and silent and there was no breath, no air, no heartbeat, no life. Oh God, what had happened? Dread fear coiled in my guts. I was stuck there beneath him. I was flattened with weight and smashed in the depth, drowning in pillowing flesh and hair and bones. How could I move him and push him and fight him for air and get him to breathe? I smacked him and shoved him and punched into his chest. I heaved and I rocked. He seemed to increase in weight until I was crushed and it took my last energy to roll him off and onto his back.

I grabbed his hair with one hand and with the other tilted his chin up to clear the airway. I checked in his mouth for any obstruction… so many fillings, but all his own teeth. He was not breathing, there was no pulse. He was all weight so I beat him three times hard in the chest with my fist, then pinched his nose and began to blow into his mouth, the contact with his unresponsive lips now so different. Thoughts vaulted into to my panicking mind one after the other. Could I leave him? Ring an ambulance? Breathe you bastard, how dare you leave me like this? 'Jude!' I screamed between breaths,

'Breathe, Jude, breathe…' and punched and kneaded his chest. I was weakening, running out of my own air, yet I couldn't give up. He might survive, I didn't know, but there was nothing, not the slightest response. I alternately breathed into his mouth and beat upon his chest and for a moment I thought his eyelids flickered, but he remained motionless. I couldn't keep going. I was slowing. He was silent. I couldn't stop. I had to get help. He was dying. I was dying. There was no one else home. I blew into his mouth and watched his chest rise, then down went his chest, and nothing else happened as finally, empty, I gave up Jude's ghost. I lay down, stretched out on top of him, to be as close as possible to him and he was warm and he hairy and still, nothing, nothing, nothing.

I was alone.

~~~~~

Phoned triple zero. The operator asked what emergency service I wanted: ambulance, police or fire? I looked over at Jude. There was no emergency, not anymore, so I put down the phone. Walked around the room and out into the flat. What to do? Who could give me advice? Thoughts flickered at the edge of my consciousness, out of reach. The ideas would slide away before I could get them into proper focus.

Opened the Yellow Pages to the entries under Doctors. My vision ran over names in Bellevue Hill, Bondi Junction, Edgecliff, Double Bay and Woollhara. How would I make a choice? Who would Jude want me to pick? Did he have a regular doctor? Then it occurred to me that doctors might not do house calls anymore. If not, how would I get Jude into the car? Get him to the waiting room? What could a doctor do for him anyway?

It became clear to me that I should report to the Department of Births, Deaths and Marriages. Found the number and they put me on hold. Then a computerised voice offered me a number of choices, none of which included reporting a death. I hung up.

Went back to the bedroom. He was still. The room was quiet, hot and airless. The curtains hung limp. I dressed and sat down beside Jude. His body was stretched out diagonally. Surprised he looked so peaceful. He even looked happy. His legs were muscular and straight, his feet slightly turned out. There was a sprinkling of sand between his toes, and grains around his toenails. His arms lay by his sides, slightly bent at the elbows, showing pale inner skin. His palms faced up and the fingers curled around an invisible cup. He was open and vulnerable. There he was on my bed and I loved him. His face was relaxed and smooth. His neck was raised up by the pillow beneath it, and creased. His chest was freckled tan and his nipples were brown. His entire body was known to me and yet now completely foreign and apart. I appraised him as if he were a sculpture—he had good bones.

Tried to close his eyes. They sprang open again. A fly buzzed around the room and landed on his chin. It walked over his lips. Another fly landed on his chest and walked, up and over his hair. The first fly marched over the bridge of his nose and onto his eyeball. Nothing twitched it away. The little fly feet made no impression on the shining eyeball. More flies arrived. I waved them away. The sun screamed in through the window as the day powered up.

Wanted to sculpt Jude. Wanted to cover him in clay. If only I could make him again, in clay, and find the magic words to bring him back to life, like a golem. I could make a golem out of Jude. I could rebuild him and sing his spirit back. We are all clay in the end. The thing I know best is clay. The thing I love best is Jude. *Was* Jude. Could I bring him back to life? Could he be my golem?

Didn't want to leave him. Wanted to bury myself in him. To wear him like a cloak. Although it was getting hotter in the room, he stayed cool. I held his hand and the memories took me over. Do memories begin? They did. They shuffled in, some with a mere modicum of life, like zombies; others bursting with bright vitality. Our meeting, our wedding, and his other weddings, pieces of pottery; memories transported me for I do not know how long.

When I came back to my senses it was because of the weather. The heat oppressed me.

My eyes focussed on one of the first things I'd ever made. The bowl was on the top of my chest of drawers. The pale-green glaze was crazed. It was useless for holding water. The shape held my attention. It was a circle. My eye travelled around the rim and found no rest. It was the circle of life. It became the symbol of everything, time without beginning and without end. Finally, my contemplation fixed on Jude. He could not stay there. I would have to act.

I rolled him in the bed sheet like a mummy. Egyptian cotton. I rolled him off the bed, thump, onto the rug. I apologised. I dragged him, still on the rug, through the living room and almost to the front door. I could not take him further like that. We would have to negotiate the stairs in a different way. He lay there, wrapped in a sheet, still and silent. As he would be, forever and ever. Amen.

I went downstairs into the workshop. Cleared the bench. Emptied the old freezer I used for storage. Wiped it down with an old tee shirt. Flicked the on switch. The little red light came on. The machine began to hum.

Went outside. Repositioned the car so as to block off access by any casual visitor. Subconsciously I must have feared an interruption, but apart from my relentless yearning for a golem, I don't think I'd formulated any plans.

Found the rusted wheelbarrow behind an old door. The wheelbarrow's tyre was deflated. Pumped it up with Peter's bicycle pump. Pulled the wheelbarrow upstairs, backwards. The steps were broad, built in the twenties, and I had room to bump the barrow from step to step.

Once back inside my flat, I positioned the barrow next to the body on the floor. Tried to lift him from the shoulders but he was too heavy. After struggling in vain to get him into the barrow, I saw I would have to drag him back into the living room, lift him onto the couch, and drop him down into the wheelbarrow. After half an hour I sat on the couch and looked at the body slumped in the wheelbarrow, his head lolled back between the handles and his legs dangling in front.

Death did not offer him dignity. I stole his dignity. I didn't mean to. I was just looking after him.

As if on remote control, I wheeled Jude out the front door. If anyone had asked me then what I thought I was doing, I wouldn't have had an answer. I would have had to say, 'What I thought best'.

The air in the stairwell was stale. I looked down the steps to the mid-point landing and sighed. I was able to bump down one step at a time. I rested on the first landing. Then bumped down to Zita's floor. Felt dizzy. Went back to my flat and picked up Jude's keys from the bedside table. Went into his bedsit and used the lavatory. Avoided looking at myself in the mirror. Splashed my face with cool water. Ran the water into my cupped hands and drank. This was my breakfast.

Returned to his body wrapped in the sheet. Jude's bulk was awkward in the wheelbarrow. Had to position his legs to one side to avoid contact with the wheel. Bumped down to Simone's level. Parked him and walked down the empty corridor. Felt like a ghost. Walked back to Jude and lifted the handles of the wheelbarrow again. Now each step was increasingly difficult. Had to lean over the barrow to prevent it twisting. Never did let him fall. When we made it to ground level, put the weight down and straightened my back. Rubbed the curve of my spine. Tightened my stomach muscles before heaving the weight once more and continuing into the workshop. Parked the wheelbarrow under the chain hoist. Stood in the middle of the room and thought.

Thought about blood. He was bound to bleed even though his heart had stopped. Opened drawers. Laid old towels on the bench. Swung the chain hoist over the body. Wound chains around the sheet and fastened the shackles. Pulled the chain loop through the first wheel of the hoist. The chains tightened and then hefted him up like a heavy pot. Locked off the lift and left him dangling above the wheelbarrow. Swung him over the workbench then ran the chain backwards through the gear. The entire parcel descended to the bench. Undid the chains and swung the hoist away. Rolled his body from side to side as I removed the sheet from his head. Laid him out on his back. His feet dangled over the end of the bench.

Could not stand to see his face. Found another old beach towel in the bench drawer. This one was faded by many washes but you could still see the *Bananas in Pyamas* coming down the stairs. Wrapped his head in the towel leaving his neck exposed. Kept him wrapped in the sheet from the neck down.

Would need to open his jugular vein, but which one was it? Found *Anatomy for Artists*. Opened the book to an illustration of a dissected arm. Stared at it. A wash of sadness rose through me. A tear dropped onto the page. Turned the pages and found the jugular there where it had always been: on the left.

Cut into the neck with a Stanley knife. I was as gentle as I could be. There was not much resistance. The knife was sharp. A little blood trickled out. I felt relief. Must have been expecting a flood. Grew calmer as I watched the small rivulet splash down into the bucket I'd placed under the bench. The blood was contained.

Jude's hair caught a few drops of the blood. His hair was white at the roots. Beyond grey. He was only fifty-seven.

I looked around at the gardening tools, the woodworking tools. Would I use the rusty hand saw? The pruning saw? What would be best to dissect a husband?

~~~~~

Up in my kitchen I was caught in a lull. I moved sluggishly. I leaned on the kitchen bench. I stared out the window. The sky was cloudless. The harbour was flat. The leaves in the park hung motionless. Then, far away, I heard a bird crying.

I had been holding my breath.

Opened drawers and found a boning knife that Jude had given me. I'd never used it before. Poultry scissors? Filleting knife?

What else would I need? Gathered gloves. Paper towels. Apron. Plastic bags. Rubbish bags. What does that say of dignity and respect for human remains? Putting them in the same wrapping as rubbish? Remembering then I had clay stored in rubbish bins. What did that say about clay?

Sat down in the chair by the door with the tools in my lap. Stared forward into my memories of Jude. My marriage was now over. All of his marriages were over. He had left for good. I felt cold and wet and dizzy. I put my head down to my knees. A knife prodded me in the ribs. It was getting dark…

Had to get to work.

Back down in the workshop I turned on the lights and looked at the shrouded figure on the bench. Reached through the sheet for Jude's hand and held it. Oh, Lord! His flesh was cold and hard; his beautiful hands with such fingernails, his hands in my memory. Traced my fingers over his hand to the wrist. Encircled his wrist with my bracelet of fingers. Then I cut through the skin with the Stanley knife.

Cut through the tendons, tough and crunchy, at the wrist. Dropped the hand into a plastic bag. Did the same with the other hand, then sealed each bag with a twist tie and put them in the freezer.

My breathing was harsh and my mouth was dry. Needed a cup of tea. Put the kettle on. Turned on the radio. The announcer, Philip Adams, called all of us Gladys and soon I was back at work. Making art. Making pottery. Finding beauty in shape and form. God's work. We are the work of thy hand. Oh Lord, Oh Khum, Oh Mami; thou art our father or mother, and thou art our culture, and thou art our potter. We are the clay. What I knew best. I was preparing the ingredients of my job. The kettle boiled. I found the teabags, put one in a mug and poured the water in. It transformed into the colour of rust. Sipped the tea and burned my mouth. Topped up the tea with cold water. I drank. I did not finish the cup. Left it by the sink when I went back to work.

The arm muscles were stiff. I had to massage them to get the arm to relax so I could bend it. Used the snippers to crunch through the tendons around the elbow. Had to twist the joint out of locking. The tendons were shiny and white.

The shoulders were simple ball and socket; the shiny joint capsule, magnificent smooth whiteness.

The ankles were mortise joints, one part fitting within the other. The bones of the leg—the tibia inside and the smaller fibula on the outside—bound to the calcaneus bone in the heel by tendons, nerves and blood vessels. I removed both feet and bagged them.

Kept the patellas with the calves, snipped the quadriceps tendon where it entered the tibia, and snipped through the cords of the cruciate tendon.

Cut around the flesh to get at the head of the femur. Used force to dislocate the hip. Pulled on the thigh. There was a suction noise as the head of the femur came away from the pelvis.

Could not force the knifepoint into the wall of sternum. Turned to the throat and, with poultry scissors, cut through the trachea between the cartilage rings. Needed to edge the point of the Stanley knife between the vertebrae to get to the spinal cord. Head surprisingly heavy. I rolled it, still wrapped in the *Bananas in Pyjamas* towel, into a plastic bag.

I remembered when I had dissected before: not a human, of course, but a frog. It was when I first met Jude. It was a simple dissection but it showed me life mechanics. How wonderful it was. At first I could not see. I was too upset at the loss of life. It had been Jude who had revealed the mysteries and focused my skittish curiosity. I heard an echo of Father Brian talking about the church as the body of Christ. How the body and the blood of Christ are in the Eucharist and how heaven is within. Paradise is inside us all.

Opened the entire front of the torso with the Stanley knife. Cut the skin from just above the pubic hair all the way up to the neck. Folded back and peeled away the skin and fatty tissue from the abdomen and ribs. Removed the lower ribs with poultry scissors.

Removed the muscles covering the abdomen to reveal intestines. Removed the liver. Cut around the anus and removed the small intestines plus colon and stomach, and put the whole mass into a large plastic bag. Tied it and placed it into the freezer.

Wiped the interior of the abdominal cavity with paper towels. Took spleen, pancreas, bladder and kidneys and added those to the genital bag. Sawed through the remaining ribs with the pruning saw. Cracked them open, and revealed the heart. Stared at it. That heart. Wondered where it had gone wrong. What fault or blockage had caused it to stop? Could feel my own heart beating. Picked up the heart in my hand. I felt the heaven contained there. Had to continue. Placed the heart into a bag and snipped around the diaphragm preparing to take both lungs. The spine was left exposed. Found a larger rubbish bag and enveloped the spine, which was still covered with considerable musculature. Finally, added the ribs to those already bagged, and put this bag in the freezer.

Became conscious of the sound of groaning. It was me. The sound was sad.

Threw towels, apron and gloves into the kiln. Turned it on low. Wiped down the bench. Moved bucket of blood to studio. Poured in thousands of tiny, dried pieces of clay and added water to fill. Covered with lid. Turned off lights.

Freezer full of husband.

~~~~~

And so I type these words, my farewell to you my readers: my son, my lover and my erstwhile harem.

These pieces of Jude have been the making of me even as I make them. It has made me as a woman, as a human being, as a soul.

'Come on!' I hear you say. 'It's only clay. How can you find soul in clay?'

Ask Adam and Eve.

~~~~~

The Anzac War Memorial in Hyde Park directs light through huge amber glass panes onto a monument called 'Sacrifice'. The entrances are roped off. 'Sacrifice' is a monolith in the middle of a room that no one may enter. Three women carry a dead soldier laid out on a shield. The soldier is naked, his head thrown back, and his arms are out-stretched over a sword. It is the three women who bear the load.

Catalina Gallery presents
The touch of earthly years
Ceramics by Constance Sonnenberg

The following is the transcript of an address given by Dr William Richards to invited guests at the opening of the exhibition.

Constance Sonnenberg worked with clay for over thirty years. During that time not only did she produce functional pots she fully expected would be used in the home, but also she created exquisite public sculptures. These ranged from the giant BHP gateway to the minuscule buttons used for Royal wedding gowns. The National Gallery, state galleries throughout Australia and our most important corporations collect and regularly display her work. She is represented internationally in major galleries including the V&A, the Smithsonian and the Tate. We are proud to present *The touch of earthly years*, her third exhibition with Catalina Gallery.

Many of you will remember *The touch of earthly years* was to be the last of a trilogy of exhibitions curated by my mother, the late Sheryl Richards. Mixed works by three women with three different areas of expertise—photographer, florist and ceramicist—were to be spearheaded by each in turn.

The first exhibition, *Light of the common day*, took place in 1996. Together with flowers and vases, the presentation focused on photography by Simone Vega-Baldwin. A year later, *The glory in the flower and the splendour in the grass* featured floral displays by Zita De Angelis-Baldwin. The program was suspended upon the death of my mother. Simone, Zita and Connie can no longer work together.

Connie continued to explore the original impulse that drove the three women to contemplate marriage and weddings—flowers, vases and photography—so very successfully. She created these pieces you see today; glazed pots, made of clay and fired in a kiln. We've all seen ceramics before. Why, then, is our response so visceral? Why do these items creep under our perception and attack our emotions?

It is a great pity that Connie is not here to present this exhibition. Her family has agreed to show it in her absence, hoping that public appreciation of her work may enable her return to those of us who love her. Her disappearance has been reported widely so I will not go into detail here. Suffice to say we found the ceramics in her abandoned studio. The chronicle, printed in the catalogue, was found on a computer owned by her ex-husband, Dr Jude Baldwin. This document purports to explain everything: the pottery, the process and her some aspects of her complex personal relationships. There is no clue as to where she has gone. Although it is unusual these days to produce such an extensive catalogue for an exhibition, I've decided, with police permission, to reprint Connie's words in their entirety and let the viewer into her world. You be the judge.

Constance Sonnenberg is an artist of the highest calibre. This exhibition showcases an extraordinary range in her skills. She is certainly not the first potter to incorporate human remains in their work. I am struck by the fact that so many of the objects are functional, rather than merely decorative.

Dr Jude Baldwin was a herpetologist of international standing. I once asked Jude about the apocryphal experiment where a frog, placed into a pot of water, perfectly capable of jumping out of its predicament, is gradually heated to boiling point without the frog noticing the change in temperature until it is too late. He told me that the result of this experiment has been shown, time after time, to be that the frog will certainly jump as it becomes uncomfortable.

I'm about to commission a new exhibition in honour of my mother. As you know, Sheryl died of an inoperable brain tumour two years ago. She was cremated, and I am planning for her ashes to be incorporated in a series of ceramic works, which will celebrate her life.

I am surprised and inspired by the gallery that Sheryl has built here in Five Ways. All of us at Catalina Gallery hope the next thirty years can be as fulfilling for curators and customers as the previous thirty were under Sheryl's direction.

I'm relying on Connie to help keep the flame alive. Applying lessons learned from English craftsmen, African women and the great Asian traditionalists, artisan potters of today strive to express simple truths in their work. If I understand Connie's philosophy correctly, she would say that life is contained in a line. Force turns the wheel. Fire changes everything.

As we commence a new millennium, I welcome you to *The touch of earthly years*. I'm sure Connie would too. If anyone has any information at all that might lead us to her, please do not hesitate to come forward.

Dr William Richards
Director, Catalina Gallery
Five Ways, Paddington
Sydney, Australia 2000

Exhibition

The Touch of Earthly Years

All prices on application

1. Torso - 1.4 m x 53 cm - Earthenware. Coiled and sculpted earthenware fired to 1200°C then fired three times to lesser temperatures for glazes.

2. Gargoyle - 40 cm x 25 cm - Earthenware. Mudgee earthenware bisque fired to 1000°C. Terra sigillata, stains, oxides. Glaze fired to 1110°C.

3. Rain jar - 1.6 m x 43 cm - Stoneware. Guglong clay. Coil-built stoneware. Bisque fired to 1000°C. Slips applied by sponge to give texture. Reduction fired with bone-ash glaze to 1260°C.

4. Birdbath - 1 m x 62 cm - Stoneware. Pedestal comprised of three wheel-thrown cylinders decorated with sprigs. The bowl is a slab, press-melded. Bisque fired then spotted with slip for surface texture. Reduction fired with bone-ash glaze to cone 8 [1250°C].

5. Footrest - 50 cm x 50 cm - Stoneware. By the door of a Japanese house, people will take off their shoes, sit on the step, and rest their feet on a stone like this one. Coiled walls, repeated sprays with terra sigillata and burnishing. Final firing to cone 8.

6. Garden stools - 45 cm x 30 cm - Terracotta. Hollow rectangular stools decorated with cut-out and indented shapes. Slabs of grogged terracotta dried to leather-hard, painted with slips for texture, glaze fired to 1170°C.

7. Bud vase - 18 cm x 6 cm - Bone china. Slip-cast with bone china. Bisque fired then majolica decoration (resist painting over white opaque glaze). Fire gradually increased to burn off wax to around 316°C, then to orange-hot 1100°C.

8. Garden table - 70 cm x 70 cm x 70 cm - Terracotta. Grogged terracotta. Slab-built, textured with stamps and cut-out shapes. Raw glaze, fired slowly to 1260° over twelve hours.

9. Decanter - 42 cm x 16 cm - Stoneware. Wheel-thrown and altered form. Stoneware, bisque fired then glaze fired to cone

10. Breadbin - 60 cm x 45 cm - Terracotta. Heavily grogged terra-cotta. Coil built on a slab base. Contrasting lid and handles.

11. Fountain - 1 m x 40 cm - Earthenware. Earthenware altered, wheel-thrown segments. Three sections spilling into three non-uniform concentric bowls joined by metal rod and pump mech-anism. Textured with slip and reduction fired.

12. Lantern - 35 cm x 18 cm - Terracotta. Slab-built with lattice-style heart piercings. Bisque fired then glaze fired to 1180°C.

13. Ashtray - 7 cm x 27 cm x 31 cm - Stoneware. Wheel-thrown and altered stoneware. Bisque fired then glaze fired to 1260°C.

14. Platter - 8.5 cm x 33 cm x 39 cm - Stoneware. Wheel-thrown and altered-shape stoneware. Slip design of warts. Bisque fired to 1000°C. Glaze fired to 1260°C.

15. Tea cups - 9 cm x 8 cm. Saucers - 3 cm x 18 cm -Bone china. Thrown and pinched. Bisque fired and then glaze fired to 1240°C.

16. Bowl - 30 cm x 16 cm - Porcelain. Coil-built porcelain. Bisque fired then glazed to 1290°C.

17. Wind chimes - 35 cm when hanging - Coloured clay. Threaded with rolled hair string. Coiled and scraped coloured clay slabs. Decorated with coloured slip texture. Fired once to 1210C°.

18. Aroma burner - 21 cm x 31 cm - Bone china. Carved from plaster then bone china slip cast.

19. Candle stick - 41 cm x 31 cm - Stoneware. Pinch, coiled and sculpted. Bisque fired to 1000°C. Glaze fired to 1200°C.

Selected bibliography and acknowledgements

Campbell, A. ed *Declines and disappearances of Australian frogs* Commonwealth of Australia 1999

Souder, W. *A plague of frogs, The horrifying true story* Hyperion New York 2000

Tyler, M. *Australian frogs, A natural history* Reed Books 1994

Bush, B., Maryan, B., Browne-Cooper, R., and Robinson, D. *Reptiles and frogs in the bush* University of Western Australian Press 2007

www.frogs.org.au/frogs/species
www.frogsaustralia.net.au/frogs
www.threatenedspecies.environment.nsw.gov.au
www.environment.gov.au/biodiversity/threatened

Correspondence with Associate Professor Michael Mahoney, Head of Discipline of Biology at the University of Newcastle.

bindiwurra - pregnant - from the wordlist of the Dharug/Eora language www.dharug.dalang.com.au/index.php/word-list

Contemporary ceramic art in Australia and NZ Janet Mansfield 1995 Craftsman House in association with G + B Arts International

A potter's book Bernard Leach 1976 London Faber

Zen and the art of pottery Kenneth R. Beittel 1989 New York Weatherhill

Ceramic art: comment and review 1882-1977 New York EP Dutton 1978

Advice from Jane Sawyer, ceramicist

Companion guide to Sydney Ruth Park 1973 Collins

The body Anthony Smith 1985 George Allen and Unwin

The anatomist; a true story of Gray's Anatomy Bill Hayes 2008 Scribe

Advice from Miss Jane Fox, surgeon
and Leanne Beatty of the Australian Funeral Directors Association

Thank you:

Philip and Felix Millar

RMIT Novel classes with Laurie Clancy, Olga Lorenzo and the girly swots

Early readers: Clare, Jane, Jane, Jo, Abbers, Peter, Jenny, Lucy, Pippa, Mark and Fred

Encouragement from Year of the Novel workshops with Andrea Goldsmith at The Victorian Writers' Centre

Mr Pernickity (aka) Martin Shepherd, copy-editor

All errors, omissions and exaggerations entirely my fault.
Victoria Osborne
www.ourrelationshipwithnature.com

www.ingramcontent.com/pod-product-compliance
Lightning Source LLC
Chambersburg PA
CBHW030531270626
47155CB00024B/2716